Dear Reader:

Ireland holds a special place in my heart. The rolling green fields under heavy skies, the crisscrossing gray of stone fences, the majestic tumble of a ruined castle most likely sacked by those damned Cromwellians. I love the way the sun can shine gold through the rain and the way the flowers bloom wildly in gardens and fields. It's a land of violent cliffs and dim, smoky pubs. Of magic and legend and heartbreak. There is a beauty even in the air.

But beyond the countryside, the most magnificent things in Ireland are the Irish. True, it's a land of poets and warriors and dreamers, but it is also a land that opens its arms to strangers. Irish hospitality is simple and kind. That is, or should be, the definition of the word *welcome*.

Writing the Irish Born Trilogy was a natural decision. Both the land and its people inspire, as well as thrive on, stories. The idea, for me, was to write of Ireland, and of family, as they intertwined in my heart. In each book of this trilogy I chose to feature one of three sisters, different in type but bound by blood. Their lives have each taken a different course, yet it is Ireland that inspires them, as it inspires me.

I hope you'll enjoy all three books—*Born in Fire*, *Born in Ice*, and *Born in Shame*—and the trip to County Clare, a land steeped in tradition, lush splendor, and enduring romance.

NORA ROBERTS

Nora Roberts

HOT ICE
SACRED SINS
BRAZEN VIRTUE
SWEET REVENGE
PUBLIC SECRETS
GENUINE LIES
CARNAL INNOCENCE
DIVINE EVIL
HONEST ILLUSIONS
PRIVATE SCANDALS
HIDDEN RICHES
TRUE BETRAYALS
MONTANA SKY
SANCTUARY
HOMEPORT

THE REEF
RIVER'S END
CAROLINA MOON
THE VILLA
MIDNIGHT BAYOU
THREE FATES
BIRTHRIGHT
NORTHERN LIGHTS
BLUE SMOKE
ANGELS FALL
HIGH NOON
TRIBUTE
BLACK HILLS
THE SEARCH
CHASING FIRE

Series

Irish Born Trilogy
BORN IN FIRE
BORN IN ICE
BORN IN SHAME

Key Trilogy
KEY OF LIGHT
KEY OF KNOWLEDGE
KEY OF VALOR

Dream Trilogy
DARING TO DREAM
HOLDING THE DREAM
FINDING THE DREAM

In The Garden Trilogy
BLUE DAHLIA
BLACK ROSE
RED LILY

Chesapeake Bay Saga
SEA SWEPT
RISING TIDES
INNER HARBOR
CHESAPEAKE BLUE

Circle Trilogy
MORRIGAN'S CROSS
DANCE OF THE GODS
VALLEY OF SILENCE

Sign of Seven Trilogy
BLOOD BROTHERS
THE HOLLOW
THE PAGAN STONE

Gallaghers of Ardmore Trilogy
JEWELS OF THE SUN
TEARS OF THE MOON
HEART OF THE SEA

Bride Quartet
VISION IN WHITE
BED OF ROSES
SAVOR THE MOMENT
HAPPY EVER AFTER

Three Sisters Island Trilogy
DANCE UPON THE AIR
HEAVEN AND EARTH
FACE THE FIRE

The Inn BoonsBoro Trilogy
THE NEXT ALWAYS

Nora Roberts & J. D. Robb

REMEMBER WHEN

J. D. Robb

Anthologies

FROM THE HEART
A LITTLE MAGIC
A LITTLE FATE

MOON SHADOWS
(with Jill Gregory, Ruth Ryan Langan, and Marianne Willman)

The Once Upon Series
(with Jill Gregory, Ruth Ryan Langan, and Marianne Willman)

ONCE UPON A CASTLE
ONCE UPON A STAR
ONCE UPON A KISS
ONCE UPON A ROSE
ONCE UPON A DREAM
ONCE UPON A MIDNIGHT

* * *

SILENT NIGHT
(with Susan Plunkett, Dee Holmes, and Claire Cross)

OUT OF THIS WORLD
(with Laurell K. Hamilton, Susan Krinard, and Maggie Shayne)

BUMP IN THE NIGHT
(with Mary Blayney, Ruth Ryan Langan, and Mary Kay McComas)

DEAD OF NIGHT
(with Mary Blayney, Ruth Ryan Langan, and Mary Kay McComas)

THREE IN DEATH
SUITE 606
(with Mary Blayney, Ruth Ryan Langan, and Mary Kay McComas)

IN DEATH
THE LOST
(with Patricia Gaffney, Mary Blayney, and Ruth Ryan Langan)

THE OTHER SIDE
*(with Mary Blayney, Patricia Gaffney, Ruth Ryan Langan,
and Mary Kay McComas)*

THE UNQUIET
*(with Mary Blayney, Patricia Gaffney, Ruth Ryan Langan,
and Mary Kay McComas)*

Also available . . .

THE OFFICIAL NORA ROBERTS COMPANION
(edited by Denise Little and Laura Hayden)

NORA ROBERTS

BORN IN FIRE

JOVE BOOKS, NEW YORK

THE BERKLEY PUBLISHING GROUP
Published by the Penguin Group
Penguin Group (USA) Inc.
375 Hudson Street, New York, New York 10014, USA
Penguin Group (Canada), 90 Eglinton Avenue East, Suite 700, Toronto, Ontario M4P 2Y3, Canada
(a division of Pearson Penguin Canada Inc.)
Penguin Books Ltd., 80 Strand, London WC2R 0RL, England
Penguin Group Ireland, 25 St. Stephen's Green, Dublin 2, Ireland (a division of Penguin Books Ltd.)
Penguin Group (Australia), 250 Camberwell Road, Camberwell, Victoria 3124, Australia
(a division of Pearson Australia Group Pty. Ltd.)
Penguin Books India Pvt. Ltd., 11 Community Centre, Panchsheel Park, New Delhi—110 017, India
Penguin Group (NZ), 67 Apollo Drive, Rosedale, North Shore 0632, New Zealand
(a division of Pearson New Zealand Ltd.)
Penguin Books (South Africa) (Pty.) Ltd., 24 Sturdee Avenue, Rosebank, Johannesburg 2196,
South Africa

Penguin Books Ltd., Registered Offices: 80 Strand, London WC2R 0RL, England

This is a work of fiction. Names, characters, places, and incidents either are the product of the author's imagination or are used fictitiously, and any resemblance to actual persons, living or dead, business establishments, events, or locales is entirely coincidental. The publisher does not have any control over and does not assume any responsibility for author or third-party websites or their content.

BORN IN FIRE

A Jove Book / published by arrangement with the author

PRINTING HISTORY
First Jove mass-market edition / October 1994

Copyright © 1994 by Nora Roberts.
Excerpt from *Naked in Death* by J. D. Robb copyright © by Nora Roberts.
Cover design by Diana Kolsky.
Cover image of dragonfly by Shutterstock (#71078239); image of claddagh by Shutterstock (#3325163).

All rights reserved.
No part of this book may be reproduced, scanned, or distributed in any printed or electronic form without permission. Please do not participate in or encourage piracy of copyrighted materials in violation of the author's rights. Purchase only authorized editions
For information, address: The Berkley Publishing Group,
a division of Penguin Group (USA) Inc.,
375 Hudson Street, New York, New York 10014.

ISBN: 978-0-515-11469-0

JOVE®
Jove Books are published by The Berkley Publishing Group,
a division of Penguin Group (USA) Inc.,
375 Hudson Street, New York, New York 10014.
JOVE® is a registered trademark of Penguin Group (USA) Inc.
The "J" design is a trademark of Penguin Group (USA) Inc.

PRINTED IN THE UNITED STATES OF AMERICA

50 49 48 47 46 45 44 43 42

If you purchased this book without a cover, you should be aware that this book is stolen property. It was reported as "unsold and destroyed" to the publisher, and neither the author nor the publisher has received any payment for this "stripped book."

To Amy Berkower,
*for a decade of
taking care of business*

I never will marry, I'll be no man's wife.
I intend to stay single for the rest of my life.

—nineteenth-century Irish ballad

ℬ Chapter One

HE would be in the pub, of course. Where else would a smart man warm himself on a frigid, wind-blown afternoon? Certainly not at home, by his own fire.

No, Tom Concannon was a smart man, Maggie thought, and wouldn't be at home.

Her father would be at the pub, among friends and laughter. He was a man who loved to laugh, and to cry and to spin improbable dreams. A foolish man some might call him. But not Maggie, never Maggie.

As she steered her racketing lorry around the last curve that led into the village of Kilmihil, she saw not a soul on the street. No wonder, as it was well past time for lunch and not a day for strolling with winter racing in from the Atlantic like a hound from icy Hades. The west coast of Ireland shivered under it and dreamed of spring.

She saw her father's battered Fiat, among other vehicles she recognized. Tim O'Malley's had a good crowd this day. She parked as close as she could to the front entrance of the pub, which was nestled in a line of several shops.

As she walked down the street the wind knocked her back, made her huddle inside the fleece-lined jacket and pull the black wool cap down lower on

her head. Color whipped into her cheeks like a
blush. There was a smell of damp under the cold,
like a nasty threat. There would be ice, thought the
farmer's daughter, before nightfall.

She couldn't remember a more bitter January, or
one that seemed so hell-bent on blowing its frosty
breath over County Clare. The little garden in front
of the shop she hurried by had paid dearly. What was
left of it was blackened by the wind and frost and lay
pitifully on the soggy ground.

She was sorry for it, but the news she held inside
her was so fearfully bright, she wondered the flowers
didn't rise up and bloom away into spring.

There was plenty of warmth in O'Malley's. She felt
it nuzzle her the moment she opened the door. She
could smell the peat burning in the fire, its red-hot
heart smoldering cheerfully, and the stew O'Malley's
wife, Deirdre, had served at lunch. And tobacco,
beer, the filmy layer that frying chips left in the air.

She spotted Murphy first, sitting at one of the tiny
tables, his boots stretched out as he eased a tune out
of an Irish accordion that matched the sweetness of
his voice. The other patrons of the pub were listening, dreaming a bit over their beer and porter. The
tune was sad, as the best of Ireland was, melancholy
and lovely as a lover's tears. It was a song that bore
her name, and spoke of growing old.

Murphy saw her, smiled a little. His black hair fell
untidily over his brow, so that he tossed his head to
clear it away. Tim O'Malley stood behind the bar, a
barrel of a man whose apron barely stretched across
the girth of him. He had a wide, creased face and
eyes that disappeared into folds of flesh when he
laughed.

He was polishing glasses. When he saw Maggie, he continued his task, knowing she would do what was polite and wait to order until the song was finished.

She saw David Ryan, puffing on one of the American cigarettes his brother sent him every month from Boston, and tidy Mrs. Logan, knitting with pink wool while her foot tapped to the tune. There was old Johnny Conroy, grinning toothlessly, his gnarled hand holding the equally twisted one of his wife of fifty years. They sat together like newlyweds, lost in Murphy's song.

The television over the bar was silent, but its picture was bright and glossy with a British soap opera. People in gorgeous clothes and shining hair argued around a massive table lit with silver-based candles and elegant crystal.

Its glittery story was more, much more than a country away from the little pub with its scarred bar and smoke-dark walls.

Maggie's scorn for the shining characters squabbling in their wealthy room was quick and automatic as a knee jerk. So was the swift tug of envy.

If *she* ever had such wealth, she thought—though, of course, she didn't care one way or the other—she would certainly know what to do with it.

Then she saw him, sitting in the corner by himself. Not separate, not at all. He was as much a part of the room as the chair he sat on. He had an arm slung over the back of that chair, while the other hand held a cup she knew would hold strong tea laced with Irish.

An unpredictable man he might be, full of starts and stops and quick turns, but she knew him. Of all the men she had known, she had loved no one with the full thrust of her heart as she loved Tom Concannon.

She said nothing, crossed to him, sat and rested her head on his shoulder.

Love for him rose up in her, a fire that warmed down to the bone but never burned. His arm came from around the chair and wrapped her closer. His lips brushed across her temple.

When the song was done, she took his hand in hers and kissed it. "I knew you'd be here."

"How did you know I was thinking of you, Maggie, my love?"

"Must be I was thinking of you." She sat back to smile at him. He was a small man, but toughly built. Like a runt bull, he often said of himself with one of his rolling laughs. There were lines around his eyes that deepened and fanned out when he grinned. They made him, in Maggie's eyes, all the more handsome. His hair had once been gloriously red and full. It had thinned a bit with time, and the gray streaked through the fire like smoke. He was, to Maggie, the most dashing man in the world.

He was her father.

"Da," she said. "I have news."

"Sure, I can see it all over your face."

Winking, he pulled off her cap so that her hair fell wildly red to her shoulders. He'd always liked to look at it, to watch it flash and sizzle. He could still remember when he'd held her the first time, her face screwed up with the rage of life, her tiny fists bunched and flailing. And her hair shining like a new coin.

He hadn't been disappointed not to have a son,

had been humbled to have been given the gift of a daughter.

"Bring me girl a drink, Tim."

"I'll have tea," she called out. "It's wicked cold." Now that she was here, she wanted the pleasure of drawing the news out, savoring it. "Is that why you're in here singing tunes and drinking, Murphy? Who's keeping your cows warm?"

"Each other," he shot back. "And if this weather keeps up, I'll have more calves come spring than I can handle, as cattle do what the rest of the world does on a long winter night."

"Oh, sit by the fire with a good book, do they?" Maggie said, and had the room echoing with laughter. It was no secret, and only a slight embarrassment to Murphy, that his love of reading was well-known.

"Now, I've tried to interest them in the joys of literature, but those cows, they'd rather watch the television." He tapped his empty glass. "And I'm here for the quiet, what with your furnace roaring like thunder day and night. Why aren't you home, playing with your glass?"

"Da." When Murphy walked to the bar, Maggie took her father's hand again. "I needed to tell you first. You know I took some pieces to McGuinness's shop in Ennis this morning?"

"Did you now?" He took out his pipe, tapped it. "You should have told me you were going. I'd have kept you company on the way."

"I wanted to do it alone."

"My little hermit," he said, and flicked a finger down her nose.

"Da, he bought them." Her eyes, as green as her father's, sparkled. "He bought four of them, and that's all I took in. Paid me for them then and there.''

"You don't say, Maggie, you don't say!" He leaped up, dragging her with him, and spun her around the room. "Listen to this, ladies and gentlemen. My daughter, my own Margaret Mary, has sold her glass in Ennis."

There was quick, spontaneous applause and a barrage of questions.

"At McGuinness's," she said, firing answers back. "Four pieces, and he'll look at more. Two vases, a bowl, and a . . . I supposed you could call the last a paperweight." She laughed when Tim set whiskeys on the counter for her and her father.

"All right then." She lifted her glass and toasted. "To Tom Concannon, who believed in me."

"Oh, no, Maggie." Her father shook his head and there were tears in his eyes. "To you. All to you." He clicked glasses and sent the whiskey streaming down his throat. "Fire up that squeeze box, Murphy. I want to dance with my daughter."

Murphy obliged with a jig. With the sounds of shouts and clapping hands, Tom led his daughter around the floor. Deirdre came out from the kitchen, wiping her hands on her apron. Her face was flushed from cooking as she pulled her husband into the dance. From jig to reel and reel to hornpipe, Maggie whirled from partner to partner until her legs ached.

As others came into the pub, drawn either by the music or the prospect of company, the news was spread. By nightfall, she knew, everyone within twenty kilometers would have heard of it.

It was the kind of fame she had hoped for. It was her secret that she wished for more.

"Oh, enough." She sank into her chair and drained her cold tea. "My heart's about to burst."

"So is mine. With pride for you." Tom's smile remained bright, but his eyes dimmed a little. "We should go tell your mother, Maggie. And your sister, too."

"I'll tell Brianna this evening." Her own mood shifted at the mention of her mother.

"All right, then." He reached down, brushed his hand over her cheek. "It's your day, Maggie Mae, nothing will spoil it for you."

"No, 'tis our day. For I never would have blown the first bubble of glass without you."

"Then we'll share it, just us two for a little while." He felt smothered for a minute, dizzy and hot. He thought he felt a little click behind his eyes before it cleared. Air, he thought. He needed a bit of air. "I'm in the mood for a drive. I want to smell the sea, Maggie. Will you come with me?"

"Of course I will." She rose immediately. "But it's freezing out, and the wind's the devil. Are you sure you want to go to the cliffs today?"

"I've a need to." He reached for his coat, then tossing a muffler around his throat, turned to the pub. All the dark, smoky colors seemed to whirl in his eyes. He thought, ruefully, that he was a little drunk. Then again, it was the day for it. "We're having us a party. Tomorrow night it'll be. With fine food, fine drink and fine music, to celebrate my daughter's success. I'll expect every one of me friends there."

Maggie waited until they were out in the cold. "A party? Da, you know she'll not have it."

"I'm still the master of my own house." His chin,

very like his daughter's, jutted out. "A party there will be, Maggie. I'll deal with your mother. Would you drive now?"

"All right." There was no arguing, she knew, once Tom Concannon had made up his mind. She was grateful for that, or she would never have been able to travel to Venice and apprentice herself in a glass house. Never have been able to take what she'd learned, and what she'd dreamed, and build her own studio. She knew her mother had made Tom pay miserably for the money it had cost. But he had stood firm.

"Tell me what you're working on now."

"Well, it's a kind of a bottle. And I want it to be very tall, very slim. Tapered you see, from bottom to top, then it should flare out. A bit like a lily. And the color should be very delicate, like the inside of a peach."

She could see it, clear as the hand she used to describe it.

"It's lovely things you see in your head."

"It's easy to see them there." She shot him a smile. "The hard work is making them real."

"You'll make them real." He patted her hand and fell into silence.

Maggie took the twisting, narrow road toward the sea. Away toward the west, the clouds were flying in, their sails whipped by the wind and darkened with storm. Clearer patches were swallowed up, then fought their way free to glow gem bright amid the pewter.

She saw a bowl, wide and deep, swirled with those warring colors, and began to fashion it in her head.

The road twisted, then straightened, as she threaded

the rattling lorry through hedgerows yellowed with winter and taller than a man. A roadside shrine to Mary stood at the outskirts of a village. The Virgin's face was serene in the cold, her arms spread in generous welcome, foolishly bright plastic flowers at her feet.

A sigh from her father had Maggie glancing over. He seemed a bit pale to her, a little drawn around the eyes. "You look tired, Da. Are you sure you don't want me to take you back home?"

"No, no." He took out his pipe, tapped it absently against his palm. "I want to watch the sea. There's a storm brewing, Maggie Mae. We'll have a show from the cliffs at Loop Head."

"We will at that."

Past the village the road narrowed alarmingly again until she was threading the lorry along like cotton through the eye of a needle. A man, bundled tight against the cold, trudged toward them, his faithful dog following stoically at his heels. Both man and dog stepped off the road into the hedges as the lorry eased by, inches from the toe of the man's boots. He nodded to Maggie and Tom in greeting.

"You know what I've been thinking, Da?"

"What's that?"

"If I could sell a few more pieces—just a few more mind—I could have another furnace. I want to work with more color, you see. If I could build another furnace, I could have more melts going. The fire-brick's not so costly, really. But I'll need more than two hundred."

"I've a bit put by."

"No, not again." On this she was firm. "I love you for it, but this I'll do on my own."

He took immediate umbrage and scowled at his pipe. "What's a father for, I'd like to know, if not to give to his children? You'll not have fancy clothes or pretty baubles, so if it's firebrick you want, then that's what you'll have."

"So I will," she shot back. "But I'll buy it myself. I've a need to do this myself. It's not the money I want. It's the faith."

"You've paid me back tenfold already." He sat back, drawing the window down a crack so that the wind whistled through as he lit his pipe. "I'm a rich man, Maggie. I have two lovely daughters, each of them a jewel. And though a man could ask for no more than that, I've a good solid house and friends to count on."

Maggie noticed he didn't include her mother in his treasures. "And always the pot at the end of the rainbow."

"Always that." He fell silent again, brooding. They passed old stone cabins, roofless and deserted on the verge of gray-green fields that stretched on, endless and impossibly beautiful in the gloomy light. And here a church, standing against the wind that was unbroken now, was blocked only by a few twisted and leafless trees.

It should have been a sad and lonely sight, but Tom found it beautiful. He didn't share Maggie's love of solitude, but when he looked out on a sight like this, with lowered sky and empty land meeting with barely a sight of man between, he understood it.

Through the whistling crack of the window, he could smell the sea. Once he'd dreamed of crossing it.

Once he'd dreamed of many things.

He had always searched for that pot of gold, and knew the failure to find it was his. He'd been a farmer by birth, but never by inclination. Now he'd lost all but a few acres of land, enough only for the flowers and vegetables his daughter Brianna grew so skillfully. Enough only to remind him that he had failed.

Too many schemes, he thought now as another sigh fetched up in his chest. His wife, Maeve, was right about that. He'd always been full of schemes, but never had the sense or the luck to make them work.

They chugged past another huddle of houses and a building whose owner boasted it was the last pub until New York. Tom's spirits lifted at the sight, as they always did.

"Shall we sail over to New York, Maggie, and have a pint?" he said, as he always did.

"I'll buy the first round."

He chuckled. A feeling of urgency came over him as she pulled the lorry to the end of the road, where it gave way to grass and rock, and at last to the windswept sea that spanned to America.

They stepped into a roar of sound that was wind and water lashing furiously against the teeth and fists of black rock. With their arms linked, they staggered like drunks, then laughing, began to walk.

"It's madness to come here on such a day."

"Aye, a fine madness. Feel the air, Maggie! Feel it. It wants to blow us from here to Dublin Town. Do you remember when we went to Dublin?"

"We saw a juggler tossing colored balls. I loved it so much you learned how yourself."

His laugh boomed out like the sea itself. "Oh, the apples I bruised."

"We had pies and cobblers for weeks."

"And I thought I could make a pound or two with my new skill and took me up to Galway to the fair."

"And spent every penny you made on presents for me and Brianna."

His color was back, she noted, and his eyes were shining. She went willingly with him across the uneven grass into the gnashing teeth of the wind. There they stood on the edge of the powerful Atlantic with its warrior waves striking at the merciless rock. Water crashed, then whipped away again, leaving dozens of waterfalls tumbling through crevices. Overhead, gulls cried and wheeled, cried and wheeled, the sound echoing on and on against the thunder of the waves.

The spray plumed high, white as snow at the base, clear as crystal in the beads that scattered in the icy air. No boat bobbed on the rugged surface of the sea today. The fierce whitecaps rode the sea alone.

She wondered if her father came here so often because the merging of sea and stone symbolized marriage as much as war to his eyes. And his marriage had been forever a battle, the constant bitterness and anger of his wife's lashing forever at his heart, and gradually, oh so gradually, wearing it away.

"Why do you stay with her, Da?"

"What?" He pulled his attention back from the sea and the sky.

"Why do you stay with her?" Maggie repeated. "Brie and I are grown now. Why do you stay where you're not happy?"

"She's my wife," he said simply.

"Why should that be an answer?" she demanded. "Why should it be an end? There's no love between you, no liking, if it comes to that. She's made your life hell as long as I can remember."

"You're too hard on her." This, too, was on his head, he thought. For loving the child so much that he'd been helpless not to accept her unconditional love for him. A love, he knew, that had left no room for understanding the disappointments of the woman who had borne her. "What's between your mother and me is as much my doing as hers. A marriage is a delicate thing, Maggie, a balance of two hearts and two hopes. Sometimes the weight's just too heavy on the one side, and the other can't lift to it. You'll understand when you've a marriage of your own."

"I'll never marry." She said in fiercely, like a vow before God. "I'll never give anyone the right to make me so unhappy."

"Don't say that. Don't." He squeezed her hard, worried. "There's nothing more precious than marriage and family. Nothing in the world."

"If that's so, how can it be such a prison?"

"It isn't meant to be." The weakness came over him again, and all at once he felt the cold deep in his bones. "We haven't given you a good example, your mother and I, and I'm sorry for it. More than I can tell you. But I know this, Maggie, my girl. When you love with all you are, it isn't unhappiness alone you risk. It's heaven, too."

She pressed her face into his coat, drew comfort from the scent of him. She couldn't tell him that she knew, had known for years, that it hadn't been heaven for him. And that he would never have bolted the door to that marital prison behind him if it hadn't been for her.

"Did you love her, ever?"

"I did. And it was as hot as one of your furnaces. You came from that, Maggie Mae. Born in fire you were, like one of your finest and boldest statues. However much that fire cooled, it burned once. Maybe if it hadn't flared so bright, so hard, we could have made it last."

Something in his tone made her look up again, study his face. "There was someone else."

Like a honeyed blade, the memory was painful and sweet. Tom looked to sea again, as if he could gaze across it and find the woman he'd let go. "Aye, there was once. But it wasn't to be. Had no right to be. I'll tell you this, when love comes, when the arrow strikes the heart, there's no stopping it. And even bleeding is a pleasure. So don't say never to me, Maggie. I want for you what I couldn't have."

She didn't say it to him, but she thought it. "I'm twenty-three, Da, and Brie's but a year behind me. I know what the church says, but I'm damned if I believe there's a God in heaven who finds joy in punishing a man for the whole of his life for a mistake."

"Mistake." His brows lowered, Tom stuck his pipe in his teeth. "My marriage has not been a mistake, Margaret Mary, and you'll not say so now, nor ever again. You and Brie came from it. A mistake—no, a miracle. I was past forty when you were born, without a thought in my head to starting a family. I think of what my life would have been like without the two of you. Where would I be now? A man near seventy, alone. Alone." He cupped her face in his hands and his eyes were fierce on hers. "I thank God every day I found your mother, and that between us we made something I can leave behind. Of all the things I've done, and not done, you and Brianna are my first and truest joys. Now there'll be no more talk of mistakes or unhappiness, do you hear?"

"I love you, Da."

His face softened. "I know it. Too much, I think, but I can't regret it." The sense of urgency came on him again, like a wind whispering to hurry. "There's something I'd ask of you, Maggie."

"What is it?"

He studied her face, his fingers molding it as if he suddenly had a need to memorize every feature— the sharp stubborn chin, the soft curve of cheek, the eyes as green and restless as the sea that clashed beneath them.

"You're a strong one, Maggie. Tough and strong, with a true heart beneath the steel. God knows you're smart. I can't begin to understand the things you know, or how you know them. You're my bright star, Maggie, the way Brie's my cool rose. I want you, the both of you, to follow where your dreams lead you. I want that more than I can say. And when you chase them down, you'll chase them as much for me as for yourself."

The roar of the sea dimmed in his ears, as did the light in his eyes. For a moment Maggie's face blurred and faded.

"What is it?" Alarmed, she clutched at him. He'd gone gray as the sky, and suddenly looked horribly old. "Are you ill, Da? Let me get you back into the lorry."

"No." It was vital, for reasons he didn't know, that

he stand here, just here at the farthest tip of his country, and finish what he'd begun. "I'm fine. Just a twinge is all."

"You're freezing." Indeed, his wiry body felt like little more than a bag of icy bones in her hands.

"Listen to me." His voice was sharp. "Don't let anything stop you from going where you need to go, from doing what you need to do. Make your mark on the world, and make it deep so it lasts. But don't—"

"Da!" Panic bubbled inside her as he staggered, fell to his knees. "Oh God, Da, what is it? Your heart?"

No, not his heart, he thought through a haze of bleary pain. For he could hear that beating hard and fast in his own ears. But he felt something inside him breaking, bursting and slipping away. "Don't harden yourself, Maggie. Promise me. You'll never lose what's inside you. You'll take care of your sister. And your mother. You'll promise me that."

"You've got to get up." She dragged at him, fighting off fear. The thrash of the sea sounded now like a storm breaking, a nightmare storm that would sweep them both off the cliff and onto the spearing rocks. "Do you hear me, Da? You've got to get up now."

"Promise me."

"Aye, I promise. I swear it before God, I'll see to both of them, always." Her teeth were chattering; stinging tears already ran down her cheeks.

"I need a priest," he gasped out.

"No, no, you need only to get out of this cold." But she knew it was a lie as she said it. He was slipping away from her; no more how tightly she held his body, what was inside him was slipping away. "Don't leave me like this. Not like this." Desperate, she scanned the fields, the beaten paths where people walked year after year to stand as they had stood. But there was nothing, no one, so she bit back a scream for help. "Try, Da, come and try now to get up. We'll get you to a doctor."

He rested his head on her shoulder and sighed. There was no pain now, only numbness. "Maggie," he said. Then he whispered another name, a stranger's name, and that was all.

"No." As if to protect him from the wind he no longer felt, she wrapped her arms tight around him, rocking, rocking, rocking as she sobbed.

And the wind trumpeted down to the sea and brought with it the first needles of icy rain.

❧ Chapter Two

THOMAS Concannon's wake would be talked about for years. There was fine food and fine music, as he'd planned for his daughter's celebration party. The house where he'd lived out his last years was crowded with people.

Tom hadn't been a rich man, some would say, but he was a man who'd been wealthy in friends.

They came from the village, and the village beyond that. From the farms and shops and cottages. They brought food, as neighbors do for such occasions, and the kitchen was quickly stocked with breads and meats and cakes. They drank to his life and serenaded his passing.

The fires burned warm to stave off the gale that rattled the windows and the chill of mourning.

But Maggie was sure she'd never be warm again. She sat near the fire in the tidy parlor while the company filled the house around her. In the flames she saw the cliffs, the boiling sea—and herself, alone, holding her dying father.

"Maggie."

Startled, she turned and saw Murphy crouched in front of her. He pressed a steaming mug into her hands.

"What is it?"

"Mostly whiskey, with a bit of tea to warm it up." His eyes were kind and grieving. "Drink it down now. There's a girl. Won't you eat a little? It would do you good."

"I can't," she said, but did as he asked and drank. She'd have sworn she felt each fiery drop slide down her throat. "I shouldn't have taken him out there, Murphy. I should have seen he was sick."

"That's nonsense, and you know it. He looked fine and fit when he left the pub. Why, he'd been dancing, hadn't he?"

Dancing, she thought. She'd danced with her father on the day he died. Would she, someday, find comfort in that? "But if we hadn't been so far away. So alone . . ."

"The doctor told you plain, Maggie. It would have made no difference. The aneurysm killed him, and it was mercifully quick."

"Aye, it was quick." Her hand trembled, so she drank again. It was the time afterward that had been slow. The dreadful time when she had driven his body away from the sea, with her breath wheezing in her throat and her hands frozen on the wheel.

"I've never seen a man so proud as he was of you." Murphy hesitated, looked down at his hands. "He was like a second father to me, Maggie."

"I know that." She reached out, brushed Murphy's hair off his brow. "So did he."

So now he'd lost a father twice, Murphy thought. And for the second time felt the weight of grief and responsibility.

"I want to tell you, to make sure you know, that if there's anything, anything a'tall you're needing, or your family needs, you've only to tell me."

"It's good of you to say so, and to mean it."

He looked up again; his eyes, that wild Celtic blue, met hers. "I know it was hard when he had to sell the land. And hard that I was the one to buy it."

"No." Maggie set the mug aside and laid her hands over his. "The land wasn't important to him."

"Your mother . . ."

"She would have blamed a saint for buying it," Maggie said briskly. "Even though the money it brought put food in her mouth. I tell you it was easier that it was you. Brie and I don't begrudge you a blade of grass, that's the truth, Murphy." She made herself smile at him, because they both needed it. "You've done what he couldn't, and what he simply didn't want to do. You've made the land grow. Let's not hear any more talk like that."

She looked around then, as if she'd just walked out of an empty room into a full one. Someone was playing the flute, and O'Malley's daughter, heavy with her first child, was singing a light, dreamy air. There was a trill of laughter from across the room, lively and free. A baby was crying. Men were huddled here and there, talking of Tom, and of the weather, of Jack Marley's sick roan mare and the Donovans' leaking cottage roof.

The women talked of Tom as well, and of the weather, of children and of weddings and wakes.

She saw an old woman, an elderly and distant cousin, in worn shoes and mended stockings, spinning a story for a group of wide-eyed youngsters while she knitted a sweater.

"He loved having people around, you know." The pain was there, throbbing like a wound in her voice. "He would have filled the house with them daily if he could. It was always a wonder to him that I preferred to be on my own." She drew in a breath and hoped her voice was casual. "Did you ever hear him speak of someone named Amanda?"

"Amanda?" Murphy frowned and considered. "No. Why do you ask?"

"It's nothing. I probably mistook it." She shrugged it away. Surely her father's dying words hadn't been a strange woman's name. "I should go help Brie in the kitchen. Thanks for the drink, Murphy. And for the rest." She kissed him and rose.

There was no easy way to get through the room, of course. She had to stop again and again, to hear words of comfort, or a quick story about her father, or in the case of Tim O'Malley, to offer comfort herself.

"Jesus, I'll miss him," Tim said, unabashedly wiping his eyes. "Never had a friend as dear to me, and never will again. He joked about opening a pub of his own, you know. Giving me a bit of competition."

"I know." She also knew it hadn't been a joke, but another dream.

"He wanted to be a poet," someone else put in while Maggie hugged Tim and patted his back. "Said he'd only lacked the words to be one."

"He had the heart of a poet," Tim said brokenly. "The heart and soul of one, to be sure. A finer man never walked this earth than Tom Concannon."

Maggie had words with the priest about funeral services set for the next morning, and finally slipped into the kitchen.

It was as crowded as the rest of the house, with women busily serving food or making it. The sounds and smells were of life here—kettles singing, soups simmering, a ham baking. Children wandered underfoot, so that women—with that uncanny maternal grace they seemed to be born with—dodged around them or scooped them up as needs demanded.

The wolfhound puppy that Tom had given Brianna on her last birthday snored contentedly under the kitchen table. Brianna herself was at the stove, her face composed, her hands competent. Maggie could see the subtle signs of grief in the quiet eyes and the soft, unsmiling mouth.

"You'll have a plate." One of the neighbor women spotted Maggie and began to heap food together. "And you'll eat or answer to me."

"I only came in to help."

"You'll help by eating some of this food. Enough for an army it is. You know your father once sold me a rooster. Claimed it was the finest cock in the county and would keep me hens happy for years to come. He had a way with him, Tom did, that made you believe what he was saying even though you knew it for nonsense." She piled great portions of food on the plate as she spoke, taking time out to pat a child out of the way without breaking rhythm. "Well, a terrible, mean bird he turned out to be, and never crew once in his miserable life."

Maggie smiled a bit and said what was expected of her, though she knew the tale well. "And what did you do with the rooster Da sold you, Mrs. Mayo?"

"I wrung the cursed cock's neck and boiled him into stew. Gave your father a bowl of it, too, I did. Said he'd never tasted better in his whole life." She laughed heartily and pressed the plate on Maggie.

"And was it?"

"The meat was stringy and tough as old leather. But Tom ate every drop. Bless him."

So Maggie ate, because there was nothing she could do but live and go on. She listened to the stories and told some of her own. When the sun went down and the kitchen slowly emptied, she sat down and held the puppy in her lap.

"He was loved," Maggie said.

"He was." Brianna stood beside the stove, a cloth in her hand and a dazed look in her eyes. There was no one left to feed or tend to, nothing to keep her mind and her hands busy. Grief swarmed into her heart like angry bees. To hold it off awhile longer, she began to put away the dishes.

She was slim, almost willowy, with a cool, controlled way of moving. If there had been money and means, she might have been a dancer. Her hair, rosy gold and thick, was neatly coiled at the nape of her neck. A white apron covered her plain black dress.

In contrast, Maggie's hair was a fiery tangle around her face. She wore a skirt she'd forgotten to press and a sweater that needed mending.

"It won't clear for tomorrow." Brianna had forgotten the dishes in her hands and stared out the window at the blustery night.

"No, it won't. But people will come, just the same, as they did today."

"We'll have them back here after. There's so much food. I don't know what we'll do with all of it. . . ." Brianna's voice trailed off.

"Did she ever come out of her room?"

Brianna stood still for a moment, then began slowly to stack plates. "She's not well."

"Oh God, don't. Her husband's dead and everyone who knew him came here today. She can't even stir herself to pretend it matters."

"Of course it matters to her." Brianna's voice tightened. She didn't think she could bear an argument now, not when her heart was swelling up like a tumor in her chest. "She lived with him more than twenty years."

"And little else she did with him. Why do you defend her? Even now."

Brianna's hand pressed a plate so hard she wondered it didn't snap in two. Her voice remained perfectly calm, perfectly reasonable. "I'm defending no one, only saying what's true. Can't we keep peace? At least until we've buried him, can't we keep peace in this house?"

"There's never been peace in this house." Maeve spoke from the doorway. Her face wasn't ravaged by tears, but it was cold and hard and unforgiving. "He saw to that. He saw to it just as he's seeing to it now. Even dead, he's making my life a hardship."

"Don't speak of him." The fury Maggie had held back all day broke through, a jagged rock through fragile glass. She shoved away from the table, sending the dog racing for cover. "Don't you dare to speak ill of him."

"I'll speak how I choose." Maeve's hand clutched at the shawl she wore, drew it tight to her throat. It was wool, and she'd always wanted silk. "He gave me nothing but grief while he lived. Now he's dead and has given me more."

"I see no tears in your eyes, Mother."

"And you won't. I'll neither live nor die a hypocrite, but speak God's own truth. He'll go to the devil for what's he's done to me this day." Her eyes, bitter and blue, shifted from Maggie to Brianna. "And as God won't forgive him, neither will I."

"Do you know God's mind now?" Maggie demanded. "Has all your prayerbook reading and rosary clacking given you a line straight to the Lord?"

"You'll not blaspheme." Maeve's cheeks reddened with temper. "You'll not blaspheme in this house."

"I'll speak how I choose." Maggie echoed her mother's words with a tight smile. "I'll tell you Tom Concannon needed none of your stingy forgiveness."

"Enough." Though her insides were trembling, Brianna laid a steadying hand on Maggie's shoulder. She took a long, careful breath to be certain her voice was calm. "I've told you, Mother, I'll give the house to you. You've nothing to worry about."

"What's this?" Maggie turned to her sister. "What about the house?"

"You heard what it said at the will reading," Brianna began, but Maggie shook her head.

"I didn't take any of it in. Lawyer's talk. I wasn't paying attention."

"He left it to her." Still trembling, Maeve lifted a finger and jabbed it out as an accusation. "He left the house to her. All the years I suffered and sacrificed, and he takes even that from me."

"She'll settle down right enough when she knows she has a sturdy roof over her head and no need to do anything to keep it," Maggie said once her mother left the room.

It was true enough. And Brianna thought she could maintain the peace. She'd had a lifetime of practice. "I'll keep the house, and she'll stay here. I can tend them both."

"Saint Brianna," Maggie murmured, but there was no malice in it. "We'll manage it between us." The new furnace would have to wait, she decided. But as long as McGuinness kept buying, there would be enough to hold the two houses together.

"I've thought about . . . Da and I talked about it a little while ago, and I've been thinking. . . ." Brianna hesitated.

Maggie pushed aside her own thoughts. "Just say it."

"It needs some fixing up, I know, and I've only a bit left of what Gran left me—and there's the lien."

"I'll be paying off the lien."

"No, that's not right."

"It's perfectly right." Maggie got up to fetch the teapot. "He took it to send me to Venice, didn't he? Mortgaged the house and weathered the gale Mother brought down on his head for doing it. I had three years of training thanks to him. And I'll pay it back."

"The house is mine." Brianna's voice firmed. "And so's the lien."

Her sister had a soft look about her, but Maggie knew Brianna could be mule stubborn when it suited her. "Well, we can argue that to death. We'll both pay it off. If you won't let me do it for you, Brie, let me do it for him. I've a need to."

"We'll work it out." Brianna took the cup of tea Maggie poured her.

"Tell me what you've been thinking."

"All right." It felt foolish. She could only hope it didn't sound so. "I want to turn the house into a B-and-B."

"A hotel!" Stunned, Maggie could only stare. "You want to have paying guests nosing about the place? You'll have no privacy at all, Brianna, and you'll be working from morning till night."

"I like having people around," Brianna said coolly. "Not everyone wants to be a hermit like you. And I've a knack for it, I think, for making people comfortable. It's in the blood." She stuck out her chin. "Granda ran a hotel, didn't he, and Gran ran it after he died. I could do it."

"I never said you couldn't, I just for the life of me can't see why you'd want to. Strangers in and out every day." Why, it gave her the shudders just to imagine it.

"I can only hope they'll come. The bedrooms upstairs will need freshening, of course." Brianna's eyes blurred as she thought through the details. "Some paint, some paper. A new rug or two. And the plumbing needs work, God knows. The fact is, we'd need another bath altogether, but I think the closet down at the end of the hall upstairs would serve. I might have a little apartment added off the kitchen here, for Mother—so she won't be disturbed. And I'd add a bit to the gardens, put up a little sign. Nothing on a grand scale, you see. Just small and tasteful and comfortable."

"You want this," Maggie murmured, seeing the light in her sister's eyes. "You truly do."

"I do, yes. I want it."

"Then do it." Maggie grabbed her hands. "Just do it, Brie. Freshen your rooms and fix your plumbing. Put up a fine sign. He wanted it for you."

"I think he did. He laughed when I talked to him about it, in that big way he had."

"Aye, he had a grand laugh."

"And he kissed me and joked about me being an innkeeper's granddaughter, and following tradition. If I started small enough, I could open for summer this year. The tourists, they come to the west counties in the summer especially, and they look for a nice, comfortable place to spend the night. I could—" Brianna shut her eyes. "Oh, listen to this talk, and we're burying our father tomorrow."

"It's just what he'd want to hear." Maggie was able to smile again. "A grand scheme like that, he'd have cheered you on!"

"We Concannons." Brianna shook her head. "We're great ones for scheming."

"Brianna, that day on the cliff, he talked of you. He called you his rose. He'd want you to bloom."

And she'd been his star, Maggie thought. She was going to do whatever she could to shine.

🍀 Chapter Three

SHE was alone—as she liked best. From the doorway of her cottage she watched the rain lashing Murphy Muldoon's fields, slashing wildly over the grass and stone while the sun beamed hopefully, stubbornly, behind her. There was the possibility of a dozen different weathers in the layered sky, all brief and fickle.

That was Ireland.

But for Margaret Mary Concannon, the rain was a fine thing. She often preferred it to the warm slant of sun and the clear brilliance of cloudless blue skies. The rain was a soft gray curtain, tucking her away from the world. Or more important, cutting out the world, beyond her view of hill and field and sleek spotted cows.

For while the farm, the stone fences and green grasses beyond the tangle of fuchsia no longer belonged to Maggie or her family, this spot with its small wild garden and damp spring air was her own.

She was a farmer's daughter, true enough. But no farmer was she. In the five years since her father's death, she'd set about making her own place—and the mark he'd asked her to make. Perhaps it wasn't so deep as yet, but she continued to sell what she made, in Galway now and Cork, as well as Ennis.

She needed nothing more than what she had. Wanted more, perhaps, but she knew that desires, no matter how deep and dragging, didn't pay the bills. She also knew that some ambitions, when realized, carried a heavy price.

If from time to time she grew frustrated or restless, she had only to remind herself that she was where she needed to be, and doing what she chose to do.

But on mornings like this, with the rain and the sun at war, she thought of her father, and of the dreams he'd never seen come true.

He'd died without wealth, without success and without the farm that had been plowed and harvested by Concannon hands for generations.

She didn't resent the fact that so much of her birthright had been sold off for taxes and debts and the high-blown fantasies of her father. Perhaps there was a tug of sentiment and regret for the hillocks and fields she had once raced over with all the arrogance and innocence of youth. But that was past. Indeed, she wanted no part of the working of it, the worrying over it. She had little of the love of growing things that stirred her sister, Brianna. True, she enjoyed her garden, the big defiant blooms and the scents that wafted from them. But the flowers grew despite her periods of neglect.

She had her place, and anything beyond it was out of her realm, and therefore, most usually, out of her mind. Maggie preferred needing no one, and certainly needing nothing she could not provide herself.

Dependence, she knew, and the longing for more than what you had, led to unhappiness and discontent. She had her parents' example before her.

Pausing there, just past the open door into the chilling rain, she breathed in the air, the damp sweetness of it tinged with spring from the black-thorn blossoms that formed a hedgerow to the east and the early roses struggling into bloom to the west. She was a small woman, shapely beneath the baggy jeans and flannel shirt. Over her shoulder-length, fiery hair she wore a slouch hat, as gray as the rain. Beneath its bill her eyes were the moody, mystical green of the sea.

The rain dampened her face, the soft curve of cheek and chin, the wide, melancholy mouth. It dewed the creamy redhead's complexion and joined the gold freckles scattered over the bridge of her nose.

She drank the strong sweet breakfast tea from a glass mug of her own design and ignored the phone that had begun to shrill from the kitchen. Ignoring the summons was as much policy as habit, particularly when her mind was drifting toward her work. There was a sculpture forming in her head, as clear as a raindrop, she thought. Pure and smooth, with glass flowing into glass in the heart of it.

The pull of the vision beckoned. Dismissing the ringing phone, she walked through the rain toward her workshop and the soothing roar of the glass furnace.

From his offices in Dublin, Rogan Sweeney listened to the ring of the phone through the receiver and swore. He was a busy man, too busy to waste his time on a rude and temperamental artist who refused to answer the sharp knock of opportunity.

He had businesses to see to, calls to answer, files to read, figures to tally. He should, while the day was young, go down to the gallery and oversee the latest shipment. The Native American pottery was, after all, his baby, and he'd spent months selecting the best of the best.

But that, of course, was a challenge already met. That particular show would once again ensure that Worldwide was a top international gallery. Meanwhile the woman, the damn, stubborn Clarewoman, was crowding his mind. Though he'd yet to meet her face-to-face, she and her genius occupied too much of his mind.

The new shipment would, of course, receive as much of his skill, energy and time as it required. But a new artist, particularly one whose work had so completely captured his imagination, excited on a different level. The thrill of discovery was as vital to Rogan as the careful development, marketing and sale of an artist's works.

He wanted Concannon, exclusively, for Worldwide Galleries. As with most of his desires, all of which Rogan deemed quite reasonable, he wouldn't rest until it was accomplished.

He'd been raised to succeed—the third generation of prosperous merchants who found clever ways to turn pence into pounds. The business his grandfather had founded sixty years before flourished under his leadership—because Rogan Sweeney refused to take no for an answer. He would achieve his goals by sweat, by charm, by tenacity or any other means he deemed suitable.

Margaret Mary Concannon and her unbridled talent was his newest and most frustrating goal.

He wasn't an unreasonable man in his own mind, and would have been shocked and insulted to discover that he was described as just that by many of his acquaintances. If he expected long hours and hard work from his employees, he expected no less of himself. Drive and dedication weren't merely virtues to Rogan, they were necessities that had been bred in his bones.

He could have handed the reins of Worldwide over to a manager and lived quite comfortably on the proceeds. Then he could travel, not for business but for pleasure, enjoying the fruits of his inheritance without sweating over the harvesting.

He could have, but his responsibility and thirsty ambition were his birthrights.

And M. M. Concannon, glass artist, hermit and eccentric was his obsession.

He was going to make changes in Worldwide Galleries, changes that would reflect his own vision, that would celebrate his own country. M. M. Concannon was his first step, and he'd be damned if her stubbornness would make him stumble.

She was unaware—because she refused to listen, Rogan thought grimly—that he intended to make her Worldwide's first native Irish star. In the past, with his father and grandfather at the helm, the galleries had specialized in international art. Rogan didn't intend to narrow the scope, but he did intend to shift the focus and give the world the best of the land of his birth.

He would risk both his money and his reputation to do it.

If his first artist was a success, as he fully intended her to be, his investment would have paid off, his instincts would have been justified and his dream, a new gallery that showcased works exclusively by Irish artists, would become reality.

To begin, he wanted Margaret Mary Concannon.

Annoyed with himself, he rose from his antique oak desk to stand by the window. The city stretched out before him, its broad streets and green squares, the silver glint that was the river and the bridges that spanned it.

Below, traffic moved in a steady stream, laborers and tourists merging on the street in a colorful stream in the sunlight. They seemed very distant to him now as they strolled in packs or twosomes. He watched a young couple embrace, a casual linking of arms, meeting of lips. Both wore backpacks and expressions of giddy delight.

He turned away, stung by an odd little arrow of envy.

He was unused to feeling restless, as he was now. There was work on his desk, appointments in his book, yet he turned to neither. Since childhood he'd moved with purpose from education to profession, from success to success. As had been expected of him. As he had expected of himself.

He'd lost both of his parents seven years before when his father had suffered a heart attack behind the wheel of his car and had smashed into a utility pole. He could still remember the grim panic, and the almost dreamy disbelief, that had cloaked him during the flight from Dublin to London, where his mother and father had traveled for business and the horrible, sterile scent of hospital.

His father had died on impact. His mother had lived barely an hour longer. So they had both been gone before he'd arrived, long before he'd been able to accept it. But they'd taught him a great deal before he'd lost them—about family and pride of heritage, the love of art, the love of business and how to combine them.

At twenty-six he'd found himself the head of Worldwide and its subsidiaries, responsible for staff, for decisions, for the art placed in his hands. For seven years he'd worked not only to make the business grow, but to make it shine. It had been more than enough for him.

This unsettled sensation, the dilemma of it, he knew had its roots in the breezy winter afternoon when he had first seen Maggie Concannon's work.

That first piece, spied during an obligatory tea with his grandmother, had started him on this odyssey to possess—no, he thought, uncomfortable with the word. To control, he corrected, he wanted to control the fate of the artistry, and the career of the artist. Since that afternoon, he'd been able to buy only two pieces of her work. One was as delicate as a daydream, a slim almost weightless column riddled with shimmering rainbows and hardly larger than the span of his hand from wrist to fingertip.

The second, and the one he could admit privately haunted and enticed him, was a violent nightmare, fired from a passionate mind into a turbulent tangle of glass. It should have been unbalanced, he thought now as he studied the piece on his desk. It should have been ugly with its wild war of colors and shapes, the grasping tendrils curling and clawing out of the squat base.

Instead, it was fascinating and uncomfortably sexual. And it made him wonder what kind of woman could create both pieces with equal skill and power.

Since he had purchased it a little more than two months before, he had tried with no success to contact the artist and interest her in patronage.

He had twice reached her by phone, but the conversation on her part had been brief to the point of rudeness. She didn't require a patron, particularly a Dublin businessman with too much education and too little taste.

Oh, that had stung.

She was, she had told him in her musical west county brogue, content to create at her own pace and sell her work when and where it suited her. She had no need for his contracts, or for someone to tell her what must be sold. It was her work, was it not, so why didn't he go back to his ledgers, of which she was certain he had plenty, and leave her to it?

Insolent little twit, he thought, firing up again. Here he was offering a helping hand, a hand that countless other artists would have begged for, and she snarled at it.

He should leave her to it, Rogan mused. Leave her to create in obscurity. It was certain that neither he nor Worldwide needed her.

But, damn it all, he *wanted* her.

On impulse, he picked up his phone and buzzed his secretary. "Eileen, cancel my appointments for the next couple of days. I'm going on a trip."

It was a rare thing for Rogan to have business in the west counties. He remembered a family holiday from childhood. Most usually his parents had preferred trips to Paris or Milan, or an occasional break in the villa they kept on the French Mediterranean. There had been trips that had combined business and pleasure. New York, London, Bonn, Venice, Boston. But once, when he had been nine or ten, they had driven to the Shannon area to take in the wild, glorious scenery of the west. He remembered it in patches, the dizzying views from the Cliffs of Mohr, the dazzling panoramas and gem-bright waters of the Lake District, the quiet villages and the endless green of farmlands.

Beautiful it was. But it was also inconvenient. He was already regretting his impulsive decision to make the drive, particularly since the directions he'd been given in the nearby village had taken him onto a pitted excuse for a road. His Aston Martin handled it well, even as the dirt turned to mud under the ceaseless driving rain. His mood didn't negotiate the potholes as smoothly as did his car.

Only stubbornness kept him from turning back. The woman would listen to reason, by God. He would see to it. If she wanted to bury herself behind hedges of furze and hawthorn, it was her business. But her art was his. Or would be.

Following the directions he'd been given at the local post office, he passed the bed-and-breakfast called Blackthorn Cottage with its glorious gardens and trim blue shutters. Farther on there were stone cabins, sheds for animals, a hay barn, a slate-roofed shed where a man worked on a tractor.

The man lifted a hand in salute, then went back to work as Rogan maneuvered the car around the narrow curve. The farmer was the first sign of life, other than livestock, he had seen since leaving the village.

How anyone survived in this godforsaken place was beyond him. He'd take Dublin's crowded streets and conveniences over the incessant rain and endless fields every day of the week. Scenery be damned.

She'd hidden herself well, he thought. He'd barely caught sight of the garden gate and the whitewashed cottage beyond it through the tumbling bushes of privet and fuchsia.

Rogan slowed, though he'd nearly been at a crawl in any case. There was a short drive occupied by a faded blue lorry going to rust. He pulled his dashing white Aston behind it and got out.

He circled around to the gate, moved down the short walk that cut between heavy-headed, brilliant flowers that bobbed in the rain. He gave the door, which was painted a bold magenta, three sharp raps, then three again before impatience had him stalking to a window to peer inside.

There was a fire burning low in the grate, and a sugan chair pulled up close. A sagging sofa covered in some wild floral print that mated reds and blues and purples teetered in a corner. He would have thought he'd mistaken the house but for the pieces of her work set throughout the small room. Statues and bottles, vases and bowls stood, sat or reclined on every available surface.

Rogan wiped the wet from the window and spied the many-branch candelabra positioned dead center of the mantel. It was fashioned of glass so clear, so pure, it might have been water frozen in place. The arms curved fluidly up, the base a waterfall. He felt the quick surge, the inner click that presaged acquisition.

Oh yes, he'd found her.

Now if she'd just answer the damn door.

He gave up on the front and walked through the

wet grass around to the back of the cabin. More flowers, growing wild as weeds. Or, he corrected, growing wild *with* weeds. Miss Concannon obviously didn't spend much time tidying her beds.

There was a lean-to beside the door under which bricks of turf were piled. An ancient bike with one flat tire was propped beside them along with a pair of Wellingtons that were muddy to the ankles.

He started to knock again when the sound coming from behind him had him turning toward the sheds. The roar, constant and low, was almost like the sea. He could see the smoke pluming out of the chimney into the leaden sky.

The building had several windows, and despite the chilly damp of the day, some were propped open. Her workshop, no doubt, Rogan thought, and crossed to it, pleased that he had tracked her down and confident of the outcome of their meeting.

He knocked and, though he received no answer, shoved the door open. He had a moment to register the blast of heat, the sharp smells and the small woman seated in a big wooden chair, a long pipe in her hands.

He thought of fairies and magic spells.

"Close the door, damn you, there's a draft."

He obeyed automatically, bristling under the sharp fury of the order. "Your windows are open."

"Ventilation. Draft. Idiot." She said nothing more, nor did she spare him so much as a glance. She set her mouth to the pipe and blew.

He watched the bubble form, fascinated despite himself. Such a simple procedure, he thought, only breath and molten glass. Her fingers worked on the pipe, turning it and turning it, fighting gravity, using it, until she was satisfied with the shape.

She thought nothing of him at all as she went about her work. She necked the bubble, using jacks to indent a shallow grove just beyond the head of the pipe. There were steps, dozens of them yet to take, but she could already see the finished work as clearly as if she held it cool and solid in her hand.

At the furnace, she pushed the bubble under the surface of the molten glass heated there to make the second gather. Back at the bench she rolled the gather in a wooden block to chill the glass and form the "skin." All the while the pipe was moving, moving, steady and controlled by her hands, just as the initial stages of the work had been controlled by her breath.

She repeated the same procedure over and over again, endlessly patient, completely focused while Rogan stood by the door and watched. She used larger blocks for forming as the shape grew. And as time passed and she spoke not a word, he took off his wet coat and waited.

The room was filled with heat from the furnace. It felt as though his clothes were steaming on his body. She seemed sublimely unaffected, centered on her work, reaching for a new tool now and then while one hand constantly revolved the pipe.

The chair on which she sat was obviously home-made, with a deep seat and long arms, hooks set here and there where tools hung. There were buckets nearby filled with water or sand or hot wax.

She took a tool, one that looked to Rogan to be a pair of sharp-pointed tongs, and placed them at the edge of the vessel she was creating. It seemed they would flow straight through, the glass so resembled water, but she drew the shape of it out, lengthening it, slimming it.

When she rose again, he started to speak, but a sound from her, something like a snarl, had him lifting a brow and keeping his silence.

Fine then, he thought. He could be patient. An hour, two hours, as long as it took. If she could stand this vicious heat, so, by Christ, could he.

She didn't even feel it, so intent was she. She dipped a punt, another gather of molten glass, onto the side of the vessel she was creating. When the hot glass had softened the wall, she pushed a pointed file, coated with wax, into the glass.

Gently, gently.

Flames sparked under her hand as the wax burned. She had to work quickly now to keep the tool from sticking to the glass. The pressure had to be exactly right for the effect she wanted. The inner wall made contact with the outer wall, merging, creating the inner form, the angel swing.

Glass within glass, transparent and fluid.

She nearly smiled.

Carefully, she reblew the form before flattening the bottom with a paddle. She attached the vessel to a hot pontil. She plunged a file into a bucket of water, dripping it onto the neck groove of her vessel. Then, with a stroke that made Rogan jolt, she struck the file against the blowpipe. With the vessel now attached to the pontil, she thrust it into the furnace to heat the lip. Taking the vessel to the annealing oven, she rapped the pontil sharply with a file to break the seal.

She set the time and the temperature, then walked directly to a small refrigerator.

It was low to the floor, so she was forced to bend down. Rogan tilted his head at the view. The baggy jeans were beginning to wear quite thin in several interesting places. She straightened, turned and tossed one of the two soft-drink cans she taken out in his direction.

Rogan caught the missile by blind instinct before it connected with his nose.

"Still here?" She popped the top on her can and drank deeply. "You must be roasting in that suit." Now that her work was out of her mind and her eyes clear of the visions of it, she studied him.

Tall, lean, dark. She drank again. Well styled hair as black as a raven's wing and eyes as blue as a Kerry lake. Not hard to look at, she mused, tapping a finger against the can as they stared at each other. He had a good mouth, nicely sculpted and generous. But she didn't think he used it often for smiling. Not with those eyes. As blue as they were, and as appealing, they were cool, calculating and confident.

A sharply featured face with good bones. Good bones, good breeding, her granny used to say. And this one, unless she was very mistaken, had blue blood beneath the bone.

The suit was tailored, probably English. The tie discreet. There was a wink of gold at his cuffs. And he stood like a soldier—the sort that had earned plenty of brass and braid.

She smiled at him, content to be friendly now that her work had gone well. "Are you lost then?"

"No." The smile made her look like a pixie, one capable of all sorts of magic and mischief. He preferred the scowl she'd worn while she'd worked. "I've come a long way to speak with you, Miss Concannon. I'm Rogan Sweeney."

Her smile tilted a few degrees into something closer to a sneer. Sweeney, she thought. The man who wanted to take over her work. "The jackeen." She used the term, not terribly flattering, for a Dubliner. "Well, you're a stubborn one, Mr. Sweeney, that's the truth. I hope you had a pleasant drive so your trip won't be wasted."

"It was a miserable drive."

"Pity."

"But I don't consider the trip wasted." Though he would have preferred a strong cup of tea, he opened the soft-drink can. "You have an interesting setup here."

He scanned the room with its roaring furnace, its ovens and benches, the jumble of metal and wooden tools, the rods, the pipes and the shelves and cupboards he imagined held her chemicals.

"I do well enough, as I believe I told you over the phone."

"That piece you were working on when I came in. It was lovely." He stepped over to a table cluttered with sketch pads, pencils, charcoal and chalk. He picked up a sketch of the glass sculpture now annealing. It was delicate, fluid.

"Do you sell your sketches?"

"I'm a glass artist, Mr. Sweeney, not a painter."

He shot her a look, set the sketch down again. "If you were to sign that, I could get a hundred pounds for it."

She let out a snort of disbelief and tossed her empty can into a waste bin.

"And the piece you've just finished? How much will you ask for it."

"And why would that be your business?"

"Perhaps I'd like to buy it."

She considered, scooting up on the edge of a bench and swinging her feet. No one could tell her the worth of her work, not even herself. But a price—a price had to be set. She knew that well. For, artist or not, she had to eat.

Her formula for figuring price was loose and flexible. Unlike her formulas for making glass and mixing colors it had very little to do with science. She would calculate the time spent on producing the piece, her own feelings toward it, then factor in her opinion of the purchaser.

Her opinion of Rogan Sweeney was going to cost him dear.

"Two hundred and fifty pounds," she decided. A hundred of that was due to his gold cuff links.

"I'll write you a check." Then he smiled, and Maggie realized she was grateful he didn't seem to use that particular weapon often. Lethal, she thought, watching the way his lips curved, his eyes darkened. Charm floated down on him, light and effortless as a cloud. "And though I'll add it to my personal collection—for sentiment, shall we say?—I could easily get double that for it at my gallery."

"'Tis a wonder you stay in business, Mr. Sweeney, soaking your clients that way."

"You underestimate yourself, Miss Concannon." He crossed to her then, as if he knew he'd suddenly gained the upper hand. He waited until she'd tipped her head back to keep her eyes level with his. "That's why you need me."

"I know exactly what I'm doing."

"In here." He lifted an arm to encompass the room. "I've seen that quite dramatically for myself. But the business world is a different matter."

"I'm not interested in business."

"Precisely," he told her, smiling again as if she'd answered a particularly thorny question. "I, on the other hand, am fascinated by it."

She was at a disadvantage, sitting on the bench with him hovering over her. And she didn't care for it. "I don't want anyone messing in my work, Mr. Sweeney. I do what I choose, when I choose, and I get along very well."

"You do what you choose, when you choose." He picked up a wooden form from the bench as if to admire the grain. "And you do it very well. What a loss it would be for someone with your talent to merely get along. As to . . . messing about with your work, I have no intention of doing so. Though watching you work was certainly interesting." His eyes cut from the mold back to her with a speed that made her jolt. "Very interesting."

She pushed off the bench, the better to stand on her own feet. To gain the room required, she shoved him aside. "I don't want a manager."

"Ah, but you need one, Margaret Mary. You need one badly."

"A lot you know about what I'd be needing," she mumbled, and began to pace. "Some Dublin sharpie with fancy shoes."

Twice as much, he'd said; her mind replayed his earlier words. Twice what she'd asked. And there was Mother to care for, and the bills to pay, and Sweet Jesus, the price of chemicals was murderous.

"What I need's peace and quiet. And room." She whirled back at him. His very presense in the studio was crowding her. "Room. I don't need someone like you coming along and telling me we need three vases for next week, or twenty paperweights, or a half dozen goblets with pink stems. I'm not an assembly line, Sweeney, I'm an artist."

Very calmly, he took a pad and a gold pen out of his pocket and began to write.

"What are you doing there?"

"I'm noting down that you're not to be given orders for vases, paperweights or goblets with pink stems."

Her mouth twitched once before she controlled it. "I won't take orders, at all.

His eyes flicked to hers. "I believe that's understood. I own a factory or two, Miss Concannon, and know the difference between an assembly line and art. I happen to make my living through both."

"That's fine for you then." She waved both arms before setting her fists on her hips. "Congratulations. Why would you be needing me?"

"I don't." He replaced the pen and pad. "But I want you."

Her chin angled up. "But I don't want you."

"No, but you need me. And there is where we'll complement each other. I'll make you a rich woman, Miss Concannon. And more than that, a famous one."

He saw something flicker in her eyes at that. Ah, he thought, ambition. And he turned the key easily in the lock. "Do you create just to hide your gift on your own shelves and cupboards? To sell a few pieces here and there to keep the wolf from the door, and

horde the rest? Or do you want your work appreci-
ated, admired, even applauded?" His voice changed,
subtly, into a tone of sarcasm so light it stabbed
bloodlessly. "Or . . . are you afraid it won't be?"

Her eyes went molten as the blade struck true.
"I'm not afraid. My work stands. I spent three years
apprenticing in a Venice glass house, sweating as a
pontil boy. I learned the craft there, but not the art.
Because the art is in me." She thumped a hand on
her chest. "It's in me, and I breathe in and out into
the glass. Any who don't like my work can jump
straight into hell."

"Fair enough. I'll give you a show at my gallery,
and we'll see how many take the jump."

A dare, damn him. She hadn't been prepared for
it. "So a bunch of art snobs can sniff around my work
while they slurp champagne."

"You are afraid."

She hissed through her teeth and stomped to the
door. "Go away. Go away so I can think. You're
crowding my head."

"We'll talk again in the morning." He picked up
his coat. "Perhaps you can recommend a place I
could stay the night. Close by."

"Blackthorn Cottage, at the end of the road."

"Yes, I saw it." He slipped into his coat. "Lovely
garden, very trim."

"Neat and tidy as a pin. You'll find the beds soft
and the food good. My sister owns it, and she has a
practical, homemaking soul."

He lifted a brow at the tone, but said nothing.
"Then I trust I'll be comfortable enough until
morning."

"Just get out." She pulled open the door to the

rain. "I'll call the cottage in the morning if I want to talk to you again."

"A pleasure meeting you, Miss Concannon." Though it wasn't offered, he took her hand, held it while he looked into her eyes. "A greater one watching you work." On an impulse that surprised both of them, he lifted her hand to his lips, lingered just a moment over the taste of her skin. "I'll be back tomorrow."

"Wait for an invitation," she said, and closed the door smartly behind him.

&. Chapter Four

AT Blackthorn Cottage, the scones were always warm, the flowers always fresh and the kettle always on the boil. Though it was early in the season for guests, Brianna Concannon made Rogan comfortable in her serenely efficient manner, as she had all the other guests she's welcomed since that first summer after her father's death.

She served him tea in the tidy, polished parlor where a fire burned cheerfully and a vase full of freesia scented the air.

"I'll be serving dinner at seven, if that suits you, Mr. Sweeney." She was already thinking of ways to stretch the chicken she'd planned to cook so it would feed one more.

"That will be fine, Miss Concannon." He sipped the tea and found it perfect, a far cry from the chilly, sugar-laden soft drink Maggie had tossed at him. "You have a lovely place here."

"Thank you." It was, if not her only pride, perhaps her only joy. "If you need anything, anything at all, you've only to ask."

"If I could make use of the phone?"

"Of course." She started to step away to give him privacy, when he held up a hand, a signal of command to anyone who has served.

"The vase there on the table—your sister's work?"

Brianna's surprise at the question showed only in the quick widening of her eyes. "It is, yes. You know of Maggie's work?"

"I do. I have two pieces myself. And I've just purchased another even as it was made." He sipped his tea again, measuring Brianna. As different from Maggie as one piece of her work was from another. Which meant, he assumed, that they were the same somewhere beneath what the eye could see. "I've just come from her workshop."

"You were in Maggie's workshop?" Only true shock would have driven Brianna to ask a question of a guest with such a tone of disbelief. "Inside?"

"Is it so dangerous, then?"

A hint of a smile crossed Brianna's face, lightening her features. "You seem to be alive and well."

"Well enough. Your sister is an immensely talented woman."

"That she is."

Rogan recognized the same undercurrent of pride and annoyance in the statement as he had when Maggie had spoken of her sister. "Do you have other pieces of hers?"

"A few. She brings them by when the mood strikes her. If you'll not be needing anything else at the moment, Mr. Sweeney, I'll see about dinner."

Alone, Rogan settled back with his excellent tea. An interesting pair, he thought, the Concannon sisters. Brianna was taller, slimmer and certainly more lovely than Maggie. Her hair was rose gold rather than flame and fell in soft curls to her shoulders. Her eyes were a wide, pale green, almost translucent. Quiet, he thought, even a trifle aloof, like her manner. Her features were finer, her limbs softer, and she'd smelled of wildflowers rather than smoke and sweat.

All in all she was much more the type of woman he found appealing.

Yet he found his thoughts trailing back to Maggie with her compact body, her moody eyes and her uncertain temper. Artists, he mused, with their egos and insecurities, needed guidance, a firm hand. He let his gaze roam over the rose-colored vase with its swirls of glass from base to lip. He was very much looking forward to guiding Maggie Concannon.

"So, is he here?" Maggie slipped out of the rain into the warm, fragrant kitchen.

Brianna continued to peel potatoes. She'd been expecting the visit. "Who is he?"

"Sweeney." Crossing to the counter, Maggie snatched a peeled carrot and bit in. "Tall, dark, handsome and rich as sin. You can't miss him."

"In the parlor. You can take in a cup and join him for tea."

"I don't want to talk to him." Maggie hitched herself up on the counter, crossed her ankles. "What I wanted, Brie, love, is your opinion of him."

"He's polite and well-spoken."

Maggie rolled her eyes. "So's an altar boy in church."

"He's a guest in my home—"

"A paying one."

"And I've no intention," Brianna went on without pause, "of gossiping about him behind his back."

"Saint Brianna." Maggie crunched down on the

carrot, gestured with the stub of it. "What if I were to tell you that he's after managing my career?"

"Managing?" Brianna's hands faltered before they picked on the rhythm again. Peelings fell steadily on the newspaper she'd laid on the counter. "In what way?"

"Financially, to start. Displaying my work in his galleries and talking rich patrons into buying it for great sums of money." She waved the remains of the carrot before finishing it off. "All the man can think about is making money."

"Galleries," Brianna repeated. "He owns art galleries?"

"In Dublin and Cork. He has interests in others in London and New York. Paris, too, I think. Probably Rome. Everybody in the art world knows Rogan Sweeney."

The art world was as removed from Brianna's life as the moon. But she felt a quick, warm pride that her sister could claim it. "And he's taken an interest in your work."

"Stuck his aristocrat's nose in is what he's done." Maggie snorted. "Calling me on the phone, sending letters, all but demanding rights to everything I make. Now today, he pops up on my doorstep, telling me that I need him. Hah."

"And, of course, you don't."

"I don't need anyone."

"You don't, no." Brianna carried the vegetables to the sink to rinse. "Not you, Margaret Mary."

"Oh, I hate that tone, all cold and superior. You sound just like Mother." She slid off the counter to stalk to the refrigerator. And because of it, she was swamped with guilt. "We're getting along well enough," she added as she pulled out a beer. "The bills are paid, there's food on the table and a roof over all our heads." She stared at her sister's stiff back and let out a sound of impatience. "It can't be what it once was, Brie."

"You think I don't know that?" Brianna's lilting voice turned edgy. "Do you think I have to have more? That I can't be content with what is?" Suddenly unbearably sad, she stared out the window toward the fields beyond. "It's not me, Maggie. 'Tisn't me."

Maggie scowled down at her beer. It was Brianna who suffered, Maggie knew. Brianna who had always been in the middle. Now, Maggie thought, she had the chance to change that. All she had to do was sell part of her soul.

"She's been complaining again."

"No." Brianna tucked a stray hair away in the knot at the nape of her neck. "Not really."

"I can tell by the look on your face she's been in one of her moods—and taking it out on you." Before Brianna could speak, Maggie waved a hand. "She'll never be happy, Brianna. You can't make her happy. The good Lord knows I can't. She'll never forgive him for being what he was."

"And what was he?" Brianna demanded as she turned around. "Just what was our father, Maggie?"

"Human. Flawed." She set her beer down and walked to her sister. "Wonderful. Do you remember, Brie, the time he bought the mule, and was going to make a fortune having tourists snap pictures of it in a peaked cap with our old dog sitting on its back?"

"I remember." Brie would have turned away, but Maggie grabbed her hands. "And I remember he lost more money feeding that cursed, bad-tempered mule than he ever did with his scheming."

"Oh, but it was fun. We went to the Cliffs of Mohr, and it was such a bright summer day. The tourists swarming about and the music playing. And there was Da holding that stupid mule, and that poor old dog, Joe, as terrified of that mule as he would have been of a roaring lion."

Brianna softened. She couldn't help it. "Poor Joe sitting and shivering with fear on that mule's back. Then that German came along, wanting a picture of himself with Joe and the mule."

"And the mule kicked." Maggie grinned and picked up her beer again for a toast. "And the German screamed in three different languages while he hopped about on one foot. And Joe, terrified, leaped off and landed right on a display of lace collars, and the mule ran, scattering tourists. Oh, what a sight. People shouting and running, ladies screaming. There was a fiddler there, remember? And he just kept playing a reel as if we'd all start dancing any moment."

"And that nice boy from Killarney caught the mule's lead and dragged him back. Da tried to sell him the mule there and then."

"And nearly did. It's a good memory, Brie."

"He made many memories worth laughing over. But you can't live on laughter alone."

"And you can't live without it, as she would. He was alive. Now it seems this family's more dead than he is."

"She's ill," Brianna said shortly.

"As she has been for more than twenty years. And

ill she'll stay as long as she has you to tend to her hand and foot."

It was true, but knowing the truth didn't change Brianna's heart. "She's our mother."

"That she is." Maggie drained the beer and set it aside. The yeasty taste warred with the bitterness on her tongue. "I've sold another piece. I'll have money for you by the end of the month."

"I'm grateful for it. So is she."

"The hell she is." Maggie looked into her sister's eyes with all the passion and anger and hurt boiling beneath. "I don't do it for her. When there's enough you'll hire a nurse and you'll move her into her own place."

"That isn't necessary—"

"It is," Maggie interrupted. "That was the agreement, Brie. I'll not stand by and watch you dance to her tune for the rest of her life. A nurse and a place in the village."

"If that's what she wants."

"That's what she'll have." Maggie inclined her head. "She kept you up last night."

"She was restless." Embarrassed, Brianna turned back to prepare the chicken. "One of her headaches."

"Ah, yes." Maggie remembered her mother's headaches well, and how well timed they could be. An argument Maeve was losing: instant headache. A family outing she didn't approve of: the throbbing began.

"I know what she is, Maggie." Brianna's own head began to ache. "That doesn't make her less of my mother."

Saint Brianna, Maggie thought again, but with

affection. Her sister might be younger than her own twenty-eight by a year, but it had always been Brianna who took responsibility. "And you can't change what you are, Brie." Maggie gave her sister a fierce hug. "Da always said you'd be the good angel and I the bad. He was finally right about something." She closed her eyes a moment. "Tell Mr. Sweeney to come by the cottage in the morning. I'll speak with him."

"You'll let him manage you, then?"

The phrase had Maggie wincing. "I'll speak with him," she repeated, and headed back into the rain.

If Maggie had a weakness, it was family. That weakness had kept her up late into the night and had awakened her early in the chill, murky dawn. To the outside world she preferred to pretend she had responsibilities only to herself and her art, but beneath the facade was a constant love of family, and the dragging, often bitter obligations that went with it.

She wanted to refuse Rogan Sweeney, first on principle. Art and business, to her mind, could not and should not mix. She wanted to refuse him secondly because his type—wealthy, confident and blue-blooded—irritated her. Thirdly, and most telling, she wanted to refuse him because to do otherwise was an admission that she lacked the skill to handle her affairs alone.

Oh, that was a pill that stuck bitterly in her throat.

She would not refuse him. She'd made the decision sometime during the long and restless night to allow Rogan Sweeney to make her rich.

It wasn't as though she couldn't support herself,

and well, too. She'd been doing just that for more than five years. Brianna's bed and breakfast was successful enough that keeping two homes was no heavy burden. But they could not between them afford a third.

Maggie's goal, indeed her Holy Grail, was to establish their mother in a separate residence. If Rogan could help clear the path to her quest, she'd deal with him. She'd deal with the very devil.

But the devil might come to regret the bargain.

In her kitchen with the rain falling soft and steady outside, Maggie brewed tea. And plotted.

Rogan Sweeney had to be cleverly handled, she mused. With just the right amount of artistic disdain and feminine flattery. The disdain would be no problem at all, but the other ingredient would be hard coming.

She let herself picture Brianna baking, gardening, curled up with a book by the fire—without the whining, demanding voice of their mother to spoil the peace. Brianna would marry, have children. Which Maggie knew was a dream her sister kept locked in her heart. And locked it would stay as long as Brianna had the responsibility of a chronic hypochondriac.

While Maggie couldn't understand her sister's need to strap herself down with a man and a half a dozen children, she would do whatever it took to help Brianna realize the dream.

It was possible, just possible, that Rogan Sweeney could play fairy godfather.

The knock on the front door of the cottage was brisk and impatient. This fairy godfather, Maggie thought as she went to answer, wouldn't make his entrance with angel dust and colored lights.

After opening the door, she smiled a little. He was wet, as he'd been the day before, and just as elegantly dressed. She wondered if he slept in a suit and tie.

"Good morning to you, Mr. Sweeney."

"And to you, Miss Concannon." He stepped inside, out of the rain and the swirl of mist.

"Shall I take your coat? It'll dry out some by the fire."

"Thank you." He slipped out of his overcoat, watched her spread it over a chair by the fire. She was different today, he thought. Pleasant. The change put him on guard. "Tell me, does it do anything but rain in Clare?"

"We enjoy good soft weather in the spring. Don't worry, Mr. Sweeney. Even a Dubliner shouldn't melt in a west-county rain." She sent him a quick, charming smile, but her eyes were wickedly amused. "I'm brewing tea, if you'd like some."

"I would." Before she could turn to the kitchen, he stopped her—a hand on her arm. His attention wasn't on her, but on the sculpture on the table beside them. It was a long, sinuous curve in a deep icy blue. The color of an arctic lake. Glass clung to glass in waves at the tip then flowed down, liquid ice.

"An interesting piece," he commented.

"Do you think so?" Maggie blocked the urge to shake off his hand. It held her lightly, with an understated possession that made her ridiculously uncomfortable. She could smell him, the subtle woodsy cologne he'd probably dashed on after shaving, with undertones of soap from his shower. When he ran a fingertip along the length of the curved glass, she suppressed a shudder. For a moment, a foolish one, it had felt as though he'd trailed a touch from her throat to her center.

"Obviously feminine," he murmured. Though his eyes stayed on the glass, he was very aware of her. The coiled tension in her arm, the quick tremble she'd tried to mask, the dark, wild scent of her hair. "Powerful. A woman about to surrender sexually to a man."

It flustered her because he was exactly right. "How do you find power in surrender?"

He looked at her then, those depthless blue eyes locked on her face. His hand remained light on her arm. "Nothing's more powerful than a woman at that instant before she gives herself." He stroked the glass again. "Obviously you're aware of that."

"And the man?"

He smiled then, just the faintest curve of lips. His grip on her arm seemed more of a caress now. A request. And his eyes, amused, interested, skimmed over her face. "That, Margaret Mary, would depend on the woman."

She didn't move, absorbed the sexual punch, acknowledged it with a slight nod. "Well, we agree on something. Sex and power generally depend on the woman."

"That's not at all what I said, or meant. What draws you to create something like this?"

"It's difficult to explain art to a man of business."

When she would have stepped back, he curled his fingers around her arm, tightened his grip. "Try."

Annoyance pricked through her. "What comes to me comes. There's no plot, no plan. It has to do with emotions, with passions and not with practicality or profit. Otherwise I'd be making little glass swans for gift shops. Jesus, what a thought."

His smile widened. "Horrifying. Fortunately I'm not interested in little glass swans. But I would like that tea."

"We'll have it in the kitchen." She started to step away again, and again his grip stopped her. Temper flashed into her eyes like lightning. "You're blocking my way, Sweeney."

"I don't think so. I'm about to clear it for you." He released her and followed her silently into the kitchen.

Her cottage was a far cry from the country comfort of Blackthorn. There were no rich smells of baking wafting in the air, no plumped pillows or gleaming woodwork. It was spartan, utilitarian and untidy. Which was why, he supposed, the art carelessly set here and there was that much more effective and striking.

He wondered where she slept, and if her bed was as soft and inviting as the one he'd spent the night in. And he wondered if he would share it with her. No, not if, he corrected himself. *When.*

Maggie set the teapot on the table along with two thick pottery mugs. "Did you enjoy your stay at Blackthorn Cottage?" she asked as she poured.

"I did. Your sister's charming. And her cooking memorable."

Maggie softened, added three generous spoons of sugar to her tea. "Brie's a homemaker in the best sense of the word. Did she make her currant buns this morning?"

"I had two of them."

Relaxed again, Maggie laughed and propped one booted foot on her knee. "Our father used to say Brie got all the gold and I the brass. I'm afraid you won't get any home-baked buns here, Sweeney, but I could probably dig out a tin of biscuits."

"No need."

"You'd probably rather get straight to business." Cupping the mug in both hands, Maggie leaned forward. "What if I were to tell you plain I'm not interested in your offer?"

Rogan considered, sipping his tea black and strong. "I'd have to call you a liar, Maggie." He grinned at the fire that erupted in her eyes. "Because if you weren't interested, you wouldn't have agreed to see me this morning. And I certainly wouldn't be drinking tea in your kitchen." He held up a hand before she could speak. "We'll agree, however, that you don't want to be interested."

A clever man, she mused, only slightly mollified. Clever men were dangerous ones. "I've no wish to be produced, or managed, or guided."

"We rarely wish for what we need." He watched her over the rim of his cup, calculating even as he enjoyed the way the faint flush seemed to silken her skin, deepen the green of her eyes. "Why don't I explain myself more clearly? Your art is your domain. I have no intention of interfering in any way with what you do in your studio. You create what you're inspired to create, when you're inspired to create it."

"And what if what I create isn't to your taste?"

"I've shown and sold a great number of pieces I wouldn't care to have in my home. That's the business, Maggie. And as I won't interfere with your art, you won't interfere with my business."

"I'll have no say in who buys my work?"

"None," he said simply. "If you have an emotional attachment to a piece, you'll have to get over it, or keep the piece for yourself. Once it's in my hands, it's mine."

Her jaw clenched. "And anyone with the money can own it."

"Exactly."

Maggie slapped the mug down and sprang up to pace. She used her whole body, a habit Rogan admired. Legs, arms, shoulders all in rhythmically angry movements. He topped off his tea and sat back to enjoy the show.

"I pull something out of myself, and I create it, make it solid, tangible, real, and some idiot from Kerry or Dublin or, God help me, London, comes in and buys it for his wife's birthday without having the least understanding of what it is, what it means?"

"Do you develop personal relationships with everyone who buys your work?"

"At least I know where it's going, who's buying it." Usually, she added to herself.

"I'll have to remind you that I bought two of your pieces before we met."

"Aye. And look where that's got me."

Temperament, he thought with a sigh. As long as he'd worked with artists he'd never understood it. "Maggie," he began, trying for the most reasonable of tones. "The reason you need a manager is to eliminate these difficulties. You won't have to worry about the sales, only the creation. And yes, if someone from Kerry or Dublin, or God help you London comes into one of my galleries and takes an interest in one of your pieces, it's his—as long as he meets the price. No résumé, no character references required. And by the end of a year, with my help, you'll be a rich woman."

"Is that what you think I want?" Insulted, infuriated, she whirled on him. "Do you think, Rogan Sweeney, that I pick up my pipe every day calculating how much profit there might be at the end of it?"

"No, I don't. That's precisely where I come in. You're an exceptional artist, Maggie. And at the risk of inflating what appears to be an already titanic ego, I'll admit that I was captivated the first time I saw your work."

"Perhaps you have decent taste," she said with a cranky shrug.

"So I've been told. My point is that your work deserves more than you're giving it. You deserve more than you're giving yourself."

She leaned back on the counter, eyeing him narrowly. "And you're going to help me get more out of the goodness of your heart."

"My heart has nothing to do with it. I'm going to help you because your work will add to the prestige of my galleries."

"And to your pocketbook."

"One day you'll have to explain to me the root of your disdain for money. In the meantime, your tea's getting cold."

Maggie let out a long breath. She wasn't doing a good job of flattering him, she reminded herself, and returned to the table. "Rogan." She let herself smile. "I'm sure you're very good at what you do. Your galleries have a reputation for quality and integrity, which I'm sure is a reflection of yourself."

She was good, he mused, and ran his tongue over his teeth. Very good. "I like to think so."

"Doubtless any artist would be thrilled to be considered by you. But I'm accustomed to dealing for myself, for handling all the aspects of my work from making the glass to selling the finished piece—or at least placing it into the hands of someone I know and trust to sell it. I don't know you."

"Or trust me?"

She lifted a hand, let it fall. "I would be a fool not to trust Worldwide Galleries. But it's difficult for me to imagine a business of that size. I'm a simple woman."

He laughed so quickly, so richly, that she blinked. Before she could recover, he was leaning forward, taking one of her hands in his. "Oh, no, Margaret Mary, simple is exactly what you are not. Canny, obstinate, brilliant, bad-tempered and beautiful you are. But simple, never."

"I say I am." She yanked her hand free and struggled not to be charmed. "And I know myself better than you do or ever will."

"Every time you finish a sculpture you're shouting out this is who I am. At least for today. That's what makes art true."

She couldn't argue with him. It was an observation she hadn't expected from a man of his background. Making money from art didn't mean you understood it. Apparently, he did.

"I'm a simple woman," she said again, daring him to contradict her a second time. "And I prefer to stay that way. If I agree to your management, there will be rules. Mine."

He had her, and he knew it. But a wise negotiator was never a smug one. "What are they?" he asked.

"I'll do no publicity, unless it suits me. And I can promise you it won't."

"It'll add to the mystery, won't it?"

She very nearly grinned before she recovered. "I'll not be after dressing up like some fashion plate for showings—if I come at all."

This time he tucked his tongue firmly in his cheek. "I'm sure your sense of style will reflect your artistic nature."

It might have been an insult, but she couldn't be sure. "And I won't be nice to people if I don't want to be."

"Temperament, again artistic." He toasted her with his tea. "Should add to sales."

Though she was amused, she sat back and crossed her arms over her chest. "I will never, never duplicate a piece or create something out of someone else's fancy."

He frowned, shook his head. "That may be a deal breaker. I had this idea for a unicorn, with a touch of gold leaf on the horn and hooves. Very tasteful."

She snickered, then gave up and laughed out loud. "All right, Rogan. Maybe by some miracle we'll be able to work together. How do we do it?"

"I'll have contracts drawn up. Worldwide will want exclusive rights to your work."

She winced at that. It felt as though she were surrendering a part of herself. Perhaps the best part. "Exclusive rights to the pieces I choose to sell."

"Of course."

She looked past him, out the window toward the fields beyond. Once, long ago, they, like her art, had felt like part of her. Now they were just part of a lovely view. "What else?"

He hesitated. She looked almost unbearably sad. "It won't change what you do. It won't change who you are."

"You're wrong," she murmured. With an effort, she shook off the mood and faced him again. "Go on. What else?"

"I'll want a show, within two months, at the Dublin gallery. Naturally, I'll need to see what you have finished, and I'll arrange for shipping. I'll also need you to keep me apprised of what you've completed over the next few weeks. We'll price the pieces, and whatever inventory is left after the show will be displayed in Dublin and our other galleries."

She took a long, calming breath. "I'd appreciate it, if you'd not refer to my work as inventory. At least in my presence."

"Done." He steepled his fingers. "You will, of course, be sent a complete itemization of pieces sold. You may, if you choose, have some input as to which ones we photograph for our catalog. Or you can leave it up to us."

"And how and when am I paid?" she wanted to know.

"I can buy the pieces outright. I have no objection to that since I have confidence in your work."

She remembered what he'd said before, about getting twice as much as what he'd paid her for the sculpture she'd just finished. She might not have been a businesswoman, but she wasn't a fool.

"How else do you handle it?"

"By commission. We take the piece, and when and if we sell it, we deduct a percentage."

More of a gamble, she mused. And she preferred a gamble. "What percentage do you take?"

Hoping for a reaction, he kept his eyes level with hers. "Thirty-five percent."

She made a strangled sound in her throat. "Thirty-five? Thirty-five? You thief. You robber." She shoved back from the table and stood. "You're a vulture, Rogan Sweeney. Thirty-five percent be damned and you with it."

"I take all the risks, I have all the expenses." He spread his hands, steepled them again. "You have merely to create."

"Oh, as if all it takes is sitting on me ass and waiting for the inspiration to come fluttering down like raindrops. You know nothing, nothing about it." She began to pace again, swirling the air with temper and energy. "I'll remind you, you'd have nothing to sell without me. And it's my work, my sweat and blood that they'll spend good money for. You'll get fifteen percent."

"I'll get thirty."

"Plague take you, Rogan, for a horse thief. Twenty."

"Twenty-five." He rose then to stand toe to toe with her. "Worldwide will earn a quarter of your sweat and blood, Maggie, I promise you."

" A quarter." She hissed through her teeth. "That's a businessman for you, preying on art."

"And making the artist financially secure. Think of it, Maggie. Your work will be seen in New York, in Rome and Paris. And no one who sees it will forget it."

"Oh, it's clever you are, Rogan, taking a quick turn from money into fame." She scowled at him then stuck out her hand. "The hell with it and you, you'll have your twenty-five percent."

Which was exactly what he'd planned on. He took her hand, held it. "We're going to do well together, Maggie."

Well enough, she hoped, to settle her mother in the village and away from Blackthorn Cottage. "If we don't, Rogan, I'll see that you pay for it."

Because he'd enjoyed the taste of her, he lifted her hand to his lips. "I'll risk it."

His lips lingered there long enough to make her pulse stutter. "If you were going to try to seduce me, you'd have been smarter to start before we had a deal."

The statement both surprised and annoyed him. "I prefer to keep personal and professional matters separate."

"Another difference between us." It pleased her to see she'd scratched the seamlessly polite exterior. "My personal and professional lives are always fusing. And I indulge both when the whim strikes." Smiling, she slipped her hand from his. "It hasn't as yet— personally speaking. I'll let you know if and when it does."

"Are you baiting me, Maggie?"

She stopped as if thinking it through. "No, I'm explaining to you. Now I'll take you to the glass house so you can choose what you want shipped to Dublin." She turned to pull a jacket from a peg by the back door. "You might want your coat. It'd be a shame to get that fancy suit wet."

He stared at her a moment, wondering why he should feel so completely insulted. Without a word he turned on his heel and strode back into the living room for his coat.

Maggie took the opportunity to step outside and cool her blood in the chilly rain. Ridiculous, she told herself, to get so sexually tied up over having her hand kissed. Rogan Sweeney was smooth, too smooth. It was a fortunate thing he lived on the other side of the country. More fortunate yet, he wasn't her type.

Not at all.

8. Chapter Five

THE high grass beside the ruined abbey made a lovely resting place for the dead. Maggie had fought to have her father buried there, rather than in the tidy and cold ground near the village church. She had wanted the peace, and the touch of royalty for her father. For once, Brianna had argued with her until their mother had sullenly closed her mouth and washed her hands of the arrangements.

Maggie visited there only twice a year, once on her father's birthday and once on her own. To thank him for the gift of her life. She never came on the anniversary of his death, nor did she allow herself to mourn in private.

Nor did she mourn him now, but sat down on the grass beside him, tucking her knees up and wrapping her arms around them. The sun fought through layers of clouds to gild the graves and the wind was fresh, smelling of wildflowers.

She hadn't brought flowers with her, never did. Brianna had planted a bed right over him, so that as spring warmed the earth, his grave sprang with color and beauty.

Tender buds were just forming on the primroses. The fairy heads of columbine nodded gently among the tender shoots of larkspur and betony. She watched a magpie dart over headstones and sway toward a field. One for sorrow, she thought, and searched the sky fruitlessly for the second that would stand for joy.

Butterflies fluttered nearby, flashing thin, silent wings. She watched them for a time, taking comfort in the color and the movement. There had been no place to bury him near the sea, but this, she thought, this place would have pleased him.

Maggie leaned back comfortably on the side of her father's headstone and closed her eyes.

I wish you were still here, she thought, so I could tell you what I'm doing. Not that I'd listen to any of your advice, mind. But it would be good to hear it.

If Rogan Sweeney's a man of his word—and I can't see how he'd be anything else—I'll be a rich woman. How you'd enjoy that. There'd be enough for you to open your own pub like you always wanted. Oh, what a poor farmer you were, darling. But the best of fathers. The very best.

She was doing her best to keep her promise to him, she thought. To take care of her mother and her sister, and to follow her dream.

"Maggie."

She opened her eyes and looked up at Brianna. Tidy as a pin, she thought, studying her sister. Her lovely hair all scooped up, her clothes neatly pressed. "You look like a schoolteacher," Maggie said, and laughed at Brianna's expression. "A lovely one."

"You look like a ragpicker," Brianna retorted, scowling at Maggie's choice of ripped jeans and a tattered sweater. "A lovely one."

Brianna knelt beside her sister and folded her hands. Not to pray, just for neatness' sake.

They sat in silence for a moment while the wind

breathed through the grass and floated through the tumbled stones.

"A lovely day for grave sitting," Maggie commented. He'd have been seventy-one today, she thought. "His flowers are blooming nicely."

"Needs some weeding." And Brianna began to do so. "I found the money on the kitchen counter this morning, Maggie. It's too much."

"It was a good sale. You'll put some of it by."

"I'd rather you enjoyed it."

"I am, knowing you're that much closer to having her out."

Brianna sighed. "She isn't a burden to me." Catching her sister's expression, she shrugged. "Not as much as you think. Only when she's feeling poorly."

"Which is most of the time. Brie, I love you."

"I know you do."

"The money's the best way I know how to show it. Da wanted me to help you with her. And the good Lord knows I couldn't live with her as you do. She'd send me to the madhouse, or I'd send myself to prison by murdering her in her sleep."

"This business with Rogan Sweeney, you did it for her."

"I did not." Maggie bristled at the thought of it. "Because of her, perhaps, which is a different matter altogether. Once she's settled and you have your life back, you'll get married and give me a horde of nieces and nephews."

"You could have your own children."

"I don't want marriage." Comfortable, Maggie closed her eyes again. "No, indeed. I prefer coming and going as it suits me and answering to no one. I'll spoil your children, and they'll come running to

Aunt Maggie whenever you're too strict with them."
She opened one eye. "You could marry Murphy."

Brianna's laugh carried beautifully over the high
grass. "It would shock him to know it."

"He was always sweet on you."

"He was, yes—when I was thirteen. No, he's a
lovely man and I'm as fond of him as I would be of
a brother. But he's not what I'm looking for in a
husband."

"You've got it all planned then?"

"I've nothing planned," Brianna said primly, "and
we're getting off the subject. I don't want you to join
hands with Mr. Sweeney because you feel obliged to
me. I might think it's the best thing you could do for
your work, but I won't have you unhappy because
you think I am. Because I'm not."

"How many times did you have to serve her a meal
in bed this month?"

"I don't keep an accounting—"

"You should," Maggie interrupted. "In any case,
it's done. I signed his contracts a week ago. I'm now
being managed by Rogan Sweeney and Worldwide
Galleries. I'll have a show in his Dublin gallery in two
weeks."

"Two weeks. That's so fast."

"He doesn't seem to be a man to waste time. Come
with me, Brianna." Maggie grabbed her sister's hands.
"We'll make Sweeney pay for a fancy hotel and we'll eat
out in restaurants and buy something foolish."

Shops. Food she hadn't cooked herself. A bed that
didn't have to be made. Brianna yearned, but only
for a moment. "I'd love to be with you, Maggie. But
I can't leave her like that."

"The hell you can't. Jesus, she can stand her own company for a few days."

"I can't." Brianna hesitated then sat back wearily on her haunches. "She fell last week."

"Was she hurt?" Maggie's fingers tightened on her sister's. "Damn it, Brie, why didn't you tell me? How did it happen?"

"I didn't tell you because it turned out to be no great matter. She was outside, went out on her own while I was upstairs tidying rooms. Lost her footing, it seems. She bruised her hip, jarred her shoulder."

"You called Dr. Hogan?"

"Of course I did. He said there was nothing to worry about. She'd lost her balance was all. And if she got more exercise, ate better and all the rest, she'd be stronger."

"Who didn't know that?" Damn the woman, Maggie thought. And damn the constant and incessant guilt that lived in her own heart. "And it's back to bed she went, I'll wager. And has stayed there ever since."

Brianna's lips twitched into a wry smile. "I haven't been able to budge her. She claims she has an inner-ear deficiency and wants to go into Cork to a specialist."

"Hah!" Maggie tossed back her head and glared at the sky. "It's typical. Never have I known anyone with more complaints than Maeve Concannon. And she's got you on a string, my girl." She jabbed a finger at Brianna.

"I won't deny it, but I haven't the heart to cut it."

"I do." Maggie stood, brushed at her knees. "The answer's money, Brie. It's what she's always wanted. God knows she made his life a misery because he couldn't hang on to it." In a gesture of protection, Maggie laid a hand on her father's headstone.

"That's true, and he made hers a misery as well. Two people less suited I've never seen. Marriages aren't always made in heaven, or in hell. Sometimes they're just stuck in purgatory."

"And sometimes people are too foolish or too righteous to walk away." The hand on the headstone stroked once, then dropped away. "I prefer fools to martyrs. Put the money by, Brie. There'll be more coming soon. I'll see to that in Dublin."

"Will you see her before you go?"

"I will," Maggie said grimly.

"I think you'll enjoy her." Rogan dipped into the clotted cream for his scone and smiled at his grandmother. "She's an interesting woman."

"Interesting." Christine Rogan Sweeney lifted one sharp white brow. She knew her grandson well, could interpret every nuance of tone and expression. On the subject of Maggie Concannon, however, he was cryptic. "In what way?"

He wasn't sure of that himself and stalled for time by stirring his tea. "She's a brilliant artist; her vision is extraordinary. Yet she lives alone in a little cottage in Clare, and the decor is anything but aesthetically unique. She's passionate about her work, but reluctant to show it. She's by turns charming and rude— and both seem to be true to her nature."

"A contradictory woman."

"Very." He settled back, a man completely content in the gracious parlor, Sèvres cup in his hand, and his head resting against the brocade cushion of a

Queen Anne chair. A fire burned quietly in the grate. The flowers and the scones were fresh.

He enjoyed these occasional teas with his grandmother as much as she did. The peace and order of her home were soothing, as was she with her perpetual dignity and softly faded beauty.

He knew she was seventy-three and took personal pride in the fact that she looked ten years younger. Her skin was pale as alabaster. Lined, yes, but the marks of age only added to the serenity of her face. Her eyes were brilliantly blue, her hair as soft and white as a first snowfall.

She had a sharp mind, unquestionable taste, a generous heart and a dry, sometimes biting wit. She was, as Rogan had often told her, his ideal woman.

It was a sentiment that flattered Christine as much as it concerned her.

He had failed her in only one way. That was to find a personal contentment that equalled his professional one.

"How are preparations for the show going?" she asked.

"Very well. It would be easier if our artist of the moment answered her damn phone." He brushed that irritation away. "The pieces that have been shipped in are wonderful. You'll have to come by the gallery and see for yourself."

"I may do that." But she was more interested in the artist than in the art. "Did you say she was a young woman?"

"Hmmm?"

"Maggie Concannon. Did you mention she was young?"

"Oh, middle twenties, I'd expect. Young, certainly, for the scope of her work."

Lord, it was like drawing teeth. "And flashy would you say? Like—what was her name—Miranda Whitfield-Fry, the one who did metal sculpture and wore all the heavy jewelry and colored scarves?"

"She's nothing like Miranda." Thank Christ. He remembered with a shudder how relentlessly, and embarrassingly, the woman had pursued him. "Maggie's more the boots and cotton shirt type. Her hair looks like she had a whack at it with kitchen shears."

"Unattractive then."

"No, very attractive—but in an unusual sense."

"Mannish?"

"No." He recalled, uncomfortably, the vicious sexual tug, the sensual scent of her, the feel of that quick, involuntary tremble under his hand. "Far from it."

Ah. Christine thought. She would definitely make time to meet the woman who put that scowl on Rogan's face. "She intrigues you."

"Certainly, I wouldn't have signed her otherwise." He caught Christine's look and raised a brow in an identical manner. "It's business, Grandmother. Just business."

"Of course." Smiling to herself, she poured him more tea. "Tell me what else you've been up to."

Rogan arrived at the gallery at eight A.M. the next morning. He'd enjoyed an evening at the theater, and a late supper with a sometimes companion. As always, he'd found Patricia charming and delightful. The widow of an old friend, she was, to his mind, more of a distant cousin than a date. They'd discussed the Eugene O'Neill play over salmon and champagne and had parted with a platonic kiss at just after midnight.

And he hadn't slept a wink.

It hadn't been Patricia's light laugh or her subtle perfume that had kept him tossing.

Maggie Concannon, he thought. Naturally the woman was in the forefront of his mind, since most of his time and effort was focused on her upcoming show. It was hardly any wonder that he was thinking of her—particularly since it was all but impossible to speak to her.

Her aversion to the phone had caused him to resort to telegrams, which he fired off to the west with blistering regularity.

Her one and only answer had been brief and to the point: STOP NAGGING.

Imagine, Rogan thought as he unlocked the elegant glass doors of the gallery. She'd accused him of nagging, like some spoiled, whiny child. He was a businessman, for God's sake, one about to give her career an astronomical boost. And she wouldn't even spare the time to pick up the damn phone and have a reasonable conversation.

He was used to artists. Sweet Mary knew he had dealt with their eccentricities, their insecurities, their often childish demands. It was his job to do so, and he considered himself adept. But Maggie Concannon was trying both his skill and his patience.

He relocked the doors behind him and breathed in the quietly scented air of the gallery. Built by his grandfather, the building was lofty and grand, a striking testament to art with its Gothic stonework and carved balusters.

The interior consisted of dozens of rooms, some

small, some large, all flowing into the next with wide archways. Stairs curved up fluidly to a second story that housed a ballroom-size space along with intimate parlors fitted with antique sofas.

It was there he would show Maggie's work. In the ballroom he would have a small orchestra. While the guests enjoyed the music, the champagne, the canapes, they could browse among her strategically placed works. The larger, bolder pieces he would highlight, showcasing smaller pieces in more intimate settings.

Imagining it, refining the pictures in his mind, he walked through the lower gallery toward the office and storage rooms.

He found his gallery manager, Joseph Donahoe, pouring coffee in the kitchenette.

"You're here early." Joseph smiled, showing the flash of one gold tooth. "Coffee?"

"Yes. I wanted to check on the progress upstairs before heading into the office."

"Coming right along," Joseph assured him. Though the two men were of an age, Joseph's hair was thinning on top. He compensated for the loss by growing it long enough to tie in a streaming ponytail. His nose had been broken once by a wayward polo mallet and so listed a bit to the left. The result was the look of a pirate in a Savile Row suit.

The women adored him.

"You look a bit washed-out."

"Insomnia," Rogan said, and took his coffee black. "Did yesterday's shipment get unpacked?"

Joseph winced. "I was afraid you'd ask." He lifted his cup and muttered into it. "Hasn't come in."

"What?"

Joseph rolled his eyes. He'd worked for Rogan for more than a decade and knew that tone. "It didn't arrive yesterday. I'm sure it'll be along this morning. That's why I came in early myself."

"What is that woman doing? Her instructions were very specific, very simple. She was to ship the last of the pieces overnight."

"She's an artist, Rogan. She probably got struck by inspiration and worked past the time to post it. We've got plenty of time."

"I won't have her dragging her feet." Incensed, Rogan snapped up the kitchen phone. He didn't have to look up Maggie's number in his address book. He already knew it by heart. He stabbed buttons and listened to the phone ring. And ring. "Irresponsible twit."

Joseph took out a cigarette as Rogan slammed down the receiver. "We have more than thirty pieces," he said as he flicked an ornate enameled lighter. "Even without this last shipment, it's enough. And the work, Rogan. Even a jaded old hand like me is dazzled."

"That's hardly the point, is it?"

Joseph blew out smoke, pursed his lips. "Actually, it is, yes."

"We agreed on forty pieces, not thirty-five, not thirty-six. Forty. And by God, forty is what I'll have."

"Rogan—where are you going?" he called out when Rogan stormed from the kitchen.

"To goddamn Clare."

Joseph took another drag on his cigarette and toasted the air with his coffee cup. "Bon voyage."

The flight was a short one and didn't give Rogan's temper time to cool. The fact that the sky was gloriously blue, the air balmy, didn't change a thing. When he slammed the door on his rental car and headed away from Shannon Airport, he was still cursing Maggie.

By the time he arrived at her cottage, he was at full boil.

The nerve of the woman, he thought as he stalked up to her front door. Pulling him away from his work, from his obligations. Did she think she was the only artist he represented?

He pounded on her door until his fist throbbed. Ignoring manners, he pushed the door open. "Maggie!" he called out, striding from the living room to the kitchen. "Damn you." Without pausing, he stamped through the back door and headed for her workshop.

He should have known she'd be there.

She glanced up from a workbench and a mountain of shredded paper. "Good, I could use some help with this."

"Why the hell don't you answer the bloody phone? Why have the damn thing if you're going to ignore it?"

"I often ask myself the same thing. Pass me that hammer, will you?"

He lifted it from the bench, hefted the weight a moment as the very pleasant image of bopping her on the head with it flitted into his brain. "Where the devil's my shipment?"

"It's right here." She dragged a hand through her untidy hair before taking the hammer from him. "I'm just packing it up."

"It was supposed to be in Dublin yesterday."

"Well, it couldn't be because I hadn't sent it yet." With quick, expert moves, she began to hammer nails into the crate on the floor. "And if you've come all this way to check on it, I have to say you don't have enough to do with your time."

He lifted her off the floor and plunked her down on the workbench. The hammer clanked on concrete, barely missing his foot. Before she'd drawn the breath to spit at him, he caught her chin in his hand.

"I have more than enough to do with my time," he said evenly. "And baby-sitting for an irresponsible, scatterbrained woman interferes with my schedule. I have a staff at the gallery, one whose timetable is carefully, even meticulously thought out. All you had to do was follow instructions and ship the damn merchandise."

She slapped his hand away. "I don't give a tinker's damn about your schedules and timetables. You signed on an artist, Sweeney, not a bleeding clerk."

"And what artistic endeavor prevented you from following a simple direction?"

She bared her teeth, considered punching him, then simply pointed. "That."

He glanced over, froze. Only the blindness of temper could have prevented him from seeing it, being struck dumb by it on entering the building.

The sculpture stood on the far side of the room, fully three feet high, all bleeding colors and twisting, sinuous shapes. A tangle of limbs, surely, he thought, unashamedly sexual, beautifully human. He crossed to it to study it from a different angle.

He could almost, almost make out faces. They seemed to melt into imagination, leaving only the sensation of absolute fulfillment. It was impossible to see where one form began and the other left off, so completely, so perfectly were they merged.

It was, he thought, a celebration of the human spirit and the sexuality of the beast.

"What do you call it?"

"*Surrender.*" She smiled. "It seems you inspired me, Rogan." Whipped by fresh energy, she pushed off the bench. She was light-headed, giddy, and felt glorious. "It took forever to get the colors right. You wouldn't believe what I've remelted and discarded. But I could see it, perfectly, and it had to be exact." She laughed and picked up her hammer to drive another nail. "I don't know when I've slept last. Two days, three." She laughed again, dragging her hands through her tousled hair. "I'm not tired. I feel incredible. Full of desperate energy. I can't seem to stop."

"It's magnificent, Maggie."

"It's the best work I've ever done." She turned to study it again, tapping the hammer against her palm. "Probably the best I'll ever do."

"I'll arrange for a crate." He tossed her a look over his shoulder. She was pale as wax, he noted, with the fatigue her bustling brain had yet to transmit to her body. "And handle the shipping personally."

"I was going to build one. It wouldn't take long."

"You can't be trusted."

"Of course I can." Her mood was so festive, she didn't even take offense. "And it'd be quicker for me to build one than for you to have one built. I already have the dimensions."

"How long?"

"An hour."

He nodded. "I'll use your phone and arrange for a truck. Your phone does work, I assume."

"Sarcasm"—chuckling, she crossed to him—"becomes you. So does that impeccably proper tie."

Before either of them had a chance to think, she grabbed his tie and hauled him toward her. Her warm mouth fixed on his, stunning him into immobility. Her free hand slid into his hair, gripped as her body pressed close. The kiss sizzled, sparked, smoldered. Then as quickly as she had initiated it, she broke away.

"Just a whim," she said, and smiled up at him. Her heart might have been jolting like a rabbit in her chest, but she would think about that later. "Blame it on sleep deprivation and excess energy. Now—"

He snagged her arm before she could turn away. She wouldn't get away so easily, he thought. Wouldn't paralyze him one moment and shrug it off the next.

"I have a whim of my own," he murmured. As he slid a hand around to cup the back of her neck, he watched her eyes register wary surprise. She didn't resist. He thought he saw a hint of amusement on her face before he lowered his mouth to hers.

The amusement faded quickly. This kiss was soft, sweet, sumptuous. As unexpected as rose petals in the blaze of a furnace, it cooled and soothed and aroused all at once. She thought she heard a sound, something between a whimper and a sigh. The fact that it had slipped from her own burning throat amazed her.

But she didn't draw away, not even when the sound came again, quiet and helpless and beguiled. No, she didn't pull away. His mouth was too clever, too gently persuasive. She opened herself to it and absorbed.

She seemed to melt against him, degree by slow degree. That first blast of heat had mellowed, ripened into a low, long burn. He forgot that he'd been angry, or that he'd been challenged, and knew only that he was alive.

She tasted dark, dangerous, and his mouth was full of her. His mind veered toward taking, toward conquering, toward ravishing. The civilized man in him, the one who had been raised to follow a strict code of ethics, stepped back, appalled.

Her head reeled. She placed a hand down on the workbench for balance as her legs buckled. One long breath followed by another helped clear her vision. And she saw him staring at her, a mixture of hunger and shock in his eyes.

"Well," she managed, "that's certainly something to think about."

It was foolish to apologize for his thoughts, Rogan told himself. Ridiculous to blame himself for the fact that his imagination had drawn erotic and vivid pictures of throwing her to the floor and tearing away flannel and denim. He hadn't acted on it. He'd only kissed her.

But he thought it was possible, even preferable, to blame her.

"We have a business relationship," he began tersely. "It would be unwise and possibly destructive to let anything interfere with that at this point."

She cocked her head, rocked back on her heels. "And sleeping together would confuse things?"

Curse her for making him sound like a fool. Curse her twice for leaving him shaken and horribly, horribly needy. "At this point I think we should concentrate on launching your show."

"Hmmm." She turned away on the pretext of tidying the workbench. In truth she needed a moment to settle herself. She wasn't promiscuous by any means, and certainly didn't tumble into bed with every man who attracted her. But she liked to think of herself as independent enough, liberated enough and smart enough to choose her lovers with care.

She had, she realized, chosen Rogan Sweeney.

"Why did you kiss me?"

"You annoyed me."

Her wide, generous mouth curved. "Since I seem to be doing that on a regular basis, we'll be spending a lot of time with our lips locked."

"It's a matter of control." He knew he sounded stiff and prim, and hated her for it.

"I'm sure you have just buckets of it. I don't." She tossed her head, folded her arms over her chest. "If I decide I want you, what are you going to do about it? Fight me off?"

"I doubt it'll come to that." The image brought on twinges of humor and desperation. "We both need to concentrate on the business at hand. This could be the turning point in your career."

"Yes." It would be wise to remember that, she thought. "So we'll use each other, professionally."

"We'll *enhance* each other, professionally," he corrected. Christ, he needed air. "I'll go in and call for that truck."

"Rogan." She waited until he reached the door and turned back to her. "I'd like to go with you."

"To Dublin? Today?"

"Yes. I can be ready to go by the time the truck arrives. I only need to make one stop, at my sister's."

She was as good as her word. Even as the shipment chugged away she was tossing a suitcase into the back of Rogan's rented car.

"If you'd just give me ten minutes," she said as Rogan started down the narrow lane, "I'm sure Brie has some tea or coffee on."

"Fine." He stopped the car by Blackthorn and went with Maggie up the walk.

She didn't knock, but stepped inside and headed straight toward the kitchen in the back. Brianna was there, a white bib apron tied at her waist and her hands coated with flour.

"Oh, Mr. Sweeney, hello. Maggie. You'll have to excuse the mess. We have guests and I'm making pies for dinner."

"I'm leaving for Dublin."

"So soon?" Brianna picked up a tea towel to dust off her hands. "I thought the show was next week."

"It is. I'm going early. Is she in her room?"

Brianna's polite smile strained a bit at the edges. "Yes. Why don't I go tell her you're here?"

"I'll tell her myself. Perhaps you could give Rogan some coffee."

"Of course." She cast one worried look at Maggie as her sister walked out of the kitchen into the adjoining apartment. "If you'll make yourself comfortable in the parlor, Mr. Sweeney, I'll bring you some coffee right away."

"Don't trouble." His curiosity was up. "I'll have a cup right here, if I won't be in your way." He added an easy smile. "And please, call me Rogan."

"You have it black as I recall."

"You have a good memory." And you're a bundle of nerves, he observed, watching Brianna reach for a cup and saucer.

"I try to remember the preferences of my guests.

Would you have some cake? It's a bit of chocolate I made yesterday."

"The memory of your cooking makes it difficult to refuse." He took a seat at the scrubbed wood table. "You do it all yourself?"

"Yes, I . . ." She heard the first raised voice and fumbled. "I do. I've a fire laid in the parlor. Are you sure you wouldn't be more comfortable?"

The clash of voices from the next room rose, bringing a flush of embarrassment to Brianna's cheeks. Rogan merely lifted his cup. "Who's she shouting at this time?"

Brianna managed a smile. "Our mother. They don't get on very well."

"Does Maggie get along with anyone?"

"Only when it suits her. But she has a heart, a wonderful, generous heart. It's only that she guards it so carefully." Brianna sighed. If Rogan wasn't embarrassed by the shouting, neither would she be. "I'll cut you that cake."

"You never change." Maeve stared at her oldest child through narrowed eyes. "Just like your father."

"If you think that's an insult to me, you're wrong."

Maeve sniffed and brushed at the lace cuffs of her bed gown. The years and her own dissatisfactions had stolen the beauty of her face. It was puffy and pale, with lines dug deeply around the pursed mouth. Her hair, once as golden as sunlight, had faded to gray and was scraped back ruthlessly into a tight bun.

She was plumped onto a mountain of pillows, her Bible at one hand and a box of chocolates at the other. The television across the room murmured low.

"So, it's Dublin, is it? Brianna told me you were going off. Frittering money away on hotels, I imagine."

"It's my money."

"Oh, and you won't let me forget it." Bitterness reared as Maeve pushed up in bed. For her whole life, someone else had held the purse strings, her parents, her husband, and now, most demeaning of all, her own daughter. "To think of all he tossed away on you, buying you glass, sending you off to that foreign country. And for what? So you could play at being an artist and superior to the rest of us."

"He tossed nothing away on me. He gave me the chance to learn."

"While I stayed on the farm, working my fingers to the bone."

"You never worked a blessed day in your life. It was Brianna who did it all while you took to your bed with one ailment after another."

"Do you think I enjoy being delicate?"

"Oh, aye," Maggie said with relish. "I think you revel in it."

"It's my cross to bear." Maeve picked up her Bible, pressed it to her chest like a shield. She had paid for her sin, she thought. A hundred times over she had paid for it. Yet if forgiveness had come, comfort had not. "That and an ungrateful child."

"What am I supposed to be grateful for? The fact that you complained every day of your life? That you made your dissatisfaction for my father and your disappointment in me clear with every word, every look."

"I gave birth to you!" Maeve shouted. "I nearly died giving you life. And because I carried you in my

womb, I married a man who didn't love me, and who
I didn't love. I sacrificed everything for you."

"Sacrificed?" Maggie said wearily. "What sacrifices
have you made?"

Maeve cloaked herself in the bitter rage of her
pride. "More than you know. And my reward was to
have children who have no love for me."

"Do you think because you got pregnant and
married to give me a name, I should overlook
everything you've done? Everything you haven't
done?" Like love me even a little, Maggie thought,
and ruthlessly pushed the ache away. "It was you on
your back, Mother. I was the result, not the cause."

"How dare you speak to me that way?" Maeve's
face flushed hot, her fingers dug into the blankets.
"You never had any respect, any kindness, any com-
passion."

"No." Because her eyes were stinging, Maggie's
voice was sharp as a whip. "And it's that lack I
inherited from you. I only came today to tell you that
you won't run Brie ragged while I'm gone. If I find
you have, I'll stop the allowance."

"You'd take food out of my mouth?"

Maggie leaned over to tap the box of chocolates.
"Yes. Be sure of it."

"Honor thy father and thy mother." Maeve hugged
the Bible close. "You're breaking a commandment,
Margaret Mary, and sending your soul to hell."

"Then I'll give up my place in heaven rather than
live a hypocrite on earth."

"Margaret Mary!" Maeve shouted when Maggie
had reached the door. "You'll never amount to
anything. You're just like him. God's curse is on you,

Maggie, for being conceived outside the sacrament of marriage.''

"I saw no sacrament of marriage in my house," Maggie tossed back. "Only the agony of it. And if there was a sin in my conception, it wasn't mine."

She slammed the door behind her, then leaned back against it a moment to steady herself.

It was always the same, she thought. They could never be in the same room together without hurling insults. She had known, since she was twelve, why her mother disliked her, condemned her. Her very existence was the reason Maeve's life had turned from dream to harsh reality.

A loveless marriage, a seven-month baby and a farm without a farmer.

It was *that* her mother had thrown in her face when Maggie had reached puberty.

It was *that* they had never forgiven each other for.

Straightening her shoulders, she walked back into the kitchen. She didn't know her eyes were still angry and overbright or her face pale. She walked to her sister and kissed her briskly on the cheek.

"I'll call you from Dublin."

"Maggie." There was too much to say, and nothing to say. Brianna only squeezed her hands. "I wish I could be there for you."

"You could if you wished it enough. Rogan, are you ready?"

"Yes." He rose. "Goodbye, Brianna. Thank you."

"I'll just walk you—" Brianna broke off when her mother called out.

"Go see to her," Maggie said, and walked quickly out of the house. She was yanking at the door of Rogan's car when he laid a hand on her shoulder.

"Are you all right?"

"No, but I don't want to talk about it." With a final tug, she jerked the door open and climbed inside.

He hurried around the hood and slipped onto the driver's seat. "Maggie—"

"Don't say anything. Anything at all. There's nothing you can do or say to change what's always been. Just drive the car and leave me alone. It would be a great favor to me." She began to weep then, passionately, bitterly, while he struggled with the urge to comfort her and the wish to comply with her request.

In the end, he drove, saying nothing, but holding her hand. They were nearing the airport when her sobs died and her tensed fingers went limp. Glancing over, he saw she was sleeping.

She didn't awaken when he carried her inside his company jet, or when he settled her in a seat. Nor did she awaken all through the flight as he watched her. And wondered.

&. Chapter Six

MAGGIE awoke in the dark. The only thing she was certain of in those first groggy minutes was that she wasn't in her own bed. The scent of the sheets, the texture of them was wrong. She didn't have to sleep on fine linen habitually to recognize the difference, or to notice the faint, restful scent of verbena that clung to the pillowslip in which she'd buried her face.

As an uncomfortable thought zeroed into her brain, she stretched out a cautious hand to make certain she was the only occupant of the bed. The mattress flowed on, a veritable lake of smooth sheets and cozy blankets. An empty lake, thank Jesus, she thought, and rolled over to the center of the bed.

Her last clear memory was of crying herself empty in Rogan's car, and the hollow feeling that had left her drifting like a broken reed in a stream.

A good purge, she decided, for she felt incredibly better—steady and rested and clean.

It was tempting to luxuriate in the soft dark on soft sheets with soft scents. But she decided she'd best find out where she was and how she'd arrived. After sliding her way over to the edge of the bed, she groped around the smooth wood of the night table, eased her fingers over and up until she located a lamp and its switch.

The light was gently shaded, a warm golden hue that subtly illuminated a large bedroom with coffered ceiling, dainty rosebud wallpaper and the bed itself, a massive four-poster.

The veritable queen of beds, she thought with a smile. A pity she'd been too tired to appreciate it.

The fireplace across the room was unlit, but scrubbed clean as a new coin and set for kindling. Long-stemmed pink roses, fresh as a summer morning, stood in a Waterford vase on a majestic bureau along with a silver brush set and gorgeous little colored bottles with fancy stoppers.

The mirror above it reflected Maggie, rumpled and heavy-eyed among the sheets.

You look a bit out of place, my girl, she decided, and grinning, tugged on the sleeve of her cotton nightshirt. Someone, it seemed, had had the good sense to change her before dumping her into the royal bed.

A maid perhaps, or Rogan himself. It hardly mattered, she thought practically, since the deed was done and she'd certainly benefited from it. In all likelihood, her clothes were gracing the carved rosewood armoire. As out of place there, she decided with a chuckle, as she was in the glorious lake of smooth linen sheets.

If she was in a hotel, it was certainly the finest that had ever had her patronage. She scrambled up, stumbled toward the closest door over a deep-piled Aubusson.

The bath was as sumptuous as the bedroom, all gleaming rose and ivory tiles, a huge tub fashioned for lounging and a separate shower constructed from a wavy glass block. With a sigh of pure greed, she stripped off her nightshirt and turned on the spray.

It was heaven, the hot water beating on the back of her neck, her shoulders, like the firm fingers of an expert masseuse. A far cry from the stingy trickle her own shower managed at home. The soap smelled of lemon and glided over her skin like silk.

She saw with some amusement that her few meager toiletries had been set out on the generous counter by the shell-shaped pink sinks. Her robe, such as it was, hung on a brass hook beside the door.

Well, someone was taking care of her, she realized, and at the moment she could find no cause for complaint.

After a steamy fifteen minutes while the water ran hot, she reached for one of the thick towels folded over a warming bar. It was big enough to wrap her from breast to calf.

She combed her wet hair back from her face, made use of the cream in a crystal decanter, then exchanged the towel for her tattered flannel robe.

Barefoot and curious, she set out to explore.

Her room was off a long wide hall. Low lights tossed shadows over the gleaming floor and its regal red runner. She heard not a sound as she wandered toward the stairs that curved graciously up to another story, and down. She chose down, letting her fingers play along the polished railing.

Quite obviously she wasn't a guest in a luxury hotel, but in a private home. Rogan's home, she concluded, with an envious glance at the art that graced the foyer and main hall. The man had a Van

Gogh and a Matisse, she realized as her mouth watered.

She found the front parlor, with its wide windows open to the balmy night, a sitting room, its chairs and sofas arranged in conversation groupings. Across the hall was what she supposed would be called the music room, as it was dominated by a grand piano and a gilded harp.

Beautiful it all was, with enough artwork to keep Maggie entranced for days. But at the moment she had another priority.

She wondered how long she would have to search before she found the kitchen.

The light under a door drew her closer. When she looked in, she saw Rogan seated behind a desk, papers arranged in tidy piles before him. It was a two-level room, with his desk on the first and steps leading up to a small sitting area. The walls were lined with books.

Acres of them, she thought at a glance, in a room smelling of leather and beeswax. The room was done in burgundies and dark woods that suited the man as much as it suited the literature.

She watched him, interested in the way he scanned the page in front of him, made quick, decisive notes. He was, for the first time in their acquaintance, without a suit coat or tie. He'd been wearing them, certainly, she mused, but now his collar was unbuttoned, the sleeves of his crisp shirt rolled up to the elbows.

His hair, glinting darkly in the lamplight, was a bit mussed. As if he'd run his hands impatiently through it while he worked. Even as she watched he did so again, raking the fingers through, scowling a bit.

Whatever he was working on absorbed him, for he

worked in a steady, undistracted rhythm that was, in some odd way, fascinating.

He wasn't a man to let his mind wander, she thought. Whatever he chose to do, he would do with the utmost concentration and skill.

She remembered the way he had kissed her. Concentration and skill indeed.

Rogan read the next clause in the proposal and frowned. The wording wasn't quite right. A modification . . . He paused, considered, crossed out a phrase and reworded it. The expansion of his factory in Limerick was crucial to his game plan, and needed to be implemented before the end of the year.

Hundreds of jobs would be created, and with the construction of moderate-income apartments that a subsidiary of Worldwide was planning, hundreds of families would have homes as well.

One branch of the business would feed directly into the other, he thought. It would be a small but important contribution to keeping the Irish—sadly, his country's biggest export—in Ireland.

His mind circled around the next clause, had nearly zeroed in, when he caught himself drifting. Something pulled at his brain, distracting it from the business at hand. Rogan glanced toward the doorway and saw it was not some*thing*, but some*one*.

He must have sensed her standing there, barefoot and sleepy-eyed in a ratty gray robe. Her hair was slicked back, shining red fire, in a style that should have been severe but instead was striking.

Unadorned and fresh-scrubbed, her face was like ivory with a blush of rose beneath. Her lashes were spiked with damp around her slumberous eyes.

His reaction was swift and brutal and human. Even as the heat blasted through him he checked it, ruthlessly.

"Sorry to interrupt." She flashed him a quick, cheeky smile that tortured his already active libido. "I was looking for the kitchen. I'm half-starved."

"It's hardly a wonder." He was forced to clear his throat. Her voice was husky, as sleepily sexy as her eyes. "When did you eat last?"

"I'm not certain." Leaning lazily on the doorjamb, she yawned. "Yesterday, I think. I'm still a bit foggy."

"No, you slept yesterday. All of yesterday—from the time we left your sister's—and all of today."

"Oh." She shrugged. "What time is it?"

"Just past eight—Tuesday."

"Well." She walked into the room and curled up in a big leather chair across from his desk, as if she'd been joining him there for years.

"Do you often sleep for thirty-odd hours straight?"

"Only when I've been up too long." She stretched her arms high to work out kinks she was just beginning to feel. "Sometimes a piece grabs you by the throat and it won't let you go until you've finished."

Resolutely, he shifted his gaze from the flesh the fall of her robe had revealed, and looked down blindly at the paperwork before him. He was appalled that he would react like some hormone-mad teenager. "It's dangerous, in your line of work."

"No, because you're not tired. You're almost unbearably alert. When you've simply worked too long, you lose the edge. You have to stop, rest. This is different. And when I'm done, I fall down and stay down until I've slept it off." She smiled again. "The kitchen, Rogan? I'm ravenous."

Instead of an answer, he reached for the phone and punched in a number. "Miss Concannon is awake," he said. "She'd like a meal. In the library, please."

"That's grand," she said when he replaced the receiver. "But I could have scrambled myself some eggs and saved your staff the bother."

"They're paid to bother."

"Of course." Her voice was dry as dust. "How smug you must be to have round-the-clock servants." She waved a hand before he could answer. "Best we don't get into that on an empty stomach. Tell me, Rogan, how exactly did I come to be in that big bed upstairs?"

"I put you there."

"Did you now?" If he was hoping for a blush or stutter, he'd be disappointed. "I'll have to thank you."

"You slept like a stone. At one point I nearly held a mirror up to your lips to be certain you were alive." She was certainly alive now, vibrant in the lamplight. "Do you want a brandy?"

"Better not, before I've eaten."

He rose, went to a sideboard and poured a single snifter from a decanter. "You were upset before we left."

She cocked her head. "Now, that's a fine and diplomatic way of phrasing it." The weeping spell didn't embarrass her. It was simply emotion, passion, as real and as human as laughter or lust. But she remembered that he had held her hand and had offered no useless words to stem the storm. "I'm sorry if I made you uncomfortable."

She had, miserably, but he shrugged it off. "You didn't want to talk about it."

"Didn't, and don't." She took a quiet breath because her voice had been sharp. He didn't deserve such rudeness after his kindness. "It's nothing to do with you, Rogan, just old family miseries. Since I'm feeling mellow, I'll tell you it was comforting to have you hold my hand. I didn't think you were the type to offer."

His eyes flicked back to hers. "It seems to me we don't know each other well enough to generalize."

"I've always considered myself a quick and accurate judge, but you may be right. So tell me"—she propped an elbow on the arm of the chair, cocked her chin on her fist—"who are you, Rogan Sweeney?"

He was relieved when the need to answer was postponed by the arrival of her dinner. A tidy, uniformed maid wheeled in a tray, settling it in front of Maggie with no more than a whisper of sound and a jingle of silverware. She bobbed once when Maggie thanked her, then disappeared the moment Rogan told her that would be all.

"Ah, what a scent." Maggie attacked the soup first, a rich, thick broth swimming with chunks of vegetables. "Do you want some?"

"No, I've eaten." Rather than go back around the desk, he sat in the chair beside hers. It was oddly cozy, he realized, to sit with her while she ate and the house seemed to settle quietly around them. "Since you're back among the living, perhaps you'd like to go by the gallery in the morning."

"Umm." She nodded, her mouth full of crusty roll. "When?"

"Eight—I have appointments midmorning, but I can take you in and leave a car at your disposal."

"A car at my disposal." Tickled, she pressed a fist to her mouth as she laughed. "Oh, I could get used to that quick enough. And what would I do with the car at my disposal?"

"What you like." God knew why her reaction annoyed him, but it did. "Or you can wander around Dublin on foot, if you prefer."

"A bit touchy this evening, are we?" She moved from the soup to the entrée of honeyed chicken. "Your cook's a treasure, Rogan. Do you think I can charm this recipe out of him—or her—for Brie?"

"Him," Rogan said. "And you're welcome to try. He's French, insolent and given to tantrums."

"Then we have all but nationality in common. Tell me, will I be moving to a hotel tomorrow?"

He'd thought about that, a great deal. It would certainly be more comfortable for him if she were tucked away in a suite at the Westbury. More comfortable, he thought, and much more dull. "You're welcome to stay in the guest room if it suits you."

"It suits me down to the ground." She studied him as she speared a tiny new potato. He looked relaxed here, she realized. Very much the complacent king of the castle. "Is it just you in this big house?"

"It is." He lifted a brow. "Does that worry you?"

"Worry me? Oh, you mean because you might come knocking on my door one lustful night?" She chuckled, infuriating him. "I'm able to say yes or no, Rogan, the same as you would be if I came knocking on yours. I only asked because it seems a lot of room for one man."

"It's my family home," he said stiffly. "I've lived here all my life."

"And a fine place it is." She pushed the tray back and rose to go to the small sideboard. Lifting the top of a decanter, she sniffed. Sighed at the fine scent of Irish whiskey. After pouring herself a glass, she came back and curled up her legs. *"Sláinte,"* she said, and tossed the whiskey back. It set a good, strong fire kindling in her gut.

"Would you like another?"

"One'll do me. One warms the soul, two warms the brain, my father often said. I'm in the mood for a cool head." She set the empty glass on the tray, shifted her body more comfortably. Her frayed flannel robe slid open at the curve of her knee. "You haven't answered my question."

"Which was?"

"Who are you?"

"I'm a businessman, as you remind me with regularity." He settled back, making a determined effort not to let his mind or his gaze wander to her bare legs. "Third generation. Born and bred in Dublin, with love and respect for art nurtured in me from the cradle."

"And that love and respect was augmented by the idea of making a profit."

"Precisely." He swirled his brandy, sipped, and looked exactly like what he was. A man comfortable with his own wealth and content with his life. "While making a profit brings its own sense of satisfaction, there's another, more spiritual satisfaction that comes from developing and promoting a new artist. Particularly one you believe in passionately."

Maggie touched her tongue to her top lip. He was entirely too confident, she decided, much too sure of himself and his place in the world. All that tidy certainty begged for a bit of shaking.

"So, I'm here to satisfy you, Rogan?"

He met her amused eyes, nodded. "I have no doubt you will, Maggie, eventually. On every level."

"Eventually." She hadn't meant, really, to steer them onto this boggy ground, but it seemed irresistible, sitting with him in the quiet room with her body so rested, her mind so alert. "Your choice of time and place, then?"

"It's traditional, I believe, for the man to choose when to advance."

"Hah!" Bristling, she leaned over to jab a finger in his chest. Any thoughts she'd had of easing into romance vanished like smoke. "Stuff your traditions in your hat and wear it well. I don't cater to them. You might be interested to know that as we approach the twenty-first century, women are doing their own choosing. The fact is we've been doing so since time began, those of us sharp enough, and men are just catching on to it." She plopped back in her chair. "I'll have you, Rogan, in my time, and in my place."

It baffled him why such an incredible statement should both arouse him and make him uneasy. "Your father was right, Maggie, about you getting the brass. You have it to spare."

"And what of it? Oh, I know your type." Contempt colored her tone. "You like a woman to sit quietly by, mooning a bit, catering to your whims, to be sure, and hoping, while her romantic heart beats desperately in her breast, that you'll look twice in her direction. She'll be proper as a saint in public, never a sour word slipping through her rosy lips. Then, of course, when you've decided on that time and that place, she's to transform herself into a veritable tiger, indulging your most prurient fantasies until the lights switch on again and she turns into a doorstop."

Rogan waited to be sure she'd run down, then hid a smile in his brandy. "That sums it up amazingly well."

"Jackass."

"Shrew," he said pleasantly. "Would you care for some dessert?"

The chuckle tickled her throat, so she set it free. Who would have thought she'd actually come to like him? "No, damn you. I'll not drag that poor maid away again from her television or her flirtation with the butler or however she spends her evenings."

"My butler is seventy-six, and well safe from flirtations with a maid."

"A lot you know." Maggie rose again and wandered toward a wall of books. Alphabetized by author, she noted, and nearly snorted. She should have known. "What's her name?"

"Whose?"

"The maid's."

"You want to know my maid's name?"

Maggie stroked a finger down a volume of James Joyce. "No, I want to see if *you* know your maid's name. It's a test."

He opened his mouth, closed it again, grateful that Maggie's back was to him. What difference did it make if he knew the name of one of his maids?

Colleen? Maureen? Hell! The domestic staff was his butler's domain. Bridgit? No, damn it, it was . . .

"Nancy." He thought—was nearly certain. "She's fairly new. I believe she's been here about five months. Would you like me to call her back in for an introduction?"

"No." Casually, Maggie moved from Joyce to Keats. "It was a curiosity to me, that's all. Tell me, Rogan, do you have anything in here other than classics? You know, a good murder mystery I might pass some time with?"

His library of first editions was considered one of the finest in the country, and she was criticizing it for lacking a potboiler. With an effort, he schooled his temper and his voice. "I believe you'll find some of Dame Agatha's work."

"The British." She shrugged. "Not bloodthirsty enough as a rule—unless they're sacking castles like those damn Cromwellians. What's this?" She bent down, peered. "This Dante's in Italian."

"I believe it is."

"Can you read it, or is it just for show?"

"I can fumble through it well enough."

She passed by it, hoping for something more contemporary. "I didn't pick up as much of the language as I should have in Venice. Plenty of slang, little of the socially correct." She glanced over her shoulder and grinned. "Artists are a colorful lot in any country."

"So I've noticed." He rose and crossed to another shelf of books. "This might be more what you're looking for." He offered Maggie a copy of Thomas Harris's *Red Dragon*. "I believe several people are murdered horribly."

"Wonderful." She tucked the book under her arm. "I'll say good night then so you can get back to work. I'm grateful for the bed and the meal."

"You're welcome." He sat behind his desk again, lifted a pen and ran it through his fingers while he watched her. "I'd like to leave at eight sharp. The dining room's down this hall and to the left. Breakfast will be served anytime after six."

"I can guarantee it won't be served to me at that hour, but I'll be ready at eight." On impulse she crossed to him, placed her hands on the arms of his chair and leaned her face close to his. "You know, Rogan, we're precisely what each other doesn't need or want—on a personal level."

"I couldn't agree more. On a personal level." Her skin, soft and white where the flannel parted at her throat, smelled like sin.

"And that's why, to my way of thinking, we're going to have such a fascinating relationship. Barely any common ground at all, wouldn't you say?"

"No more than a toehold." His gaze lowered to her mouth, lingered, rose to hers again. "A shaky one at that."

"I like dangerous climbs." She leaned forward a little more, just an inch, and nipped his bottom lip with her teeth.

A spear of fire arrowed straight to his loins. "I prefer having my feet on the ground."

"I know." She leaned back again, leaving him with a tingle on his lips and the heat in his gut. "We'll try it your way first. Good night."

She strolled out of the room without looking back. Rogan waited until he was certain she was well away before he lifted his hands and scrubbed them over his face.

Good Christ, the woman was tying him into knots, slippery tangled knots of pure lust. He didn't believe on acting on lust alone, at least not since his adolescence. He was, after all, a civilized man, one of taste and breeding.

He respected women, admired them. Certainly he'd developed relationships that had culminated in bed, but he'd always tried to wait until the relationships had developed before making love. Reasonably, mutually and discreetly. He wasn't an animal to be driven by instinct alone.

He wasn't even certain he liked Maggie Concannon as a person. So what kind of man would he be if he did what he was burning to do at this moment? If he stalked up those stairs, threw open the door to her bedroom and ravished her good and proper.

A satisfied man, he thought with grim humor.

At least until morning when he had to face her, and himself, and the business they had to complete.

Perhaps it was more difficult to take the high road. Perhaps he would suffer, as he was damn well certain she expected him to. But when the time came for him to take her to bed, he would have the upper hand.

That, most certainly, was worth something.

Even, he thought as he shoved papers aside, a miserably sleepless night.

Maggie slept like a baby. Despite the images evoked by the novel Rogan had given her, she'd dropped off to sleep just after midnight and had slept dreamlessly until nearly seven.

Flushed with energy and anticipation, she searched out the dining room and was pleased to see a full Irish breakfast warming on the sideboard.

"Good morning, miss." The same maid who had served her the night before scurried in from the kitchen. "Is there anything I can get for you?"

"Thank you, no. I can serve myself." Maggie picked up a plate from the table and moved toward the tempting scents on the sideboard.

"Shall I pour you coffee or tea, miss?"

"Tea would be lovely." Maggie took the lid off a silver warmer and sniffed appreciately at the thick rashers of bacon. "Nancy, is it?"

"No, miss, it's Noreen."

Failed that test, Squire Sweeney, Maggie mused. "Would you tell the cook, Noreen, that I've never had a better meal than my dinner last night."

"I'd be happy to, miss."

Maggie moved from server to server, heaping her plate. She often skipped meals altogether, so indifferent was her own cooking. But when food was available in such quantity, and food of such quality, she made up for it.

"Will Mr. Sweeney be joining me for breakfast?" she asked as she carried her plate back to the table.

"He's already eaten, miss. Mr. Sweeney breakfasts every day at half-six, precisely."

"A creature of habit, is he?" Maggie winked at the maid and slathered fresh jam on her warmed toast.

"He is, yes," Noreen answered, flushing a bit. "I'm to remind you, miss, he'll be ready to leave at eight."

"Thank you, Noreen, I'll keep it in mind."

"You've only to ring if you need anything."

Quiet as a mouse, Noreen faded back into the

kitchen. Maggie applied herself to a breakfast she felt was fit for a queen and perused the copy of the *Irish Times* that had been neatly folded beside her plate.

A cozy way to live, she supposed, with servants only the snap of a finger away. But didn't it drive Rogan mad to know they were always about the house? That he was never alone?

The very idea made her wince. She'd go mad for sure, Maggie decided, without solitude. She looked over the room with its dark and glossy wainscoting, the glitter from the twin crystal chandeliers, the gleam from the silver on the antique sideboard, the sparkle of china and Waterford glass.

Yes, even in this lush setting, she'd go stark, raving mad.

She lingered over a second cup of tea, read the paper from back to front and cleaned every crumb from her plate. From somewhere in the house a clock chimed the hour. She debated having just one more serving of bacon, called herself a glutton and resisted.

She took a few moments to study the art on the walls. There was a watercolor she found particularly exquisite. Taking a last, leisurely turn around the room, she started out, down the hall.

Rogan stood in the foyer, immaculate in a gray suit and navy tie. He studied her, studied his watch. "You're late."

"Am I?"

"It's eight past the hour."

She lifted her brows, saw he was serious and dutifully muffled a chuckle. "I should be flogged."

He skimmed a gaze up her, from the half boots

and dark leggings to the mannish white shirt that reached to midthigh and was cinched with two leather belts. Glittering translucent stones swung at her ears, and she had, for once, added a touch of makeup. She hadn't, however, bothered with a watch.

"If you don't wear a timepiece, how can you be on time?"

"You've a point there. Perhaps that's why I don't."

Still watching her, he took out a pad and his pen.

"What are you doing?"

"Noting down that we have to supply you with a watch, as well as a phone-answering machine and a calendar."

"That's very generous of you, Rogan." She waited until he opened the door and gestured her out. "Why?"

"The watch so you'll be prompt. The answering machine so I'll at least be able to leave a damn message when you ignore the phone, and the calendar so you'll know what the bloody day is when I request a shipment."

He'd bitten off the last word as if it were stringy meat, Maggie thought. "Since you're in such a bright and cheerful mood this morning, I'll risk telling you that none of those things will change me a whit. I'm irresponsible, Rogan. You've only to ask what's left of my family." She turned around, ignoring his hiss of impatience, and studied his house.

It overlooked a lovely, shady green—St. Stephen's, she was to learn later—and stood proudly, a trifle haughtily, against a dreamy blue sky.

Though the stone was aged, the lines were as graceful as a young woman's body. It was a combination of dignity and elegance Maggie knew only the rich could afford. Every window, of which there were many, glistened like diamonds in the sun. The lawn, smooth and green, gave way to a lovely front garden, tidy as a church and twice as formal.

"A pretty spot you have here. I missed it, you know, on my way in."

"I'm aware of that. You'll have to wait for the tour, Margaret Mary. I don't like to be late." He took her arm and all but dragged her to the waiting car.

"Do you get docked for tardiness, then?" She laughed when he said nothing, and settled back to enjoy the ride. "Are you by nature surly of a morning, Rogan?"

"I'm not surly," he snapped at her. Or he wouldn't be, he thought, if he'd gotten above two hours' sleep. And the responsibility for that, damn all women, fell solidly on her head. "I have a lot to accomplish today."

"Oh, to be sure. Empires to build, fortunes to win."

That did it. He didn't know why, but the light undertone of disdain broke the last link on control. He swerved to the side of the road, causing the driver who had been cruising behind him to blast rudely on his horn. Grabbing Maggie by the collar, he hauled her half out of her seat and crushed his mouth to hers.

She hadn't been expecting quite that reaction. But that didn't mean she couldn't enjoy it. She could meet him on even ground when he wasn't quite so controlled, quite so skillful. Her head might have spun, but the sensation of power remained. No seduction here, only raw needs, rubbing together like live wires and threatening to flare.

He dragged her head back and plundered her mouth. Just once, he promised himself. Only once to relieve some of this vicious tension that coiled inside him like a snake.

But kissing her didn't relieve it. Instead, the complete and eager response of her, the total verve of it, wrapped his tension only tighter until he couldn't breathe.

For a moment he felt as though he were being sucked into some velvet-lined, airless tunnel. And he was terrified that he'd never want or need light again.

He jerked away, fastened his hands like vises on the wheel. He eased back onto the road like a drunk trying to negotiate a straight line.

"I'm assuming that was an answer to something." Her voice was unnaturally quiet. It wasn't his kiss that had unnerved her nearly as much as the way he had ended it.

"It was that or throttle you."

"I prefer being kissed to strangled. Still, I'd like it better if you weren't angry about wanting me."

He was calmer now, concentrating on the road and making up the time she'd cost him that morning. "I explained myself before. The timing's inappropriate."

"Inappropriate. And who's in charge of propriety?"

"I prefer knowing whom I'm sleeping with. Having some mutual affection and respect."

Her eyes narrowed. "There's a long way between a kiss on the lips and a tumble in the sheets, Sweeney. I'll have you know I'm not one to leap onto the mattress at the blink of an eye."

"I never said—"

"Oh, didn't you, now?" She was all the more insulted because she knew how quickly she would have leaped onto a mattress with him. "As far as I can see, you've decided I'm plenty loose enough. Well, I won't be explaining my past history to you. And as for affection and respect, you've yet to earn them from me, boy-o."

"Fine, then. We're agreed."

"We're agreed you can go straight to hell. And your maid's name is Noreen."

That distracted him enough to have him taking his eyes off the road and staring. "What?"

"Your maid, you dolt, you narrow-nosed aristocrat. 'Tisn't Nancy. It's Noreen." Maggie folded her arms and stared resolutely out the side window.

Rogan only shook his head. "I'm grateful to you for clearing that up. God knows what an embarrassment it would have been to me if I'd had to introduce her to the neighbors."

"Blue-blooded snob," she muttered.

"Wasp-tongued viper."

They settled into an angry silence for the rest of the drive.

8. Chapter Seven

IT was impossible not to be impressed by Worldwide Gallery, Dublin. The architecture alone was worth a visit to the place. Indeed, photographs of the building had appeared in dozens of magazines and art books around the world as a shining example of the Georgian style that was part of Dublin's architectural legacy.

Though Maggie had seen it reproduced in glossy pages, the sight of it, the sheer grandeur of it in three dimensions, took her breath away.

She'd spent hours of her free time during her apprenticeship in Venice haunting galleries. But nothing compared in splendor with Rogan's.

Yet she made no comment at all while he unlocked the imposing-looking front doors and gestured her inside.

She had to resist the urge to genuflect, such was the churchlike quiet, the play of light, the scented air in the main room. The Native American display was beautifully and carefully mounted—the pottery bowls, the gorgeous baskets, the ritual masks, shaman rattles and beadwork. On the walls were drawings at once primitive and sophisticated. Maggie's attention and her admiration focused on a buckskin dress the color of cream, adorned with beads and smooth, bright stones. Rogan had ordered it hung like a tapestry. Maggie's fingers itched to touch.

"Impressive" was all she said.

"I'm delighted you approve."

"I've never seen American Indian work outside of books and such." She leaned over a water vessel.

"That's precisely why I wanted to bring the display to Ireland. We too often focus on European history and culture and forget there's more to the world."

"Hard to believe people who could create this would be the savages we see in those old John Wayne movies. Then again"—she smiled as she straightened—"my ancestors were savage enough, stripping naked and painting themselves blue before they screamed into battle. I come from that." She tilted her head to study him, the perfectly polished businessman. "We both do."

"One could say that such tendencies become more diluted in some than in others over the centuries. I haven't had the urge to paint myself blue in years."

She laughed, but he was already checking his watch again.

"We're using the second floor for your work." He started toward the stairs.

"For any particular reason?"

"For several particular reasons." Impatience shimmering like a wave of heat around him, he paused until she joined him on the staircase. "I prefer a show like this to have some sense of a social occasion. People tend to appreciate art, at least feel it's more accessible, if they're relaxed and enjoying themselves." He stopped at the top of the steps, lifting a brow at her expression. "You've a problem with that?"

"I'd like people to take my work seriously, not think of it as a party favor."

"I assure you, they'll take it seriously." Particularly with the prices he'd decided to demand for it, the strategy he intended to employ. "And the marketing of your work is, after all, my province." He turned, sliding open double pocket doors, then stepped back so that Maggie could enter first.

She quite simply lost her voice. The wonderfully enormous room was flooded with light from the domed central skylight above. It poured down over the dark, polished floor and tossed back stunning reflections, almost mirrorlike, of the work Rogan had chosen to display.

In all of her dreams, in her wildest and most secret hopes, she'd never imagined that her work would be showcased so sensitively, or so grandly.

Thick-based pedestals of creamy white marble stood around the room, lifting the glass to eye level. Rogan had chosen only twelve pieces to grace the lofty space. A canny move, she realized, as it made each piece seem all the more unique. And there, in the center of the room, glistening like ice heated by a core of fire, was Maggie's *Surrender*.

There was a dull ache in her heart as she studied the sculpture. Someone would buy it, she knew. Within days someone would pay the price Rogan was asking and steal it completely and finally from her life.

The price of wanting more, she thought, seemed to be the loss of what you already had. Or perhaps of what you were.

When she said nothing, only walked through the

room with her boots echoing, Rogan stuck his hands in his pockets. "The smaller pieces are displayed in what we call the upper sitting rooms. It's a more intimate space." He paused, waiting for some response, then hissed through his teeth when he received none. Damn the woman, he thought. What did she want? "We'll have an orchestra at the show. Strings. And champagne and canapes, of course."

"Of course," Maggie managed. She kept her back to him, wondering why she should stand in such a magnificent room and want to weep.

"I'll ask you to attend, at least for a short time. You needn't do or say anything that would compromise your artistic integrity."

Her heart was beating much too loudly for her to catch his tone of annoyance. "It looks . . ." She couldn't think of a word. Simply couldn't. "Fine," she said lamely. "It all looks fine."

"Fine?"

"Yes." She turned back, sober-eyed and, for the first time in recent memory, terrified. "You have a nice aesthetic sense."

"A nice aesthetic sense," he repeated, amazed at her tepid response. "Well, Margaret Mary, I'm so gratified. It's only taken three incredibly difficult weeks and the combined efforts of more than a dozen highly qualified people to make everything look 'fine.'"

She ran an unsteady hand through her hair. Couldn't he see she was speechless, that she was completely out of her realm and scared as a rabbit faced by a hound? "What do you want me to say? I've done my job and given you the art. You've done yours and utilized it. We're both to be congratulated, Rogan. Now perhaps I should look about in your more intimate rooms."

He stepped forward, blocking her path as she started for the doorway. The fury that rose up in him was so molten, so intense, he was surprised it didn't melt her glass into puddles of shine and color.

"You ungrateful peasant."

"A peasant, am I?" Emotions swirled inside her, contradictory and frightening. "You're right enough on that, Sweeney. And if I'm ungrateful because I don't fall at your feet and kiss your boots, then it's ungrateful I'll stay. I don't want or expect any more from you than what it said in your cursed contracts with your bloody exclusive clauses, and you'll get no more from me."

She could feel the hot tears boiling up, ready to erupt. She was certain that if she didn't get out of the room quickly, her lungs would quite simply collapse from the strain. In her desperation to escape, she shoved at him.

"I'll tell you what I expect." He snagged her shoulder, whirled her around. "And what I'll have."

"I beg your pardon," Joseph said from the doorway. "I seem to be interrupting."

He couldn't have been more amused, or more fascinated, as he watched his coolheaded boss spit fire and rage at the small, dangerous-eyed woman whose fists had already raised as if for a bout.

"Not at all." Using every ounce of willpower, Rogan released Maggie's arm and stepped back. In the wink of an eye, he had gone from fury to calmness. "Miss Concannon and I were just discussing the terms of our contract. Maggie Concannon, Joseph Donahoe, the curator of this gallery."

"A pleasure." All charm, Joseph stepped forward to take Maggie's hand. Though it trembled a bit, he kissed it lavishly, dashingly, and set his gold tooth flashing with a grin. "A pure pleasure, Miss Concannon, to meet the person behind the genius."

"And a pleasure for me, Mr. Donahoe, to meet a man so sensitive to art, and to the artist."

"I'll be leaving Maggie in your capable hands, Joseph. I have appointments."

"You'll be doing me an honor, Rogan." Joseph's eyes twinkled as he kept Maggie's hand lightly in his.

The gesture wasn't lost on Rogan, nor was the fact that Maggie made no move to break the contact. She was, in fact, smiling up at Joseph flirtatiously.

"You've only to tell Joseph when you require the car," Rogan said stiffly. "The driver's at your disposal."

"Thank you, Rogan," she said without looking at him. "But I'm sure Joseph can keep me entertained for some time."

"There's no way I'd rather spend the day," Joseph quickly put in. "Have you seen the sitting rooms, Miss Concannon?"

"I haven't, no. You'll call me Maggie, I hope."

"I will." His hand still linked with hers, Joseph drew her through the doorway. "I believe you'll appreciate what we've done here. With the showing only days away, we want to be certain you're happy. Any suggestions you have will be most welcomed."

"That'll be a change." Maggie paused, glanced over her shoulder to where Rogan remained standing. "Don't let us keep you from your business,

Rogan. I'm sure it's pressing." With a toss of her head, she beamed at Joseph. "I know a Francis Donahoe, from near Ennis. A merchant he is, with the same look around the eyes as you. Would you be related?"

"I've cousins in Clare, on my father's side, and my mother's. They'd be Ryans."

"I know scores of Ryans. Oh." She stopped, sighed as she stepped through an archway into a tidy little room complete with fireplace and love seat. Several of her smaller pieces, including the one Rogan had bought at their first meeting, graced the antique tables.

"An elegant setting, I think." Joseph moved inside to switch on the recessed lighting. The glass jumped into life under the beams, seemed to pulse. "The ballroom makes a breathless statement. This, a delicate one."

"Yes." She sighed again. "Do you mind if I sit a moment, Joseph? For the truth is I have lost my breath." She settled on the love seat and closed her eyes. "Once when I was a child, my father bought a billy goat, with some idea of breeding. I was in the field with it one morning, paying it no mind, and it got its dander up. Butted me hard, he did, and sent me flying. I felt just that way when I stepped into that other room. As if something had butted me hard and sent me flying."

"Nervous, are you?"

She opened her eyes and saw the understanding in Joseph's. "I'm frightened to death. And damned if I'll let himself know it. He's so damned cocksure, isn't he?"

"He's confident, our Rogan. And with reason

enough. He's got an uncanny sense for buying the right piece, or patronizing the right artist." A curious man, and one who enjoyed a good gossip, Joseph made himself comfortable beside her. He stretched out his legs, crossed them at the ankle in a posture inviting relaxation and confidence. "I noticed the two of you were butting heads, so to speak, when I interrupted."

"We don't seem to have a lot of common ground." Maggie smiled a little. "He's pushy, our Rogan."

"True enough, but usually in such a subtle way one doesn't know one's been pushed."

Maggie hissed through her teeth, "He hasn't been subtle with me."

"I noticed. Interesting. You know, Maggie, I don't think I'd be giving away any corporate secrets if I told you Rogan was determined to sign you with Worldwide. I've worked for him for more than ten years, and never recall seeing him more focused on a single artist."

"And I should be flattered." She sighed and closed her eyes again. "I am, most of the time, when I'm not busy being infuriated with his bossy ways. Always prince to peasant."

"He's used to having things his way."

"Well, he won't be having me his way." She opened her eyes and rose. "Will you show me the rest of the gallery?"

"I'd be happy to. And perhaps you'll tell me the story of your life."

Maggie cocked her head and studied him. A mischief maker, she thought, with his dreamy eyes and piratical demeanor. She'd always enjoyed a mischief-making friend. "All right, then," she said, and linked her arm through his as they strolled through the next archway. "There once was a farmer who wanted to be a poet. . . ."

There were just too damn many people in Dublin for Maggie's taste. You could hardly take a step without bumping into someone. It was a pretty city, she couldn't deny it, with its lovely bay and spearing steeples. She could admire the magnificence of its architecture, all the red brick and gray stone, the charm of its colorful storefronts.

She was told by her driver, Brian Duggin, that the early Dubliners had a sense of order and beauty as keen as their sense of profit. And so, she thought, the city suited Rogan even as he suited it.

She settled back in the quiet car to admire the dazzling front gardens and copper cupolas, the shady greens and the busy River Liffey, which split the city in two.

She felt her pulse quicken to the pace around her, respond to the crowds and the hurry. But the bustle excited her only briefly before it exhausted. The sheer number of people on O'Connell Street, where everyone seemed to be in a desperate rush to get somewhere else, made her yearn for the lazy, quiet roads of the west.

Still, she found the view from O'Connell Bridge spectacular, the ships moored at the quays, the majestic dome of the Four Courts glinting in the sun. Her driver seemed happy enough to obey her request simply to cruise, or to pull over and wait while she walked through parks and squares.

She stopped on Grafton Street among the smart shops and bought a pin for Brianna, a simple silver crescent with a curve of garnets. It would, Maggie thought as she tucked the box in her purse, suit her sister's traditional taste.

For herself, she mooned briefly over a pair of earrings, long twists of gold and silver and copper, accented top and bottom with fire opals. She had no business spending good money on such frivolous baubles. No business at all, she reminded herself, when she had no real guarantee when she might sell another piece.

So, of course, she bought the earrings, and sent her budget to the devil.

To round off her day, she visited museums, wandered along the river and had tea in a tiny shop off FitzWilliam Square. She spent her last hour watching the sunlight and reflections from Half Penny Bridge and sketching in a pad she'd picked up in an art store.

It was after seven when she returned to Rogan's house. He came out of the front parlor and stopped her before she'd reached the stairs.

"I'd begun to wonder if you'd had Duggin drive you all the way back to Clare."

"I thought of it once or twice." She pushed back her untidy hair. "It's been years since I've visited Dublin." She thought of the juggler she'd seen, and of course, of her father. "I'd forgotten how noisy it is."

"I assume you haven't eaten."

"I haven't, no." If she didn't count the biscuit she'd had with her tea.

"Dinner's ordered for seven-thirty, but I can have it put back until eight if you'd like to join us for cocktails."

"Us?"

"My grandmother. She's anxious to meet you."

"Oh." Maggie's mood plummeted. Someone else to meet, to talk to, to be with. "I wouldn't want to hold you up."

"It's not a problem. If you'd like to change, we'll be in the parlor."

"Change for what?" Resigned, she tucked her sketchbook under her arm. "I'm afraid I left all my formal attire at home. But if my appearance embarrasses you, I can have a tray in my room."

"Don't put words in my mouth, Maggie." Taking her firmly by the arm, Rogan steered her into the parlor. "Grandmother." He addressed the woman sitting regally in the high back brocaded chair. "I'd like you to meet Margaret Mary Concannon. Maggie, Christine Sweeney."

"An absolute delight." Christine offered a fine-boned hand, accented with one gleaming sapphire. Matching ones dripped from her ears. "I take full credit for you being here, my dear, as I bought the first piece of your work that intrigued Rogan."

"Thank you. You're a collector, then?"

"It's in the blood. Please sit. Rogan, get the child something to drink."

Rogan moved to the glittering decanters. "What would you like, Maggie?"

"Whatever you're having." Resigned to being polite for an hour or two, Maggie set her sketchpad and purse aside.

"It must be thrilling to be having your first major show," Christine began. Why, the girl was striking, she thought. All cream and fire, as eye-catching in a shirt and tights as dozens of women would attempt to be in diamonds and silks.

"To be honest, Mrs. Sweeney, it's hard for me to imagine it." She accepted the glass from Rogan and hoped its contents would be enough to brace her for an evening of making conversation.

"Tell me what you thought of the gallery."

"It's wonderful. A cathedral to art."

"Oh." Christine reached out again, squeezing Maggie's hand. "How my Michael would have loved to hear you say that. It's exactly what he wanted. He was a frustrated artist, you know."

"No." Maggie slanted Rogan a glance. "I didn't."

"He wanted to paint. He had the vision, but not the aptitude. So he created the atmosphere and the means to celebrate others who did." Christine's smoky silk suit rustled as she sat back. "He was a wonderful man. Rogan takes after him, in looks and temperament."

"That must make you very proud."

"It does. As I'm sure what you've done with your life has made your family proud of you."

"I don't know as pride's quite the word." Maggie sipped her drink, discovered Rogan had served her sherry and struggled not to grimace. Fortunately, the butler came to the doorway at that moment to announce dinner.

"Well, that's handy." Grateful, Maggie set her glass aside. "I'm starved."

"Then we'll go straight in." Rogan offered his grandmother his arm. "Julien is delighted you're enjoying his cuisine."

"Oh, he's a fine cook, that's the truth. I wouldn't

have the heart to tell him I'm such a poor one myself I'll eat anything I don't have to prepare."

"We won't mention it." Rogan drew out a chair for Christine, then for Maggie.

"We won't," Maggie agreed. "Since I've decided to try to barter some of Brie's recipes for his."

"Brie is Maggie's sister," Rogan explained as the soup course was served. "She runs a B-and-B in Clare, and from personal experience, I can attest that her cuisine is excellent."

"So, your sister's an artist in the kitchen rather than the studio."

"She is," Maggie agreed, finding herself much more comfortable in Christine Sweeney's company than she'd expected to be. "It's a magic touch Brianna has with hearth and home."

"In Clare, you say." Christine nodded as Rogan offered her wine. "I know the area well. I come from Galway myself."

"You do?" Surprise and pleasure flitted across Maggie's face. It was another reminder to her of how much she missed home. "What part?"

"Galway City. My father was in shipping. I met Michael through his business deals with my father."

"My own grandmother—on my mother's side— came from Galway." Though under most circumstances, Maggie would rather eat than talk, she was enjoying the combination of excellent food and conversation. "She lived there until she married. That would be about sixty years ago. She was a merchant's daughter."

"Is that so. And her name?"

"She was Sharon Feeney before her marriage."

"Sharon Feeney." Christine's eyes brightened, as

deep now and as sparkling as her sapphires. "Daughter of Colin and Mary Feeney?"

"Aye. You knew her, then?"

"Oh, I did. We lived minutes from each other. I was a bit younger than she, but we spent time together." Christine winked at Maggie, then looked at Rogan to draw him into the conversation. "I was madly in love with Maggie's great-uncle Niall, and used Sharon shamelessly to be around him."

"Surely you needed to use nothing and no one to get any man's attention," Rogan said.

"Oh, you've a sweet tongue." Christine laughed and patted his hand. "Mind yourself around this one, Maggie."

"He doesn't waste much sugar on me."

"It dissolves in vinegar," Rogan retorted in the most pleasant of tones.

Deciding to ignore him, Maggie turned back to Christine. "I haven't seen my uncle in years, but I've heard he was a fine, handsome man in his youth, and had a way with the ladies."

"He was, and he did." Christine laughed again, and the sound was young and gay. "I spent many a night dreaming of Niall Feeney when I was a girl. The truth is"—she turned her brilliant eyes on Rogan, and there was a hint of mischief in them that Maggie admired—"if Michael hadn't come along and swept me off my feet, I'd have fought to the death to marry Niall. Interesting, isn't it? You two might have been cousins had things worked out differently."

Rogan glanced at Maggie, lifted his wine. Horrifying was all he could think. Absolutely horrifying.

Maggie snickered and polished off her soup.

"Niall Feeney never married, you know, and lives a bachelor's life in Galway. Perhaps, Mrs. Sweeney, you broke his heart."

"I'd like to think so." The bone-deep beauty so evident in Christine Sweeney's face was enhanced by a flattering blush. "But the sad truth is, Niall never noticed me."

"Was he blind, then?" Rogan asked, and earned a beaming smile from his grandmother.

"Not blind." Maggie sighed at the scents as the fish course was set before her. "But a man perhaps more foolish than most."

"And never married, you say?" Christine's inquiry, Rogan noted with a slight frown, was perhaps just a tad too casual.

"Never. My sister corresponds with him." A wicked twinkle gleamed in Maggie's eye. "I'll have her mention you in her next letter. We'll see if his memory's better than his youthful judgment."

Though her smile was a bit dreamy, Christine shook her head. "Fifty-five years it's been since I left Galway for Dublin, and for Michael. Sweet Mary."

The thought of the passing years brought a pleasant sadness, the same she might have felt on watching a ship sail out of port. She still missed her husband, though he'd been gone for more than a dozen years. In an automatic gesture Maggie found touching, Christine laid a hand over Rogan's.

"Sharon married a hotelier, did she not?"

"She did, yes, and was widowed for the last ten years of her life."

"I'm sorry. But she had her daughter to comfort her."

"My mother. But I don't know as she was a

comfort." The dregs of bitterness interfered with the delicate flavor of the trout in Maggie's mouth. She washed them away with wine.

"We wrote for several years after Sharon married. She was very proud of her girl. Maeve, isn't it?"

"Aye." Maggie tried to envision her mother as a girl, and failed.

"A lovely child, Sharon told me, with striking golden hair. The temper of a devil, she would say, and the voice of an angel."

Maggie swallowed hurriedly, gaped. "The voice of an angel? My mother?"

"Why, yes. Sharon said she sang like a saint and wanted to be a professional. I believe she was, at least for a time." Christine paused, thinking, while Maggie simply stared. "Yes, I know she was. In fact she came up to Gort to sing, but I couldn't get down to see her. I had some clippings Sharon sent me, must have been thirty years past." She smiled, curious. "She no longer sings?"

"No." Maggie let out a quiet baffled breath. She had never heard her mother raise her voice in anything other than complaint or criticism. A singer? A professional, with a voice like an angel? Surely they must be speaking of different people.

"Well," Christine went on, "I imagine she was happy raising her family."

Happy? That was surely a different Maeve Feeney Concannon than had raised her. "I suppose," Maggie said slowly, "she made her choice."

"As we all do. Sharon made hers when she married and moved from Galway. I must say I missed her sorely, but she loved her Johnny, and her hotel."

With an effort, Maggie put thoughts of her mother

aside. She would have to pick through them later, carefully. "I remember Gran's hotel from childhood. We worked there one summer, Brie and I, as girls. Tidying and fetching. I didn't take to it."

"A fortunate thing for the art world."

Maggie acknowledged Rogan's compliment. "Perhaps, but it was certainly a relief to me."

"I've never asked you how you became interested in glass."

"My father's mother had a vase—Venetian glass it was, flute-shaped, of pale, hazy green. The color of leaves in bud. I thought it was the most beautiful thing I'd ever seen. She told me it had been made with breath and fire." Maggie smiled at the memory, lost herself in it a moment, so that her eyes became as hazy as the vase she described. "It was like a fairy tale to me. Using breath and fire to create something you could hold in your hand. So she brought me a book that had pictures of a glass house, the workers, the pipes, the furnaces. I think from that moment there was nothing else I wanted to do but make my own."

"Rogan was the same," Christine murmured. "So sure at such a young age of what his life would be." She let her gaze wander from Maggie to her grandson and back. "And now you've found each other."

"So it would seem," Rogan agreed, and rang for the next course.

😵 Chapter Eight

MAGGIE couldn't stay away from the gallery. There seemed to be no reason to. Joseph and the rest of the staff were welcoming enough, even going so far as asking for her opinion on some of the displays.

However much it might have pleased her, she couldn't improve on Rogan's eye for detail and placement. She left the staff to carry out his orders and set herself up unobtrusively to sketch the Native American artwork.

It fascinated her—the baskets and headdresses, the meticulous beading, the intricacies of the ritual masks. Ideas and visions leaped around in her head like gazelles, bounding, soaring, so that she rushed to transfer them to paper.

She preferred burying herself in work to everything else. Whenever she took too much time to think, her mind veered back to what Christine had told her about Maeve. Just how much, she'd wondered, was beneath the surface of her parents' lives that she'd been ignorant of? Her mother with a career, her father loving some other woman. And the two of them trapped—because of her—in a prison that had denied them their deepest wishes.

She needed to find out more, and yet she was afraid, afraid that whatever she learned would only further demonstrate the fact that she hadn't really known the people who had created her. Hadn't known them at all.

So she put that need aside and haunted the gallery.

When no one objected, she used Rogan's office as a temporary studio. The light was good, and as the room was tucked away in the back of the building, she was rarely disturbed. Roomy, it was not. Obviously Rogan had elected to utilize every space he could find for the showing of art.

She couldn't argue with that decision.

She covered his gleaming walnut desk with a sheet of plastic and thick pads of newspaper. The charcoal-and-pencil sketches she had made were only a start. She worked now by adding splashes of color. She'd picked up a few acrylics in a shop near the gallery, but often her impatience with the imperfections of her materials caused her to use other materials at hand, and she would dip her brush into coffee dregs or dampened ashes, or stroke bolder lines with lipstick or eyebrow pencils.

She considered her sketches merely a first step. While she believed herself an adequate enough draftsman, Maggie would never have termed herself a master with brush and paint. This was only a way to keep her vision alive from conception to execution. The fact that Rogan had arranged for several of her sketches to be matted and hung for the show embarrassed her more than pleased her.

Still, she reminded herself that people would buy anything if they were made to believe in its quality and value.

She'd become a cynic, she thought, narrowing her

eyes as she studied her work. And a bean counter as well, tallying up profits before they were made. God help her, she'd been caught up in the gossamer dream Rogan had spun, and she'd hate herself, even more than she would hate him, if she went back home a failure.

Did failure run in her blood? she wondered. Would she be like her father and fail to achieve the goal that mattered most to her? She was so intent on her work, and on her darkening thoughts, that she hissed in surprise and annoyance as the office door opened.

"Out! Out! Do I have to lock the damn thing?"

"My thoughts exactly." Rogan closed the door at his back. "What the hell are you doing?"

"An experiment in nuclear physics," she snapped back. "What does it look like?" Frustrated by the interruption, she blew her choppy bangs out of her eyes and glared. "What are you doing here?"

"I believe this gallery, which includes this office, belongs to me."

"There's no forgetting that." Maggie dipped her brush in a mixture of paint she'd daubed on an old board. "Not with the first words out of everyone's mouth around here being Mr. Sweeney this and Mr. Sweeney that." Inspired by this little verbal foray, she washed color over the thick paper she'd tacked to another board.

As she did so his gaze dropped from her face to her hands, and for a moment he was struck speechless. "What in sweet hell are you about?" Dumbfounded, he lunged forward. His priceless and well-loved desk was covered with paint-splattered newspapers, jars of brushes, pencils and—unless he had very much mistaken the sharp smell—bottles of turpentine. "You're a madwoman. Do you realize this desk is a George II?"

"It's a sturdy piece," she responded, with no respect for the dead English king. "You're in my light." Distracted, she waved a paint-flecked hand at him. He avoided it out of instinct. "And well protected," she added. "I've a sheet of plastic under the newspaper."

"Oh well, that makes it all right, then." He grabbed a handful of her hair and tugged ruthlessly. "If you'd wanted a bloody easel," he said when they were nose to nose, "I'd have provided you with one."

"I don't need an easel, only a bit of privacy. So if you'd make yourself scarce, as you've done brilliantly for the past two days—" She gave him a helpful shove. They both looked down at the bold red smudges she'd transferred to his pin-striped lapel.

"Oops," she said.

"Idiot." His eyes narrowed into dangerous cobalt slits when she chuckled.

"I'm sorry. Truly." But the apology was diluted by a strangled laugh. "I'm messy when I work, and I forgot about my hands. But from what I've seen, you've a warehouse full of suits. You won't be missing this one."

"You think not." Quick as a snake, he dipped his fingers in paint and smeared it over her face. Her squeal of surprise was intensely satisfying. "The color becomes you."

She swiped the back of her hand over her cheek and spread the paint around. "So you want to play, do you?" Laughing, she snatched up a tube of canary yellow.

"If you dare," he said, torn between anger and amusement, "I'll make you eat it, tube and all."

"A Concannon never ignores a challenge." Her grin spread as she prepared to squeeze. Retaliation on both sides was interrupted as the office door opened.

"Rogan, I hope you're not—" The elegant woman in the Chanel suit broke off, pale blue eyes widening. "I beg your pardon." Obviously baffled, she smoothed back her soft swing of sable hair. "I didn't know you were . . . engaged."

"Your interruption's timely." Cool as a spring breeze, Rogan ripped a sheet of newspaper and rubbed at the paint on his fingertips. "I believe we were about to make fools of ourselves."

Perhaps, Maggie thought, setting aside the tube of paint with a ridiculous sense of regret. But it would have been fun.

"Patricia Hennessy, I'd like to present Margaret Mary Concannon, our featured artist."

This? Patricia thought, though her fragile, well-bred features revealed nothing but polite interest. This paint-smeared, wild-haired woman was M. M. Concannon? "How lovely to meet you."

"And you, Miss Hennessy."

"It's Missus," Patricia told her with the faintest of smiles. "But please call me Patricia."

Like a single rose behind glass, Maggie thought, Patricia Hennessy was lovely, delicate and perfect. And, she mused, studying the elegant oval face, unhappy. "I'll be out of your way in a moment or two. I'm sure you want to talk to Rogan alone."

"Please don't hurry on my account." Patricia's smile curved her lips but barely touched her eyes.

"I've just been upstairs with Joseph, admiring your work. You have an incredible talent."

"Thank you." Maggie snatched Rogan's handkerchief from his breast pocket.

"Don't—" The order died on his lips as she soaked the Irish linen in turpentine. With something resembling a snarl, he took it back and scrubbed the rest of the paint from his hands. "My office seems to have been temporarily transformed into an artist's garret."

"Sure and I've never worked in a garret in me life," Maggie announced, deliberately broadening her brogue. "I've annoyed himself by disturbing sacred ground here, don't you know. If you've been acquainted with Rogan long, you'll understand he's a finicky man."

"I'm not finicky," he said between his teeth.

"Oh, of course not," Maggie responded with a roll of the eyes. "A wild man he is, as unpredictable as the colors of a sunrise."

"A sense of organization and control is not generally considered a flaw. A complete lack of it normally is."

They'd turned toward each other again, effectively, if unintentionally, closing Patricia out, even in the small room. There was tension in the air, and it was obvious to Patricia. She couldn't forget the time when he had desired her keenly. She couldn't forget it because she was in love with Rogan Sweeney.

"I'm sorry if I've come at a bad time." She hated the fact that her voice was stiff with formality.

"Not at all." Rogan's scowl was easily transformed into a charming smile as he turned to her. "It's always a delight to see you."

"I just dropped in thinking you might be done with business for the day. The Carneys invited me for drinks and hoped you could join us."

"I'm sorry, Patricia." Rogan looked down at his ruined handkerchief, then dropped it onto the spread-out sheets of newspaper. "With the show tomorrow, I've dozens of details yet to see to."

"Nonsense." Maggie shot Rogan a wide grin. "I wouldn't want to interfere with your social hour."

"It's not your fault—I've simply other obligations. Give my apologies to Marion and George."

"I will." Patricia offered her cheek for Rogan to kiss. The scent of turpentine clashed with, then overwhelmed, her delicate floral perfume. "It was nice to meet you, Miss Concannon. I'm looking forward to tomorrow night."

"It's Maggie," she said, with a warmth that came from innate female understanding. "And thank you. We'll hope for the best. Good day to you, Patricia." Maggie hummed to herself as she cleaned her brushes. "She's lovely," she commented after Patricia left. "Old friend?"

"That's right."

"Old married friend."

He only lifted a brow at the implication. "An old widowed friend."

"Ah."

"A very significant response." For reasons he couldn't fathom, he became defensive. "I've known Patricia for more than fifteen years."

"My, you're a slow one, Sweeney." Propping a hip on the desk, Maggie tapped a pencil to her lips. "A beautiful woman, of obvious taste—a woman of your own class, I may add, and in fifteen years you haven't made a move."

"A move?" His tone iced like frost on glass. "A particularly unattractive phrase, but ignoring your infelicitous phrasing for the moment, how do you know I haven't?"

"Such things show." With a shrug, Maggie eased off the desk. "Intimate relationships and platonic ones give off entirely different signals." Her look softened. He was, after all, only a man. "I'll wager you think you're terribly good friends."

"Naturally I do."

"You dolt." She felt a rush of sympathy for Patricia. "She's more than half in love with you."

The idea, and the casually confident way Maggie presented it, took him aback. "That's absurd."

"The only thing absurd about it is that you haven't a clue." Briskly, she began to gather her supplies. "Mrs. Hennessy has my sympathy—or part of it. Hard for me to offer it all when I'm interested in you myself, and I don't fancy the idea of you popping from her bed to mine."

She was, he thought, exasperated, the damnedest woman. "This is a ridiculous conversation, and I have a great deal of work to do."

It was rather endearing, the way his voice could go so grandly formal. "On my account at that, so I shouldn't be holding you up. I'll spread these drawings out in the kitchen to dry, if that's all right with you."

"As long as they're out of my way." And their creator with them, he thought. He made the mistake of glancing down, focusing. "What have you done here?"

"Made a bit of a mess, as you've already pointed out, but it'll tidy quick enough."

Without a word, he picked up one of her drawings by the edges. He could see clearly what had inspired her, how she meant to employ the Native American art and turn it into something boldly and uniquely her own.

No matter how much or how often she exasperated him, he was struck time and again by her talent.

"You haven't been wasting time, I see."

"It's one of the little things we have in common. Do you want to tell me what you think?"

"That you understand pride and beauty very well."

"A good compliment, Rogan." She smiled over it. "A very good one."

"Your work exposes you, Maggie, and makes you all the more confusing. Sensitive and arrogant, compassionate, pitiless. Sensual and aloof."

"If you're saying I'm moody, I won't argue." The tug came again, quick and painful. She wondered if there would come a time when he would look at her the way he looked at her work. And what they would create between them when, and if, he did. "It's not a flaw to me."

"It only makes you difficult to live with."

"No one has to but myself." She lifted a hand, disconcerting him by stroking it down his cheek. "I'm thinking of sleeping with you, Rogan, and we both know it. But I'm not your proper Mrs. Hennessy, looking for a husband to guide the way."

He curled his fingers around her wrist, surprised and darkly pleased when her pulse bumped unsteadily. "What are you looking for?"

She should have had the answer. It should have

been on the tip of her tongue. But she'd lost it somewhere between the question and the hard, fast stroke of her own heart. "I'll let you know when I find out." She leaned forward, rising on her toes to brush her mouth over his. "But that does fine for now."

She took the painting from him and gathered up others.

"Margaret Mary," he said as she started for the door. "I'd wash that paint from my face if I were you."

She twitched her nose, looked cross-eyed down at the red smear. "Bloody hell," she muttered, and slammed the door on her way out.

The parting shot may have soothed his pride, but he wasn't steady and bitterly resented that she could turn him inside out with so little effort. There was simply no time for the complications she could cause in her personal life. If there were time, he would simply drag her off to some quiet room and empty all of this frustration, this lust, this maddening hunger, into her until he was purged of it.

Surely once he'd taken control of her, or at least of the situation, he'd find his balance again.

But there were priorities, and his first, by legal contract and moral obligation, was to her art.

He glanced down at one of the paintings she'd left behind. It looked hurriedly executed, carelessly brilliant, with quick strokes and bold colors demanding attention.

Like the artist herself, he mused, it simply wouldn't be ignored.

Deliberately he turned his back on it and started

out. But the image remained, teasing his brain just as the taste of her remained, teasing his senses.

"Mr. Sweeney. Sir."

Rogan stopped in the main room, bit back a sigh. The thin, grizzled-looking man standing there, clutching a ragged portfolio, was no stranger.

"Aiman." He greeted the roughly dressed man as politely as he would have a silk-draped client. "You haven't been in for a while."

"I've been working." A nervous tic worked around Aiman's left eye. "I've a lot of new work, Mr. Sweeney."

Perhaps he had been working, Rogan mused. He'd most certainly been drinking. The signs were all there in the flushed cheeks, the red-rimmed eyes, the trembling hands. Aiman was barely thirty, but drink had made him old, frail and desperate.

He stayed just inside the door, off to the side, so that visitors to the gallery wouldn't be distracted by him. His eyes pleaded with Rogan. His fingers curled and uncurled on the old cardboard portfolio.

"I was hoping you'd have time to look, Mr. Sweeney."

"I've a show tomorrow, Aiman. A large one."

"I know. I saw it in the paper." Nervously, Aiman licked his lips. He'd spent the last of the money he'd earned from sidewalk sales in the pub the night before. He knew it was crazy. Worse, he knew it was stupid. Now he desperately needed a hundred pounds for rent or he'd be out on the street within the week. "I could leave them with you, Mr. Sweeney. Come back on Monday. I've—I've done some good work here. I wanted you to be the first to see it."

Rogan didn't ask if Aiman was out of money. The answer was obvious and the question would only

have humiliated the man. He had shown promise
once, Rogan remembered, before fears and whiskey
had leveled him.

"My office is a bit disrupted at the moment,"
Rogan said kindly. "Come upstairs and show me what
you've done."

"Thank you." Aiman's bloodshot eyes brightened
with a smile, with hope as pathetic as tears. "Thank
you, Mr. Sweeney. I won't take up much of your time.
I promise you."

"I was about to have a bit of tea." Unobtrusively,
Rogan took Aiman's arm to steady him as they
started upstairs. "You'll join me while we look over
your work?"

"I'd be pleased to, Mr. Sweeney."

Maggie eased back so that Rogan wouldn't see her
watching as he took the curve of the stairs. She'd
been certain, absolutely certain, that he would boot
the scruffy artist out the door. Or, she mused, have
one of his underlings do his dirty work for him.
Instead he'd invited the man to tea and had led him
upstairs like a welcomed guest.

Who would have thought Rogan Sweeney had
such kindness in him?

He'd buy some of the paintings as well, she
realized. Enough so that the artist could keep his
pride, and a meal or two in his belly. The gesture was
more impressive to her, more important than a
dozen of the grants and donations she imagined
Worldwide made annually.

He cared. The realization shamed her even as it
pleased her. He cared as much about the very
human hands that created art as he did the art itself.

She went back into his office to tidy, and to try to assimilate this new aspect of Rogan to all the others.

Twenty-four hours later Maggie sat on the edge of her bed in Rogan's guest room. She had her head between her knees and was cursing herself for being vilely ill. It was humiliating to admit, even to herself, that nerves could rule her. But there was no denying it, with the nasty taste of sickness still in her throat and her body shivering with the chills.

It won't matter, she told herself again. It won't matter a whit what they think. What I think is what counts.

Oh God, oh God, why did I let myself be pulled into this?

On long, careful breaths, she raised her head. The wave of dizziness slapped her, made her grit her teeth. In the cheval glass across the room, her image shot back at her.

She was wearing nothing but her underwear, and her skin was shockingly white against the lacy black she'd chosen. Her face was pasty looking, her eyes red-rimmed. A shuddering moan escaped her as she lowered her head again.

A fine mess she looked. And it was nothing but a spectacle she was going to make of herself. She'd been happy in Clare, hadn't she? It was there she belonged, alone and unfettered. Just herself and her glass, with the quiet fields and the morning mists. It was there she would be if it hadn't been for Rogan Sweeney and all his fancy words tempting her away.

He was the devil, she thought, conveniently forgetting that she'd begun to change her mind about him. A monster he was, who preyed on innocent artists for his own greedy ends. He would squeeze her dry, then cast her aside like an empty tube of paint.

She would have murdered him if she'd had the strength to stand.

When the knock came softly at her door, she squeezed her eyes shut. Go away, she shouted in her mind. Go away and leave me to die in peace.

It came again, followed by a quiet inquiry. "Maggie, dear, are you nearly ready?"

Mrs. Sweeney. Maggie pressed the heels of her hands to her gritty eyes and bit back a scream. "No, I'm not." She fought to make her voice curt and decisive, but it came out in a whimper. "I'm not going at all."

With a swish of silk, Christine slipped into the room. "Oh, sweetheart." Instantly maternal, she hurried to Maggie and draped an arm over her shoulders. "It's all right, darling. It's just nerves."

"I'm fine." But Maggie abandoned pride and turned her face into Christine's shoulder. "I'm just not going."

"Of course you are." Briskly, Christine lifted Maggie's face to hers. She knew exactly which button needed to be pushed, and did so, ruthlessly. "You don't want them to think you're afraid, do you?"

"I'm not afraid." Maggie's chin came up, but the nausea swam like oil in her stomach. "I'm just not interested."

Christine smiled, stroked Maggie's hair and waited.

"I can't face it, Mrs. Sweeney," Maggie blurted out. "I just can't. I'll humiliate myself, and I hate that more than anything. I'd sooner be hanged."

"I understand completely, but you'll not humiliate

yourself." She took Maggie's frozen hands in hers. "It's true it's yourself on display as much as your work. That's the foolishness of the art world. They'll wonder about you, and talk about you and speculate. Let them."

"It's not that so much—though that's part of it. I'm not used to being wondered over, and I don't think I'll like it, but it's my work. . . ." She pressed her lips together. "It's the best part of me, Mrs. Sweeney. If it's found wanting. If it's not good enough—"

"Rogan thinks it is."

"A lot he knows," Maggie muttered.

"That's true. A lot he does know." Christine tilted her head. The child needed a bit of mothering, she decided. And mothering wasn't always kind. "Do you want me to go down and tell him you're too afraid, too insecure to attend the show?"

"No!" Helpless, Maggie covered her face with her hands. "He's trapped me. The tricky snake of a man. The damned greedy—I beg your pardon." Going stiff, Maggie lowered her hands.

Christine made certain to swallow the chuckle. "That's quite all right," she said soberly. "Now, you wait here and I'll go down and tell Rogan to go on without us. He's already wearing a trench in the hallway with his pacing."

"I've never seen anyone so obsessed with time."

"It's a Sweeney trait. Michael drove me mad with it, God bless him." She patted Maggie's hand. "I'll be right back up to help you dress."

"Mrs. Sweeney." Desperate, Maggie grabbed at Christine's sleeve. "Couldn't you just tell him I've died? They could make a lovely wake out of the showing. And as a rule, you make more of a profit off a dead artist than a live one."

"There, you see." Christine dislodged Maggie's clutching fingers. "You're feeling better already. Now run along and wash your face."

"But—"

"I'm standing in for your gran tonight," Christine said firmly. "I believe Sharon would have wanted me to. And I said go wash your face, Margaret Mary.

"Yes, ma'am. Mrs. Sweeney?" With no place else to go, Maggie got shakily to her feet. "You won't tell him . . . I mean, I'd be grateful to you if you didn't mention to Rogan that I'd . . ."

"On one of the most important evenings of her life, a woman's entitled to linger over dressing."

"I suppose." A ghost of a smile played around Maggie's mouth. "It makes me sound like a frivolous fool, but it's better than the alternative."

"Leave Rogan to me."

"There's just one other thing." She'd been putting this off, Maggie admitted. She might as well face it now when she was feeling as low as she imagined she could possibly feel. "Do you think you might be able to find those clippings you spoke of? The ones about my mother?"

"I think I could. I should have thought of it myself. Of course, you'd like to read them."

"I would, yes. I'd be grateful."

"I'll see that you get them. Now go fix your face. I'll scoot Rogan along." She sent Maggie a bolstering smile before closing the door.

When Christine found him, Rogan was still furiously pacing in the foyer. "Where the devil is she?" he demanded the moment he spotted his grandmother. "She's been primping up there for two hours."

"Well, of course she has." Christine gestured grandly. "The impression she makes tonight is vital, isn't it?"

"It's important, naturally." If she made the wrong one, his dreams would slide down the drain along with Maggie's. He needed her here, now, and ready to dazzle. "But why should it take her so long? She's only to put on her clothes and fuss with her hair."

"You've been a single man too long, my darling, if you truly believe such nonsense." Affectionately, Christine reached out to straighten his already perfect tie. "How handsome you look in a tuxedo."

"Grandmother, you're stalling."

"No, not at all." Beaming at him, she brushed at his spotless lapels. "I've just come down to tell you to go along without us. We'll follow when Maggie's ready."

"She should be ready now."

"But she's not. Besides, how much more effective might it be if she arrived just late enough to make an entrance? You appreciate the theater of these events, Rogan."

There was truth in that. "All right then." He checked his watch, swore lightly. If he didn't go within the minute he'd most certainly be late. It was his responsibility to be there, he reminded himself, to see to any last minute details, no matter how much he wanted to wait and take Maggie to the gallery himself. "I'll leave her in your more than capable hands. I'll have the car come back for you as soon as I've been dropped off. See that she's there within the hour, won't you?"

"You can count on me, darling."

"I always do." He kissed her on the cheek, stepped back. "By the way, Mrs. Sweeney, I haven't mentioned how beautiful you look."

"No, you haven't. I was quite deflated."

"You will be, as always, the most stunning woman in the room."

"Well said. Now, run along with you and leave Maggie to me."

"With pleasure." He shot one look up the stairs as he headed for the door. It was not a gentle look. "I wish you good luck with her."

As the door closed Christine let out a sigh. She thought she might need all the luck she could get.

Chapter Nine

No detail had been overlooked. The lighting was perfect, leaping and bounding off the curves and swirls of glass. The music, a waltz now, flowed as softly as happy tears through the room. Fizzing glasses of champagne crowded the silver trays carried gracefully by liveried waiters. The sound of clinking crystal and murmuring voices set up a gracious counterpoint to the weeping violins.

It was, in a word, perfect, not a detail missing. Except, Rogan thought grimly, the artist herself.

"It's wonderful, Rogan." Patricia stood beside him, elegant in a narrow white gown shivering with bugle beads. "You have a smashing success."

He turned to her, smiling. "So it would seem."

His eyes lingered on hers long enough, intensely enough, to make her uneasy. "What is it? Have I smudged my nose?"

"No." He lifted his own glass quickly, cursing Maggie for putting ridiculous thoughts in his head and making him wary of one of his oldest friends.

In love with him? Absurd.

"I'm sorry. I suppose my mind was wandering. I can't imagine what's keeping Maggie"

"I'm sure she'll be along any moment." Patricia

laid a hand on his arm. "And in the meantime, everyone's being dazzled by our combined efforts."

"It's a lucky thing. She's always late," he added under his breath. "No more than a child's sense of time."

"Rogan, dear, there you are. I see my Patricia found you."

"Good evening, Mrs. Connelly." Rogan took Patricia's mother's delicate hand in his own. "I'm delighted to see you. No gallery showing can be a success without your presence."

"Flatterer." Pleased, she swept up her mink stole. Anne Connelly held on as tightly to her beauty as she did to her vanity. She considered it as much a woman's duty to preserve her looks as it was to make a home and bear children. Ann never, never neglected her duties, and as a result, she had the dewy skin and the youthful figure of a girl. She fought a constant battle with the years and had, for half a century, emerged the victor.

"And your husband?" Rogan continued. "Did Dennis come with you?"

"Naturally, though he's already off somewhere puffing on one of his cigars and discussing finance." She smiled when Rogan signaled for a waiter and offered her a glass of champagne. "Even his fondness for you doesn't change his apathy toward art. This is fascinating work." She gestured to the sculpture beside them, an explosion of color, mushrooming up from a twisted base. "Gorgeous and disturbing all at once. Patricia tells me she met the artist briefly yesterday. I'm dying to do so myself."

"She's yet to arrive," Rogan covered his own impatience smoothly. "You'll find Miss Concannon as contradictory and as interesting, I think, as her work."

"And I'm sure as fascinating. We haven't seen nearly enough of you lately, Rogan. I've badgered Patricia unmercifully about bringing you by." She shot her daughter a veiled look that spoke volumes. *Get a move on, girl,* it said. *Don't let him slip away from you.*

"I'm afraid I've been so obsessed with getting this show together quickly that I've neglected my friends."

"You're forgiven, as long as we can expect you to dine with us one evening next week."

"I'd love to." Rogan caught Joseph's eye. "Excuse me just a moment, won't you?"

"Must you be so obvious, Mother?" Patricia murmured into her wine as Rogan slipped through the crowd.

"Someone has to be. Merciful heavens, girl, he treats you like a sister." Beaming a smile across the room at an acquaintance, Anne continued to speak in undertones. "A man doesn't marry a woman he thinks of as his sister, and it's time you were wed again. You couldn't ask for a better match. Keep loitering around, and someone else will scoop him up from under your nose. Now smile, will you? Must you always look as though you're in mourning?"

Dutifully, Patricia forced her lips to curve.

"Did you reach them?" Rogan demanded the moment he'd cornered Joseph.

"On the car phone." Joseph's gaze skimmed the room, brushed over Patricia, lingered, then moved on. "They'll be here any moment."

"More than an hour late. Typical."

"Be that as it may, you'll be pleased to know that

we have sales on ten pieces already, and at least that many offers on *Surrender*."

"That piece is not for sale." Rogan studied the flamboyant sculpture that stood in the center of the room. "We'll tour it first, in our galleries in Rome, Paris and New York, but along with the other pieces we've chosen it is not to be sold."

"It's your decision," Joseph said easily enough. "But I should tell you that General Fitzsimmons offered us twenty-five thousand pounds for it."

"Did he? Make sure that gets around, won't you?"

"Count on it. In the meantime I've been entertaining some of the art critics. I think you should . . ." Joseph trailed off when he saw Rogan's eyes darken as he looked intently at something over his shoulder. Joseph turned, saw the object of his boss's gaze and let out a low whistle. "She may be late, but she's certainly a showstopper."

Joseph looked back at Patricia and saw from the expression on her face that she, too, had noted Rogan's reaction. His heard bled a little for the woman. He knew from personal experience how miserable it was to love someone who thought of you as only a friend.

"Shall I go take her around?" Joseph asked.

"What? No—no. I'll do it myself."

Rogan had never imagined Maggie could look like that—sleek and stunning and sensual as sin. She'd chosen black, unrelieved and unadorned. The dress took all its style from the body it covered. It draped from throat to ankle, but no one would call it prim, not with the glossy black buttons that swirled the length of it, the buttons that she'd left daringly unfastened to the swell of her breast, and up to the top of one slim thigh.

Her hair was a tousled crown of fire, carelessly curled around her face. As he drew closer he saw that her eyes were already scanning, assessing and absorbing everything in the room.

She looked fearless, defiant and completely in control.

And so she was . . . now. The bout of nerves had served to embarrass her so much that she'd beaten them back with nothing more than sheer willfulness.

She was here. And she meant to succeed.

"You're impossibly late." The complaint was a last line of defense, delivered in a mutter as he took her hand and raised it to his lips. Their eyes met. "And incredibly beautiful."

"You approve of the dress?"

"That's not the word I would have chosen, but yes, I do."

She smiled then. "You were afraid I'd wear boots and torn jeans."

"Not with my grandmother standing guard."

"She's the most wonderful woman in the world. You're lucky to have her."

The emotional force of the statement more than the words caused Rogan to study her curiously. "I'm aware of that."

"You can't be. Not really, for you've never known any different." She took a deep breath. "Well." There were eyes on her already, dozens of them, bright with curiosity. "It's into the lions' den, isn't it? You needn't worry," she said before he could speak. "I'll behave. My future depends on it."

"This is only the beginning, Margaret Mary."

As he drew her into the room with its whirl of light and color, she was very much afraid he was right.

But behave she did. The evening seemed to go well as she shook hands, accepted compliments, answered questions. The first hour seemed to float by like a dream, what with the sparkle of wine, the glitter of glass and the flash of jewels. Drifting through it was easy, as Maggie felt slightly removed from the reality, somewhat disconnected, as much audience as actor in a sumptuously produced play.

"This, ah this." A bald man with a drooping mustache and a fussy British accent expounded on a piece. It was a series of glowing blue spears trapped within a sheer glass globe. "*Imprisoned,* you call it. Your creativity, your sexuality, fighting to set itself free. Man's eternal struggle, after all. It's triumphant, even as it's melancholy."

"It's the six counties," Maggie said simply.

The bald man blinked. "I beg your pardon."

"The six counties of Ireland," she repeated with a wicked rebel gleam in her eyes. "Imprisoned."

"I see."

Standing beside this would-be critic, Joseph muffled a laugh. "I found the use of color here so striking, Lord Whitfield. The translucence of it creates an unresolved tension between its delicacy and its boldness."

"Just so." Lord Whitfield nodded, cleared his throat. "Quite extraordinary. Excuse me."

Maggie watched him retreat with a broad smile. "Well, I don't think he'll be after buying it and setting it in his den, do you, Joseph?"

"You're a wicked woman, Maggie Concannon."

"I'm an Irishwoman, Joseph." She winked at him. "Up the rebels."

He laughed delightedly and, slipping an arm around her waist, led her around the room. "Ah, Mrs. Connelly." Joseph gave Maggie a subtle squeeze to signal her. "Looking stunning as always."

"Joseph, always a smooth word. And this—" Anne Connelly shifted her attention from Joseph, whom she considered a mere factotum to Maggie. "This is the creative drive. I'm thrilled to meet you, my dear. I'm Mrs. Dennis Connelly—Anne. I believe you met my daughter, Patricia, yesterday."

"I did, yes." Maggie found Anne's handclasp as delicate and soft as a brush of satin.

"She must be off with Rogan somewhere. They're a lovely couple, aren't they?"

"Very." Maggie lifted a brow. She knew a warning when she heard one. "Do you live in Dublin, Mrs. Connelly?"

"I do indeed. Only a few houses away from the Sweeney mansion. My family has been a part of Dublin society for generations. And you're from the west counties?"

"Clare, yes."

"Lovely scenery. All those charming quaint villages and thatched roofs. Your family are farmers, I'm told?" Anne lifted a brow, obviously amused.

"Were."

"This must be so exciting for you, particularly with your rural upbringing. I'm sure you've enjoyed your visit to Dublin. You'll be going back soon?"

"Very soon, I think."

"I'm sure you miss the country. Dublin can be very

confusing to one unused to city life. Almost like a foreign land."

"At least I understand the language," Maggie said equably. "I hope you'll enjoy your evening, Mrs. Connelly. Excuse me, won't you?"

And if Rogan thought he would sell that woman anything that Maggie Concannon created, Maggie thought as she walked away, he'd hang for it.

Exclusive rights be damned. She'd smash every last piece into dust before she saw any in Anne Connelly's hands. Talking to her as though she were some slack-jawed milkmaid with straw in her hair.

She held her temper back as she made her way out of the ballroom and toward one of the sitting rooms. Each was crowded with people, talking, sitting, laughing, discussing her. Her head began to throb as she marched down the stairs. She'd get herself a beer out of the kitchen, she decided, and have a few minutes of peace.

She strode straight in, only to come up short when she saw a portly man puffing on a cigar and nursing a pilsner.

"Caught," he said, and grinned sheepishly.

"That makes two of us then. I was coming down for a quiet beer myself."

"Let me fetch you one." Gallantly, he heaved his bulk out of the chair and pulled a bottle out for her. "You don't want me to put out the cigar, do you?"

The plea in his voice made her laugh. "Not at all. My father used to smoke the world's worst pipe. Stunk to high heaven. I loved it."

"There's a lass." He found her a beer and a glass. "I hate these things." He jerked his thumb toward the ceiling. "M'wife drags me."

"I hate them, too."

"Pretty enough work, I suppose," he said as she drank. "Like the colors and shapes. Not that I know a damn thing about it. Wife's the expert. But I liked the look of it, and that should be enough, I'd say."

"And I."

"Everyone's always trying to explain it at these blasted affairs. What the artist had in mind and such. Symbolism." He rolled his tongue over the word as if it were a strange dish he wasn't quite ready to sample. "Don't know what the devil they're talking about."

Maggie decided the man was half-potted and that she loved him. "Neither do they."

"That's it!" He raised his glass and drank deeply. "Neither do they. Just blustering. But if I was to say that to Anne—that's my wife—she'd give me one of those looks."

He narrowed his eyes, lowered his brows and scowled. Maggie hooted with laughter.

"Who cares what they think anyway?" Maggie propped her elbow on the table and held a fist to her chin. "It's not as if anyone's life depended on it." Except mine, she thought, and pushed the idea away. "Don't you think affairs like this are just an excuse for people to get all dressed up and act important?"

"I do absolutely." So complete was his agreement that he rapped his glass sharply to hers. "As for me, do you know what I wanted to be doing tonight?"

"What?"

"Sitting in my chair, with my feet on the hassock and Irish in my glass, watching the television."

He sighed, regretfully. "But I couldn't disappoint Anne—or Rogan, for that matter."

"You know Rogan, then?"

"Like my own son. A fine man he's turned out to be. He wasn't yet twenty when I saw him first. His father and I had business together, and the boy couldn't wait to be part of it." He gestured vaguely to encompass the gallery. "Smart as a whip, he is."

"And what business are you in?"

"Banking."

"Excuse me." A female voice interrupted them. They looked up to see Patricia standing in the doorway, her hands folded neatly.

"Ah, there's my love."

While Maggie looked on, goggle-eyed, the man lunged out of his chair and enfolded Patricia in a hug that could have felled a mule. Patricia's reaction, rather than stiff rejection or cool disgust, was a quick, musical laugh.

"Daddy, you'll break me in half."

Daddy? Maggie thought. Daddy? Patricia Henessy's father? Anne's husband? This delightful man was married to that—that icy stick of a woman? It only went to prove, she decided, that the words *till death do us part* were the most foolish syllables human beings were ever forced to utter.

"Meet my little girl." With obvious pride, Dennis whirled Patricia around. "A beauty, isn't she? My Patricia."

"Yes, indeed." Maggie rose, grinning. "It's nice to see you again."

"And you. Congratulations on the wonderful success of your show."

"Your show?" Dennis said blankly.

"We never introduced ourselves." Laughing now, Maggie stepped forward and offered Dennis her hand. "I'm Maggie Concannon, Mr. Connelly."

"Oh." He said nothing for a moment as he racked his brain trying to recall if he'd said anything insulting. "A pleasure," he managed to say as his brain stalled.

"It was, truly. Thank you for the best ten minutes I've had since I walked in the door."

Dennis smiled. This woman seemed downright human, for an artist. "I do like the colors, and the shapes," he offered hopefully.

"And that's the nicest compliment I've had all evening."

"Daddy, Mother's looking for you." Patricia brushed a stray ash from his lapel. The gesture, one she had carelessly used with her own father countless times, arrowed straight into Maggie's heart.

"I'd better let her find me, then." He looked back at Maggie, and when she grinned at him, he grinned back. "I hope we meet again, Miss Concannon."

"So do I."

"Won't you come up with us?" Patricia asked.

"No, not just now," Maggie answered, not wishing to socialize further with Patricia's mother.

The bright look faded the moment their footsteps died away on the polished floor. She sat down, alone, in the light-flooded kitchen. It was quiet there, so quiet she could nearly fool herself into believing the building was empty but for her.

She wanted to believe she was alone. More, she wanted to believe the sadness she suddenly felt was just that she missed the solitude of her own green fields and quiet hills, the endless hours of silence with only the roar of her own kiln and her own imagination to drive her.

But it wasn't only that. On this, one of the brightest nights of her life, she had no one. None of the chattering, brilliant crowd of people upstairs knew her, cared for her, understood her. There was no one abovestairs waiting for Maggie Concannon.

So she had herself, she thought, and rose. And that was all anyone needed. Her work was well received. It wasn't so difficult to cut through all the fancy and pompous phrases to the core. Rogan's people liked what she did, and that was the first step.

She was on her way, she told herself as she swung out of the kitchen. She was rushing down the path toward fame and fortune, the path that had eluded the Concannons for the last two generations. And she would do it all herself.

The light and the music sparkled down the staircase like fairy dust along the curve of a rainbow. She stood at the foot of the stairs, her hand clutched on the rail, her foot on the first tread. Then, with a jerk, she turned to hurry outside, into the dark.

When the clock struck one, Rogan yanked at his elegant black tie and swore. The woman, he thought as he paced the darkened parlor, deserved murder and no less. She'd vanished like smoke in the middle of a crowded party arranged for her benefit. Leaving him, he remembered with boiling resentment, to make foolish excuses.

He should have known that a woman of her temperament couldn't be trusted to behave reasonably. He certainly should have known better than to give her such a prominent place in his own ambitions, his hopes for the future of his business.

How in hell could he hope to build a gallery for Irish art when the first Irish artist he'd personally selected, groomed and showcased had fled her own opening like an irresponsible child?

Now it was the middle of the night, and he'd not had a word from her. The brilliant success of the show, his own satisfaction with a job well done, had clouded over like her precious west county sky. There was nothing he could do but wait.

And worry.

She didn't know Dublin. For all its beauty and charm there were still sections dangerous to a woman alone. And there was always the possibility of an accident—the thought of which brought on a vicious, throbbing headache at the base of his skull.

He'd taken two long strides toward the phone to telephone the hospitals when he heard the click of the front door. He pivoted and rushed into the hallway.

She was safe, and under the dazzle of the foyer chandelier, he could see she was unharmed. Visions of murder leaped back into his aching head.

"Where in the sweet hell have you been?"

She'd hoped he be out at some high-class club, clinking glasses with his friends. But since he wasn't, she offered him a smile and a shrug. "Oh, out and about. Your Dublin's a lovely city at night."

As he stared at her, his hands closed into ready fists. "You're saying you've been out sightseeing until one in the morning?"

"Is it so late then? I must have lost track. Well then, I'll say good night."

"No, you won't." He took a step toward her. "What you will do is give me an explanation for your behavior."

"That's something I don't have to explain to anyone, but if you'd be more clear, perhaps I'd make an exception."

"There were nearly two hundred people gathered tonight for your benefit. You were unbelievably rude."

"I was nothing of the kind." More weary than she wanted to admit, she strolled past him into the parlor, slipped out of the miserably uncomfortable heels and propped her tired feet on a tassled stool. "The truth is, I was so unbelievably polite, my teeth nearly fell out of my head. I hope to Christ I don't have to smile at another bloody soul for a month. I wouldn't mind one of your brandies now, Rogan. It's chilly out this time of night."

He noticed for the first time that she wore nothing over the thin black dress. "Where the devil is your wrap?"

"I didn't have one. You'll have to mark that down in your little book. Acquire Maggie a suitable evening wrap." She reached up for the snifter he'd poured.

"Damn it, your hands are frozen. Have you no sense?"

"They'll warm quick enough." Her brows arched as he stalked over to the fireplace and crouched down to start a fire. "What, no servants?"

"Shut up. The one thing I won't tolerate from you tonight is sarcasm. I've taken all I plan to take."

Flames licked into life to eat greedily at dry wood. In the shifting light Maggie saw that his face was tight with anger. The best way to meet temper, she'd always thought, was to match it.

"I've given you nothing to take." She sipped the brandy, would have sighed over the welcome heat of the liquor if she and Rogan hadn't been glaring at each other. "I went to your showing, didn't I? In a proper dress, with a proper foolish smile pasted on my face."

"It was your showing," he shot back. "You ungrateful, selfish, inconsiderate brat."

However weary her body, she wouldn't allow him to get away with such language. She stood rigidly and faced him. "I won't contradict you. I'm exactly as you say, and have been told so most of my life. Fortunately for both of us, it's only my work you have to be concerned about."

"Do you have any idea the time and effort and expense that went into putting that show together?"

"That's your province." Her voice was as stiff as her spine. "As you're always so quick to tell me. And I was there, stayed above two hours, rubbing elbows with strangers."

"You'd better learn that a patron is never a stranger, and that rudeness is never attractive."

The quiet, controlled tone cut through her defensive armor like a sword. "I never agreed to stay the whole evening. I needed to be alone, that's all."

"And to wander the streets all night? I'm responsible for you while you're here, Maggie. For God's sake, I'd nearly called out the garda."

"You're not responsible for me, I am." But she could see now that it wasn't simply anger darkening his eyes, but concern as well. "If I caused you worry, I'll apologize. I simply went for a walk."

"You went out strolling and left your first major show without a by-your-leave?"

"Yes." The snifter was out of her hand and hurtling toward the stone hearth before she realized it. Glass shattered, rained like bullets. "I had to get out! I couldn't breathe. I couldn't bear it. All those people, staring at me, at my work, and the music, the lights. Everything so lovely, so perfect. I didn't know it would scare me so. I thought I'd gotten over it since that first day you showed me the room, and my work set up like something out of a dream."

"You were frightened."

"Yes, yes, damn you. Are you happy to hear it? I was terrified when you opened the door and I looked inside and saw what you'd done. I could barely speak. You did this to me," she said furiously. "You opened this Pandora's box and let out all my hopes and my fears and my needs. You can't know what it's like to have needs, terrible ones, you don't even think you should have."

He studied her now, ivory and flame in a slim black dress. "Oh, but I can," he said quietly. "I can. You should have told me, Maggie." His voice was gentle now as he stepped toward her.

She threw up both hands to ward him off. "No, don't. I couldn't bear you to be kind just now. Especially when I know I don't deserve it. It was wrong of me to leave that way. It was selfish and ungrateful." She dropped her hands helplessly at her sides. "But there was no one for me up those stairs. No one. And it broke my heart."

She looked so delicate all at once, so he did what she asked and didn't touch her. He was afraid if he did, however gently, she might snap in his hands. "If you'd let me know how important it was to you, Maggie, I'd have arranged to have your family here."

"You can't arrange Brianna. God knows you can't bring my father back." Her voice broke, shaming her. With a strangled sound she pressed a hand to her mouth. "I'm overtired, that's all." She fought a bitter war to control her voice. "Overstimulated with all the excitement. I owe you an apology for leaving the way I did, and gratitude for all the work you did for me."

He preferred her raging or weeping to this stilted politeness. It left him no choice but to respond in kind. "The important thing is that the show was a success."

"Yes." Her eyes glittered in the firelight. "That's the important thing. If you'll excuse me now, I'll go up to bed."

"Of course. Maggie? One more thing."

She turned back. He stood before the fire, the flames leaping gold behind him. "Yes?"

"I was there for you, up those stairs. Perhaps next time you'll remember that, and be content."

She didn't answer. He heard only the rustle of her dress as she hurried across the hall and up the stairs, then the quick click of her bedroom door closing.

He stared at the fire, watched a log break apart, cut through by flame and heat. Smoke puffed once, stirred by the wind. He continued to stare as a shower of sparks rained against the screen, scattered over stone and winked out.

She was, he realized, every bit as capricious, moody and brilliant as that fire. As dangerous and as elemental.

And he was, quite desperately, in love with her.

💮 Chapter Ten

"WHAT do you mean, gone?" Rogan pushed away from his desk and scraped Joseph with a look of outrage. "Of course she's not gone."

"But she is. She stopped by the gallery to say goodbye only an hour ago." Reaching into his pocket, Joseph drew out an envelope. "She asked me to give you this."

Rogan took it, tossed it on his desk. "Are you saying she's gone back to Clare? The morning after her show?"

"Yes, and in a tearing hurry. I didn't have time to show her the reviews." Joseph reached up to fiddle with the tiny gold hoop in his ear. "She'd booked a flight to Shannon. Said she only had a moment to say goodbye and God bless, gave me the note for you, kissed me and ran out again." He smiled. "It was a bit like being battered by a small tornado." He lifted his shoulders, let them fall. "I'm sorry, Rogan, if I'd known you wanted her to stay, I'd have tried to stop her. I believe I'd have been flattened, but I'd have tried."

"It doesn't matter." He lowered carefully into his chair again. "How did she seem?"

"Impatient, rushed, distracted. Very much as usual. She wanted to be back home, was all she told me, back at work. I wasn't sure you knew, so I thought I'd come by and tell you in person. I have an appointment with General Fitzsimmons, and it was on my way."

"I appreciate it. I should be by the gallery by four. Give the general my regards."

"I'll give him the business," Joseph said with a flashing grin. "By the way, he went up another five thousand on *Surrender*."

"Not for sale."

Rogan picked up the note on his desk after Joseph closed the door behind him. Ignoring his work, Rogan split the envelope with his ebony-handled letter opener. The creamy stationery from his own guest room was dashed over with Maggie's hurried and beautiful scrawl.

Dear Rogan,

I imagine you'll be annoyed that I've left so abruptly, but it can't be helped. I need to be home and back at work, and I won't apologize for it. I will thank you. I'm sure you'll start firing wires my way, and I'll warn you in advance I intend to ignore them, at least for a time. Please give my best to your grandmother. And I wouldn't mind if you thought of me now and again.

Maggie

Oh, one more thing. You might be interested to know that I'm taking home a half dozen of Julien's recipes—that's your cook's name, if you don't know. He thinks I'm charming.

Rogan skimmed the letter a second time before setting it aside. It was for the best, he decided. They would both be happier and more productive with the whole of Ireland between them. Certainly, he would be. It was difficult to be productive around a woman when you were in love with her, and when she frustrated you on every possible level.

And with any luck, any at all, these feelings that had grown in him would ease and fade with time and distance.

So . . . He folded the letter and set it aside. He was glad she'd gone back, satisfied that they'd accomplished the first stage of his plans for her career, happy that she'd inadvertently given him time to deal with his own confused emotions.

The hell, he thought. He missed her already.

The sky was the color of a robin's egg and clear as a mountain stream. Maggie sat on the little stoop at her front door, elbows on knees, and just breathed. Beyond her own garden gate and the trailing, flowering fuchsia, she could see the lush green of hill and valley. And farther, since the day was so clear, so bright, she glimpsed the distant dark mountains.

She watched a magpie dart across her line of vision, flashing over the hedge and up. Straight as an arrow he went, until even the shadow of him was lost in the green.

One of Murphy's cows lowed and was answered by another. There was a humming echo that would be his tractor, and the more insistent sealike roar of her furnaces, which she'd fired the moment she'd arrived.

Her flowers were brilliant in the sunshine, vivid red begonias tangled with the late-blooming tulips and dainty spears of larkspur. She could smell rose-mary and thyme and the strong perfume of the wild roses that swayed like dancers in the mild, sweet breeze.

A wind chime she'd made out of scraps of glass sang musically above her head.

Dublin, with its busy streets, seemed very far away.

On the ribbon of road in the valley below, she saw a red truck, tiny and bright as a toy, rumble along, turn into a lane and climb toward a cottage.

Home for tea, she thought, and let out a sigh of pure contentment.

She heard the dog first, that full-throated echoing bark, then the rustle of brush that told her he'd flushed out a bird. Her sister's voice floated out on the air, amused, indulgent.

"Leave the poor thing alone, Con, you great bully."

The dog barked again and, moments later, leaped at the garden gate. His tongue lolled happily when he spotted Maggie.

"Get down from there," Brianna ordered. "Do you want her to come home and find her gate crashed in, and . . . Oh." She stopped, laying a hand on the wolfhound's massive head as she saw her sister. "I didn't know you were home." The smile came first as she tugged open the gate.

"I've just arrived." Maggie spent the next few minutes being greeted by Concobar, wrestling and accepting his lavish licks until he responded to Brianna's command to sit. Sit he did, his front paws over Maggie's feet, as if to ensure that she would stay put.

"I had a little time," Brianna began. "So I thought I'd come down and tend to your garden."

"It looks fine to me."

"You always think so. I've brought you some bread I baked this morning. I was going to put it in your freezer." Feeling awkward, Brianna held out the basket. There was something here, she realized. Something behind the cool, calm look in her sister's eyes. "How was Dublin?"

"Crowded." Maggie set the basket beside her on the stoop. The scent beneath the neat cloth was so tempting that she lifted the cloth aside and broke off a warm hunk of brown bread. "Noisy." She tore off a bit of bread and tossed it. Concobar nipped it midair, swallowed it whole and grinned. "Greedy bastard, aren't you?" She tossed him another piece before she rose. "I have something for you."

Maggie turned into the house, leaving Brianna standing on the path. When she came back, she handed Brianna a box and a manila envelope.

"You didn't have to get me anything—" Brianna began, but stopped. It was guilt she felt, she realized. And guilt she was meant to feel. Accepting it, she opened the box. "Oh, Maggie, it's lovely. The loveliest thing I've ever had." She held the pin up to the sun and watched it glint. "You shouldn't have spent your money."

"It's mine to spend," Maggie said shortly. "And I hope you'll wear it on something other than an apron."

"I don't wear an apron everywhere," Brianna said evenly. She replaced the pin carefully in the box, slipped the box into her pocket. "Thank you. Maggie, I wish—"

"You haven't looked at the other." Maggie knew what her sister wished, and didn't care to hear it.

Regrets that she hadn't been in Dublin for the show hardly mattered now.

Brianna studied her sister's face, found no sign of softening. "All right, then." She opened the envelope, drew out a sheet. "Oh! Oh my." However bright and lovely the pin, it was nothing compared with this. They both knew it. "Recipes. So many. Soufflés and pastries, and—oh, look at this chicken. It must be wonderful."

"It is." Maggie shook her head at Brianna's reaction, nearly sighed. "I've tasted it myself. And the soup there—the herbs are the trick to it, I'm told."

"Where did you get them?" Brianna caught her bottom lip between her teeth, studied the handwritten pages as if they were the treasures of all the ages.

"From Rogan's cook. He's a Frenchman."

"Recipes from a French chef," Brianna said reverently.

"I promised him you'd send a like number of your own in trade."

"Of mine?" Brianna blinked, as if coming out of a dream. "Why, he couldn't want mine."

"He can, and he does. I praised your Irish stew and your berry pie to the moon and back. And I gave him my solemn word you'd send them."

"I will, of course, but I can't imagine—thank you, Maggie. It's a wonderful gift." Brianna stepped forward for an embrace, then back again, cut to the quick by the coolness of Maggie's response. "Won't you tell me how it went for you? I kept trying to imagine it, but I couldn't."

"It went well enough. There were a lot of people. Rogan seems to know how to tickle their interest. There was an orchestra and waiters in white suits serving flutes of champagne and silver platters of fancy finger food."

"It must have been beautiful. I'm so proud of you."

Maggie's eyes chilled. "Are you?"

"You know I am."

"I know I needed you there. Damn it, Brie, I needed you there."

Con whined at the shout and looked uneasily from Maggie to his mistress.

"I would have been there if I could."

"There was nothing stopping you but her. One night of your life was all I asked. One. I had no one there, no family, no friends, no one who loved me. Because you chose her as you always have, over me, over Da, even over yourself."

"It wasn't a matter of choosing."

"It's always a matter of choosing," Maggie said coldly. "You've let her kill your heart, Brianna, just as she killed his."

"That's cruel, Maggie."

"Aye, it is. She'd be the first to tell you that cruel is just what I am. Cruel, marked with sin and damned to the devil. Well, I'm glad to be bad. I'd chose hell in a blink over kneeling in ashes and suffering silently for heaven as you do." Maggie stepped back, curled a stiff hand around the doorknob. "Well, I had my night without you, or anyone, and it went well enough. I should think they'll be some sales out of it. I'll have money for you in a few weeks."

"I'm sorry I hurt you, Maggie." Brianna's own pride stiffened her voice. "I don't care about the money."

"I do." Maggie shut the door.

*   *   *

For three days she was undisturbed. The phone didn't ring, no knock came at the door. Even if there had been a summons, she would have ignored it. She spent nearly every waking minute in the glass house, refining, perfecting, forming the images in her brain and on her sketchpad into glass.

Despite Rogan's claim as to their worth, she hung her drawings on clothespins or on magnets, so that a corner of the studio soon came to resemble a dark room, with prints drying.

She'd burned herself twice in her hurry, once badly enough to make her stop for some hastily applied first aid. Now she sat in her chair, carefully, meticulously, turning her sketch of an Apache breastplate into her own vision.

It was sweaty work, and viciously exacting. Bleeding color into color, shape into shape as she wanted required hundreds of trips to the glory hole.

But here, at least, she could be patient.

White-hot flames licked through open furnace doors, blasting out heat. The exhaust fan hummed like an engine to keep the fumes coating the glass—and not her lungs—to an iridescent hue.

For two days she worked with chemicals, mixing and experimenting like a mad scientist until she'd perfected the colors she desired. Copper for the deep turquoise, iron for the rich golden yellow, manganese for a royal, bluish purple. The red, the true ruby she wanted, had given her trouble, as it did any glass artist. She was working with that now, sandwiching that section between two layers of clear glass. She'd used copper again, with reducing agents in the melt to ensure a pure color. Though it was poisonous, and potentially dangerous even under controlled conditions, she'd chosen sodium cyanide.

Even with this the casing was necessary to prevent the red from going livery.

The first gather of the new section was blown, rotated, then carefully trailed from the iron. She used long tweezers to draw the molten, taffylike glass into a subtly feathery shape.

Sweat dripped down onto the cotton bandanna she'd tied around her brow as she worked the second gather, repeated the procedure.

Again and again, she went to the glory hole to reheat, not only to keep the glass hot, but to ensure against thermal strains that could break any vessel— and the heart of the artist.

To prevent searing her hands, she dripped water over the pipe. Only the tip needed to be kept hot.

She wanted the wall of the breastplate thin enough so that light could seep and be refracted through it. This required additional trips for heating and careful patient work with tools for flattening and for adding the slight curve she envisioned.

Hours after she'd blown the first gather, she placed the vessel in the annealing oven and struck the pontil.

It wasn't until she'd set both temperature and time that she felt the cramps in her hands, the knots in her shoulders and neck.

And the emptiness in her belly.

No scraping out of a can tonight, she decided. She would celebrate with a meal and a pint at the pub.

Maggie didn't ask herself why, after pining for solitude, she now hurried toward company. She'd been home for three days and had spoken to no one but Brianna. And then only briefly and angrily.

Maggie was sorry for it now, sorry that she hadn't tried harder to understand Brianna's position. Her sister was always in the middle, the unlucky second child of a flawed marriage. Instead of leaping for her sister's throat, she should have taken her oversolicitousness toward their mother in stride. And she should have told Brianna what she'd learned from Christine Sweeney. It would be interesting to gauge Brianna's reaction to the news of their mother's past.

But that would have to wait. She wanted an undemanding hour with people she knew, over a hot meal and a cold beer. It would take her mind off the work that had been driving her for days, and off the fact that she'd yet to hear from Rogan.

Because the evening was fine and she wanted to work out the worst of her kinks, she straddled her bicycle and began the three-mile trek into the village.

The long days of summer had begun. The sun was brilliant and pleasantly warm, keeping many of the farmers out in their fields long after their supper was over. The curving narrow road was flanked on both sides by high hedgerows that provided no shoulder and gave Maggie the impression of riding down a long, sweet-smelling tunnel. She passed a car, gave the driver a wave and felt the breeze of its passing flutter her jeans.

Pedaling hard, more for the fun than because she was in a hurry, she burst out of the tunnel of hedges into the sheer breathless beauty of the valley.

The sun dashed off the tin roof of a hay barn and dazzled her eyes. The road was smoother now, if no wider, but she slowed, simply to enjoy the evening breeze and the lingering sunlight.

She caught the scent of honeysuckle, of hay, of sweet mown grass. Her mood, which had been manic and restless since her return, began to mellow.

She passed houses with clothes drying on the line and children playing in the yard, and the ruins of castles, majestic still with their gray stones and legends of ghostly inhabitants, a testament to a way of life that still lingered.

She took a curve, caught the bright flash that was the river flowing through high grass and turned away from it toward the village.

The houses were more plentiful now and stood closer together. Some of the newer ones made her sigh with disappointment. They were blocky and plain to her artist's eye, and usually drab in color. Only the gardens, lush and vivid, saved them from ugliness.

The long last curve took her into the village proper. She passed the butcher's, the chemist's, O'Ryan's little food store and the tiny, neat hotel that had once belonged to her grandfather.

Maggie paused to study the building a moment, trying to imagine her mother living there as a girl. A lovely girl, according to Christine Sweeney's report, with the voice of an angel.

If it were true, why had there been so little music in the house? And why, Maggie wondered, had there never been a mention, a hint of Maeve's talent?

She would ask, Maggie decided. And there was likely no place better than O'Malley's.

As she pulled her bike to the curb Maggie noticed a family of tourists wandering on foot, shooting videos and looking enormously pleased with themselves to be committing a quaint Irish village onto tape.

The woman held the small, clever little camera and laughed as she focused on her husband and two children. Maggie must have stepped into the frame, for the woman lifted her hand and waved.

"Good evening, miss."

"And to you."

To her credit, Maggie didn't even snicker when the woman whispered to her husband, "Isn't her accent wonderful? Ask her about food, John. I'm dying to get more of her on tape."

"Ah . . . excuse me."

Tourism couldn't hurt the village, Maggie decided, and turned back to play the game. "Can I help you with something this evening?"

"If you wouldn't mind. We were wondering about a place to eat in town. If you could recommend something."

"And sure I could do that." Because they looked so delighted with her, she layered a bit more west county into her speech. "Now, if you're after wanting something fancy, you couldn't do better but to drive along this road another, oh, fifteen minutes, and you could have the very king of meals at Dromoland Castle. It'll be hard on your wallet, but your taste buds will be in heaven."

"We're not dressed for a fancy meal," the woman put in. "Actually, we were hoping for something simple right here in the village."

"If you're in the mood for a bit of pub grub"—she winked at the two children, who were eyeing her as if she'd stepped off a light-flashing UFO—"you'll find O'Malley's to your liking, I'm sure. His chips are as good as anyone's."

"That's means french fries," the woman translated. "We just arrived this morning, from America," she told Maggie. "I'm afraid we don't know much about the local customs. Are children permitted in the bars—pubs?"

"This is Ireland. Children are welcome anywhere, anywhere a'tall. That's O'Malley's there." She gestured toward the low plastered block building with dark trim. "I'm going there meself. They'd be pleased to have you and your family for a meal."

"Thank you." The man beamed at her, the children stared and the woman had yet to take the camera from in front of her face. "We'll give it a try."

"Enjoy your meal, then, and the rest of your stay." Maggie turned and sauntered down the sidewalk and into O'Malley's. It was dim, smoky and smelled of frying onions and beer.

"And how are you, Tim?" Maggie asked as she settled herself at the bar.

"And look who's dragged herself in." Tim grinned at her as he built a pint of Guinness. "And how are you, Maggie?"

"I'm fit and hungry as a bear." She exchanged greetings with a couple at a postage-stamp-sized table behind her and at the two men who nursed pints at the bar. "Will you fix me one of your steak sandwiches, Tim, with a pile of chips, and I'll have a pint of Harp while I'm waiting."

The proprietor stuck his head around the back of the bar and shouted out Maggie's order. "Well now, how was Dublin City?" he asked while he drew her a pint.

"I'll tell you." She propped her elbows on the bar and began to describe her trip for the patrons of the bar. While she talked the American family came in and settled at a table.

"Champagne and goose liver?" Tim shook his head. "Isn't that a wonder? And all those people come to see your glass. Your father'd be proud of you, Maggie girl. Proud as a peacock."

"I hope so." She sniffed deeply when Tim slid her plate in front of her. "But the truth is, I'd rather have your steak sandwich than a pound of goose liver."

He laughed heartily. "That's our girl."

"It turns out that the grandmother of the man who's managing things for me was a friend of my gran, Gran O'Reilly."

"You don't mean it?" With a sigh, Tim rubbed his belly. "Sure and it's a small world."

"It is," Maggie agreed, making it casual. "She's from Galway and knew Gran when they were girls. They wrote letters for years after Gran moved here, keeping up, you know?"

"That's fine. No friend like an old friend."

"Gran wrote her about the hotel and such, the family. Mentioned how it was my mother used to sing."

"Oh, that was a time ago." Remembering, Tim picked up a glass to polish. "Before you were born, to be sure. Fact is, now that I think of it, she sang here in this very pub one of the last times before she gave it up."

"Here? You had her sing here?"

"I did, yes. She had a sweet voice, did Maeve. Traveled all over the country. Hardly saw a bit of her for, oh, more than ten years, I'd say, then she came back to stay a time. It seems to me Missus O'Reilly was ailing. So I asked Maeve if maybe she'd like to sing an evening or two, not that we've as grand a place as some in Dublin and Cork and Donnegal where she'd performed."

"She performed? For ten years?"

"Oh well, I don't know as she made much of it at first. Anxious to be off and away was Maeve, as long as I remember. She wasn't happy making beds in a hotel in a village like ours, and let us know it." He winked to take the sting out of his words. "But she was doing well by the time she came back and sang here. Then she and Tom . . . well, they only had eyes for each other the moment he walked in and heard her singing."

"And after they married," Maggie said carefully, "she didn't sing any longer?"

"Didn't care to. Wouldn't talk of it. Fact is, it's been so long, till you brought it up, I'd nearly forgotten."

Maggie doubted her mother had forgotten, or could forget. How would she herself feel if some twist in her life demanded that she give up her art? she wondered. Angry, sad, resentful. She looked down at her hands, thought of how it would be if she couldn't use them again. What would she become if suddenly, just as she was about to make her mark, it was all taken away?

If relinquishing her career wasn't an excuse for the bitter years that had passed with her mother, at least it was a reason.

Maggie needed time to shift through it, to talk to Brianna. She toyed with her beer and began to put the pieces of the woman her mother had been together with the personality of the woman she'd become.

How much of both, Maggie wondered, had Maeve passed on to her daughter?

"You're to eat that sandwich," Tim ordered as he slid another pint down the bar. "Not study it."

"I am." To prove her point, Maggie took a healthy bite. The pub was warm and comforting. Time enough tomorrow, she decided, to wipe the film off old dreams. "Will you get me another pint, Tim?"

"That I'll do," he said, then lifted a hand when the pub door opened again. "Well, it's a night for strangers. Where've you been, Murphy?"

"Why missing you, boy-o." Spotting Maggie, Murphy grinned and joined her at the bar. "I'm hoping I can sit by the celebrity."

"I suppose I can allow it," she returned. "This once, at any rate. So, Murphy, when are you going to court my sister?"

It was an old joke, but still made the pub patrons chuckle. Murphy sipped from Maggie's glass and sighed. "Now, darling, you know there's only room in my heart for you."

"I know you're a scoundrel." She took back her beer.

He was a wildly handsome man, trim and strong and weathered like an oak from the sun and wind. His dark hair curled around his collar, over his ears, and his eyes were as blue as the cobalt bottle in her shop.

Not polished like Rogan, she thought. Rough as a Gypsy was Murphy, but with a heart as wide and sweet as the valley he loved. Maggie had never had a brother, but Murphy was the nearest to it.

"I'd marry you tomorrow," he claimed, sending the pub, except for the Americans who looked on avidly, into whoops of laughter. "If you'd have me."

"You can rest easy, then, for I won't be having the likes of you. But I'll kiss you and make you sorry for it."

She made good on her word, kissing him long and hard until they drew back and grinned at one another. "Have you missed me, then?" Maggie asked.

"Not a whit. I'll have a pint of Guinness, Tim, and the same thing our celebrity's having." He stole one of her chips. "I heard you were back."

"Oh." Her voice cooled a little. "You saw Brie?"

"No, I *heard* you were back," he repeated. "Your furnace."

"Ah."

"My sister sent me some clippings, from Cork."

"Mmm. How is Mary Ellen?"

"Oh, she's fit. Drew and the children, too." Murphy reached in his pocket, frowned, patted another. "Ah, here we go." He took out two folded pieces of newspaper. "'Clarewoman triumphs in Dublin,'" he read. "'Margaret Mary Concannon impressed the art word at a showing at Worldwide Gallery, Dublin, Sunday night.'"

"Let me see that." Maggie snatched the clipping out of his hand. "'Miss Concannon, a free-blown-glass artist, drew praise and compliments from attendees of the show with her bold and complex sculptures and drawings. The artist herself is a diminutive'—diminutive, hah!" Maggie editorialized.

"Give it back." Murphy tugged the clipping away and continued to read it aloud himself. "'A diminutive young woman of exceptional talent and beauty.'"

Hah, yourself," Murphy added, sneering at her.
"'The green-eyed redhead of ivory complexion and
considerable charm was as fascinating as her work to
this art lover. Worldwide, one of the top galleries in
the world, considers itself fortunate to display Miss
Concannon's work.

"'"I believe she's only begun to tap her creativity,"
stated Rogan Sweeney, president of Worldwide. "Bringing Miss Concannon's work to the attention of the
world is a privilege."'"

"He said that?" She reached for the clipping again,
but Murphy held it out of reach.

"He did. It's here in black and white. Now let me
finish. People want to hear."

Indeed, the pub had gone quiet. Every eye was on
Murphy as he finished the review.

"'Worldwide will be touring several of Miss Concannon's pieces over the next year, and will keep
others, personally selected by the artist and Mr.
Sweeney, on permanent display in Dublin.'" Satisfied, Murphy placed the clipping on the bar, where
Tim craned over to see it.

"And there's pictures," he added, unfolding the
second clipping. "Of Maggie with the ivory complexion and some of her fancy glass. Nothing to say,
Maggie?"

She let out a long breath, dragged at her hair. "I
guess I'd better say 'drinks for all my friends.'"

"You're quiet, Maggie Mae."

Maggie smiled over the nickname, one her father
had used for her. She was more than comfortable in
Murphy's lorry, with her bike stowed in the bed and

the engine purring, as did all of Murphy's machinery, like a satisfied cat.

"I'm thinking I'm a wee bit drunk, Murphy." She stretched and sighed. "And that I like the feeling quite a lot."

"Well, you earned it." She was more than a wee bit drunk, which was why he'd hauled her bike into his lorry before she could think to argue. "We're all proud of you, and I for one will look upon that bottle you made me with more respect from now on."

"'Tis a weed pot, I've told you, not a bottle. You put pretty twigs or wild flowers in it."

Why anyone would bring twigs, pretty or otherwise, into the house was beyond him. "So are you going back to Dublin, then?"

"I don't know—not for a time, anyway. I can't work there and work's what I want to do right now." She scowled at a tumble of furze, silvered now by the rising moon. "He never acted like it was a privilege, you know."

"What's that?"

"Oh, no, it was always that *I* should be privileged he'd taken a second look at me work. The great and powerful Sweeney giving the poor, struggling artist a chance for fame and fortune. Well, did I ask for fame and fortune, Murphy? That's what I want to know? Did I ask for it?"

He knew the tone, the belligerent, defensive slap of it, and answered cautiously. "I can't say, Maggie. But don't you want it?"

"Of course I do. Do I look like a fleabrain? But ask for it? No, I did not. I never once asked him for a blessed thing, except at the start to leave me alone. And did he? Hah!" She folded her arms across her chest. "Not much he did. He tempted me, Murphy, and the devil himself couldn't have been more sly and persuasive. Now I'm stuck, you see, and can't go back."

Murphy pursed his lips and pulled smoothly to a stop by her gate. "Well, are you wanting to go back?"

"No. And that's the worst of it. I want exactly what he says I can have, and want it so it hurts my heart. But I don't want things to change either, that's the hell of it. I want to be left alone to work and to think, and just to be. I don't know as I can have both."

"You can have what you want, Maggie. You're too stubborn to take less."

She laughed at that and turned to kiss him sloppily. "Oh, I love you, Murphy. Why don't you come out into the field and dance with me in the moonlight?"

He grinned, ruffled her hair. "Why don't I put your bike away and tuck you into bed?"

"I'll do it meself." She climbed out of the lorry, but he was quicker. He lifted out her bike and set it on the road. "Thank you for escorting me home, Mr. Muldoon."

"The pleasure was mine, Miss Concannon. Now get yourself to bed."

She wheeled her bike through the gate as he began to sing. Stopping just inside the garden, she listened as his voice, a strong, sweet tenor, drifted through the night quiet and disappeared.

"Alone all alone by the wave wash strand, all alone in a crowded hall. The hall it is gay, and the waves they are grand, but my heart is not here at all."

She smiled a little and finished the rest in her

mind. *It flies far away, by night and by day, to the times and the joys that are gone.*

"Slievenamon" was the ballad, she knew. Woman of the Mountain. Well, she wasn't standing on a mountain, but she thought she understood the soul of the tune. The hall in Dublin had been gay, yet her heart hadn't been there. She'd been alone. All alone.

She wheeled her bike around the back, but instead of going inside, Maggie headed away from the house. It was true she was a little light-headed and none too steady on her feet, but she didn't want to waste such a night in bed. Alone in bed.

And drunk or sober, day or night, she could find her way over the land that had once been hers.

She heard the hoot of an owl and the rustle of something that hunted or hid by night in the higher grass to the east. Overhead, the moon, just past full, shone like a bright beacon in a swimming sea of stars. The night whispered around her, secretly. A brook to the west babbled in answer.

This, this, was part of what she wanted. What she needed as much as breath was the glory of solitude. Having the green fields flowing around her, silvered now in moon- and star-light, with only the faint glow in the distance that was the lamp in Murphy's kitchen.

She remembered walking here with her father, her child's hand clutched warmly in his. He hadn't talked of planting or plowing, but of dreams. Always, he had spoken of dreams.

He'd never really found his.

Sadder somehow, she thought, was that she was

beginning to see that her mother had found hers, only to lose it again.

How would it be, she wondered, to have what you wanted as close as your fingertips, then have it slip away? Forever.

And wasn't that exactly what she herself was so afraid of?

She lay on her back on the grass, her head spinning with too much drink and too many dreams of her own. The stars wheeled in their angels' dance, and the moon, shiny as a silver coin, looked down on her. The air was sweetened by the lilt of a nightingale. And the night was hers alone.

She smiled, shut her eyes and slept.

❧ Chapter Eleven

Iᴛ was the cow that woke her. The big, liquid eyes studied the sleeping form curled in the pasture. There was little thought in a cow's head other than food and the need to be milked. So she sniffed once, twice, at Maggie's cheek, snorted, then began to crop grass.

"Oh God have mercy, what's the noise?"

Her head throbbing like a large drum being beaten, Maggie rolled over, bumped solidly into the cow's foreleg and opened bleary, bloodshot eyes.

"Sweet Jesus Christ!" Maggie's squeal reverberated in her head like a gong, causing her to catch hold of her ears as if they were about to explode as she scrambled away. The cow, as startled as she, mooed and rolled her eyes. "What are you doing here?" Keeping a firm hold on her head, Maggie made it to her knees. "What am I doing here?" When she dropped back on her haunches, she and the cow studied each other doubtfully. "I must've fallen asleep. Oh!" In pitiful defense against a raging hangover, she shifted her hands from her ears to her eyes. "Oh, the penance paid for one drink over the limit. I'll just sit right here for a minute, if you don't mind, until I have the strength to stand."

The cow, after one last roll of her eyes, began to graze again.

The morning was bright and warm, and full of sound. The drone of a tractor, the bark of a dog, the cheerful birdsong rolled in Maggie's sick head. Her mouth tasted as if she'd spent the night dining on a peat bog, and her clothes were coated with morning dew.

"Well, it's a fine thing to pass out in a field like a drunken hobo."

She made it to her feet, swayed once and moaned. The cow swished its tail in what might have been sympathy. Cautious, Maggie stretched. When her bones didn't shatter, she worked out the rest of the kinks and let her gritty eyes scan the field.

More cows, uninterested in their human visitor, grazed. In the next field, she could see the circle of standing stones, ancient as the air, that the locals called Druid's Mark. She remembered now kissing Murphy good night and, with his fading song playing in her head, wandering under the moon.

And the dream she'd had, sleeping under its silver light, came back to her so vividly, so breathlessly, that she forgot the throbbing in her head and the stiffness in her joints.

The moon, glowing with light, pulsing like a heartbeat. Flooding the sky, and the earth beneath it with cold white light. Then it had burned, hot as a torch until it ran with color, bled blues and reds and golds so lovely that even in sleep she had wept.

She had reached up, and up, and up, until she had touched it. Smooth it had been, and solid and cool as she cupped it in her hands. In that sphere she had seen herself, and deep, somewhere deep within those swimming colors, had been her heart.

The vision whirling in her head was more than a match for a hangover. Driven by it, she ran from the field, leaving the placid cows to their grazing and the morning to its birdsong.

Within the hour she was in her studio, desperate to turn vision into reality. She needed no sketch, not with the image so boldly imprinted in her mind. She'd eaten nothing, didn't need to. With the thrill of discovery glittering over her like a cloak, she made the first gather.

She smoothed it on the marble to chill and center it. Then she gave it her breath.

When it was heated and fluid again, she marvered the bubble over powdered colorants. Into the flames it went again until the color melted into the vessel wall.

She repeated the process over and over, adding glass, fire, breath, color. Turning and turning the rod both against and with gravity, she smoothed the glowing sphere with paddles to maintain its shape.

Once she'd transferred the vessel from pipe to pontil, she heated it strongly in the glory hole. She would employ a wet stick now, holding it tightly to the mouth of her work so that the steam pressure enlarged the form.

All of her energies were focused. She knew that the water on the stick would vaporize. The pressure could blow out the vessel walls. She would have done with a pontil boy now, someone to be another pair of hands, to fetch tools, to gather more glass, but she had never hired anyone for the job.

She began to mutter to herself as she was forced to make the trips herself, back to the furnace, back to the marver, back to the chair.

The sun rose higher, streaming through the windows and crowning her in a nimbus of light.

That was how Rogan saw her when he opened the door. Sitting in the chair, with a ball of molten color under her hands and sunlight circling her.

She spared him one sharp glance. "Take off that damn suit coat and tie. I need your hands."

"What?"

"I need your hands, damn it. Do exactly what I tell you and don't talk to me."

He wasn't sure he could. He wasn't often struck dumb, but at that moment, with the blast of fire, the flash of sun, she looked like some sort of fierce, fiery goddess creating new worlds. He set his briefcase aside and stripped off his coat.

"You'll hold this steady," she told him as she slipped out of the chair. "And you'll turn the pontil just as I am. You see? Slowly, constantly. No jerks or pauses or I'll have to kill you. I need a prunt."

He was so stunned that she would trust him with her work that he sat in her chair without a word. The pipe was warm in his hands, heavier than he'd expected. She kept hers over his until she felt he had the rhythm.

"Don't stop," she warned him. "Believe me, your very life depends on it."

He didn't doubt her. She went to the furnace, gathered a prunt and came back.

"Do you see how I did that? Nothing to that part. I want you to do it for me next time." Once the wall was softened, she took jacks and pushed into the glass.

"Do it now." She took the pipe from him and continued to work it. "I can shear it off if you gather too much."

The heat from the furnace stole his breath. He dipped the pipe in, following her terse directions, rolled it under the melt. He watched the glass gather and cling, like hot tears.

"You'll bring it to me from the back of the bench and to the right." Anticipating him, she snatched up a pair of tongs and took control of the pontil even as he angled it toward her.

She repeated the process, sending off sparks from the wax, merging glass into glass, color into color. When she was satisfied with the interior design, she reblew the vessel, urging it into a sphere again, shaping it with air.

What Rogan saw was a perfect circle, the size perhaps of a soccer ball. The interior of the clear glass orb exploded with colors and shapes, bled and throbbed with them. If he had been a fanciful man, he would have said the glass lived and breathed just as he did. The colors swirled, impossibly vivid, at the center, then flowed to the most delicate hues as they trailed to the wall.

Dreams, he thought. It's a circle of dreams.

"Bring me that file," she snapped out.

"The what?"

"The file, blast it." She was already moving to a bench covered with fireproof pads. As she braced the pontil on a wooded vise, she held out her hand, like a surgeon demanding a scalpel. Rogan slapped a file into it.

He heard her slow steady breathing pause, hold, just as she struck the glass bond with the file. She struck the pontil. The ball rolled comfortably onto the pad. "Gloves," she ordered. "The heavy ones by my chair. Hurry up."

With her eyes still on the ball, she jerked the gloves on. Oh, she wanted to hold it. To cup it in her naked palms as she had in her dream. Instead, she chose a metal fork, covered with asbestos, and carried the sphere to the annealing oven.

She set the timer, then stood for a minute, staring blankly into space.

"It's the moon, you see," she said softly. "It pulls the tides, in the sea, in us. We hunt by it and harvest by it and sleep by it. And if we're lucky enough, we can hold it in our hands and dream by it."

"What will you call it?"

"It won't have a name. Everyone should see what they want most in it." As if coming out of a dream herself, she lifted a hand to her head. "I'm tired." She trudged wearily back to her chair, sat and let her head fall back.

She was milk pale, Rogan noticed, drained of the energized glow that had covered her while she'd worked. "Have you worked through the night again?"

"No, I slept last night." She smiled to herself. "In Murphy's field, under the bright, full moon."

"You slept in a field?"

"I was drunk." She yawned, then laughed and opened her eyes. "A little. And it was such a grand night."

"And who," Rogan asked as he crossed to her, "is Murphy?"

"A man I know. Who would have been a bit surprised to find me sleeping in his pasture. Would you get me a drink?" At his lifted brow, she laughed. "A soft one, if you will. From the refrigerator there. And help yourself," she added when he obliged her. "You make a passable pontil boy, Sweeney."

"You're welcome," he said, taking that for a thanks. As she tipped the can he gave her back, he scanned the room. She hadn't been idle, he noted. There were several new pieces tucked away, her interpretations of the Native American display. He studied a shallow wide-lipped dish, decorated with deep, dull colors.

"Lovely work."

"Mmm. An experiment that turned out well. I combined opaque and transparent glass." She yawned again, broadly. "Then tin-fumed it."

"Tin-fumed? Never mind," he said when he saw that she was about to launch into a complicated explanation. "I wouldn't understand what you were talking about, anyway. Chemistry was never my forte. I'll just be pleased with the finished product."

"You're supposed to say it's fascinating, just as I am."

He glanced back at her and his lips twitched. "Been reading your reviews, have you? God help us now. Why don't you go get some rest? We'll talk later. I'll take you to dinner."

"You didn't come all this way to take me to dinner."

"I'd enjoy it just the same."

There was something different about him, she decided. Some subtle change somewhere deep in those gorgeous eyes of his. Whatever it was, he had it under control. A couple of hours with her ought to fix that, Maggie concluded, and smiled at him.

"We'll go in the house, have some tea and a bite to eat. You can tell me why you've come."

"To see you, for one thing."

Something in his tone told her to sharpen her work-dulled wits. "Well, you've seen me."

"So I have." He picked up his briefcase and opened the door. "I could use that tea."

"Good, you can brew it." She shot a look over her shoulder as she stepped outside. "If you know how."

"I believe I do. Your garden looks lovely."

"Brie's tended it while I was gone. What's this?" She tapped a foot against a cardboard box at her back door.

"A few things I brought with me. Your shoes for one. You left them in the parlor."

He handed her the briefcase and hauled the box into the kitchen. After dumping it on the table, he looked around the kitchen.

"Where's the tea?"

"In the cupboard above the stove."

While he went to work she slit the box open. Moments later she was sitting down, holding her belly as she laughed.

"Trust you never to forget a thing. Rogan, if I won't answer the phone, why should I listen to a silly answering machine?"

"Because I'll murder you if you don't."

"There's that." She rose again and pulled out a wall calendar. "French Impressionists," she murmured, studying the pictures above each month. "Well, at least it's pretty."

"Use it," he said simply, and set the kettle to boil. "And the machine, and this." He reached into the box himself and pulled out a long velvet case. Without ceremony he flipped it open and took out a slim gold watch, its amber face circled by diamonds.

"God, I can't wear that. It's a lady's watch. I'll forget I have it on and shower with it."

"It's waterproof."

"I'll break it."

"Then I'll get you another." He took her arm, began to unbutton the cuff of her shirt. "What the hell is this?" he demanded when he hit the bandage. "What have you done?"

"It's a burn." She was still staring at the watch and didn't see the fury light in his eyes. "I got a bit careless."

"Damn it, Maggie. You've no right to be careless. None at all. Am I to be worried about you setting yourself afire now?"

"Don't be ridiculous. You'd think I severed my hand." She would have pulled her hand away, but his grip tightened. "Rogan, for pity sake, a glass artist gets a burn now and again. It's not fatal."

"Of course not," he said stiffly. He forced back the anger he was feeling at her carelessness and clasped the watch on her wrist. "I don't like to hear you've been careless." He let her hand go, slipped his own in his pockets. "It's not serious, then?"

"No." She watched him warily when he went to answer the kettle's shrill. "Shall I make us a sandwich?"

"As you like."

"You didn't say how long you'd be staying."

"I'll go back tonight. I wanted to speak with you in person rather than try to reach you by phone." In control again, he finished making the tea and brought the pot to the table. "I've brought the clippings you asked my grandmother about."

"Oh, the clippings." Maggie stared at his briefcase. "Yes, that was good of her. I'll read them later." When she was alone.

"All right. And there was something else I wanted to give you. In person."

"Something else." She sliced through a loaf of Brianna's bread. "It's a day for presents."

"This wouldn't qualify as a present." Rogan opened his briefcase and took out an envelope. "You may want to open this now."

"All right, then." She dusted off her hands, tore open the envelope. She had to grab the back of a chair to keep her balance as she read the amount on the check. "Mary, mother of God."

"We sold every piece we'd priced." More than satisfied by her reaction, he watched her sink into the chair. "I would say the showing was quite successful."

"Every piece," she echoed. "For so much."

She thought of the moon, of dreams, of changes. Weak, she laid her head on the table.

"I can't breathe. My lungs have collapsed." Indeed, she could hardly talk. "I can't get my breath."

"Sure you can." He went behind her, massaged her shoulders. "Just in and out. Give yourself a minute to let it take hold."

"It's almost two hundred thousand pounds."

"Very nearly. With the interest we'll generate from touring your work, and offering only a portion of it to the market, we'll increase the price." The strangled sound she made caused him to laugh. "In and out, Maggie love. Just push the air out and bring it in again. I'll arrange for shipping for those pieces you've finished. We'll set the tour for the fall, because you've so much completed already. You may want to take some time off to enjoy yourself. Have a holiday."

"A holiday." She sat up again. "I can't think about that yet. I can't think at all."

"You've time." He patted her head, then moved around her to pour the tea. "You'll have dinner with me tonight, to celebrate?"

"Aye," she murmured. "I don't know what to say, Rogan. I never really believed it would . . . I just didn't believe it." She pressed her hands to her mouth. For a moment he was afraid she would begin to sob, but it was laughter, wild and jubilant, that burst out of her mouth. "I'm rich! I'm a rich woman, Rogan Sweeney." She popped out of the chair to kiss him, then whirled away. "Oh, I know it's a drop in the bucket to you, but to me—to me, it's freedom. The chains are broken, whether she wants them to be or not."

"What are you talking about?"

She shook her head, thinking of Brianna. "Dreams, Rogan, wonderful dreams. Oh, I have to tell her. Right away." She snatched up the check and impulsively stuffed it in her back pocket. "You'll stay, please. Have your tea, make some food. Make use of the phone you're so fond of. Whatever you like."

"Where are you going?"

"I won't be long." There were wings on her feet as she whirled back and kissed him again. Her lips missed his in her hurry and caught his chin. "Don't go." With that she was racing out of the door and across the fields.

She was puffing like a steam engine by the time she scrambled over the stone fence that bordered Brianna's land. But then, she'd been out of breath before she'd begun the race. She barely missed trampling her sister's pansies—a sin she would have paid for dearly—and skidded on the narrow stone path that wound through the velvety flowers.

She drew in air to shout, but didn't waste it as she spotted Brianna in the little path of green beyond the garden, hanging linen on the line.

Clothespins in her mouth, wet sheets in her hands, Brianna stared across the nodding columbines and daisies while Maggie pressed her hands to her thudding heart. Saying nothing, Brianna snapped the sheet expertly and began to clip it to the line.

There was hurt in her sister's face still, Maggie observed. And anger. All chilled lightly with Brianna's special blend of pride and control. The wolfhound gave a happy bark and started forward, only to stop short at Brianna's quiet order. He settled, with what could only be a look of regret at Maggie, back at his mistress's feet. She took another sheet from the basket beside her, flicked it and clipped it neatly to dry.

"Hello, Maggie."

So the wind blew cold from this quarter, Maggie mused, and tucked her hands into her back pockets. "Hello, Brianna. You've guests?"

"Aye. We're full at the moment. An American couple, an English family and a young man from Belgium."

"A virtual United Nations." She sniffed elaborately. "You've pies baking."

"They're baked and cooling on the windowsill." Because she hated confrontations of any kind, Brianna kept her eyes on her work as she spoke. "I thought about what you said, Maggie, and I want to say I'm sorry. I should have been there for you. I should have found a way."

"Why didn't you?"

Brianna let out a quick breath, her only sign of agitation. "You never make it easy, do you?"

"No."

"I have obligations—not only to her," she said before Maggie could speak. "But to this place. You're not the only one with ambitions, or with dreams."

The heated words that burned on Maggie's tongue cooled, then slid away. She turned to study the back of the house. The paint was fresh and white; the windows, open to the summer afternoon, were glistening. Lace curtains billowed, romantic as a bridal veil. Flowers crowded the ground and poured out of pots and tin buckets.

"You've done fine work here, Brianna. Gran would have approved."

"But you don't."

"You're wrong." In an apology of her own, she laid a hand on her sister's arm. "I don't claim I understand how you do it, or why you want to, but that's not for me to say. If this place is your dream, Brie, you've made it shine. I'm sorry I shouted at you."

"Oh, I'm used to that." Despite her resigned tone, it was clear that she had thawed. "If you'll wait till I've finished here, I'll put on some tea. I've a bit of trifle to go with it."

Maggie's empty stomach responded eagerly, but she shook her head. "I haven't time for it. I left Rogan back at the cottage."

"Left him? You should have brought him along with you. You can't leave a guest kicking his heels that way."

"He's not a guest, he's . . . well, I don't know what we'd call him, but that doesn't matter. I want to show you something."

Though her sense of propriety was offended, Brianna took out the last pillowslip. "All right, show me. Then get back to Rogan. If you've no food in the house, bring him here. The man's come all the way from Dublin after all, and—"

"Will you stop worrying about Sweeney?" Maggie cut in impatiently, and pulled the check out of her pocket. "And look at this?"

One hand on the line, Brianna glanced at the paper. Her mouth dropped open and the clothespin fell out to plop on the ground. The pillowslip floated after it.

"What is it?"

"It's a check, are you blind? A big, fat, beautiful check. He sold all of it, Brie. All he'd set out to sell."

"For so much?" Brianna could only gape at all the zeros. "For so much? How can that be?"

"I'm a genius." Maggie grabbed Brianna's shoulders and whirled her around. "Don't you read my reviews? I have untapped depths of creativity." Laughing, she dragged Brianna into a lively hornpipe. "Oh, and there's something more about my soul and my sexuality. I haven't memorized it all yet."

"Maggie, wait. My head's spinning."

"Let it spin. We're rich, don't you see?" They tumbled to the ground together, Maggie shrieking with laughter and Con jumping in frantic circles around them. "I can buy that glass lathe I've been wanting, and you can have that new stove you've been pretending you don't need. And we'll have a holiday. Anywhere in the world, anywhere a'tall. I'll have a new bed." She plopped back on the grass to wrestle with Con. "And you can add a whole wing onto Blackthorn if you've a mind to."

"I can't take it in. I just can't take it in."

"We'll find a house." Pushing herself up again, Maggie hooked an arm around Con's neck. "Whatever kind she wants. And hire someone to fetch and carry for her."

Brianna shut her eyes and fought back the first guilty flare of elation. "She might not want—"

"It will be what she wants. Listen to me." Maggie grabbed Brianna's hands and squeezed. "She'll go, Brie. And she'll be well taken care of. She'll have whatever pleases her. Tomorrow we'll go into Ennis and talk to Pat O'Shea. He sells houses. We'll set her up as grandly as we can, and as quickly. I promised Da I'd do my best by both of you, and that's what I'm going to do."

"Have you no consideration?" Maeve stood on the garden path, a shawl around her shoulders despite the warmth of the sun. The dress beneath it was starched and pressed—by Brianna's hand, Maggie had no doubt. "Out here shouting and shrieking while a body's trying to rest." She pulled the shawl closer and jabbed a finger at her younger daughter. "Get up off the ground. What's wrong with you? Behaving like a hoyden, and you with guests in the house."

Brianna rose stiffly, brushed at her slacks. "It's a fine day. Perhaps you'd like to sit in the sun."

"I might as well. Call off that vicious dog."

"Sit, Con." Protectively, Brianna laid a hand on the dog's head. "Can I bring you some tea?"

"Yes, and brew it properly this time." Maeve shuffled

to the chair and table Brianna had set up beside the garden. "That boy, that Belgian, he's clattered up the stairs twice today. You'll have to tell him to mind the racket. It's what comes when parents let their children traipse all over the country."

"I'll have the tea in a moment. Maggie, will you stay?"

"Not for tea. But I'll have a word with Mother." She sent her sister a steely look to prevent any argument. "Can you be ready to drive into Ennis by ten tomorrow, Brie?"

"I—yes, I'll be ready."

"What's this?" Maeve demanded as Brie walked toward the kitchen door. "What are the two of you planning?"

"Your future." Maggie took the chair beside her mother's, kicked out her legs. She'd wanted to go about it differently. After what she'd begun to learn, she'd hoped she and her mother could find a meeting ground somewhere beyond the old hurts. But already the old angers and guilts were working in her. Remembering last night's moon and her thoughts about lost dreams, she spoke quietly. "We're after buying you a house."

Maeve made a sound of disgust and plucked at the fringe of her shawl. "Nonsense. I'm content here, with Brianna to look after me."

"I'm sure you are, but it's about to end. Oh, I'll hire you a companion. You needn't worry that you'll have to learn to do for yourself. But you won't be using Brie any longer."

"Brianna understands the responsibilities of a child to her mother."

"More than," Maggie agreed. "She's done everything in her power to make you content, Mother. It hasn't been enough, and maybe I've begun to understand that."

"You understand nothing."

"Perhaps, but I'd like to understand." She took a deep breath. Though she couldn't reach out to her mother, physically or emotionally, her voice softened. "I truly would. I'm sorry for what you gave up. I learned of the singing only—"

"You won't speak of it." Maeve's voice was frigid. Her already pale skin whitened further with the shock of a pain she'd never forgotten, never forgiven. "You will never speak of that time."

"I wanted only to say I'm sorry."

"I don't want your sorrow." With her mouth tight, Maeve looked aside. She couldn't bear to have the past tossed in her face, to be pitied because she had sinned and lost what had mattered most to her. "You will not speak of it to me again."

"All right." Maggie leaned forward until Maeve's gaze settled on her. "I'll say this. You blame me for what you lost, and maybe that comforts you somehow. I can't wish myself unborn. But I'll do what I can. You'll have a house, a good one, and a respectable, competent woman to see to your needs, someone I hope can be a friend to you as well as a companion. This I'll do for Da, and for Brie. And for you."

"You've done nothing for me in your life but cause me misery."

So there would be no softening, Maggie realized. No meeting on new ground. "So you've told me, time and again. We'll find a place close enough so that Brie can visit you, for she'll feel she should. And

I'll furnish the place as well, however you like. You'll have a monthly allowance—for food, for clothes, for whatever it is you need. But I swear before God you'll be out of his house and into your own before a month is up."

"Pipe dreams." Her tone was blunt and dismissive, but Maggie sensed a little frisson of fear beneath. "Like your father, you are full of empty dreams and foolish schemes."

"Not empty, and not foolish." Again, Maggie drew the check out of her pocket. This time she had the satisfaction of seeing her mother's eyes go wide and blank. "Aye, it's real, and it's mine. I earned it. I earned it because Da had the faith in me to let me learn, to let me try."

Maeve's eyes flicked to Maggie's, calculating. "What he gave you belonged to me as well."

"The money for Venice, for schooling and for the roof over my head, that's true. What else he gave me had nothing to do with you. And you'll get your share of this." Maggie tucked the check away again. "Then I'll owe you nothing."

"You owe me your life," Maeve spat.

"Mine meant little enough to you. I may know why that is, but it doesn't change how it makes me feel inside. Understand me, you'll go without complaint, without making your last days with Brianna a misery for her."

"I'll not go at all." Maeve dug in her pocket for a lace-edged hanky. "A mother needs the comfort of her child."

"You've no more love for Brianna than you do for me. We both know it, Mother. She might believe differently, but here, now, let's at least be honest.

You've played on her heart, it's true, and God knows she's deserving of any love you have in that cold heart of yours." After a long breath, she pulled out the trump card she'd been holding for five years. "Would you have me tell her why Rory McAvery went off to America and broke her heart?"

Maeve's hands gave a quick little jerk. "I don't know what you're talking about?"

"Oh, but you do. You took him aside when you saw he was getting serious in his courting. And you told him that you couldn't in good conscience let him give his heart to your daughter. Not when she'd given her body to another. You convinced him, and he was only a boy, after all, that she'd been sleeping with Murphy."

"It's a lie." Maeve's chin thrust out, but there was fear in her eyes. "You're an evil, lying child, Margaret Mary."

"You're the liar, and worse, much worse than that. What kind of a woman is it that steals happiness from her own blood because she has none herself? I heard from Murphy," Maggie said tersely. "After he and Rory beat each other to bloody pulps. Rory didn't believe his denial. Why should he, when Brianna's own mother had tearfully told him the tale?"

"She was too young to marry," Maeve said quickly. "I wouldn't have her making the same mistake as I did, ruining her life that way. The boy wasn't right for her, I tell you. He'd never have amounted to anything."

"She loved him."

"Love doesn't put bread on the table." Maeve fisted her hands, twisting the handkerchief in them. "Why haven't you told her?"

"Because I thought it would only hurt her more. I asked Murphy to say nothing, knowing Brianna's pride, and how it would be shattered. And maybe because I was angry that he would have believed you, that he didn't love her enough to see the lie. But I will tell her now. I'll walk right into that kitchen and tell her now. And if I have to, I'll drag poor Murphy over to stand with me. You'll have no one then."

She hadn't known the flavor of revenge would be so bitter. It lay cold and distasteful on Maggie's tongue as she continued. "I'll say nothing if you do as I say. And I'll promise you that I will provide for you as long as you live and do whatever I can to see that you're content. I can't give you back what you had, or wanted to have before you conceived me. But I can give you something that might make you happier than you've been since. Your own home. You've only to agree to my offer in order to have everything you've always wanted—money, a fine house and a servant to tend you."

Maeve pressed her lips together. Oh, it crushed the pride to bargain with the girl. "How do I know you'll keep your word?"

"Because I give it to you. Because I swear these things to you on my father's soul." Maggie rose. "That will have to content you. Tell Brianna I'll be by to pick her up at ten tomorrow." And with these words, Maggie turned on her heel and walked away.

🍀 Chapter Twelve

SHE took her time walking back, again choosing the fields rather than the road. As she went she gathered wildflowers, the meadowsweet and valerian that sunned themselves among the grass. Murphy's well-fed cows, their udders plump and nearly ready for milking, grazed unconcernedly as she climbed over the stone walls that separated pasture from plowed field and field from summer hay.

Then she saw Murphy himself, atop his tractor, with young Brian O'Shay and Dougal Finnian with him, all to harvest the waving hay. They called it *comhair* in Irish, but Maggie knew that here, in the west, the word meant much more than its literal translation of "help." It meant community. No man was alone here, not when it came to haying, or opening a bank of peat or sowing in the spring.

If today O'Shay and Finnian were working Murphy's land, then tomorrow, or the day after, he would be working theirs. No one would have to ask. The tractor or plow or two good hands and a strong back would simply come, and the work would be done.

Stone fences might separate one man's fields from another, but the love of the land joined them.

She lifted a hand to answer the salute of the three

farmers and, gathering her flowers, continued on to her home.

A jackdaw swooped overhead, complaining fiercely. A moment later Maggie saw why as Con barreled through the verge of the hay, his tongue lolling happily.

"Helping Murphy again, are you?" She reached down to ruffle his fur. "And a fine farmer you are, too. Go on back, then."

With a flurry of self-important barks, Con raced back toward the tractor. Maggie stood looking around her, the gold of the hay, the green of the pasture with its lazy cows and the shadows cast by the sun on the circle of stones that generations of Concannons, and now Murphy, had left undisturbed for time out of mind. She saw the rich brown of the land where potatoes had been dug. And over it all, a sky as blue as a cornflower in full blossom.

A quick laugh bubbled up in her throat, and she found herself racing the rest of the way.

Perhaps it was the pure pleasure of the day, coupled with the giddy excitement of her first major success that made her blood pump fast. It might have been the sound of birds singing as if their hearts would break, or the scent of wildflowers gathered by her own hands. But when she stopped just outside her own door and looked into her own kitchen, she was breathless with more than a quick scramble over the fields.

He was at the table, elegant in his English suit and handmade shoes. His briefcase was open, his pen out. It made her smile to see him work there, amid the clutter, on a crude wooden table he might have used for firewood at home.

The sun streamed through the windows and open door, flashing gold off his pen as he wrote in his neat hand. Then his fingers tapped over the keys of a calculator, hesitated, tapped again. She could see his profile, the faint line of concentration between the strong black brows, the firm set of his mouth.

He reached for his tea, sipped as he studied his figures. Set it down again. Wrote, read.

Elegant, he was. And beautiful, she thought, in a way so uniquely male, and as wonderfully competent and precise as the handy little machine he used to run his figures. Not a man to run across sunny fields or lie dreaming under the moon.

But he was more than she'd first imagined him to be, much more, she now understood.

The overpowering urge came over her to loosen that careful knot in his tie, unbutton that snug collar and find the man beneath.

Rarely did Maggie refuse her own urges.

She slipped inside. Even as her shadow fell over his papers, she was straddling his lap and fastening her mouth to his.

Shock, pleasure and lust speared into him like a three-tipped arrow, all sharp, all true to aim. The pen had clattered from his fingers and his hands had dived into her hair before he took the next breath. Through a haze he felt the tug on his tie.

"What?" he managed in something like a croak. The need for dignity had him clearing his throat and pressing her back. "What's all this?"

"You know. . . ." She punctuated her words by feathering light kisses over his face. He smelled expensive, she realized, all fine soap and starched linen. "I've always thought a tie a foolish thing, a sort of punishment for a man for simply being a man. Doesn't it choke you?"

It didn't, unless his heart was in his throat. "No." He shoved her hands away, but the damage was already done. Under her quick fingers, his tie was loose and his collar undone. "What are you about, Maggie?"

"That should be obvious enough, even to a Dubliner." She laughed at him, her eyes wickedly green. "I brought you flowers."

The latter were, at that moment, crushed between them. Rogan glanced down at the bruised petals. "Very nice. They could use some water, I imagine."

She tossed back her head and laughed. "It's always first things first with you, isn't it? But Rogan, from where I'm sitting, I'm aware there's something on your mind other than fetching a vase."

He couldn't deny his obvious, and very human reaction. "You'd harden a dead man," he muttered, and put his hands firmly on her hips to lift her away. She only wriggled closer, torturing him.

"Now, that's a pretty compliment, to be sure. But you're not dead, are you?" She kissed him again, using her teeth to prove her point. "Are you thinking you've work to finish up, and no time to waste?"

"No." His hands were still on her hips, but the fingers had dug in and had begun to knead. She smelled of wildflowers and smoke. All he could see was her face, the white skin with its blush of rose, dusting of gold freckles, the depthless green of her eyes. He made an heroic effort to level his voice. "But I'm thinking this is a mistake." A groan sounded in his throat when she moved her lips to his ear. "That there's a time and a place."

"And that you should choose it," she murmured as her nimble fingers flipped open the rest of the buttons on his shirt.

"Yes—no." Good God, how was a man supposed to think? "That we should both choose it, after we've set some priorities."

"I've only one priority at the moment." Her hands cruised up his chest, crushing wildflowers petals against his skin. "I'm going to have you now, Rogan." Her laugh came again, low and challenging, before her lips sank into his. "Go ahead, fight me off."

He hadn't meant to touch her. That was his last coherent thought before his hands streaked up and filled themselves with her breasts. Her throaty moan spilled into his mouth like wine, rich and drugging.

Then he was tugging away her shirt and shoving back from the table all at once. "To hell with it," he muttered against her greedy mouth, and was lifting her.

Her arms and legs wrapped around him like silken rope, her shirt dangling from one wrist where the buttons held. Beneath, she wore a plain cotton camisole as erotic to him as ivory lace.

She was small and light, but with the blood trumpeting in his brain, he thought he could have carried a mountain. Her busy mouth never paused, racing from cheek to jaw to ear and back, while sexy little whimpers purred in her throat.

He started out of the kitchen, stumbled over a loose throw rug and knocked her back against the doorjamb. She only laughed, breathlessly now, and tightened the vise of her legs around his waist.

Their lips fused again in a rough, desperate kiss. With the doorway and her own limbs bracing her, he tore his mouth free to fasten it on her breast, suckling greedily through cotton.

The pleasure of it, dark and damning, lanced like a spear through her system. This was more, she realized as the blood sizzling through her veins began to hum like an engine. More than she'd expected. More than she might have been ready for. But there was no turning back.

He whirled away from the wall.

"Hurry," was all she could say as he strode toward the stairs. "Hurry."

Her words pumped like a pulse of his blood. *Hurry. Hurry.* Against his thundering heart, hers beat in furious response. With Maggie clinging like a bur, he all but leaped up the stairs, leaving a trail of broken flowers in their wake.

He turned unerringly to the left, into the bedroom where the sun poured gold and the fragrant breeze lifted the open curtains. He fell with her onto already tumbled sheets.

If it was madness that overcame him, it ruled her as well. There was no thought, or need, in either of them for gentle caresses, for soft words or slow hands. They tore at each other, mindless as beasts, dragging at clothes, pulling, tugging, kicking off shoes, all the while feeding greedily with violent kisses.

Her body was like an engine, fueled to race. She bucked and rolled and reared while her breath seared out in burning gasps. Seams ripped, needs exploded.

His hands were smooth. Another time they might have glided over her body like water. But now they grasped and bruised and plundered, bringing her unspeakable pleasure that tore through her over-charged system like lightning tears a darkened sky. He filled his palms with her breast again, and now, without barriers, drew the rigid tips into his mouth.

She cried out, not in pain at the rough scrape of his teeth and tongue, but in glory as the first harsh, vicious orgasm struck like a blow.

She hadn't expected it to slap her so quick and hard, nor had she ever experienced the utter help-lessness that followed so fast on the heels of the storm. Before she could do more than wonder, fresh needs coiled whiplike inside her.

She spoke in Gaelic, half-remembered words she hadn't known she'd held in her heart. She'd never believed, never, that hunger could swallow her up and leave her trembling. But she shook under his hands, under the wild demand of his mouth. For another dazed interlude she was totally vulnerable, her bones molten and her mind reeling, stunned into surrender by the punch of her own climax.

He never felt the change. He knew only that she vibrated beneath him like a plucked bow. She was wet and hot and unbearably arousing. Her body was smooth, soft, supple, all the lovely dips and curves his to explore. He knew only the desperate desire to conquer, to possess, and so gorged himself on the flavor of her flesh until it seemed the essence of her raced through his veins like his own blood.

He clasped her limp hand in his and ravaged until she cried out once again, and his name was like a sob in the air.

With the room spinning like a carousel around her, she dragged her hands from his, tangled her fingers in his hair. Need spurted through her again, voraciously. She thrust her hips up.

"Now!" The demand broke from her throat. "Rogan, for God's sake—"

But he had already plunged inside her, deep and hard. She arched back, arched up, in glorious welcome as fresh pleasure geysered through her in one lancing, molten flash. Her body mated with his, matching rhythms, stroke for desperate stroke. The bite of her nails on his back was unfelt.

With vision blurred and dimmed, he watched her, saw each stunning sensation flicker over her face. It won't be enough, he thought dizzily. Even as the sorrow nicked through the burnished shield of passion, she opened her eyes and said his name again.

So he drowned in that sea of green, and burying his face in the fire of her hair, surrendered. With one last flash of glorious greed, he emptied himself into her.

In a war of any kind, there are casualties. No one, Maggie thought, knew the glory, the sorrow or the price of battle better than the Irish. And if, as she was very much afraid at the moment, her body was paralyzed for life as the result of this wonderful little war, she wouldn't count the cost.

The sun was still shining. Now that her heart had ceased to crash like thunder in her head, she heard the twitter of birds, the roar of her furnace, and the hum of a bee buzzing by the window.

She lay across the bed, her head clear off the mattress and dragged down by gravity. Her arms were aching. Perhaps because they were still wrapped like vises around Rogan, who was splayed over her, still as death.

She felt, when she held her own breath, the quicksilver race of his heart. It was, she decided, a wonder they hadn't killed each other. Content with his weight, and the drouzy feel of cobwebs in her brain, she watched the sun dance on the ceiling.

His own mind cleared slowly, the red haze mellowing, then fading completely until he became aware again of the quiet light and the small, warm body beneath his. He shut his eyes again and lay still.

What were the words he should say? he wondered. If he told her that he'd discovered, to his own shock and confusion, that he loved her, why should she believe it? To say those words now, when they were both still sated and dazed from sex, would hardly please a woman like Maggie, or make her see the bare truth of them.

What words were there, after a man had tossed a woman down and plundered like an animal? Oh, he'd no doubt she'd enjoyed it, but that hardly changed the fact that he'd completely lost control, of his mind, of his body, of whatever it was that separated the civilized from the wild.

For the first time in his life, he'd taken a woman without finesse, without care and, he thought with a sudden start, without a thought about the consequences.

He started to shift, but she murmured in protest and tightened her already fierce grip.

"Don't go away."

"I'm not." He realized her head was unsupported and, cupping a hand beneath it, rolled to reverse their positions. And nearly sent them over the other edge. "How do you sleep on a bed this size? Hardly big enough for a cat."

"Oh, it's done well enough for me. But I'm thinking of buying another now that I've money to spare. A fine big one, like the one in your house."

He thought of a Chippendale four-poster in the tiny loft and smiled. Then his thoughts veered back and wiped the smile away. "Maggie." Her face was glowing, her eyes half-shut. There was a smug little smile on her face.

"Rogan," she said in the same serious tone, then laughed. "Oh, you're not going to start telling me you're sorry to have trampled my honor or some such thing? If anyone's honor was trampled, after all, it was yours. And I'm not a bit sorry for it."

"Maggie," he said again, and brushed the tousled hair from her cheek. "What a woman you are. It's hard to be sorry for trampling, or for being trampled when I—" He broke off. He'd lifted her hand as he spoke, started to kiss her fingers, when his gaze landed on the dark smudges on her arm. Appalled, he started. "I've hurt you."

"Mmm. Now that you mention it, I'm beginning to feel it." She rolled her shoulder. "I must have hit the doorway pretty hard. Now, you were about to say?"

He shifted off of her. "I'm terribly sorry," he said in an odd voice. "It's inexcusable. An apology's hardly adequate for my behavior."

Her head tilted, and she took a good long look at him. Breeding, she thought again. How else could a buck-naked man sitting on a rumpled bed appear so dignified. "Your behavior?" she repeated. "I'd say it was more *our* behavior, Rogan, and that it was well done on both parts." Laughing at him, she pushed herself up and locked her arms around his neck. "Do you think a few bruises will wilt me like a rose, Rogan? They won't, I promise you, especially when I earned them."

"The point is—"

"The point is we tumbled each other. Now stop acting as though I'm a fragile blossom that can't admit to having enjoyed a good, hot bout of sex. Because I enjoyed it very much, and so, my fine fellow, did you."

He trailed a fingertip over the faint bruise above her wrist. "I'd rather I hadn't marked you."

"Well, it's not a brand that's permanent."

No, it wasn't. But there was something else, in his carelessness, that could be. "Maggie, I wasn't thinking before, and I certainly didn't leave Dublin today planning on ending up like this. It's a little late to be thinking of being responsible now." In frustration he dragged a hand through his hair. "Could I have gotten you pregnant?"

She blinked, sat back on her haunches. Let out a long breath. Born in fire. She remembered her father had told her she'd been born in fire. And this was what he'd meant. "No." She said it flatly, her emotions too mixed and unsteady for her to explore. "The timing's wrong. And I'm responsible for myself, Rogan."

"I should have seen to it." He reached over to rub his knuckles down her cheek. "You dazzled me, Maggie, sitting on my lap with your wildflowers. You dazzle me now."

Her smile came back, lighting her eyes first, then curving her lips. "I was coming across the fields away from my sister's and toward home. The sun was bright, Murphy was haying in his field, and there were flowers at my feet. I haven't felt so happy since my father died five years ago. Then I saw you in the kitchen, working. And it may be I was dazzled as well."

She knelt again, rested her head on his shoulder. "Must you go back to Dublin tonight, Rogan?"

All the minute and tedious details of his schedule ran like a river through his brain. Her scent, mixed with his own, settled over them like a mist. "I can rearrange some things, leave in the morning."

She leaned back, smiled. "And I'd rather not go out to dinner."

"I'll cancel the reservations." He glanced around the room. "Don't you have a phone up here?"

"For what? So it can ring in my ear and wake me up?"

"I can't think why I asked." He eased away to tug on the wrinkled slacks of his suit. "I'll go down, make some calls." He looked back to where she knelt in the center of the narrow, rumpled bed. "Very quick calls."

"They could wait," she shouted after him.

"I don't intend to be interrupted by anything until morning." He hurried down, sentimentally scooping up a tattered meadowsweet as he went.

Upstairs, Maggie waited five minutes, then six before climbing out of bed. She stretched, wincing a bit at the aches. She considered the robe that was tossed carelessly over a chair, then humming to herself, strolled downstairs without it.

He was still on the phone, the receiver cocked on his shoulder as he made notes in his book. The light, softer now, pooled at his feet. "Reschedule that for eleven. No, eleven," he repeated. "I'll be back in the office by ten. Yes, and contact Joseph, will you, Eileen? Tell him I've having another shipment sent from Clare. Concannon's work, yes. I . . ."

He heard the sound behind him, glanced back. Maggie stood like some flame-crowned goddess, all alabaster skin, sleek curves and knowing eyes. His secretary's voice buzzed in his ear like an annoying fly.

"What? The what?" His eyes, their expression dazed at first, then heated, skimmed up, then down, then up again to lock on Maggie's face. "I'll deal with it when I get back." His stomach muscles quivered when Maggie stepped forward and jerked down the zipper of his slacks. "No," he said in a strangled voice. "You can't reach me anymore today. I'm . . ." The breath hissed between his teeth when Maggie took him in her long, artist's fingers. "Sweet Jesus. Tomorrow," he said with the last of his control. "I'll see you tomorrow."

He slapped the receiver into the cradle, where it jiggled then slipped off to crash against the counter.

"I interrupted your call," she began, then laughed when he dragged her against him.

It was happening again. He could almost stand outside himself and watch the animal inside take over. With one desperate yank, he pulled her head back by the hair and savaged her throat, her mouth. The need to take her was raging, some fatal drug that stabbed into his veins, speeding up his heartbeat and clouding his mind.

He would hurt her again. Even knowing it, he couldn't stop. With a sound, part rage, part triumph, he pushed her back on the kitchen table.

He had the dark, twisted satisfaction of seeing her eyes widen in surprise. "Rogan, your papers."

He jerked her hips from the edge of the wood, raising them with his hands. His eyes were warrior bright on hers as he drove himself into her.

Her hand flailed out, knocked the cup from its saucer and sent both flying to the floor. China shattered, even as the jolting table sent his open briefcase crashing to the ground.

Stars seemed to explode in front of Maggie's eyes as she gave herself up to the delirium. She felt the rough wood on her back, the sweat that bloomed up to slicken her skin. And when he braced her legs higher and thrust himself deep, she could have sworn she felt him touch her heart.

Then she felt nothing at all but the wild wind that tossed her up and up and over that jagged-edged peak. She gasped for air like a woman drowning, then expelled it on a long, languorous moan.

Later, sometime later, when she found she could speak, she was cradled in his arms. "Did you finish your calls, then?"

He laughed and carried her out of the kitchen.

It was early when he left her. A sunshower tossed wavering rainbows into the morning sky. She'd made some sleepy offer to brew him tea, then had drifted off again. So he'd gone to the kitchen alone.

There'd been a miserable jar of hardening instant coffee in her cupboard. Though he'd winced, Rogan had settled for it, and for the single egg in her refrigerator.

He was gathering up, and trying to sort out, his scattered papers when she stumbled into the kitchen.

She was heavy-eyed and rumpled, and barely grunted at him as she headed for the kettle.

So much, he thought, for loverlike farewells.

"I used what appeared to be your last clean towel."

She grunted again and scooped out tea.

"And you ran out of hot water in the middle of my shower."

This time she only yawned.

"You don't have any eggs."

She muttered something that sounded like "Murphy's hens."

He tapped his wrinkled papers together and stacked them in his briefcase. "I've left the clippings you wanted on the counter. There'll be a truck by this afternoon to pick up the shipment. You'll need to crate it before one o'clock."

When he made no answer at all to this, he snapped his briefcase closed. "I have to go." Annoyed, he strode to her, took her chin firmly in hand and kissed her. "I'll miss you, too."

He was out the front door before she could gather her wits and chase after him. "Rogan! For pity's sake, hold up a moment. I've barely got my eyes open."

He turned just as she launched herself at him. Off balance, he nearly tumbled them both into the flower bed. Then she was caught close and they were kissing each other breathless in the soft, luminous rain.

"I will miss you, damn it." She pressed her face into his shoulder, breathed deep.

"Come with me. Go throw some things in a bag and come with me."

"I can't." She drew back, surprised at how sorry she

was to have to refuse. "I've some things I need to do. And I—I can't really work in Dublin."

"No," he said after a long moment. "I don't suppose you can."

"Could you come back? Take a day or two."

"It's not possible now. In a couple of weeks, perhaps I could."

"Well, that's not so long." It seemed like eternity. "We can both get what needs to be done done, and then . . ."

"And then." He bent to kiss her. "You'll think of me, Margaret Mary."

"I will."

She watched him go, carrying his briefcase to the car, starting the engine, backing out into the road.

She stood for a long time after the sound of the car had faded, until the rain stopped and the sun gilded the morning.

🍀 Chapter Thirteen

MAGGIE walked across the empty living room, took a long look out of the front window, then retraced her steps. It was the fifth house she had considered in a week, the only one not currently occupied by hopeful sellers, and the last one she intended to view.

It was on the outskirts of Ennis, a bit farther away than Brianna might have liked—and not far enough to Maggie's taste. It was new, which was in its favor, a box of a house with the rooms all on one floor.

Two bedrooms, Maggie mused as she walked through yet again. A bath, a kitchen with room for eating, a living area with plenty of light and tidy brick hearth.

She took one last glance, set her fists on her hips. "This is it."

"Maggie, it's certainly the right size for her." Brianna nibbled her lip as she scanned the empty room. "But shouldn't we have something closer to home?"

"Why? She hates it there in any case."

"But—"

"And this is closer to more conveniences. Food shops, the chemist, places to eat out if she's of a mind to."

"She never goes out."

"It's time she did. And since she won't have you jumping at every snap of her finger, she'll have to, won't she?"

"I don't jump." Spine stiff, Brianna walked to the window. "And the fact of the matter is, she's likely to refuse to move here in any case."

"She won't refuse." Not, Maggie thought, with the ax I hold over her head. "If you'll let go of that guilt you love wrapping about you for a moment, you'll admit this is best for everyone. She'll be happier in her own place—or as happy as a woman of her nature can be. You can give her whatever she wants out of the house if that eases your conscience, or I'll give her money to buy new. Which is what she'd rather."

"Maggie, the place is charmless."

"And so is our mother." Before Brianna could retort, Maggie crossed to her and swung an arm around the stiffened shoulders. "You'll make a garden, right outside the door there. We'll have the walls painted or papered or whatever it takes."

"It could be made nice."

"No one's better suited to do that than you. You'll draw out whatever money it takes until the two of you are satisfied."

"It's not fair, Maggie, that you should bear all this expense."

"Fairer than you might think." The time had come, Maggie decided, to speak to Brianna about their mother. "Did you know she used to sing? Professionally?"

"Mother?" The idea was so farfetched, Brianna laughed. "Where did you get a notion like that?"

"It's true. I learned of it by accident, and I've checked to be sure." Reaching into her purse, Maggie pulled out the yellowed clippings. "You can see for yourself, she was even written up a few times."

Speechless, Brianna scanned the newsprint, stared at the faded photo. "She sang in Dublin," she murmured. "She had a living. 'A voice as clear and sweet as church bells on Easter morning,' it says. But how can this be? She's never once spoken of it. Nor Da either."

"I've thought of it quite a lot in the last few days." Turning away, Maggie walked to the window again. "She lost something she wanted, and got something she didn't. All this time she's punished herself, and all of us."

Dazed, Brianna lowered the clipping. "But she never sang at home. Not a note. Ever."

"I'm thinking she couldn't bear to, or considered her refusal penance for her sin. Probably both." A weariness came over Maggie and she struggled to fight it back. "I'm trying to excuse her for it, Brie, to imagine how devastated she must have been when she learned she was pregnant with me. And being what she is, there'd have been nothing for her but marriage."

"It was wrong of her to blame you, Maggie. It always was. That's no less true today."

"Perhaps. Still, it gives me more of an understanding as to why she's never loved me. Never will."

"Have you . . ." Carefully Brianna folded the clippings and slipped them into her own purse. "Have you spoken to her of it?"

"I tried to. She won't talk about it. It could have been different." Maggie whirled back, hating the burden of guilt she couldn't shake. "It could have been. If she couldn't have the career she wanted, there could have been music still. Did she have to shut off everything because she couldn't have it all?"

"I don't know the answer. Some people aren't content with less than all."

"It can't be changed," Maggie said firmly. "But we'll give her this, we'll give all of us this."

How quickly money dribbled away, Maggie thought a few days later. It seemed the more you had, the more you needed. But the deed to the house was now in Maeve's name, and the details, the dozens of them that came from establishing a home, were being dealt with, one by one.

A pity the details of her own life seemed to hang in limbo.

She'd barely spoken to Rogan, she thought as she sulked at her kitchen table. Oh, there'd been messages relayed through his Eileen and Joseph, but he rarely bothered to contact her directly. Or to come back, as he'd said he would.

Well, that was fine, she thought. She was busy in any case. There were any number of sketches that were begging to be turned into glass. If she was a bit late getting started this morning, it was only because she'd yet to decide which project to pursue first.

It certainly wasn't because she was waiting for the blasted phone to ring.

She got up and started to the door when she saw Brianna through the window, the devoted wolfhound at her heels.

"Good. I hoped I'd catch you before you started

for the day." Brianna took the basket from her arm as she stepped into the kitchen.

"You did, just. Is it going well?"

"Very." Brisk and efficient, Brianna uncovered the steaming muffins she'd brought along. "Finding Lottie Sullivan's like a gift from God." She smiled, thinking of the retired nurse they'd hired as Maeve's companion. "She's simply wonderful, Maggie. Like part of the family already. Yesterday, when I was working on the front flower beds, Mother was carrying on about how it was too late in the year for planting and how the paint on the outside of the house was the wrong color. And, oh, just being contrary. And Lottie was standing there laughing, disagreeing with everything she said. I swear, the two of them were having the time of their lives."

"I wish I'd seen it." Maggie broke open a muffin. The smell of it, and the picture Brianna had put in her head, almost made up for postponing her morning's work. "You found a treasure there, Brie. Lottie'll keep her in line."

"It's more than that. She really enjoys doing it. Every time Mother says something horrid, Lottie just laughs and winks and goes about her business. I never thought I'd say it, Maggie, but I really believe this is going to work."

"Of course it's going to work." Maggie tossed a bit of muffin to the patiently hopeful Con. "Did you ask Murphy if he'd help move her bed and the other things she wants?"

"I didn't have to. Word's out that you've bought her a house near Ennis. I've had a dozen people drop by in the last two weeks, casuallike. Murphy already offered his back and his lorry."

"Then she'll be moved tidily in with Lottie before the next week is up. I've bought us a bottle of champagne, and we're going to drink ourselves drunk when it's done."

Brianna's lips twitched, but her voice was sober. "It's not something to celebrate."

"Then I'll just drop in, casuallike," Maggie said with a sly grin. "With a bottle of bubbly under me arm."

Though Brianna smiled back, her heart wasn't in it. "Maggie, I tried to talk to her about her singing." She was sorry to see the light go out of her sister's eyes. "I thought I should."

"Of course you did." Losing her appetite for the muffin, Maggie tossed the rest to Con. "Did you have better luck than I?"

"No. She wouldn't talk to me, only got angry." It wasn't worth recounting the verbal blows punch by punch, Brianna thought. To do so would only serve to spread the unhappiness more thickly. "She went off to her room, but she took the clippings with her."

"Well, that's something. Perhaps they'll comfort her." Maggie jolted when the phone rang and scrambled out of her chair so quickly that Brianna gaped. "Hello. Oh, Eileen, is it?" The disappointment in her voice was unmistakable. "Yes, I've the photos you sent for the catalog. They look more than fine. Perhaps I should tell Mr. Sweeney myself that— oh, a meeting. No, that's all right, then, you can tell him I approved of them. You're welcome. Goodbye."

"You answered the phone," Brianna commented.

"Of course I did. It rang, didn't it?"

The waspish tone of her sister's voice had Brianna's brow arching. "Were you expecting a call?"

"No. Why would you think so?"

"Well, the way you went leaping up, like you were after snatching a child from in front of a car."

Oh, had she? Maggie thought. Had she done that? It was humiliating. "I don't like the damn thing ringing my ears off, that's all. I've got to get to work." With that as a fare-thee-well, she stalked out of the kitchen.

It didn't matter a tinker's damn to her whether he called or not, Maggie told herself. Maybe it had been three weeks since he'd gone back to Dublin, maybe she'd only spoken to him twice in all that time, but it hardly mattered to her. She was much too busy to be bothered chattering over the phone, or entertaining him if he came to see her.

As he'd bloody well said he would, she added silently, and slammed the shop door behind her.

She didn't need Rogan Sweeney's company, or anyone's. She had herself.

Maggie picked up her pipe and went to work.

The Connellys' formal dining room would have reminded Maggie of a set she had seen on the glossy soap opera that had been on television the day her father died. Everything gleamed and sparkled and shone. Wine of the very best vintage glimmered gold in the crystal, shooting rainbows into the facets. Candles, slim and white, added to the elegance of light showered down from the five-tiered chandelier.

The people surrounding the lace-decked table were every bit as polished as the room. Anne, in sapphire silk and her grandmother's diamonds, was the picture of the gracious hostess. Dennis, flushed from the good meal and better company, beamed at his daughter. Patricia looked particularly lovely, and as delicate as the pastel pink and creamy pearls she wore.

Across from her, Rogan sipped at his wine and struggled to keep his mind from wandering west, toward Maggie.

"It's so nice to have a quiet family meal." Anne picked at the miserly portion of pheasant on her plate. The scale had warned her that she'd added two pounds in the last month, and that would never do. "I hope you're not disappointed I didn't invite a party, Rogan."

"Of course not. It's a pleasure, a rare one for me these days, to spend a quiet evening with friends."

"Exactly what I've been telling Dennis," Anne went on. "Why, we've hardly seen you in months. You work much too hard, Rogan."

"A man can't work too hard at something he loves," Dennis put in.

"Ah, you and your man's work." Anne laughed lightly and barely resisted kicking her husband smartly under the table. "Too much business makes a man tense, I say. Especially if he has no wife to soothe him."

Knowing just where this was leading, Patricia did her best to change the subject. "You had a wonderful success with Miss Concannon's showing, Rogan. And I've heard the American Indian art has been very well received."

"Yes, on both counts. The American art is moving to the Cork gallery this week, and Maggie's—Miss Concannon's—moves on to Paris shortly. She's finished some astonishing pieces this past month."

"I've seen a few of them. I believe Joseph covets the globe. The one with all the colors and shapes inside. It's quite fascinating really." Patricia folded her hands in her lap as the dessert course was served. "I wonder how it was done."

"As it happens, I was there when she made it." He remembered the heat, the bleeding colors, the sizzling sparks. "And I still can't explain it to you."

The look in his eyes put Anne on full alert. "Knowing too much about the artistic process can spoil the enjoyment, don't you think? I'm sure it's all routine to Miss Concannon, after all. Patricia, you haven't told us about your little project? How is the day school going?"

"It's coming along nicely, thank you."

"Imagine our little Patricia starting a school." Anne smiled indulgently.

Rogan realized with a guilty start that he hadn't asked Patricia about her pet project in weeks. "Have you found a location, then?"

"Yes, I have. It's a house off Mountjoy Square. The building will require some renovation, of course. I've hired an architect. The grounds are more than suitable, with plenty of space for play areas. I hope to have it ready for children by next spring."

And she could imagine it. The babies and toddlers whose mothers needed a reliable place to leave their children while they worked. The older children who would come after school and before the close of business. It would fill some of the ache, she thought, and the emptiness that throbbed inside her. She and Robert hadn't had children. They had been so sure there was plenty of time. So sure.

"I'm sure Rogan could help you with the business end of it, Patricia," Anne went on. "After all, you've no experience."

"She's my daughter, isn't she?" Dennis interjected with a wink. "She'll do fine."

"I'm sure she will." Again Anne itched to connect her foot with her husband's shin.

She waited until she was in the parlor with her daughter and the men were lingering over glasses of port in the dining room—a custom Anne refused to believe was outdated. She dismissed the maid who had wheeled in coffee, and rounded on her daughter.

"What are you waiting for, Patricia? You're letting the man slip between your fingers."

"Please, don't start this." Already Patricia could feel the dull, insistent throb of a headache in progress.

"You want to be a widow all your life, I suppose." Grim-eyed, Anne added cream to her cup. "I'm telling you it's been time enough."

"You've been telling me that since a year after Robbie died."

"And it's no more than the truth." Anne sighed. She'd hated to watch her daughter grieve, had wept long and hard herself, not only over the loss of the son-in-law she'd loved, but for the pain she'd been unable to erase from Patricia's eyes. "Darling, as much as we all wish it wasn't so, Robert's gone."

"I know that. I've accepted it and I'm trying to move on."

"By starting a day-care service for other people's children?"

"Yes, in part. I'm doing that for myself, Mother. Because I need work, the satisfaction of it."

"I've finished trying to talk you out of that." In a

gesture of peace, Anne raised her hands. "And if it's what you want, truly, than it's what I want as well."

"Thank you for that." Patricia's face softened as she leaned over to kiss her mother's cheek. "I know that you only want the best for me."

"I do. Which is exactly why I want Rogan for you. No, don't close up on me, girl. You can't tell me you don't want him as well."

"I care for him," Patricia said carefully. "Very much. I always have."

"And he for you. But you're standing back, all too patiently, and waiting for him to take the next step. And while you're waiting he's becoming distracted. A blind woman could see that he's interested in more than that Concannon woman's art. And she's not the type to wait," Anne added with a wag of the finger. "Oh, no, indeed. She'll see a man of Rogan's background and means and snap him up before he can blink."

"I very much doubt Rogan can be snapped up," Patricia said dryly. "He knows his own mind."

"In most areas," Anne agreed. "But men need to be guided, Patricia. Allured. You haven't set yourself out to allure Rogan Sweeney. You've got to make him see you as a woman, not as his friend's widow. You want him, don't you?"

"I think—"

"Of course you do. Now see to it that he wants you, too."

Patricia said little when Rogan drove her home. Home to the house she'd shared with Robert, the house she couldn't give up. She no longer walked into a room expecting to find him waiting for her, or suffered those silvery slashes of pain at odd moments when she suddenly remembered their life together.

It was simply a house that held good memories.

But did she want to live in it alone for the rest of her life? Did she want to spend her days caring for other women's children while there were none of her own to brighten her life?

If her mother was right and Rogan was what she wanted, then what was wrong with a little allure.

"Won't you come in for a while?" she asked when he walked her to the door. "It's early still, and I'm restless."

He thought of his own empty house, and the hours before the workday began. "If you'll promise me a brandy."

"On the terrace," she agreed, and walked inside.

The house reflected the quiet elegance and faultless taste of its mistress. Though he'd always felt completely at home there, Rogan thought of Maggie's cluttered cottage and narrow rumpled bed.

Even the brandy snifter reminded him of Maggie. He thought of the way she'd smashed one against the hearth in a rage of passion. And of the package that had come days later, holding the one she'd made to replace it.

"It's a lovely night," Patricia said, and snagged his wandering attention.

"What? Oh, yes. Yes, it is." He swirled the brandy, but didn't drink.

A crescent moon rode the sky, misted by clouds, then glowing white and thin as the breeze nudged them clear. The air was warm and fragrant, disturbed only by the muffled sound of traffic beyond the hedges.

"Tell me more about the school," he began. "What architect have you chosen?" She named a firm he approved of. "They do good work. We've used them ourselves."

"I know. Joseph recommended them. He's been wonderfully helpful, though I feel guilty taking his mind off his work."

"He's well able to do a half-dozen things at once."

"He never seems to mind my dropping into the gallery." Testing him, herself, Patricia moved closer. "I've missed you."

"Things have been hectic." He tucked her hair behind her ear, an old gesture, an old habit he wasn't even aware of. "We'll have to make some time. We haven't been to the theater in weeks, have we?"

"No." She caught his hand, held it. "But I'm glad we have time now. Alone."

A warning signal sounded in his head. He dismissed it as ridiculous and smiled at her. "We'll make more. Why don't I come by that property you've bought, look it over for you?"

"You know I value your opinion." Her heart beat light, quick, in her chest. "I value you."

Before she could change her mind, she leaned forward and pressed her mouth to his. If there had been alarm in his eyes, she refused to see it.

No sweet, platonic kiss this time. Patricia curled her fingers into his hair and poured herself into it. She wanted, desperately wanted, to feel something again.

But his arms didn't come around her. His lips didn't heat. He stood, still as a statue. It wasn't pleasure, nor was it desire that trembled between them. It was the chilly air of shock.

She drew back, saw the astonishment and, worse, much worse, the regret in his eyes. Stung, she whirled away.

Rogan set his untouched brandy down. "Patricia."

"Don't." She squeezed her eyes tight. "Don't say anything."

"Of course I will. I have to." His hands hesitated over her shoulders and finally settled gently. "Patricia, you know how much I . . ." What words were there? he thought frantically. What possible words? "I care about you," he said, and hated himself.

"Leave it at that." She gripped her hands together until her fingers ached. "I'm humiliated enough."

"I never thought—" He cursed himself again and, because he felt so miserable, cursed Maggie for being right. "Patty," he said helplessly. "I'm sorry."

"I'm sure you are." Her voice was cool again, despite his use of her old nickname. "And so am I, for putting you in such an awkward position."

"It's my fault. I should have understood."

"Why should you?" Chilled, she stepped away from his hands, made herself turn. In the dappled starlight, her face was fragile as glass, her eyes as blank. "I'm always there, aren't I? Dropping by, available for whatever evening you might have free. Poor Patricia, at such loose ends, dreaming up her little projects to keep herself busy. The young widow who's content with a pat on the head and an indulgent smile."

"That's not at all true. It's not the way I feel."

"I don't know how you feel." Her voice rose, cracked, alarming them both. "I don't know how I feel. I only know I want you to go, before we say things that would embarrass us both more than we already are."

"I can't leave you this way. Please come inside, sit down. We'll talk."

No, she thought, she would weep and complete her mortification. "I mean it, Rogan," she said flatly. "I want you to go. There's nothing for either of us to say but good night. You know the way out." She swept past him, into the house.

Damn all women, Rogan thought as he strode into the gallery the following afternoon. Damn them for their uncanny ability to make a man feel guilty and needy and idiotic.

He'd lost a friend, one who was very dear to him. Lost her, he thought, because he'd been blind to her feelings. Feelings, he remembered with growing resentment, that Maggie had seen and understood in the blink of an eye.

He stalked up the stairs, furious with himself. Why was it he had no idea how to handle two of the women who meant so much to him?

He'd broken Patricia's heart, carelessly. And Maggie, God cursed her, had the power to break his.

Did people never fall in love with anyone who was eager to return it?

Well, he wouldn't be fool enough to toss his feelings at Maggie's feet and have her crush them. Not now. Not after he'd inadvertently done some crushing of his own. He could get along very well on his own, thank you.

He stepped into the first sitting room and scowled. They'd put a few more pieces of her work on display. A mere glimpse of what would be toured over the next twelve months. The globe she'd created in front of his eyes gleamed back at him, seeming to contain all the dreams she'd claimed were held inside, dreams that now mocked at him as he stared into its depths.

It was just as well she hadn't answered the phone when he'd called the night before. Perhaps he'd needed her at that moment while the miserable guilt over Patricia had clawed at him. He'd needed to hear her voice, to soothe himself with it. Instead he'd heard his own, clipped and precise on the answering machine. She'd refused to make the recording herself.

So instead of a quiet, perhaps intimate late-night conversation, he'd left a terse message that would, no doubt, annoy Maggie as much as it annoyed him.

God, he wanted her.

"Ah, just the man I wanted to see." Cheerful as a robin, Joseph popped into the room. "I've sold *Carlotta.*" Joseph's self-satisfied smile faded into curiosity when Rogan turned. "Bad day, is it?"

"I've had better. *Carlotta,* you say? To whom?"

"To an American tourist who strolled in this morning. She was absolutely enthralled by *Carlotta.* We're having her shipped—the painting, that is—to someplace called Tucson."

Joseph sat on the corner of the love seat and lighted a celebratory cigarette. "The American claimed that she adores primitive nudes, and our *Carlotta* was certainly primitive. I'm quite fond of nudes myself, but Carlotta was never my type. Too heavy at the hip—and the brush strokes. Well, the artist lacked subtlety, shall we say."

"It was an excellent oil," Rogan said absently.

"Of its type. Since I prefer something a bit less obvious, I won't be sorry to ship *Carlotta* off to Tucson." He pulled a little flip-top ashtray out of his pocket and tapped his cigarette in it. "Oh, and that watercolor series, from the Scotsman? Arrived an hour ago. It's beautiful work, Rogan. I think you've discovered another star."

"Blind luck. If I hadn't been checking on the factory in Inverness, I never would have seen the paintings."

"A street artist." Joseph shook his head. "Well, not for long, I can guarantee that. There's a wonderfully mystical quality to the work, rather fragile and austere." His tooth flashed in a grin. "And a nude as well, to make up for the loss of *Carlotta*. More to my taste, I'll have to say. She's elegant, rather delicate and just a bit sad-eyed. I fell hopelessly in love."

He broke off, flushing a little around the collar as he saw Patricia in the doorway. His heart trembled hopelessly. Out of your reach, boy-o, he reminded himself. Way out of your reach. His smile was dashing as he rose.

"Hello, Patricia. How lovely to see you."

Rogan turned, decided he should be flogged for putting those shadows under her eyes.

"Hello, Joseph. I hope I'm not disturbing you."

"Not at all. Beauty is always welcome here." He took her hand, kissed it, and called himself an idiot. "Would you like tea?"

"No, don't trouble."

"It's no problem, no problem at all. It's near to closing."

"I know. I'd hoped . . ." Patricia braced herself.

"Joseph, would you mind? I need to have a moment alone with Rogan."

"Of course not." Fool. Dolt. Imbecile. "I'll just go on down. I'll put the kettle on if you change your mind."

"Thank you." She waited until he'd gone, then shut the door. "I hope you don't mind my coming, since it's so near closing."

"No, of course not." Rogan wasn't prepared, again, he discovered, to handle himself. "I'm glad you came."

"No, you're not." She smiled a little as she said it, to ease the sting. "You're standing there, frantically trying to think of what to say, how to behave. I've known you too long, Rogan. Can we sit?"

"Yes, of course." He started to offer a hand, then let it fall back to his side. Patricia lifted a brow at the movement. She sat, folded her hands in her lap. "I've come to apologize."

Now his distress was complete. "Please, don't. There's no need."

"There's every need. You'll do me the courtesy of hearing me out."

"Patty." He sat as well, felt his stomach lurch. "I've made you cry." It was all too obvious now that they were close. However careful her makeup, he could see the signs.

"Yes, you did. And after I'd finished crying, I began to think. For myself." She sighed. "I've had much too little practice thinking for myself, Rogan. Mother and Daddy took such close care of me. And they had such expectations. I was always afraid I couldn't meet them."

"That's absurd—"

"I've asked you to hear me out," she said in a tone that had him staring in surprise. "And you will. You were always there, from the time I was what— fourteen, fifteen? And then there was Robbie. I was so in love there was no need to think, no room for it. It was all him, and putting the house together, making a home. When I lost him, I thought I would die, too. God knows I wanted to."

There was nothing else Rogan could do but take her hand. "I loved him, too."

"I know you did. And it was you who got me through it. You who helped me grieve, then move past the grieving. I could talk about Robbie with you, and laugh or cry. You've been the best of friends to me, so it was natural that I'd love you. If seemed sensible for me to wait until you began to see me as a woman instead of an old friend. Then, wouldn't it be natural enough for you to fall in love with me, ask me to marry you?"

His fingers moved restlessly under hers. "If I'd paid closer attention—"

"You'd have still seen nothing I didn't wish you to see," she finished. "For reasons I'd rather not discuss, I decided I'd take the next step myself, last night. When I kissed you, I expected to feel, oh, stardust and moonbeams. I threw myself into kissing you, expecting it to be everything I'd been waiting for, all those wonderful, terrifying tugs and pulls. I wanted so much to feel them again. But I didn't."

"Patricia, it's not that I—" He broke off, eyes narrowing. "I beg your pardon?"

She laughed, confusing him all the more. "When I'd finished my well-deserved bout of weeping, I thought through the whole episode. It wasn't just you who was taken by surprise, Rogan. I realized I'd felt nothing at all when I'd kissed you."

"Nothing at all," he repeated after a moment.

"Nothing more than embarrassment for having put us both in such a potentially dreadful situation. It came to me that while I love you dearly, I'm not in love with you at all. I was simply kissing my closest friend."

"I see." It was ridiculous to feel as though his manhood had been impugned. But he was, after all, a man. "That's lucky, isn't it?"

She did know him well. Laughing, she pressed his hand to her cheek. "Now I've insulted you."

"No, you haven't. I'm relieved we've sorted this out." Her bland look had him cursing. "All right, damn it, you have insulted me. Or at least nicked my masculine pride." He grinned back at her. "Friends, then?"

"Always." She let out a long breath. "I can't tell you how relieved I am that *that's* over. You know, I think I'll take Joseph up on that tea. Can you join us?"

"Sorry. We've just gotten in a shipment from Inverness I want to look over."

She rose. "You know, I have to agree with Mother on one thing. You're working too hard, Rogan. It's beginning to show. You need a few days to relax."

"In a month or two."

Shaking her head, she leaned down to kiss him. "You always say that. I wish I thought you meant it this time." She tilted her head, smiled. "I believe your villa in the south of France is an excellent place not only to relax, but for creative inspiration. The colors and the textures would undoubtedly appeal to an artist."

He opened his mouth, closed it again. "You do know me too well," he murmured.

"I do. Give it some thought." She left him brooding and went down to the kitchen. Since Joseph was in the main gallery with a few lingering clients, she began to brew the tea herself.

Joseph came in just as she was pouring the first cup. "I'm sorry," he said. "They wouldn't be hurried along, nor could they be seduced into parting with a single pound. Here I thought I'd end the day by selling that copper sculpture. You know, the one that looks a bit like a holly shrub, but they got away from me."

"Have some tea and console yourself."

"I will, thanks. Have you—" He stopped when she turned to him and he saw her face in the full light. "What is it? What's wrong?"

"Why, nothing." She brought the cups to the table, nearly dropping them both when he caught her by the arms.

"You've been crying," he said in a tight voice. "And there're shadows under your eyes."

On an impatient breath she set the jostling cups down. "Why are cosmetics so damn expensive if they don't do the job? A woman can't indulge herself in a good weeping spell if she can't depend on her powder." She started to sit, but his hands remained firm on her shoulders. Surprised, she looked up at him. What she saw in his eyes had her fumbling. "It's nothing—really nothing. Just some foolishness. I'm . . . I'm fine now."

He didn't think. He'd held her before, of course. They'd danced together. But there was no music now. Only her. Slowly, he lifted a hand, brushed a thumb gently over the faint smudges under her eyes. "You still miss him. Robbie."

"Yes. I always will." But her husband's face, so well loved, blurred. She saw only Joseph. "I wasn't crying for Robbie. Not really. I'm not sure exactly what I was crying for."

She was so lovely, he thought. Her eyes so soft and confused. And her skin—he'd never dared touch her like this before—was like silk. "You mustn't cry, Patty," he heard himself say. Then he was kissing her, his mouth homing to hers like an arrow, his hand scooping up into that soft swing of hair.

He lost himself, drowning in the scent of her, aching at the way her lips parted in surprise to allow him one long, full-bodied taste of her.

Her body gave to his, a delicate sway of fragility that aroused unbearable and conflicting needs. To take, to protect, to comfort and to possess.

It was her sigh, part shock, part wonder, that snapped him back like a faceful of ice water.

"I—I beg your pardon." He fumbled over the words, then went rigid with regret when she only stared at him. Emotions churned sickly inside of him as he stepped back. "That was inexcusable."

He turned on his heel and walked away before her head stopped spinning.

She took one step after him, his name on her lips. Then she stopped, pressed her hand to her racing heart and let her shaking legs buckle her into a chair.

Joseph? Her hand crept up from her breast to her flushed cheek. Joseph, she thought again, staggered. Why, it was ridiculous. They were no more than casual friends who shared an affection for Rogan and for art. He was . . . well, the closest thing she knew to a bohemian, she decided. Charming, certainly, as every woman who walked into the gallery would attest.

And it had only been a kiss. Just a kiss, she told herself as she reached for her cup. But her hand trembled and spilled tea onto the table.

A kiss, she realized with a jolt, that had given her those moonbeams, the stardust, and all the wonderful and terrifying tugs and pulls she had hoped for.

Joseph, she thought again, and raced out of the kitchen to find him.

She caught a glimpse of him outside and darted past Rogan with barely a word.

"Joseph!"

He stopped, swore. Here it was, he thought bitterly. She'd slap him down good and proper, and—since he hadn't made a quick enough exit—in public as well. Resigned to facing the music, he turned, tossed his streaming hair back over his shoulder.

She skidded to a halt inches in front of him. "I—" She completely forgot what she'd hoped to say.

"You've every right to be angry," he told her. "It hardly matters that I never meant—that is, I'd only wanted to . . . Goddamn it, what do you expect? You come in looking so sad and beautiful. So lost. I forgot myself, and I've apologized for it."

She had been feeling lost, she realized. She wondered if he would understand what it was like to know just where you were, and to believe you knew where you were going, but to be lost just the same. She thought he might.

"Will you have dinner with me?"

He blinked, stepped back. Stared. "What?"

"Will you have dinner with me?" she repeated. She felt giddy, almost reckless. "Tonight. Now."

"You want to have dinner?" He spoke slowly, spacing each word. "With me? Tonight?"

He looked so baffled, so leery, that she laughed. "Yes. Actually, no, that isn't what I want at all."

"All right, then." He nodded stiffly and headed down the street.

"I don't want dinner," she called out, loudly enough to have heads turn. Almost reckless? she thought. Oh, no, completely reckless. "I want you to kiss me again."

That stopped him. He turned back, ignored the wink and encouraging word from a man in a flowered shirt. Like a blind man feeling his way, he walked toward her. "I'm not sure I caught that."

"Then I'll speak plainly." She swallowed a foolish bubble of pride. "I want you to take me home with you, Joseph. And I want you to kiss me again. And unless I've very much mistaken what we're both feeling, I want you to make love with me." She took the last step toward him. "Did you understand that, and is it agreeable to you?"

"Agreeable?" He took her face in his hands, stared hard into her eyes. "You've lost your mind. Thank God." He laughed and swooped her against him. "Oh, it's more than agreeable, Patty darling. Much more."

❧ Chapter Fourteen

MAGGIE dozed off at her kitchen table, her head on her folded arms.

Moving day had been sheer hell.

Her mother had complained constantly, relentlessly, about everything from the steady fall of rain to the curtains Brianna had hung at the wide front window of the new house. But it was worth the misery of the day to see Maeve at last settled in her own place. Maggie had kept her word, and Brianna was free.

Still, Maggie hadn't expected the wave of guilt that swamped her when Maeve had wept—her back bent, her face buried in her hands and the hot fast tears leaking through her fingers. No, she hadn't expected to feel guilty, or to feel so miserably sorry for the woman who'd barely finished cursing her before she collapsed into sobs.

In the end it was Lottie, with her brisk, unflappable cheerfulness who had taken control. She scooted both Brianna and Maggie out of the house, telling them not to worry, no, not to worry a bit, as the tears were as natural as the rain. And what a lovely place it was, she'd gone on to say, all the while nudging and pushing them along. Like a dollhouse and just as tidy. They'd be fine. They'd be cozy as cats.

She'd all but shoved them into Maggie's lorry.

So it was done, and it was right. But there would be no opening of champagne bottles that night.

Maggie had downed one bracing whiskey and simply folded into a heap of exhausted emotions at the table while the rain drummed on the roof and dusk deepened the gloom.

The phone didn't awaken her. It rang demandingly while she dozed. But Rogan's voice stabbed through the fatigue and had her jolting up, shaking off sleep.

"I'll expect to hear from you by morning, as I've neither the time nor the patience to come fetch you myself."

"What?" Groggy, she blinked like an owl and stared around the darkened room. Why, she'd have sworn he'd been right there, badgering her.

Annoyed that her nap had been interrupted, and that the interruption reminded her she was hungry and there was no more to eat in the house than would satisfy a bird, she pushed away from the table.

She'd go down to Brie's, she decided. Raid her kitchen. Perhaps they could cheer each other up. She was reaching for a cap when she saw the impatient red blip on the answering machine.

"Bloody nuisance," she muttered, but stabbed the buttons until the tape rewound, then played.

"Maggie." Again, Rogan's voice filled the room. It made her smile as she realized he had been the one to wake her after all. "Why the devil don't you ever answer this thing? It's noon. I want you to call the moment you come in from your studio. I mean it.

There's something I need to discuss with you. So—I miss you. Damn you, Maggie, I miss you."

The message clicked off, and before she could feel too smug about it, another began.

"Do you think I've nothing better to do than spend my time talking to this blasted machine?"

"I don't," she answered back, "but you're the one who put it here."

"It's half four now, and I need to go by the gallery. Perhaps I didn't make myself clear. I need to speak with you, today. I'll be at the gallery until six, then you can reach me at home. I don't give a damn how wrapped up you are in your work. Damn you for being so far away."

"The man spends more time damning me than anything else," she muttered. "And you're just as far away from me as I am from you, Sweeney."

As if in answer, his voice came again. "You irresponsible, idiotic, insensitive brat. Am I supposed to worry now that you've blown yourself up with your chemicals and set your hair on fire? Thanks to your sister, who does answer her phone, I know perfectly well you're there. It's nearly eight, and I have a dinner meeting. Now you listen to me, Margaret Mary. Get yourself to Dublin, and bring your passport. I won't waste my time explaining why, just do as you're told. If you can't arrange a flight, I'll send the plane for you. I expect to hear from you by morning, as I've neither the time nor the patience to fetch you myself."

"*Fetch me?* As if you could." She stood for a moment, scowling at the machine. So she was supposed to get herself to Dublin, was she? Just because he demanded it. Never a please or a will you, just do what you're told.

Ice would flow in hell before she'd give him the satisfaction.

Forgetting her hunger, she stormed from the room and up the stairs. Get herself to Dublin, she fumed. The nerve of the man, ordering her about.

She yanked the suitcase out of her closet and heaved it onto the bed.

Did he think she was so eager to see him that she'd drop everything and scramble off to do his bidding? He was going to find out differently. Oh, yes, she decided as she tossed clothes into the case. She was going to tell him differently, in person. Face-to-face.

She doubted he'd thank her for it.

"Eileen, I'll need Limerick to fax me those adjusted figures before the end of the day." Behind his desk, Rogan checked off a line of his list, rubbed at the tension at the base of his neck. "And I'll want to see the report on the construction there the moment it comes in."

"It was promised by noon." Eileen, a trim brunette who managed the office as skillfully as she did her husband and three children, jotted a note. "You've a two o'clock meeting with Mr. Greenwald. That's *re* the changes in the London catalog."

"Yes, I've got that. He'll want martinis."

"Vodka," Eileen said. "Two olives. Should I see about a cheese tray to keep him from staggering out?"

"You'd better." Rogan drummed his fingers on the desk. "Has there been no call from Clare?"

"None this morning." She shot a quick, interested

look from under her lashes. "I'll be sure to let you know the moment Miss Concannon calls."

He made a sound, the vocal equivalent of a shrug. "Go ahead and put that call through to Rome if you will."

"Right away. Oh, and I have that draft of the letter to Inverness on my desk if you want to approve it."

"Fine. And we'd best send a wire to Boston. What's the time there?" He started to check his watch when a blur of color in the doorway stopped him. "Maggie."

"Aye. Maggie." She tossed her suitcase down with a thud and fisted her hands on her hips. "I've a few choice words for you, Mr. Sweeney." She bit down on her temper long enough to nod at the woman rising from the chair in front of Rogan's desk. "You'd be Eileen?"

"Yes. It's a pleasure to meet you at last, Miss Concannon."

"It's nice of you to say so. I must say you look remarkably well for a woman who works for a tyrant." Her voice rose on the last word.

Eileen's lips twitched. She cleared her throat, closed her steno pad. "It's nice of you to say so. Is there anything else, Mr. Sweeney?"

"No. Hold my calls please."

"Yes, sir." Eileen walked out, closing the door discreetly behind her.

"So." Rogan leaned back in his chair, tapped his pen against his palm. "You got my message."

"I got it."

She walked across the room. No, Rogan thought, she swaggered across it, hands still fisted on hips, eyes flashing.

He wasn't ashamed to admit that his mouth watered at the sight of her.

"Who in this wide world do you think you are?" She slapped her palms on his desk, rattling pens. "I signed my work to you, Rogan Sweeney, and aye, I slept with you—to my undying regret. But none of it gives you the right to order me about or swear at me every five minutes."

"I haven't spoken to you in days," he reminded her. "So how can I have sworn at you?"

"Over your hideous machine—which I tossed into the garbage this very morning."

Very calmly, he made a note on a pad.

"Don't start that."

"I'm merely noting down that you need a replacement for your answering machine. You had no trouble getting a flight in, I see."

"No trouble? You've been nothing but trouble to me since the moment you walked into my glass house. Nothing but. You think you can just take over everything, not just my work—which is bad enough—but me as well. I'm here to tell you that you can't. I won't—where in the hell are you going? I haven't finished."

"I never thought you had." He continued to the door, locked it, turned back.

"Unlock that door."

"No."

The fact that he was smiling as he came back toward her didn't help her nerves. "Don't you put your hands on me."

"I'm about to. In fact, I'm about to do something I haven't done in the twelve years I've worked in this office."

Her heart began a fast hard tattoo in her throat. "You are not."

So, he thought, he'd finally shocked her. He watched her gaze slide to the door, then made his grab. "You can rage at me once I've finished with you."

"Finished with me?" Even as she took a swing at him he was crushing his mouth to hers. "Get off me, you ham-handed brute."

"You like my hands." And he used them to tug her sweater up. "You told me so."

"That's a lie. I won't have this, Rogan." But the denial ended in a moan as his lips skimmed hot over her throat. Then, "I'll shout down the roof," once she got her breath back.

"Go ahead." He bit her, none too gently. "I like it when you shout."

"Curse you," she muttered, and went willingly when he lowered her to the floor.

It was fast and hot, a frantic coupling that was over almost as soon as it had begun. But the speed didn't diminish the power. They lay tangled together a moment longer, limbs vibrating. Rogan turned his head to press a kiss to her jaw.

"Nice of you to drop by, Maggie."

She summoned up the strength to bounce her fist off his shoulder. "Get off of me, you brute." She would have shoved him, but he was already shifting, drawing her with him until she was straddled across his lap.

"Better?"

"Than what?" She grinned, then remembered she was furious with him. Pushing away, she sat on the rug and tidied her clothes. "You've a nerve, you do, Rogan Sweeney."

"Because I dragged you to the floor?"

"No." She snapped her jeans. "It'd be foolish to say that when it's obvious I enjoyed it."

"Very obvious."

She sent him a steely look as he rose and offered her a hand.

"That's neither here nor there. Who do you think you are, ordering me about, telling me what to do without a will you or a won't you?"

He bent down and pulled her to her feet. "You're here, aren't you?"

"I'm here, you swine, to tell you that I won't tolerate it. Here it's been nearly a month since you walked away from my door whistling, and—"

"You missed me."

She hissed at him. "I did not. I have more than enough to keep my time filled. Oh, straighten that silly tie. You look like a drunkard."

He obliged her. "You missed me, Margaret Mary, though you never bothered to say so whenever I managed to reach you by phone."

"I can't talk on the phone. How am I supposed to say anything to someone I can't see? And you're evading the issue."

"What is the issue?" He leaned back comfortably against his desk.

"I won't be given orders. I'm not one of your servants or one of your staff, so get that through your head. Mark it down in that fancy leather notebook of yours if you need reminding. But don't you ever tell me what to do again." She let out a short, satisfied breath. "Now that I've made that clear, I'll be on my way."

"Maggie. If you'd no intention to stay, why did you pack a suitcase?"

He had her there. Patiently he waited while annoyance, dismay and confusion flitted across her face.

"Maybe I've a mind to stay in Dublin for a day or two. I can come and go as I please, can't I?"

"Mmm. Did you bring your passport?"

She eyed him warily. "And what if I did?"

"Good." He circled around his desk, sat. "It'll save time. I thought you might have been stubborn and left it at home. It would have been a nuisance to go back and get it." He leaned back, smiling. "Why don't you sit down? Shall I ask Eileen to bring in some tea?"

"I don't want to sit, and I don't want tea." Folding her arms, she turned away from him and stared hard at the Georgia O'Keeffe on the wall. "Why didn't you come back?"

"There were a couple of reasons. One, I've been swamped here. I had several matters I wanted to clear up so I'd have a block of free time. Second, I wanted to stay away from you for a while."

"Oh, did you?" She kept her eyes trained on the bold colors. "Did you now?"

"Because I didn't want to admit how much I wanted to be with you." He waited, shook his head. "No response to that, I see. No I-wanted-to-be-with-you-as-well?"

"I did. Not that I don't have a life of my own. But there were odd moments when I would have liked your company."

And he would, it seemed, have to settle for that. "You're about to get it. Would you sit now, Maggie? There are some things we need to discuss."

"All right, then." She turned back, sat in front of his desk. He looked perfect there, she thought. Dignified, competent, in charge. Not at all like a man who would have indulged in a wild tussle on the office rug. The idea made her smile.

"What?"

"I was just wondering what your secretary might be thinking out there."

He lifted a brow. "I'm sure she assumes we're having a civilized business discussion."

"Hah! She looked like a sensible woman to me, but you go right on believing that." Pleased by the way his eyes flickered to the door, she propped her ankle on her knee. "So, what business are we about to discuss?"

"Ah—your work over the last few weeks has been exceptional. As you know, we held back ten pieces from the first showing with the purpose of touring them over the next year. I would like to keep a few of your newest pieces in Dublin, but the rest is already on its way to Paris."

"So your very efficient and very sensible Eileen told me." She began to tap her fingers on her ankle. "You didn't call me all the way to Dublin to tell me again—nor do I think you called me here for a spot of hot sex on the office rug."

"No, I didn't. I would have preferred discussing the plans with you over the phone, but you never bothered to return my calls."

"I was out a good deal of the time. You may have

exclusive rights to my work, but not to me, Rogan. I do have my own life, as I've already explained."

"A number of times." He could feel the temper seeping back into him. "I'm not interfering with your life. I'm managing your career. And to that purpose, I'll be traveling to Paris to oversee the display, and the showing."

Paris. She'd barely had an hour with him and he was already talking about leaving. Distressed by her own plummeting heart, she spoke crisply. "'Tis a wonder you keep your business thriving, Rogan. I'd think you'd be hiring people capable of handling details like that without you feeling the need to peek over their shoulders."

"I assure you, I have very competent people. As it happens, I have a vested interest in your work, and I want to handle those details myself. I want it done right."

"Which means you want it done your way."

"Precisely. And I want you to come with me."

The sarcastic little comment that had sprung to her lips slipped off. "With you? To Paris?"

"I realize you have some artistic or possibly moral objection to promoting your own work, but you did well enough at the Dublin show. It would be advantageous to have you appear, however briefly, at your first international show."

"My first international show," she repeated, dumbfounded as the phrase sank into her head. "I don't—I don't speak French."

"That won't be a problem. You'll have a look at the Paris gallery, dispense a bit of charm and have plenty of time to see the sights." He waited for her answer, received nothing but a blank stare. "Well?"

"When?"

"Tomorrow."

"Tomorrow." The first skitter of panic had her pressing a hand to her stomach. "You want me to go with you to Paris tomorrow?"

"Unless you've some pressing previous engagement."

"I don't, no."

"Then it's settled." The relief was almost brutal. "After we've satisfied ourselves that the Paris show is successful, I'd like you to go south with me."

"South?"

"I've a villa on the Mediterranean. I want to be alone with you, Maggie. No distractions, no interruptions. Just you."

Her eyes lifted to his. "The block of time you've been working on for these weeks?"

"Yes."

"I wouldn't have shouted at you if you'd explained it to me."

"I had to explain it to myself first. Will you come?"

"Yes, I'll come with you." She smiled. "You'd only to ask."

An hour later she burst into the gallery, only to stop and simmer with frustration as she waited for Joseph to finish with a client. While he charmed a woman old enough to be his mother, Maggie wandered around the main room, noting that the American Indian display had been replaced by a selection of metal sculptures. Intrigued by the shapes, she lost her sense of urgency in admiration.

"A German artist," Joseph said from behind her.

"This particular work is, I feel, both visceral and joyous. A celebration of elemental forces."

"Earth, fire, water, the suggestion of wind in the feathering of the copper." She put on an airy accent to match his. "Powerful indeed in scope, but with an underlying mischief that suggests satire."

"And it can be yours for a mere two thousand pounds."

"A bargain. A pity I'm without a farthing to me name." She turned, laughing, and kissed him. "You're looking fit, Joseph. How many hearts have you broken since I left you?"

"Nary a one. Since mine belongs to you."

"Hah! A good thing for us both that I know you're full of blarney. Have you a minute to spare?"

"For you, days. Weeks." He kissed her hand. "Years."

"A minute will do me. Joseph, what do I need for Paris?"

"A tight black sweater, a short skirt and very high heels."

"That'll be the day. Really, I'm to go, and I haven't a clue what I'll need. I tried to reach Mrs. Sweeney, but she's out today."

"So I'm your second choice. You devastate me." He signaled to one of his staff to take the room. "All you need for Paris, Maggie, is a romantic heart."

"Where can I buy one?"

"You have your own. You can't hide it from me, I've seen your work."

She grimaced, then slipped her arm through his. "Listen now, I'd not admit this to just anyone, but I've never traveled. In Venice I only had to worry about learning and not wearing anything that would catch fire. And paying the rent. If I'm going to have a trip to Paris, I don't want to make a fool of myself."

"You won't. You'll be going with Rogan, I take it, and he knows Paris as well as a native. You've only to act a bit arrogant, a bit bored, and you'll fit right in."

"I've come to you for fashion advice. Oh, it's humiliating to say it, but I can't go looking like this. Not that I want to paint myself up like a mannequin, but I don't want to look like Rogan's country cousin either."

"Hmm." Joseph took the question seriously, drawing her back to arm's length for a slow, careful study. "You'd do just fine as you are, but . . ."

"But?"

"Buy yourself a silk blouse, very tailored, but soft. Vivid colors, my girl, no pastels for you. Slacks of the same type. Use your eye for color. Go for the clash. And that short skirt is a must. You've got that black dress?"

"I didn't bring it with me."

He clucked his tongue like a maiden aunt. "You should always be prepared. All right, that's out, so go for glitter this time. Something that dazzles the eye." He tapped the sculpture beside them. "These metal tones would suit you. Don't go for classic, go for bold." Pleased with the thought, he nodded. "How's that?"

"Confusing. I'm ashamed to find it matters to me."

"There's nothing shameful about it. It's simply a matter of presentation."

"That may be, but I'd be grateful to you if you didn't mention this to Rogan."

"Consider me your confessor, darling." He looked

over her shoulder, and Maggie saw joy leap into his eyes.

Patricia came in, hesitated, then crossed the glossy tiles. "Hello, Maggie. I didn't know you were coming to Dublin."

"Neither did I." What change was this? Maggie wondered. Gone was the shadowed sadness, the fragile reserve. It only took a moment, seeing the way Patricia's eyes lighted on Joseph's, to give her the answer. Aha, she thought. So there's where the wind blows.

"I'm sorry to interrupt. I just wanted to tell Joseph . . ." Patricia sputtered to a halt. "Ah, that is, I was passing by and remembered the business we'd discussed. The seven o'clock appointment?"

"Yes." Joseph dipped his hands into his pockets to keep them from reaching for her. "Seven o'clock."

"I'm afraid I have to make it seven-thirty. I've a bit of a conflict. I wanted to be sure that wouldn't upset the schedule."

"I'll adjust it."

"Good. That's good." She stood for a moment, staring foolishly at him before she remembered Maggie and her manners. "Will you be in town long?"

"No, actually, I'm leaving tomorrow." The way the air was sizzling, Maggie thought, it was a wonder the sculptures didn't melt. "In fact, I'm leaving now."

"Oh, no, please, don't run off on my account. I've got to go." Patricia sent one more longing look in Joseph's direction. "I've people waiting for me. I just wanted to—well, goodbye."

Maggie waited one beat. "Are you just going to

stand here?" she hissed at Joseph as Patricia headed for the door.

"Hmm? What? Excuse me." He made the dash to the door in two seconds flat. She watched Patricia turn, blush, smile. Then they were in each other's arms.

The romantic heart Maggie refused to believe she had, swelled. She waited until Patricia hurried out and Joseph stood staring after her like a man recently struck by lighting.

"So your heart belongs to me, does it?"

The dazed look cleared from his eyes. "She's beautiful, isn't she?"

"There's no denying it."

"I've been in love with her so long, even before she married Robbie. I never thought, never believed . . ." He laughed a little, still dazzled by love. "I thought it was Rogan."

"So did I. It's plain to see you make her happy." She kissed his cheek. "I'm glad for you."

"It's—we're trying to keep it between us. At least until . . . for a while. Her family . . . I can guarantee her mother won't approve of me."

"The hell with her mother."

"Patricia said nearly the same thing." It brought a smile to his lips to remember it. "But I'll not be the cause of any trouble there. So I'd appreciate it if you'd say nothing."

"Not to Rogan either?"

"I work for him, Maggie. He's a friend, yes, but I work for him. Patricia's the widow of one of his oldest friends, a woman he's escorted himself. A great many people thought she'd become his wife."

"I don't believe Rogan was among them."

"Be that as it may, I'd rather tell him myself when the time's right."

"It's your business, Joseph. Yours and Patricia's. So we'll trade confession for confession."

"I'm grateful to you."

"No need. If Rogan's stiff-necked enough to disapprove, he deserves to be fooled."

🍂 Chapter Fifteen

PARIS was hot, muggy and crowded. The traffic was abominable. Cars, buses, motorbikes screeched and swerved and sped, their drivers seemingly bent on challenging each other to endless roadway duels. Along the sidewalks, people strolled and swaggered in a colorful pedestrian parade. Women in those short skirts Joseph seemed so fond of looked lean and bored and impossibly chic. Men, equally fashionable, watched them from little café tables where they sipped red wine or strong black coffee.

Flowers bloomed everywhere—roses, gladiolus, marigolds, snapdragons, begonias tumbling out of vendors' stalls, sunning on banks, spilling out of the arms of young girls whose legs flashed bright as blades in the sunshine.

Boys skated by with yards of golden bread spearing up out of bags. Packs of tourists aimed cameras like so many shotguns to blast away at their shutter view of Paris life.

And there were dogs. The city seemed a veritable den of them, prancing on leashes, skulking in alleyways, darting by shops. Even the lowliest cur appeared exotic, wonderfully foreign and arrogantly French.

Maggie took it all in from her window overlooking the Place de la Concorde.

She was in Paris. The air was full of sound and scent and gaudy light. And her lover was sleeping like a stone in the bed behind her.

Or so she thought.

He'd been watching her watch Paris for some time. She leaned out of the grand window, heedless of the cotton nightshirt falling off her left shoulder. She'd acted wholly indifferent to the city when they'd arrived the evening before. Her eyes had widened at the lush lobby of the Hôtel de Crillon, but she'd made no comment when they'd checked in.

She'd said little more when they entered the plush and lofty suite, and wandered away when Rogan tipped the bellman.

When he asked her if the room suited her, she'd simply shrugged and said it would do well enough.

It made him laugh and drag her off to bed.

But she wasn't quite so blasé now, he noted. He could all but see the excitement shimmering around her as she stared out at the street and absorbed the bustling life of the city. Nothing could have pleased him more than to give her Paris.

"If you lean out much farther, you'll stop traffic."

She jolted and, dragging her hair from her eyes, looked around to where he lay among rumpled sheets and a mountain of pillows.

"A bomb couldn't stop that traffic. Why do they want to kill each other?"

"It's a matter of honor. What do you think of the city in daylight?"

"It's crowded. Worse than Dublin." Then she

relented and grinned at him. "It's lovely, Rogan. Like an old, bad-tempered woman holding court. There's a vendor down there with an ocean of flowers. And every time someone stops to look or buy, he ignores them, like it's beneath his dignity to notice them. But he takes their money, and counts every coin."

She crawled back into bed and stretched herself over him. "I know exactly how he feels," she murmured. "Nothing makes you more irritable than selling what you love."

"If he didn't sell them, they'd die." He tipped up her chin. "If you didn't sell what you love, part of you would die, too."

"Well, the part that needs to eat would without a doubt. Are you going to call up one of those fancy waiters and have him bring us breakfast?"

"What would you like?"

Her eyes danced. "Oh, everything. Starting with this . . ."

She tugged the sheets away and fell on him.

Quite a bit later she stepped out of the shower, wrapping herself in the plush white robe that had hung on the back of the door. She found Rogan at a table by the parlor window, pouring coffee and reading the paper.

"That newspaper's in French." She sniffed at a basket of croissants. "You read French and Italian?"

"Mmm." His brows were knit over the financial pages. He was thinking of calling his broker.

"What else?"

"What else what?"

"What else do you read—speak. Language I mean."

"Some German. Enough Spanish to get by."

"Gaelic?"

"No." He turned the page, scanning for news of art auctions. "Do you?"

"My father's mother spoke it, so I learned." Her shoulders moved restlessly as she slathered jam onto a steaming croissant. "It's not much good, I suppose, except for cursing. It won't get you the best table in a French restaurant."

"It's valuable. We've lost a considerable amount of our heritage." Which was something he thought about, often. "It's a pity that there are only pockets in Ireland where you can hear Irish spoken." Because this reminded him of an idea he'd been toying with, he folded his paper and set it aside. "Say something in Gaelic."

"I'm eating."

"Say something for me, Maggie, in the old tongue."

She made a little sound of impatience, but obliged him. It was musical, exotic and as foreign to him as Greek.

"What did you say?"

"That you've a pleasing face to see of a morning." She smiled. "You see it's a language as useful for flattery as it is for cursing. Now say something to me in French."

He did more than speak. He leaned over, touched his lips softly to hers, then murmured, *"Me reveiller à côté de toi, c'est le plus beau de tous les rêves."* Her heart did a long, slow swirl in her chest.

"What does it mean?"

"That waking beside you is more lovely than any dream."

She lowered her eyes. "Well. It seems French is a

tongue more given to pretty sounds than plain English."

Her quick, unplanned feminine reaction both amused and allured. "I've touched you. I should have tried French before."

"Don't be foolish." But he *had* touched her, deeply. She combated the uneasy weakness by attacking her meal. "What am I eating?"

"Eggs Benedict."

"It's good," she said with her mouth full. "A bit on the rich side, but good. What are we after doing today, Rogan?"

"You're still blushing, Maggie."

"I'm not." She met his eyes narrowly, in a dare. "I'd like to know what the plans are. I'm assuming this time you'll discuss them with me first instead of just tugging me along like an idiot dog."

"I'm growing very fond of that wasp you call a tongue," he said pleasantly. "I'm probably losing my mind. And before you sting me again, I thought you'd enjoy seeing some of the city. You'd no doubt enjoy the Louvre. So I've left the morning quite clear for sight-seeing, or shopping, or whatever you'd like. Then we'll go by the gallery later this afternoon."

The notion of strolling through the great museum pleased her. She topped off Rogan's coffee, then heated up her own cup of tea. "I'd like to wander about, I suppose. As for shopping, I'll want to find something to take back for Brie."

"You should have something for Maggie as well."

"Maggie doesn't need anything. Besides, I can't afford it."

"That's absurd. You've no need to deny yourself a present or two. You've earned it."

"I've spent what I've earned." She grimaced over her cup. "Do they have the nerve to call this tea?"

"What do you mean you've spent it?" He set down his fork. "Only a month ago I gave you a check in the six figures. You can hardly have frittered that away."

"Frittered?" She gestured dangerously with her knife. "Do I look like a fritterer?"

"Good God, no."

"And what's that supposed to mean? That I haven't the taste or style to spend my money well?"

He held up a hand for peace. "It means nothing more than no. But if you've wasted the money I gave you, I'd like to know how."

"I wasted nothing, as if it were your business to begin with."

"You are my business. If you can't manage your money, I'll do it for you."

"You'll not. Why you pompous, penny-pinching ass, 'tis mine, isn't it? And it's gone, or most of it. So you'll just have to see that you sell my work and get me more."

"That's precisely what I'll do. Now, where did it go?"

"Away." Infuriated, embarrassed, she shoved back from the table. "I've expenses, don't I? I needed supplies, and I was foolish enough to buy a dress."

He folded his hands. "You spent, in a month's time, nearly two hundred thousand pounds on supplies and a dress."

"I had a debt to pay," she raged at him. "And why should I have to explain to you? It says nothing of how I spend my money in your bloody contract."

"The contract has nothing to do with it," he said patiently, because he could see it wasn't anger so much as mortification that was driving her. "I'm asking you where the money went. But you're certainly under no legal obligation to tell me."

His reasonable tone only pinched harder at her humiliation. "I bought my mother a house, though she'll never thank me for it. And I had to furnish it for her, didn't I? She'd have taken every stick and cushion from Brianna otherwise." Frustrated, she dragged both hands through her hair and sent it into fiery tufts. "And I had to hire Lottie, and see they had a car. And she'll have to be paid every week, so I gave Brie enough for six months in salary and for food and such. Then there was the lien, though Brie will be furious when she finds I've paid it off. But it was mine to pay, as Da took it out for me. So it's done. I kept my word to him and I won't have you telling me what I should or shouldn't do with my own money."

She'd stormed around the room while she spoke and came to a halt now by the table where Rogan continued to sit, silently, patiently.

"If I might summarize?" he said. "You bought a house for your mother, furnished it, purchased a car and hired a companion for her. You've paid off a lien, which will displease your sister, but which you felt was your responsibility. You've given Brianna enough to keep your mother for six months, bought supplies. And with what was left, you bought yourself a dress."

"That's right. That's what I said. What of it?"

She stood there, trembling with fury, her eyes sharp and bright and eager for battle. He could, he mused, tell her he admired her incredible generosity, her loyalty to her family. But he doubted that she'd appreciate the effort.

"That explains it." He picked up his coffee again. "I'll see that you get an advance."

She wasn't at all sure she could speak. When she did, her voice came out in a dangerous hiss. "I don't want your bloody advance. I don't want it. I'll earn my own keep."

"Which you're doing—and quite well. It's not charity, Maggie, or even a loan. It's a simple business transaction."

"Be damned to your business." Her face was pink with embarrassment now. "I'll not take a penny until I've earned it. I've just gotten myself out of debt, I won't go into it again."

"God, you're stubborn." He tapped his fingers on the table as he thought her reaction through, trying to understand her display of passion. If it was pride she needed so badly, he could help her keep it. "Very well, we'll do this another way entirely. We've had several offers on your *Surrender*, which I've turned down."

"Turned down?"

"Mmm. The last, I believe, was thirty thousand."

"Pounds!" The word erupted from her. "I was offered thirty thousand pounds for it, and you turned it down? Are you mad? It may seem like little or nothing to you, Rogan Sweeney, but I could live handsomely on that amount for more than a year. If this is how you manage—"

"Be quiet." And because he said it so casually, so absently, she did just that. "I refused the offer because I intended to buy the piece myself, after we'd toured it. I'll simply buy it now and it will continue on the tour as part of my collection. We'll make it thirty-five thousand."

He tossed off the amount as though it was loose change casually dropped on a bureau.

Something inside her was trembling like the heart of a frightened bird. "Why?"

"I can't, ethically, purchase it for myself at the same amount offered by a client."

"No, I mean why do you want it?"

He stopped his mental calculations and looked up at her. "Because it's beautiful work, intimate work. And because whenever I look at it, I remember making love with you the first time. You didn't want to sell it. Did you think I couldn't see that in your face the day you showed it to me? Did you really think I couldn't understand how much it hurt you to give it up?"

Unable to speak, she simply shook her head and turned away.

"It was mine, Maggie, even before you finished it. As much, I think, as it was yours. And it'll go to no one else. I never intended it to go to anyone else."

Still silent, she walked to the window. "I don't want you to pay me for it."

"Don't be absurd—"

"I don't want your money," she said quickly, while she could. "You're right—that piece was terribly special to me, and I'd be grateful if you'd accept it." She let out a long breath, staring hard through the glass. "I'd be pleased to know it was yours."

"Ours," he said in a tone that drew her gaze back to his like a magnet. "As it was meant to be."

"Ours, then." She sighed. "How can I stay angry

with you?" she said quietly. "How can I fight what you do to me?"

"You can't."

She was afraid he was right about that. But she could, at least, take a stand on a smaller matter. "I'm grateful to you for offering an advance, but I don't want it. It's important to me to take only what I make, when I make it. I've enough left to get by. I want no more than that for now. What needed to be done is done. From this point on, what comes will be mine."

"It's only money, Maggie."

"So easy to say when you've more than you've ever needed." The edge in her voice, so much like her mother's, stopped her cold. She took a deep breath and let out what was in her own heart. "Money was like an open wound in my house—the lack of it, my father's skill for losing it, and my mother's constant nagging for more. I don't want to depend on pounds for my happiness, Rogan. And it frightens and shames me that I might."

So, he thought, studying her, this was why she'd fought him every step of the way. "Didn't you tell me once that you didn't pick up your pipe each day thinking about the profit on the other end of it?"

"Yes, but—"

"Do you think of it now?"

"No. Rogan—"

"You're arguing against shadows, Maggie." He rose to cross to her. "The woman you are has already decided that the future will be very different from the past."

"I can't go back," she murmured. "Even if I wanted to, I couldn't go back."

"No, you can't. You'll always be one to go forward." He kissed her softly on the brow. "Will you get dressed now, Maggie? Let me give you Paris."

He did. For nearly a week he gave her everything the city had to offer, from the magnificence of Notre Dame to the intimacy of dim cafés. He bought her flowers from the tight-lipped street vendor every morning until the suite smelled like a garden. They strolled along the Seine in the moonlight, Maggie with her shoes in her hand and the river's breeze on her cheeks. They danced in clubs to poorly played American music, and dined on glorious food and wine at Maxim's.

She watched him pore over the sidewalk art, searching always for another diamond in the rough. And though he winced when she bought an undoubtedly bad painting of the Eiffel Tower, she only laughed and told him art was in the soul, not always in the execution.

The hours she spent in the Paris gallery were just as exciting to her. While Rogan ordered, directed and arranged she saw her work shine under his vigilant eye.

A vested interest, he'd said. She couldn't deny that he tended his interests well. He was as passionate and attentive to her art during those afternoons as he was to her body during the nights.

When it was done, and the last piece was set to shine under the lights, she thought that the show was every bit as much a result of his efforts as of her own.

But partnership didn't always equal harmony.

"Damn it, Maggie, if you keep fussing in there

we'll be late." For the third time in as many minutes, Rogan knocked on the bedroom door she'd locked.

"And if you keep bothering me, we'll be later still," she called out. "Go away. Better yet, go on to the gallery yourself. I can get myself there when I'm ready."

"You can't be trusted," he muttered, but her ears were sharp.

"I don't need a keeper, Rogan Sweeney." She was breathless from struggling to reach the low zipper of her dress. "I've never seen a man so ruled by the hands of a clock."

"And I've never seen a woman more careless of time. Would you unlock this door? It's infuriating to have to shout through it."

"All right, all right." By nearly dislocating her arm, she managed to fasten the dress. She wriggled her feet into ridiculously high bronze heels, cursed herself for being fool enough to take Joseph's advice, then twisted the lock. "I wouldn't have taken so long if they made women's clothes with the same consideration they make men's. Your zippers are within easy reach." She stopped, tugged once on the short hem of the dress. "Well? Is it all right or not?"

He said nothing at all, only twirled his finger to indicate he wanted her to circle. Rolling her eyes to heaven, she complied.

The dress was strapless, nearly backless, with a skirt that halted teasingly at midthigh. It glittered, bronze, copper, gold, sparking fire at every breath. Her hair echoed the tone so that she seemed like a candle flame, slim and bright.

"Maggie. You take my breath away."

"The seamstress wasn't generous with material."

"I admire her parsimony."

When he continued to stare, she lifted her brows. "You said we were in a hurry."

"I've changed my mind."

Her brows lifted higher as he started toward her. "I'm warning you, if you get me out of this dress, it'll be your responsibility to get me back in."

"As attractive as that sounds, it'll have to wait. I've a present for you, and it seems that the fates guided my hand. I believe this will complement your dress nicely."

He reached into the inside pocket of his tux and took out a slim velvet box.

"You've already bought me a present. That huge bottle of scent."

"That was for me." He leaned over to sniff her bare shoulder. The smoky perfume might have been created with her in mind. "Very much for me. This is for you."

"Well, since it's too small to be another answering machine, I'll take it." But when she opened the box, the chuckle died in her throat. Rubies, square flames of them, simmered with white-hot diamonds in a three-tiered choker tied together by twists of glinting gold. No delicate bauble, but a bold flash, a lightning flash of color and heat and gleam.

"Something to remember Paris by," Rogan told her as he slipped it from the box. The necklace ran like blood and water through his fingers.

"It's diamonds. Rogan, I can't wear diamonds."

"Of course you can." He brought it to her throat, his eyes on hers as he fastened the clasp. "Not alone perhaps. They'd be cold and wouldn't suit you. But with the other stones . . ." He stepped back to take in the effect. "Yes, exactly right. You look like a pagan goddess."

She couldn't stop her hand from reaching up, from running across the gems. They felt warm against her skin. "I don't know what to say to you."

"Say thank you, Rogan. It's lovely."

"Thank you, Rogan." Her smile bloomed and spread. "It's a great deal more than lovely. It's dazzling."

"And so are you." He leaned into the kiss, then patted her bottom. "Now get a move on, or we'll be late. Where's your wrap?"

"I haven't got one."

"Typical," he murmured, and pulled her out the door.

Maggie thought she handled her second showing with a great deal more panache than she had the first. Her stomach wasn't nearly as jittery, her temper not nearly as short. If she did, once or twice, think wistfully of escape, she covered it well.

And if she pined for something she couldn't have, she reminded herself that success sometimes had to be enough in itself.

"Maggie."

She turned from the heavily accented ramblings of a Frenchman whose eyes had rarely left her cleavage and stared dumbstruck at her sister.

"Brianna?"

"It certainly is." Smiling, Brianna gathered her astonished sister in an embrace. "I would have been here an hour ago, but there was a delay at the airport."

"But how? How are you here at all?"

"Rogan sent his plane for me."

"Rogan?" Baffled, Maggie scanned the room until she found him. He only smiled at her, then at Brianna, before returning his attention to an enormous woman in fuchsia lace. Maggie nudged her sister to a corner of the room. "You came on Rogan's plane?"

"I thought I would have to let you down again, Maggie." More than a little overwhelmed by the sight of Maggie's work glittering in a roomful of exotic strangers, Brianna slipped her hand into her sister's. "I was trying to think of how to manage it. Mother's fine with Lottie, of course, and I knew I could leave Con with Murphy. I even asked Mrs. McGee if she'd look after Blackthorn for a day or two. But then there was the how to get here."

"You wanted to come," Maggie said softly. "You wanted to."

"Of course I did. I wanted nothing more than to be with you. But I never imagined it would be like this." Brie stared at the white-coated waiter who offered her champagne from his silver tray. "Thank you."

"I didn't think it mattered to you." To clear the emotion from her throat, Maggie drank deeply. "I was, just now, standing here thinking I wished it mattered to you."

"I'm proud of you, Maggie, so proud. I've told you."

"I didn't believe you. Oh God." She felt the tears well up and blinked them furiously away.

"You should be ashamed of yourself, thinking so little of my feelings," Brie scolded.

"You never showed any interest," Maggie fired back.

"I showed all the interest I could. I don't understand what you do, but that doesn't mean it doesn't make me proud that you do it." Coolly, Brianna tipped back her glass. "Oh," she murmured, staring at the bubbling wine, "but that's lovely. Who'd have thought anything could taste like that?"

With a hoot of laughter, Maggie kissed her sister hard on the mouth. "Jesus save us, Brie, what are we doing here? The two of us, drinking champagne in Paris."

"I for one am going to enjoy it. I have to thank Rogan. Do you think I could interrupt him for a moment?"

"After you've told me the rest. When did you call him?"

"I didn't, he called me. A week ago."

"He called you?"

"Aye, and before I could wish him good morning, he was telling me what I would do and how I would do it."

"That's Rogan."

"He said he'd be sending the plane, and that I was to meet his driver at the airport in Paris. I tried to get a word in, but he rolled right over me. The driver would take me to the hotel. Have you ever seen the like of that place, Maggie? It's like a palace."

"I nearly swallowed my tongue when I walked in. Go on."

"Then, I was to get myself ready, and the driver would bring me here. Which he did, though I thought for certain he'd kill me along the way. And there was this in the hotel room, with a note from him telling me it would please him if I'd wear it." She brushed a hand down the misty blue silk of the evening suit she wore. "I wouldn't have taken it, but he put the request in such a way I'd have felt rude not to."

"He's good at that. And you look wonderful in it."

"I *feel* wonderful in it. I confess, my head's still spinning from planes and cars and all this. All of this," she said again, staring around the room. "These people, Maggie, they're all here for you."

"I'm glad you are. Shall I take you around so you can charm them for me?"

"They're charmed already, just seeing the two of you." Rogan stepped beside them and took Brianna's hand. "It's delightful to see you again."

"I'm grateful to you for arranging it. I can't begin to thank you."

"You just have. You don't mind if I introduce you around? Mr. LeClair—there, the rather flamboyant-looking man by Maggie's *Momentum*? He's just confessed to me that he's fallen in love with you."

"He certainly falls easily, but I'll be pleased to meet him. I'd like to wander about as well. I've never seen Maggie's work shown like this."

It took only minutes before Maggie was able to draw Rogan aside again. "Don't tell me I need to circulate," she said before he could do just that. "I have something I need to say to you."

"As long as you say it quickly. It doesn't do for me to monopolize the artist."

"It won't take long for me to tell you that this was the kindest thing anyone has every done for me. I'll never forget it."

He ignored the distraction of the rapid French a

woman chattered at his shoulder and took Maggie's hand to his lips. "I didn't want you unhappy again, and it was the simplest thing in the world to arrange for Brianna to be here."

"It might have been simple." She remembered the ragged artist he'd escorted up the elegant steps of the gallery. That, too, had been simple. "That doesn't make it any less kind. And to show you what it means to me, I'll not only stay through the whole evening, until the last guest toddles out the door, I'll talk to every one of them."

"Nicely?"

"Nicely. No matter how often I hear the word *visceral*."

"That's my girl." He kissed the tip of her nose. "Now get to work."

🦢 Chapter Sixteen

IF Paris had staggered her, the south of France with its sweep of beaches and snow-covered mountains left Maggie awestruck. There was no rattle of traffic here in Rogan's sparkling villa overlooking the searing blue waters of the Mediterranean, no crowds bustling toward shops or cafés.

The people who dotted the beach were no more than part of the painting that encompassed water and sand, bobbing boats and an endless, cloudless sky.

The countryside, which she could see from one of the many terraces that graced the villa, spread out in neat square fields bordered by stone fences like the ones she saw from her own doorway in Clare. But here, the ground rose up in terraced slopes, from orchards on sunny embankments to the higher green of the forests and on to the foothills of the magnificent Alps.

Rogan's grounds were lush with blooms and flowering herbs, exotic with olive and box trees and the sparkle of fountains. The quiet was disturbed only by the call of gulls and the music of falling water.

Content, Maggie lounged in one of the padded chaises on a sun-washed terrace and sketched.

"I thought I'd find you here." Rogan stepped out

and dropped a kiss, both casual and intimate, on the top of her head.

"It's impossible to stay inside on such a day." She squinted up at him until he took the shaded glasses she'd tossed on a table and slipped them on her nose. "Did you finish your business?"

"For now." He sat beside her, shifting so as not to block her view. "I'm sorry I've been so long. One call seemed to lead to another."

"No matter. I like being on my own."

"I've noticed." He peeked into the sketchbook. "A seascape?"

"It's irresistible. And I thought I'd draw some of the scenery, so Brie could see it. She had such a wonderful time in Paris."

"I'm sorry she could only stay one day."

"One lovely day. It's hard to believe I strolled along the Left Bank with my sister. The Concannon sisters in Paris." It still made her laugh to think of it. "She'll not forget it, Rogan." Tucking her pencil behind her ear, Maggie took his hand. "Neither will I."

"You've thanked me, both of you. And the truth is I did nothing more than make a few calls. Speaking of calls, one that kept me away just now was from Paris." Reaching over, Rogan selected a sugared grape from the basket of fruit beside them. "You've an offer, Maggie, from the Comte de Lorraine."

"De Lorraine?" Lips pursed, she searched her memory. "Ah, the skinny old man with a cane who talked in whispers."

"Yes." Rogan was amused to hear her describe one of the wealthiest men in France as a skinny old man. "He'd like to commission you to make a gift for his granddaughter's wedding this December."

Her hackles rose instinctively. "I'll take no commissions, Rogan. I made that clear from the start."

"You did, yes." Rogan took another grape and popped it into Maggie's mouth to keep her quiet. "But it's my obligation to inform you of any requests. I'm not suggesting you agree, though it would be quite an impressive feather in your—and Worldwide's—cap. I'm simply fulfilling my duties as your manager."

Eyeing him, Maggie swallowed the grape. His tone, she noted, was as sugarcoated as the fruit. "I'll not do it."

"Your choice, naturally." He waved the entire matter away. "Shall I ring for something cold? Lemonade perhaps, or iced tea?"

"No." Maggie took the pencil from behind her ear, tapped it on her pad. "I'm not interested in made-to-order."

"And why should you be?" he responded, all reason. "Your Paris showing was every bit as successful as the one in Dublin. I have every confidence that this will continue in Rome and beyond. You're well on your way, Margaret Mary." He leaned down and kissed her. "Not that the comte's request has anything to do with made-to-order. He's quite willing to leave it completely in your hands."

Cautious, Maggie tipped down her glasses and studied him over the tip. "You're trying to sweet-talk me into it."

"Hardly." But, of course, he was. "I should add, however, that the comte—a very well-respected art connoisseur, by the way—is willing to pay handsomely."

"I'm not interested." She shoved her glasses in place again, then swore. "How much is handsome?"

"Up to the equivalent of fifty thousand pounds. But I know how adamant you are about the money angle, so you needn't give it a thought. I told him it was unlikely you'd be interested. Would you like to go down to the beach? Take a drive?"

Before he could rise, Maggie snagged his collar. "Oh, you're a sneaky one, aren't you, Sweeney?"

"When needs be."

"It would be whatever I choose to make? Whatever came to me?"

"It would." He traced a finger over her bare shoulder, which was beginning to turn the color of a peach in the sun. "Except . . ."

"Ah, here we are."

"Blue," Rogan said, and grinned. "He wants blue."

"Blue, is it?" The laugh began to shake her. "Any particular shade?"

"The same as his granddaughter's eyes. He claims they are as blue as the summer sky. It seems she's his favorite, and after he saw your work in Paris, nothing would do but that she have something made for her alone from your lovely hands."

"His words or yours?"

"A bit of both," Rogan answered, kissing one of those lovely hands.

"I'll think about it."

"I'd hoped you would." No longer concerned with blocking her view, he leaned over to nibble at her lips. "But think about it later, will you?"

"Excusez-moi, monsieur." A bland-faced servant stood on the edge of the terrace, his hands at his sides and his eyes discreetly aimed toward the sea.

"Oui, Henri?"

"*Vous et mademoiselle, voudriez-vous déjeuner sur la terrasse maintenant?*"

"*Non, nous allons déjeuner plus tard.*"

"*Très bien, monsieur.*" Henri faded away, silent as a shadow into the house.

"And what was that about?" Maggie asked.

"He wanted to know if we wanted lunch. I said we'd eat later." When Rogan started to lean down again, Maggie stopped him with a hand slapped to his chest. "Problem?" Rogan murmured. "I can call him back and tell him we're ready after all."

"No, I don't want you to call him." It made her uneasy to think of Henri, or any of the other servants, lurking in a corner, waiting to serve. She wriggled off the chaise. "Don't you ever want to be alone?"

"We are alone. That's exactly why I wanted to bring you here."

"Alone? You must have six people puttering around the house. Gardeners and cooks, maids and butlers. If I were to snap my fingers right now, one of them would come running."

"Which is exactly the purpose in having servants."

"Well, I don't want them. Do you know one of those little maids wanted to wash out my underwear?"

"That's because it's her job to tend to you, not because she wanted to riffle your drawers."

"I can tend to myself. Rogan, I want you to send them away. All of them."

He rose at that. "You want me to fire the help?"

"No, for pity sakes, I'm not a monster, tossing innocent people out on the street. I want you to send them off, that's all. On a holiday, or whatever you'd call it."

"I can certainly give the staff a day off, if you'd like."

"Not a day, the week." She blew out a breath, seeing his puzzlement. "It doesn't make any sense to you, and why should it? You're so used to them, you don't even see them."

"His name was Henri, the cook is Jacques, the maid who so cheekily offered to wash your lingerie is Marie." Or possibly, he thought, Monique.

"I wasn't after starting a quarrel." She came forward, her hands reaching for his. "I can't relax as you do with all these people hovering about. I'm just not used to it—I don't think I want to be. Do this for me, please, Rogan. Give them a few days off."

"Wait here a moment."

When he left, she stood on the terrace, feeling foolish. Here she was, she mused, lounging in a Mediterranean villa with anything she could ask for within her reach. And she still wasn't satisfied.

She'd changed, she realized. In the few short months since she met Rogan, she had changed. She not only wished for more now, she coveted more of what she didn't have. She wanted the ease and the pleasure money could bring, and not just for her family. She wanted it for herself.

She'd worn diamonds and had danced in Paris.

And she wanted to do so again.

Yet, deep within her, there remained that small, hot need to be only herself, to need nothing and no one. If she lost that, Maggie thought with a whip of panic, she would have lost everything.

She snatched up her sketch pad, flipped pages.

But for a moment, a terrifying moment, her mind was as blank as the sheet in front of her. Then she began to draw frantically, with a violent intensity that burst from her like a gale.

It was herself she drew. The two parts, twisted together, pulled apart and so desperately trying to meet again. But how could they, when one was so completely opposed to the other?

Art for art's sake, solitude for sanity, independence for pride. And on the other side—ambition, hungers and needs.

She stared at the completed sketch, dumbfounded that it had poured out of her so swiftly. And now that it had, she was oddly calm. Perhaps it was those two opposing forces that made her what she was. And perhaps if she were ever really at peace, she'd be less than she could be.

"They've gone."

Her mind still drifting, she looked blankly up at Rogan. "What? Who's gone?"

On a half laugh, he shook his head. "The staff. That's what you wanted, isn't it?"

"The staff? Oh." Her mind cleared, settled. "You've sent them off? All of them?"

"I did, though God alone knows how we'll eat over the next few days. Still—" He broke off when she leaped into his arms. As she'd shot at him like a bullet from a gun, he staggered back, overbalancing to keep them from crashing through the beveled-glass door behind him and nearly tumbling them over the railing.

"You're a wonderful man, Rogan. A prince of a man."

He shifted her in his arms and looked wearily at the drop over the rail. "I was nearly a dead man."

"We're alone? Completely?"

"We are, and I've earned the undying gratitude of everyone from the butler down. The parlor maid wept with joy." As he supposed she should, with the holiday bonus he'd given her and the rest of the servants. "So now they're off to the beach or to the country or to wherever their hearts lead them. And we've the house to ourselves."

She kissed him, hard. "And we're about to use every inch of it. We'll start with that sofa in the room just through there."

"Will we?" Amused, he made no protest as she began unbuttoning his shirt. "You're full of demands today, Margaret Mary."

"The business with the servants was a request. The sofa's a demand."

He cocked a brow. "The chaise is closer."

"So it is." She laughed as he lowered her to it. "So it is."

Over the next few days they sunned on the terrace, walked on the beach or swam lazy laps in the lagoonlike pool to the music of the fountains. There were ill-prepared meals to be eaten in the kitchen and afternoon drives through the countryside.

There were also, to Maggie's mind, entirely too many telephones.

It might have been a holiday, but Rogan was never farther than a phone or a fax away from business. There was something about a factory in Limerick, something else about an auction in New York, and unintelligible mutters about property he was looking for in order to add another branch to Worldwide Galleries.

It might have annoyed her if she hadn't begun to see that his work was as much a part of his identity as her work was to hers. All differences aside, she could hardly complain about him spending an hour or two closeted in his office when he took her absorption in her sketches in stride.

If she had believed in a man and woman finding the kind of harmony that was needed to last a lifetime, she might have believed she'd found it with Rogan.

"Let me see what you've done."

With a contented yawn, Maggie offered him her sketchbook. The sun was setting, drowning colors sweeping the western sky. Between them the bottle of wine he'd chosen from his cellar nestled in a silver bucket frosty with ice. Maggie lifted her glass, sipped and settled back to enjoy her last evening in France.

"You'll be busy when you get home," Rogan commented as he studied each sketch. "How will you choose which one to work on first?"

"It will choose me. And as much as I've enjoyed being lazy, I'm itching to get back and fire up my furnace."

"I can have the ones you've drawn up for Brianna matted and framed. For simple pencil sketches they're quite good. I particularly like . . ." He trailed off when he turned a page and came across something entirely different from a sketch of the sea or a landscape. "And what have we here?"

Almost too lazy to move, she glanced over. "Oh,

yes, that. I don't do portraits often, but that one was irresistible."

It was himself, stretched over the bed, his arm flung out as if he'd been reaching for something. For her.

Taken by surprise and not entirely pleased, he frowned down at the sketch. "You drew this while I was asleep."

"Well, I didn't want to wake you and spoil the moment." She hid her grin in her glass. "You were sleeping so sweetly. Perhaps you'd like to hang that one in your Dublin gallery."

"I'm naked."

"*Nude* is the word, I'll remind you. When it's art. And you look very artistic nude, Rogan. I've signed it, you see, so you may get a nice price for it."

"I think not."

She tucked her tongue in her cheek. "As my manager it's your duty to market my work. You're always saying so yourself. And this, if I do say so, is one of my finest drawings. You'll note the light, and the way it plays on the muscles of your—"

"I see," he said in a strangled voice. "And so would everyone else."

"No need to be modest. You've a fine form. I think I captured it even better in this other one."

His blood, quite simply, ran cold. "Other one?"

"Aye. Let's see now." She reached over to flip pages herself. "Here we are. Shows a bit more . . . contrast when you're standing, I think. And a bit of that arrogance comes through as well."

Words failed him. She'd drawn him standing on the terrace, one arm resting on the rail behind him, the other cupping a brandy snifter. And a smile—a particularly smug smile—on his face. It was all he was wearing.

"I never posed for this. And I've never stood naked on the terrace drinking brandy."

"Artistic license," she said airly, delighted that she'd flummoxed him so completely. "I know your body well enough to draw it from memory. It would have spoiled the theme to bother with clothes."

"The theme? Which is?"

"Master of the house. I thought that's what I'd title it. Both of them actually. You might offer them as a set."

"I won't be selling them."

"And why not? I'd like to know? You've sold several of my other drawings that aren't nearly as well done. Those I didn't want you to sell, but I'd signed on the dotted line, so you did. I *want* you to market these." Her eyes danced. "In fact, I insist, as I believe is my right, contractually speaking."

"I'll buy them myself, then."

"What's your offer? My dealer tells me my price is rising."

"You're blackmailing me, Maggie."

"Oh, aye." She toasted him then sipped more wine. "You'll have to meet my price."

He glanced at the sketch again before firmly closing the book. "Which is?"

"Let's see now. . . . I think if I was taken upstairs and made love to until moonrise, we might have a deal."

"You've a shrewd business sense."

"I've learned it from a master." She started to

stand, but he shook his head and scooped her into his arms.

"I want no slipping through loopholes on this deal. I believe your terms were that you be taken upstairs."

"Right you are. I suppose that's why I need a manager." She wound a lock of his hair around her fingers as he carried her into the house. "You know, of course, if I'm not satisfied with the rest of the terms, the deal's off."

"You'll be satisfied."

At the top of the stairs he stopped to kiss her. Her response was, as always, fast and urgent, and as always, it quickened his blood. He stepped into the bedroom, where the softened light of sunset swam through the windows. Soon the light would go gray with dusk.

Their last night alone would not be spent in the dark.

Thinking this, he laid her on the bed, and when she reached for him, he slipped away to light candles. They were scattered through the room, some stubs, some slim tapers, all burned down to varying lengths. Maggie knelt on the bed while Rogan struck the flames and sent the light dancing gold.

"Romance." She smiled and felt oddly touched. "It seems a spot of blackmail's been well worth the effort."

He paused, a flaring match between his fingers. "Have I given you so little romance, Maggie?"

"I was only joking." She tossed back her breeze-ruffled hair. His voice had been much too serious. "I've no need for romance. Honest lust is quite good enough for me."

"Is that what we have?" Thoughtfully he set the match to the wick then shook it out. "Lust."

Laughing, she held out her arms. "If you'd stop wandering about the room and come over here, I'll show you exactly what we have."

She looked dazzling in the candle glow with the last colors of day bleeding through the windows beside the bed. Her hair afire, her skin kissed by her days in the sun and her eyes aware, mocking and unquestionably inviting.

On other days and other nights he would have dived into that invitation, accepted it, reveled in it and the firestorm they could make between them. But his mood had shifted. He crossed slowly to her, taking her hands before they could tug him eagerly into the bed with her, lifting them to his lips as his eyes watched her.

"That wasn't the bargain, Margaret Mary. I was to make love to you. It's time I did." He kept her hands in his, drawing her arms down to her sides as he leaned forward to toy with her lips. "It's time you let me."

"What foolishness is that?" Her voice wasn't steady. He was kissing her as he had once before, slowly, gently, and with the utmost concentration. "I've done more than let you a great many times before."

"Not like this." He felt her hands flex against his, her body draw back. "Are you so afraid of tenderness, Maggie?"

"Of course I'm not." She couldn't get her breath, yet she could hear it, feel it coming slow and heavy through her lips. Her whole body was tingling, yet he was barely touching her. Something was slipping away from her. "Rogan, I don't want to—"

"To be seduced?" He took his lips from hers, let them roam leisurely over her face.

"No, I don't." But her head tilted back as he skimmed his mouth down her throat.

"You're about to be."

He released her hands then to draw her closer. No fevered embrace this time, but an inescapable possession. Her arms seemed impossibly heavy as she wound them round his neck. She could do no more than cling as he stroked her hair, her face, with gentle fingertips that felt no more substantial than a whisper on the air.

His mouth came back to hers in a moist, deep, sumptuous kiss that went on endlessly, endlessly, until she was as pliant as wax in his arms.

He'd cheated both of them, Rogan realized as he laid her back on the bed. By letting only the fire take them, he'd kept them both from experiencing all the warm, waiting wells of tenderness.

Tonight it would be different.

Tonight he would take her through a labyrinth of dreams before the flames.

The taste of him seeped into her, stunning her, staggering her with tenderness. The greed that had always been so much a part of their lovemaking had mellowed into a lazy patience she could neither resist nor refuse. Long before he opened her blouse and skimmed those smooth, clever fingertips over her skin, she was floating.

Limply her hands slid from his shoulders. Her breath caught and expelled as he laved his tongue over her, seeking small secret tastes, lingering over them. Savoring. Drifting on that slow sweep of sensation, she was aware of every pulse point he awakened, of the long, quiet pull from deep inside her. So different from an explosion. So much more devastating.

She murmured his name when he cupped a hand under her head and lifted her melting body to his.

"You're mine, Maggie. No one else will ever take you here."

She should have objected to this new demand for exclusivity. But she couldn't. For his mouth was journeying over her again as if he had years, decades, to complete the exploration.

The candlelight flickered dreamily against her heavy lids. She could smell the flowers she'd picked only that morning and had placed in a blue vase by the window. She heard the breeze heralding the Mediterranean night with the scents of blossoms and water in its wake. Beneath his fingers and lips her skin softened and her muscles quivered.

How could he not have known he'd wanted her like this? All the fires banked, only glowing embers and drifting smoke. She moved under his hands helplessly, unable to do anything but absorb what he gave her, follow where he led. Even as the blood pounded in his head, in his loins, he kept the caresses light, teasing, waiting for her, watching her slide from one into the next melting sensation.

When she trembled, when a new sighing moan slipped through her lips, he took her hands again, braceleting them in one of his so that he was free to urge her over the first edge.

Her body bowed, her lashes fluttered. He watched as that first velvet fist took her breath. Then she went fluid again, languid and limp. Her pleasure welled inside of him.

The sun sank. Candles guttered. He guided her up again, a higher peak that made her cry out weakly. The sound echoed away into sighs and murmurs. When her heart was so full that it, too, seemed to weep, he slipped into her, taking her tenderly while the moon rose.

Perhaps she slept. She knew she dreamed. When she opened her eyes again, the moon was up and the room was empty. Languid as a cat, she considered curling up again. But even as she nuzzled into the pillow she knew she would not sleep without him.

She rose, floating a little as though her mind was dazed with wine. She found a robe, a thin swatch of silk that Rogan had insisted on giving her. It settled smoothly against her skin as she went to find him.

"I should have known you'd be here."

He was in the kitchen, standing shirtless in front of the gleaming stove in the brilliant white-and-black kitchen. "Thinking of your stomach?"

"And of yours, my girl." He turned off the fire under the skillet before he turned. "Eggs."

"What else?" It was all either of them could competently cook. "I won't be surprised if we're cackling when we get back to Ireland tomorrow." Because she felt unexpectedly awkward, she raked a hand through her hair once, then twice. "You should have made me get up and fix it."

"Made you?" He reached up for plates. "That would be a first."

"What I mean is, I'd have done it. After all, I don't feel I did my part before."

"Before?"

"Upstairs. In bed. I didn't exactly do my share."

"A bargain's a bargain." He scooped eggs into plates. "And from my point of view, you did very well indeed. Watching you unravel was an incredible pleasure for me." One he intended to experience again, very soon. "Why don't you sit down and eat. The moon'll be up for some time yet."

"I suppose it will." More at ease, she joined him at the table. "And this may just give me my energy back. Do you know," she said with her mouth full. "I'd no idea that sex could make you so weak."

"It wasn't just sex."

Her fork paused halfway to her lips at his tone. There was hurt beneath the sharp annoyance, and she was sorry to have caused it. Amazed that she could. "I didn't mean it that way, Rogan. Not so impersonally. When two people are fond of each other—"

"I'm a great deal more than fond of you, Maggie. I'm in love with you."

The fork slipped from her fingers and clattered on the plate. Panic tore at her throat in sharp, hungry fangs. "You're not."

"I am." He said it calmly, though he was cursing himself for making his declaration in a brightly lit kitchen over badly cooked eggs. "And you're in love with me."

"It's not—I'm not—you can't tell me what I am."

"I can when you're too foolish to say so yourself. What's between us is far more than physical attraction. If you weren't so pigheaded, you'd stop pretending it was."

"I'm not pigheaded."

"You are, but I find that's one of the things I like about you." He was thinking coolly now, pleased to be back in control. "We might have discussed all this under more atmospheric circumstances, but knowing you, it hardly matters. I'm in love with you, and I want you to marry me."

❧ Chapter Seventeen

MARRIAGE? The word stuck in her throat, threatened to choke her. She didn't dare repeat it.

"You're out of your mind."

"Believe me, I've considered the possibility." He picked up his fork and ate with the appearance of sanity. But the hurt, unexpected and raw, scraped at him. "You're stubborn, often rude, more than occasionally self-absorbed and not a little temperamental."

For a moment her mouth worked like a guppy's. "Oh, am I?"

"You most certainly are, and a man would have to have taken leave of his senses to want that sort of baggage for a lifetime. But"—he poured out the tea he'd had steeping—"there you are. I believe it's customary to use the bride's church, so we'll be married in Clare."

"Customary? Hang your customs, Rogan, and you with them." Was this panic she felt, skidding along her spine like jagged ice? Surely not, she told herself. It had to be temper. She had nothing to fear. "I'm not marrying you or anyone. Ever."

"That's absurd. Of course you'll marry me. We're amazingly well suited, Maggie."

"A moment ago I was stubborn and temperamental and rude."

"So you are. And it suits me." He took her hand, ignored her resistance and tugged it to his lips. "And it suits me beautifully."

"Well, it doesn't suit me. Not at all. Perhaps I've softened toward your arrogance, Rogan, but that's changing by the second. Understand me." She yanked her hand free of his. "I'll be no man's wife."

"No man's but mine."

She hissed out a curse. When he only grinned at that, she took a hard grip on her temper. A fight, she thought, might be satisfying, but it would solve nothing. "You brought me here for this, didn't you?"

"No, actually, I didn't. I'd thought to take more time before tossing my feelings at your feet." Very carefully, very deliberately, he shifted his plate aside. "Knowing very well you'd kick them back at me." His eyes stayed on hers, level, patient. "You see I know you very well, Margaret Mary."

"You don't." Temper, and the panic she didn't want to admit, leaked out of her, leaving room for sorrow. "I've reasons for keeping my heart whole, Rogan, and for not ever considering the possibility of marriage."

It interested and soothed him to understand that it wasn't marriage to him that seemed to appall her, but marriage itself. "What are they?"

She lowered her gaze to her cup. After a moment's hesitation she added her usual three cubes of sugar and stirred. "You lost your parents."

"Yes." His brow furrowed. This certainly wasn't the tack he'd expected her to take. "Almost ten years ago."

"It's hard losing family. It strips away a whole layer of security, exposes you to the simple cold fact of mortality. You loved them?"

"Very much. Maggie—"

"No, I'd like to hear what you have to say about this. It's important. They loved you?"

"Yes, they did."

"How did you know it?" She drank now, holding the cup in two hands. "Was it because they gave you a good life, a fine home?"

"It had nothing to do with material comfort. I knew they loved me because I felt it, because they showed it. And I could see they loved each other as well."

"There was love in your house. And laughter? Was there laughter, Rogan?"

"Quite a bit of it." He could remember it still. "I was devastated when they died. So sudden, so brutally sudden . . ." His voice tapered off, then strengthened again. "But after, when the worst of it had passed, I was glad they'd gone together. Each of them would have been only half-alive without the other."

"You've no notice how lucky you are, what a gift you were given growing up in a loving, happy home. I've never known that. I never will. There was no love between my parents. There was anger and blame and guilt and there was duty, but no love. Can you imagine what it was like, growing up in a house where the two people who had made you cared nothing for each other? Were only there because their marriage was a prison barring them in with conscience and church law."

"No, I can't." He covered her hand with his. "I'm sorry you can."

"I swore, when I was still a girl, I swore I'd never be locked in a prison like that."

"Marriage isn't only a prison, Maggie," he said gently. "My own parents' was a joy."

"And you may make one for yourself one day. But not I. You make what you know, Rogan. And you can't change what you've come from. My mother hates me."

He would have protested, but she'd said it so matter-of-factly, so simply, he could not.

"Even before I was born she hated me. The fact that I grew inside her ruined her life, which she tells me as often as possible. All these years I never knew how deep it truly went, until your grandmother told me my mother had had a career."

"A career?" He cast his mind back. "The singing? What does that have to do with you?"

"Everything. What choice did she have but to give up her career? What career would she have had left as a single, pregnant woman in a country like ours? None." Cold, she shivered and let out a shaky breath. It hurt to say it aloud this way, to say it all aloud. "She wanted something for herself. I understand that, Rogan. I know what it is to have ambitions. And I can imagine, all too well, what it would be like to have them dashed. You see, they never would have married if I hadn't been conceived. A moment of passion, of need, that was all. My father more than forty, and she past thirty. She dreaming, I suppose, of romance and he seeing a lovely woman. She was lovely then. There are pictures. She was lovely before the bitterness ate it all away. And I was the seed of it, the seven-month baby that humiliated her and ruined her dreams. And his, too. Aye and his."

"You can hardly blame yourself for being born, Maggie."

"Oh, I know that. Don't you think I know? Up here?" Suddenly fierce, she tapped her head. "But in my heart—can't you see? I know that my very existence and every breath I take burdened the lives of two people beyond measure. I came from passion only, and every time she looked at me, it reminded her that she'd sinned."

"That's not only ridiculous, it's foolish."

"Perhaps it is. My father said he'd loved her once, and perhaps it was true." She could imagine him, walking into O'Malley's, seeing Maeve, hearing her and letting his romantic heart take flight.

But it had crashed soon enough. For both of them.

"I was twelve when she told me that I hadn't been conceived within marriage. That's how she puts it. Perhaps she'd begun to see that I was making that slow shift from girl to woman. I'd begun to look at boys, you see. Had practiced my flirting on Murphy and one or two others from the village. She caught me at it, standing by the hay barn with Murphy, trying out a kiss. Just a kiss, that was all, beside the hay on a warm summer afternoon, both of us young and curious. It was my first kiss, and it was lovely— soft and shy and harmless.

"And she found us." When Maggie shut her eyes, the scene played back vividly. "She went white, bone white, and screamed and raged, dragged me into the house. I was wicked, she said, and sinful, and because my father wasn't home to stop her, she whipped me."

"Whipped you?" Shock had him rising out of his

chair. "Are you telling me she hit you because you'd kissed a boy?"

"She beat me," Maggie said flatly. "It was more than the back of her hand that I'd been used to. She took a belt and laid into me until I thought she'd kill me. While she did she shouted scripture and raged about the branding of sin."

"She had no right to treat you so." He knelt in front of her, cupped her face in his hands.

"No, no one has such a right, but it doesn't stop them. I could see the hate in her then, and the fear, too. The fear, I came to understand, was that I would end up as she had, with a baby in my belly and emptiness in my heart. I'd known always that she didn't love me as mothers were meant to love their children. I'd known that she was easier, a bit softer on Brie. But until that day, I hadn't known why."

She couldn't sit any longer. Rising, she went to the door that led out to a little stone patio decked with clay pots filled with brilliant geraniums.

"There's no need for you to talk about this anymore," Rogan said from behind her.

"I'll finish." The sky was studded with stars, the breeze a gentle whisper through the trees. "She told me that I was marked. And she beat me so that the mark would be on the outside as well, so that I would understand what a burden a woman bears because it's she who carries the child."

"That's vile, Maggie." Unable to clamp down on his own emotions, he whirled her around, his hands hard on her shoulders, his eyes icy blue and furious. "You were just a girl."

"If I was, I stopped being one that day. Because I

understood, Rogan, that she meant exactly what she said."

"It was a lie, a pitiful one."

"Not to her. To her it was sterling truth. She told me I was her penance, that God had punished her for her night of sin, with me. She believed that, fully, and every time she looked at me she was reminded of it. That even the pain and misery of birthing me wasn't enough. Because of me she was trapped in a marriage she despised, bound to a man she couldn't love and mother to a child she'd never wanted. And, as I've found out just recently, the ruin of everything she really wanted. Perhaps the ruin of everything she was."

"She's the one who should have been whipped. No one has the right to abuse a child so, and worse to use some warped vision of God as the strap."

"Funny, my father said nearly the same thing when he came home and saw what she'd done. I thought he would strike her. It's the only time in my life I'd ever seen him close to violence. They had a horrible fight. It was almost worse than the beating to listen to it. I went up to the bedroom to get away from the worst of it, and Brie came in with salve. She tended to me like a little mother, talking nonsense all the while the shouts and curses boomed up the stairs. Her hands were shaking."

She didn't object when Rogan drew her into his arms, but her eyes remained dry, her voice calm. "I thought he would go then. They said such vicious things to each other, I thought no two people could live under the same roof after. I thought if he'd just take us with him, if Brie and I could just go with him, anywhere at all, it would be all right again. Then I heard him say that he was paying, too. That he was paying for ever having believed that he loved and wanted her. That he'd go to his grave paying. Of course, he didn't go."

Maggie pulled away again. Stepped back. "He stayed more than ten years longer, and she never touched me again. Not in any way. But neither of us forgot that day—I think neither of us wanted to. He tried to make up for it by giving me more, loving me more. But he couldn't. If he'd left her, if he taken us and left her, it would have changed things. But that he couldn't do, so we lived in that house, like sinners in hell. And I knew no matter how he loved me that there were times he must have thought if it hadn't been—if *I* hadn't been, he'd have been free."

"Do you honestly blame the child, Maggie?"

"The sins of the fathers . . ." She shook her head. "One of my mother's favorite expressions that. No, Rogan, I don't blame the child. But it doesn't change the results." She took a deep breath. She was better for having said it all. "I'll never risk locking myself in that prison."

"You're too smart a woman to believe what happened to your parents happens to everyone."

"Not to everyone, no. One day, now that she's not hobbled by my mother's demands, Brie will marry. She's a woman who wants family."

"And you don't."

"I don't," she said, but the words sounded hollow. "I've my work, and a need to be alone."

He caught her chin in his hand. "You're afraid."

"If I am, I've a right to be." She shook free of him. "What kind of wife or mother would I make with what I've come from?"

"Yet you've just said your sister will be both."

"It affected her differently than it did me. She has as much need for people and for a home as I have to do without them. You were right enough when you said I was stubborn and rude and self-absorbed. I am."

"Maybe you've had to be. But that's not all you are, Maggie. You're compassionate and loyal and loving. It's not just part of you I fell in love with, but the whole. I want to spend my life with you."

Something trembled inside her, fragile as crystal struck by a careless hand. "Haven't you listened to a word I've said?"

"Every word. Now I know that you don't just love me. You need me."

She dragged both hands through her hair, fingers digging in and pulling in frustration. "I don't need anyone."

"Of course you do. You're afraid to admit it, but that's understandable." He was sorry, bitterly, for the child she'd been. But he couldn't allow that to change his plans for the woman. "You've locked yourself in a prison, Maggie. Once you admit those needs, the door will open."

"I'm happy with the way things are. Why do you have to change them?"

"Because I want more than a few days a month with you. I want a life with you, children with you." He skimmed a hand over her hair to cup the back of her neck. "Because you're the first and only woman I've ever loved. I won't lose you, Maggie. And I won't let you lose me."

"I've given you all I can give, Rogan." Her voice was shaky, but she held her ground. "It's more than

I've given anyone else. Be content with what I'm able to give, for if you can't, I'll have to end it."

"Can you?"

"I'll have to."

His hand squeezed once at the base of her neck, then released and fell away. "Stubborn," he said with a trace of amusement to hide the ache. "Well, so am I. I can wait for you to come to me. No, don't tell me you won't," he went on as she opened her mouth to protest. "It will only make it more difficult on you when you do. We'll leave things as they are, Maggie. With one alteration."

The relief she'd felt shifted into wariness. "Which is?"

"I love you." He pulled her into his arms, covered her mouth with his. "You'll have to get used to hearing it."

She was glad to be home. At home she could savor the solitude, enjoy her own company and the long, long days where the light clung to the sky until ten. At home, she didn't have to think of anything but work. To prove it, she gave herself three days in her glass house, three days without interruption.

She was productive, pleased with the results she saw cooling in the annealing oven. And she was, for the first time in her memory, lonely.

That was on his head, she thought as she watched the twilight grow and deepen and slip beautifully toward night. He'd tricked her into enjoying his company, into enjoying the whirl of cities and people. He'd made her want too much.

She wanted him too much.

Marriage. The thought made her shudder as she

gathered what she wanted from the kitchen table. That, at least, he could never make her want. She was certain, given a little time, he would see it her way. If not . . .

She stepped outside, shut the door. It was best not to think about any if-nots. Rogan was, above all, a sensible man.

She took the walk to Brianna's slowly as night settled around her. A slow mist gathered at her feet, and a breeze holding a warning chill whispered through the trees.

Like a welcoming beacon, the light in Brianna's kitchen glowed against the night. Maggie shifted the sketches she'd framed and quickened her steps.

As she approached, a low growl sounded out of the shadows of the sycamore. Maggie called out softly and was answered by a happy bark. Con leaped out of the shadows, through the mist, and would have jumped on her to show his love and devotion had she not held out a hand to stop him.

"I'd rather not be knocked over, thank you." She rubbed his head, his neck, while his swinging tail tore the thin fog like rags. "Guarding your princess tonight, are you? Well, let's go in and find her."

The moment Maggie opened the kitchen door, Con shot through in a blur of fur and muscle. He paused across the room at the door that led into the hallway, tail thumping.

"Out there, is she?" Maggie set the sketches aside and walked to the door. She heard voices through it, a soft laugh, a British accent. "She has guests," she said to Con, and disappointed the dog thoroughly when she backed away from the door. "We won't disturb her, so you're stuck with me." To make the prospect a bit more hopeful, she went to the cupboard where Brianna kept Con's biscuits. "Well, what trick will you do for me, boy-o?"

Con eyed the biscuit she was holding, smacked his lip. With restrained dignity he padded to Maggie, sat and lifted a paw.

"Well done, lad."

Once he had the treat between his teeth, Con pranced to the rug in front of the kitchen hearth, circled three times, then settled down with a sigh to enjoy himself.

"I could do with something myself."

A quick snoop around the kitchen revealed a treasure. A square of gingerbread, half-gone, rested under a protecting cloth. Maggie ate one slice while the kettle was heating, and sat down to another with a homey pot of tea.

When Brianna came in, Maggie was scraping crumbs from the plate.

"I wondered when you'd come by." Brianna reached down to pet the dog, who'd risen to press himself against her legs.

"It would have been sooner, if I'd known this was waiting. You've guests, I see."

"Yes, a couple from London, a student from Derry and two sweet ladies down from Edinburgh. How did you enjoy your holiday?"

"It was a beautiful place, hot, sunny days, warm nights. I drew you some pictures so you'd see for yourself." She gestured to them.

Brie lifted the pictures and her face lit up with joy. "Oh, they're wonderful."

"I thought you'd like them more than a postcard."

"I do. Thank you, Maggie. I've some clippings about your show in Paris."

Maggie was surprised. "Oh, how did you get them?"

"I asked Rogan to send them to me. Would you like to see?"

"Not now, no. They'll just give me a nervous stomach, and my work's going too well."

"Will you be going to Rome when the show moves on?"

"I don't know. I haven't thought about it. All that part of it seems a long way from here."

"Like a dream." Brianna sighed as she sat down. "I can hardly believe I was in Paris."

"You could travel more now, if you'd like."

"Mmm." Perhaps there were places she'd like to see, but home held her. "Alice Quinn had a boy. David they're calling him. He was christened just yesterday. He wailed all through the service."

"And Alice probably fluttered around like a bird."

"No, she held little David and soothed him, then took him off to nurse. Marriage and motherhood have changed her. You wouldn't think it was the same Alice."

"Marriage always changes people."

"Often for the better." But Brianna knew what Maggie was thinking. "Mother's getting along well."

"I didn't ask."

"No," Brianna said evenly. "But I'm telling you. Lottie's badgered her into sitting out in the garden every day, and into taking walks."

"Walking?" Despite herself, Maggie's interest was snagged. "Mother, walking?"

"I don't know how she does it, but Lottie has a way

with her. The last time I visited Mother was holding yarn while Lottie balled it. When I came in, she tossed it down and began to rant about how the woman would drive her into the grave. Claimed she fired Lottie twice, but Lottie wouldn't go. All the while Mother complained, Lottie rocked in her chair, smiling and rolling her yarn.''

"If the woman drives Lottie away—"

"No, let me finish." Brianna leaned forward, her eyes dancing. "I stood there, making excuses and apologies and waiting for the worst. And after a while Lottie stopped rocking. 'Maeve,' she said, 'stop pestering the girl. You sound like a magpie.' And she handed the yarn back to her and told me how she was after teaching Mothing to knit.''

"Teaching her to—oh, that'll be the day.''

"The thing was, Mother kept muttering under her breath and arguing with Lottie. But she seemed to be enjoying it. You were right about her having her own place, Maggie. She may not realize it yet, but she's happier there than she's been most of her life.''

"The point is she's out of here." Restless, Maggie rose to prowl around the kitchen. "I don't want you deluding yourself into thinking I did it out of the goodness of my heart.''

"But you did," Brianna said quietly. "If you want no one but me to know it, that's your choice.''

"I didn't come here to talk about her, but to see how you were getting on. Have you moved into the room off the kitchen?''

"Yes. It gives me another room upstairs free for guests.''

"It gives you some privacy.''

"There's that. I've a place for a desk in there so I

can do the books and the paperwork. I like having a window right over the garden. Murphy said I could have a door put in, if I want, so I could come in and out without going through the rest of the house."

"Good." Maggie lifted a jar of currants, set it down again. "Have you enough for the labor?"

"I've enough. It's been a good summer. Maggie, won't you tell me what's troubling you?"

"Nothing is," Maggie answered abruptly. "I've a lot on my mind, that's all."

"Have you quarreled with Rogan?"

"No." It couldn't be called a quarrel, she thought. "Why should you assume I'd be thinking of him?"

"Because I saw you together, saw how much you care for each other."

"That should be enough, shouldn't it?" Maggie demanded. "I care for him and he for me. The business we have together is successful and will likely continue to be. That should be enough."

"I don't know the answer to that. Are you in love with him?"

"I'm not." Wouldn't be. "He thinks I am, but I can't be responsible for what the man thinks. Nor will I change my life for him, or anyone. He's already made it change." She hugged her arms close, feeling suddenly cold. "And, damn him, I can't go back."

"Back to what?"

"To being what I was, what I thought I was. He's made me want more. I know I always did, but he's made me admit it. It's not enough for me to believe in my work, I need him to. He's made himself a part of it, and if I fail, I don't fail alone. When I succeed, the satisfaction isn't mine alone either. And I think

I've compromised myself because I've given part of me, the best of me, into his hands.''

"Is it your art you're talking about, Maggie, or is it your heart?" Brianna stared hard at her sister as she asked the question.

Maggie sat again, defeated. "I don't have one without the other. So it seems I've given him a piece of both.''

Rogan would have been surprised to hear it. He'd decided, after a great deal of thought, to treat his relationship with Maggie as he would any business merger with a reluctant company. He'd made his offer. Now it was time to stand back, to distance himself while the other party considered.

There was no professional reason to contact her. The show in Paris would remain for another two weeks before moving to Rome. The pieces had been chosen, the groundwork laid.

For the foreseeable future, she had her work and he had his. Any business contact could be made through his staff.

He would, in other words, let her stew.

It was important to his pride and his plans not to let her know how much her rejection of his feelings had hurt. Apart, they could each evaluate their future objectively. Together, they would simply end up in bed. That was no longer enough.

Patience and a firm hand was what was required. Rogan was sure of it. And if Maggie remained so foolishly obstinate after a reasonable amount of time, he'd use whatever means were at his disposal.

Rogan knocked briskly on his grandmother's door. It wasn't their usual time for visiting, but after being back in Dublin for a week, he needed the comfort of family.

He nodded at the maid who opened the door. "Is my grandmother at home?"

"Yes, Mr. Sweeney. She's in the front parlor. I'll tell her you're here."

"No need." He strode down the hall and through the open parlor doors. Christine rose immediately and opened her arms to him.

"Rogan! What a lovely surprise."

"I had a meeting canceled, so I thought I'd drop in and see how you were." He drew her back, lifting a brow as he studied her face. "You look exceptionally well."

"I feel exceptionally well." She laughed and led him to a chair. "Shall I get you a drink?"

"No. I don't have very long, and I only came for the company."

"I've heard how well it went in Paris." Christine sat beside him, soothed down the skirt of her linen dress. "I had lunch with Patricia last week, and she told me it was a rousing success."

"It was. Though I can't say how Patricia would know." He thought of his friend with a lingering trickle of guilt. "She's well?"

"Oh, very. Blooming, you could say. And I believe she said Joseph had told her about the Paris business. She's working very hard on her day school, and Joseph is giving her a bit of help."

"Good. I haven't had much time at the gallery this past week, I'm afraid. The fact is the expansion in Limerick is taking most of my efforts."

"How is that going?"

"Well enough. I've had some complications, so I'll have to take a trip down to sort them out."

"But you've hardly gotten back."

"It shouldn't take more than a day or two." He cocked his head, watching his grandmother tug at her skirt, brush at her hair. "Is something wrong?"

"No." She smiled brightly and forced her hands to still. "Not at all, though there is something I want to discuss with you. You see . . ." She trailed off, calling herself a miserable coward. "How is Maggie? Did she enjoy France?"

"She seemed to."

"It's a beautiful time of year to holiday at the villa. Was the weather good?"

"It was. Is it weather you want to discuss, Grandmother?"

"No, I was just—are you sure you don't want that drink?"

A trickle of alarm skidded down his back. "If something's wrong, I want you to tell me."

"There's nothing wrong, darling. Nothing at all wrong."

To his amazement she blushed like a schoolgirl. "Grandmother—"

He was interrupted by a clatter on the stairs and a shout. "Chrissy? Where have you gone off to, girl?"

Rogan stood slowly as a man popped into the doorway. He was burly of chest, bald as an egg and dressed in an ill-fitting suit the color of marigolds. His face was round and wrinkled. It beamed like a moon.

"There you are, my darling girl. I thought I'd lost you."

"I was about to ring for tea." Christine's blush

deepened as the man strode into the room and kissed both her fluttering hands.

"Rogan, this is Niall Feeney. Niall, my grandson, Rogan."

"So, this be himself." Rogan found his hand enveloped and pumped heartily. "Well, it's delighted I am to be meeting you at long last. Chrissy's told me all about you, lad. Why, you're the very apple of her eye."

"I'm—pleased to meet you, Mr. Feeney."

"No, no, now, none of that formality between us. Not with all our family connections." He winked and laughed until his belly jiggled.

"Connections?" Rogan said weakly.

"Aye, with me growing up no farther than a toad could spit from Chrissy here. Fifty years pass, begad, and now fate has it that you're handling all that pretty glass my niece makes."

"Your niece?" Realization struck like a fist. "You're Maggie's uncle."

"I am indeed." Niall sat, very much at home, his substantial belly sagging over his belt. "Proud as a peacock of the girl, I'll say, though I don't understand a bloody thing about what she's doing. I have to take Chrissy's word that it's fine."

"Chrissy," Rogan repeated in a small voice.

"Isn't it lovely, Rogan?" Christine's nervous smile hurt her face. "It seems Brianna wrote to Niall in Galway to tell him Maggie and you were working together. Of course, she mentioned that you were my grandson. Niall wrote me back, and one thing led to another. He's come to visit awhile."

"Visit. In Dublin?"

"A fine city it is, to be sure." Niall smacked a hand

on the delicate arm of the sofa. "With the prettiest girls in all of Ireland." He winked at Christine. "Though, in truth, I've only eyes for one."

"Go on with you, Niall."

Rogan stared at the pair of them, all but billing and cooing before his eyes. "I believe I'll have that drink after all," he said. "A whiskey."

🌷 Chapter Eighteen

IT was a very subdued Rogan who left his grandmother's parlor and swung by the gallery just past closing. He didn't want to believe he'd seen what he knew he'd seen. Just as Maggie had once said, when a couple is intimate, they throw off signals.

His grandmother, for God's sake, was flirting with Maggie's moon-faced uncle from Galway.

No, he decided as he let himself into the gallery, it didn't bear thinking of. Signals there might have been, but undoubtedly he'd read them incorrectly. His grandmother was, after all, over seventy, a woman of faultless taste, unblemished character, impeccable style.

And Niall Feeney was . . . was simply indescribable, Rogan decided.

What he needed was a couple of hours of perfect peace and quiet in his gallery office—away from people and phones and anything remotely personal.

He shook his head as he crossed the room. He was sounding entirely too much like Maggie.

The raised voices stopped him before his hand met the knob. An argument was in full swing on the other side of the door. While manners might have urged him to retreat, curiosity turned the tide.

He opened the door on Joseph and Patricia in full steam.

"I tell you, you're not using the head God gave you," Joseph shouted. "I won't be the cause of an estrangement between you and your mother."

"I don't give a bloody pin for what my mother thinks," Patricia shouted right back, causing Rogan's mouth to fall open. "This has nothing to do with her."

"The fact that you could say so proves my point. You're not using your head. She's—Rogan." Joseph's furious face went still as a stone. "I didn't expect you in."

"Obviously." Rogan looked cautiously from Joseph to Patricia. "I seem to have interrupted."

"Perhaps you can talk your way through that pride of his." Eyes glinting with emotion, Patricia tossed back her hair. "I can't."

"This has nothing to do with Rogan." Joseph's voice was quiet, with the steel of warning beneath.

"Oh, no, we mustn't let anyone know." The first tear spilled over. Patricia dashed it away. "We should keep sneaking around like—like adulterers. Well, I won't do it any longer, Joseph. I'm in love with you and I don't care who knows." She whirled on Rogan. "Well? What do you have to say about it?"

He held up a hand as if to regain his balance. "I think I should leave you alone."

"No need." She fumbled for her purse. "He won't listen to me. It was my mistake to believe he would. That he was the only one who really would."

"Patricia."

"Don't Patricia me in that tone," she snapped at Joseph. "All my life I've been told what to do and how to do it. What's proper, what's acceptable, and I'm sick to death of it. I tolerated the criticism over opening my school, and the damnable unspoken belief of my friends and family that I'd fail. Well, I won't fail." She whirled on Rogan again as if he'd spoken. "Do you hear, I won't fail. I'll do exactly what I wish, and I'll do it well. What I won't tolerate is criticism of my choice of lovers. Not from you, not from my mother, and most certainly not from the lover I've chosen."

Chin up, she looked back at Joseph with tear-drenched eyes. "If you don't want me, then be honest and say so. But don't you dare tell me what's best for me."

Joseph stepped toward her, but she was already darting out the door. "Patty! Damn it." Better to let her go, Joseph told himself. Better for her. "I'm sorry, Rogan," he said stiffly. "I would have found a way to have avoided that scene if I'd known you were coming in."

"Since you didn't, perhaps you might explain it." Equally stiff, Rogan rounded his desk and sat, assuming the position of authority. "In fact, I insist."

Joseph didn't bat an eye at Rogan's seamless switch from friend to employer. "It's obvious I've been seeing Patricia."

"I believe the term she used was *sneaking about.*"

The color washed back into Joseph's face. "We—I thought it best if we were discreet."

"Did you?" A fire kindled in Rogan's eyes. "And treating a woman like Patricia like one of your casual affairs was your idea of discretion?"

"I was prepared for your disapproval, Rogan."

Beneath his tailored jacket, Joseph's shoulders were rigid as steel. "I expected it."

"And well you should have," Rogan said evenly.

"So I did, just as I expected the reaction I got from her mother when Patricia talked me into dining with them last evening." His hands tightened into fists. "A gallery manager without a drop of blue in his blood. She might as well have said it, for it was in her eyes. Her daughter could do better. And by Christ she can. But I won't stand here and have you say that what's between us is a casual affair." His voice had risen to a shout by the time he was finished.

"Then what is it?"

"I'm in love with her. I've been in love with her since the first time I saw her, nearly ten years ago. But then there was Robert . . . and there was you."

"There was never me." Baffled, Rogan rubbed his hands over his face. Was the world going mad? he wondered. His grandmother and Maggie's uncle, himself and Maggie and now Joseph and Patricia. "When did this happen?"

"The week before you left for Paris." Joseph remembered those giddy hours, those wonderful days and nights before reality had set in. "I didn't plan it, but that hardly changes anything. I realize you may want to make other arrangements now."

Rogan dropped his hands. "What other arrangements?"

"For managing the gallery."

What he needed, Rogan thought, was to go home and find a bottle of aspirin. "Why?" he asked wearily.

"I'm your employee."

"You are, and I hope you'll remain so. Your private life has nothing to do with your work here. Good

Christ, do I look like some kind of monster who would fire you for claiming to be in love with a friend of mine?" He indulged his now throbbing head a moment by pressing the heels of his hands to his eyes. "I walk in here—into my own office, I'll remind you—and find the two of you snapping like terriers. Before I can take the next breath, Patricia's clawing at me for not believing her capable of running a school." He shook his head and dropped his hands. "I never thought she was incapable of anything. She's one of the most intelligent women I know."

"You just got caught in the backlash," Joseph murmured, and gave in to the desperate need for a cigarette.

"So it seems. You've a right to tell me it's none of my business, but as someone who's known you for ten years, and Patricia longer than that, I do take an interest. What the devil were you fighting about?"

Joseph huffed out smoke. "She wants to elope."

"Elope?" If Joseph had told him Patricia wanted to dance naked in St. Stephen's Square, he'd have been no more staggered. "Patricia?"

"She's cooked up some mad scheme about us driving up to Scotland. It seems she had a row with her mother and came storming straight over here."

"I've never known Patricia to storm anywhere. Her mother's not in favor of the relationship, I take it."

"Anything but." He offered a weak smile. "The truth is, she thinks Patricia should hang out for you."

Rogan was hardly surprised at this news. "She's doomed to disappointment there," he said. "I've other plans. If it helps matters, I'll make them clear to her."

"I don't know as it could hurt." Joseph hesitated, then sat as he was used to, on the corner of Rogan's desk. "You don't mind, then? It doesn't bother you?"

"Why should it? And as far as Anne's concerned, Dennis will bring her around."

"That's what Patricia said." Joseph studied the cigarette smoldering between his fingers, then pulled out his little flip-top ashtray and crushed it out. "She seemed to think if we just ran off and got married, her mother would soon fall in with the idea as if it had been hers all along."

"I'd lay odds on it. She wasn't keen on Robbie at first either."

"Wasn't she?" Joseph had the look of a man who was beginning to see the light.

"Not at all sure he was good enough for her darling daughter." Speculating, Rogan rocked back in his chair. "It didn't take long for her to begin to dote on him. Of course, he didn't wear an earring."

Joseph's grin flashed as he lifted a hand to his ear. "Patty likes it."

"Hmm," was all Rogan could think of to say. "Anne might be a bit difficult." He ignored Joseph's rude snort. "But in the end, all she wants is her daughter's happiness. If you're the answer to that, Anne will want you as well. You know, we could manage well enough around here if you took a sudden trip to Scotland."

"I couldn't. It wouldn't be fair to her."

"Your business, of course. But . . ." Rogan stretched back in his chair again. "It seems to me a woman might find a wild ride over the border, a ceremony in some musty chapel and a honeymoon in the Highlands very romantic."

"I don't want her to regret it." Joseph was beginning to sound less certain.

"The woman who walked out of here just now looked to me to know her own mind."

"She does, and she's come to know mine all too quickly." He pushed away from the desk. "I'd better go find her." He stopped at the door, tossed a grin over his shoulder. "Rogan, can you spare me for a week?"

"Take two. And kiss the bride for me."

The wire that came three days later, telling Rogan that Mr. and Mrs. Joseph Donahoe were well and happy proved to him that he wasn't a hard-hearted man. In fact, he liked to believe he'd done his part to speed the two lovers on their way.

But there were two other lovers he'd have given much to see go their separate paths. In fact, he fantasized daily about booting Niall Feeney all the way back to Galway. At first Rogan tried to ignore the situation. When more than a week had passed and Niall was still cozily ensconced in Christine Sweeney's home, he tried patience. After all, he told himself, how long would a woman of his grandmother's taste and sensibilities be duped by a charmless, borish west-county sharpie?

After two weeks, he decided it was time to try reason.

Rogan waited in the parlor—the parlor, he reminded himself that reflected the style and breeding of a lovely, sensible and generous woman.

"Why, Rogan." Christine glided into the room looking, her grandson thought, entirely too attrac-

tive for a woman of her age. "What a lovely surprise.
I thought you were on your way to Limerick."

"I am. I've just stopped in on the way to the
airport." He kissed her, glanced over her shoulder to
the doorway. "So . . . you're alone?"

"Yes, Niall's out running some errands. Do you
have time for a bite to eat before you go? Cook's
baked some lovely tarts. Niall's charmed her so, that
she's been baking treats daily."

"Charmed her?" As his grandmother sat Rogan
rolled his eyes.

"Oh, yes. He's always popping into the kitchen to
tell her what a way she has with soup, or the duck or
some dish or other. She can't do enough for him."

"He certainly looks like a man who eats well."

Christine's smile was indulgent. "Oh, he loves his
food, Niall does."

"I'm sure it goes down easy, when it's free."

The comment had Christine raising a brow. "Would
you have me bill a friend for a meal, Rogan?"

"Of course not. He's been in town some time
now," he said, changing tacks. "I'm sure he must miss
his home, and his business."

"Oh, he's retired. As Niall says, a man can't work
all his life."

"If he's worked at all," Rogan said under his
breath. "Grandmother, I'm sure it's been nice for
you to visit with a friend from your childhood,
but—"

"It has. It's been truly wonderful. Why, I feel young
again." She laughed. "Like a girl. Just last night we
went dancing. I'd forgotten what a fine dancer Niall
is. And when we go to Galway—"

"We?" Rogan felt himself pale. "*We* go to Galway?"

"Yes, next week we're planning to take a long drive back to the west. A bit of nostalgia for me. Of course, I'm interested in seeing Niall's home."

"But you can't. It's absurd. You can't go traipsing off to Galway with the man."

"Why ever not?"

"Because it's—you're my grandmother, for God's sake. I won't have you . . ."

"Won't have me what?" she asked very quietly.

The tone, reflecting the sort of anger she rarely directed at him, had Rogan reining in. "Grandmother, I realize you've let yourself be swept away by the man, by the memories. I'm sure there's no harm in it. But the idea of you going off with a man you haven't seen for more than fifty years is ludicrous."

How young he was, Christine thought. And how distressingly proper. "I believe, at my age, I'd enjoy doing something ludicrous. However, I don't believe taking a trip back to my childhood home with a man I'm very fond of, a man I knew long before you were born, fits into that category. Now, perhaps," she said, holding up a hand before he could speak, "you find that the idea of my having a relationship, an adult, satisfying relationship with Niall, does fit that category."

"You're not telling me—you're not saying—you haven't actually . . ."

"Slept with him?" Christine leaned back, tapping her well-manicured nails on the arm of the love seat. "That's certainly my business, isn't it? And I don't require your approval."

"Of course not." He heard himself beginning to babble. "I'm just concerned, naturally."

"Your concern is noted." She rose, regally. "I'm

sorry that you're shocked by my behavior, but it can't be helped."

"I'm not shocked—damn, of course I'm shocked. You can't just . . ." He could hardly say the words, could he? In his grandmother's parlor. "Darling, I know nothing about the man."

"I know about him. I haven't any definite plans on how long we'll be in Galway, but we will be stopping in to see Maggie and her family on the way. Shall I give her your regards?"

"You can't have thought this through."

"I know my own mind and heart better, it seems, than you think. Have a safe trip, Rogan."

Dismissed, he had no choice but to kiss her cheek and leave. The moment he was in the car, he yanked at the phone. "Eileen, reschedule Limerick for tomorrow. . . . Yes, there's a problem," he muttered. "I have to go to Clare."

When the first touch of fall caressed the air and gilded the trees, it seemed a sin not to enjoy it. After two solid weeks of work, Maggie decided she deserved a day off. She spent the morning in the garden, weeding with a vigor that would have made Brianna proud. To reward herself, she decided to bike to the village for a late lunch at O'Malley's.

There was a bite to the air, and the layered clouds to the west promised rain before nightfall. She pulled on her cap, pumped up her rear tire, which was going flat, then guided the bike around the house and through the gate.

She set off at a leisurely pace, dreaming a bit over the harvesting in the fields. The fuchsia continued to bloom in teardrops of red despite the threat of early frost. The landscape would change as soon as winter set it, become barren and swept by a bitter wind. But it would still be beautiful. The nights would lengthen, urging people to their fires. The rains would come, sweeping across the Atlantic with the wail of the wind.

She looked forward to it, and to the work she would do in the chilly months ahead.

She wondered if she could convince Rogan to come west during the winter, and if she did, would he find charm in the rattling windows and smoky fires. She hoped that he would. And when he stopped punishing her, she hoped that they could go back to the way things had been before that last night in France.

He'd see reason, she told herself, and leaned low over the bike against the wind. She'd make him see it. She'd even forgive him for being high-handed, overconfident and dictatorial. The moment they were together again, she would be calm and cool and sweet-tongued. They'd put this foolish disagreement behind them, and—

She had time to squeal, barely, and to swerve into the hedgerows as a car barreled around the curve. Brakes screamed, the car veered, and Maggie ended up bottom first in the blackthorn.

"Jesus, Mary and Joseph, what kind of a blind, ignorant fool is it who tries to run down innocent people?" She shoved the cap back that had fallen over her eyes and glared. "Oh, of course. It would be you."

"Are you hurt?" Rogan was out of the car and beside her in an instant. "Don't try to move."

"I can move, curse you." She batted his exploring

hands away. "What do you mean driving at that horrible speed? This isn't a raceway."

The heart that had lodged hard in his throat freed itself. "I wasn't driving that fast. You were in the middle of the road, daydreaming. If I'd come around that turn a second sooner, I'd have flattened you like a rabbit."

"I wasn't daydreaming. Minding my own business was what I was doing, not expecting some jackeen to come speeding along in a fancy car." She brushed off the seat of her pants, then kicked her bike. "Now see what you've done. I've a puncture."

"You're lucky it's the tire that's flat and not yourself."

"What are you doing?" she demanded.

"I'm putting this excuse for transportation in the car." Once he'd done so, he turned back to her. "Come on, I'll drive you back home."

"I wasn't going home. If you had any sense of direction, you'd see I was going to the village, where I was going to have a meal."

"That'll have to wait." He took her arm in the proprietary manner she forgot she'd found amusing.

"Oh, will it? Well, you can drive me to the village or nowhere at all, because I'm hungry."

"I'll drive you home," he said again. "I have something to discuss with you, privately. If I'd been able to get through to you this morning, I could have told you I was coming and you wouldn't have been riding that bike in the middle of the road."

With this, he slammed the car door behind her and skirted the hood.

"If you'd been able to get through this morning,

and had had this nasty way about you, I'd have told you not to bother to come at all."

"I've had a difficult morning, Maggie." He resisted the urge to rub at the headache drumming behind his temples. "Don't push me."

She began to, then saw that he'd said no more than the truth. There was trouble in his eyes. "Is it a problem at work?"

"No. Actually, I do have some complications with a project in Limerick. I'm on my way there."

"So you're not staying."

"No." He glanced at her. "I'm not staying. But it isn't the factory expansion I need to speak with you about." He stopped at her gate, shut off the car. "If you've nothing to eat, I'll run into the village and bring something back."

"It's not a problem. I can make do." She relented enough to close a hand over his. "I'm glad to see you, even though you nearly ran me down."

"I'm glad to see you." He lifted the hand to his lips. "Even though you nearly ran into me. I'll get your bike out."

"Just leave it in front." After striding up the walk, she turned. "Have you a proper kiss for me?"

It was hard to resist that quick flash of smile, or the way she reached up to link her hands behind his head. "I've a kiss for you, proper or not."

It was easy to meet the heat, to draw the energy in. What was difficult was to check the need, that instant desire to back her through the door and take it all.

"Perhaps I was daydreaming a bit before," she said, tugging on his lips. "I was thinking of you, and wondering how much longer you'd punish me."

"How do you mean?"

"By staying away from me." She spoke airily as she pushed through the door.

"I wasn't punishing you."

"Just staying away, then."

"Distancing myself, to give you time to think."

"And time to miss you."

"To miss me. And to change your mind."

"I have missed you, but I haven't changed my mind or anything else. Why don't you sit? I need to get some more turf for the fire."

"I love you, Maggie."

That stopped her, had her closing her eyes a moment before she turned back. "I believe you might, Rogan, and though something in me warms to it, it changes nothing." She hurried out.

He hadn't come to beg, he reminded himself. He'd come to ask her to help him with a problem. Though from her reaction, he believed things were changing more than she was ready to admit.

He paced to the window, to the sagging sofa, back again.

"Will you sit?" she demanded when she came back with her arms piled with turf blocks. "You'll wear out the floor. What's this business in Limerick?"

"A few complications, that's all." He watched as she knelt at the hearth and expertly stacked fuel. It occurred to him that he'd never seen anyone build a turf fire before. A restful sight, he mused, that drew a man close to seek that warm red heart. "We're expanding the factory."

"Oh, and what do you make at your factory?"

"China. For the most part the inexpensive sort that's fashioned into mementos."

"Mementos?" She paused at her work, leaned back

on her haunches. "Souvenirs, you mean? Not those little bells and teacups and such in the tourist shops?"

"They're very well done."

She tossed back her head and laughed. "Oh, it's rich. I've hired myself a man who makes little plates with shamrocks all over them."

"Have you any idea what percent of our economy depends on tourism, on the sale of little plates with shamrocks on them, or hand-knit sweaters, linen, lace, bloody postcards?"

"No." She snorted behind her hand. "But I'm sure you can tell me, down to the pence. Tell me, Rogan, do you do much business in plaster leprechauns, or plastic shillelaghs?"

"I didn't come here to justify my business to you, or to discuss the fact that this expansion—which will allow us to manufacture some of the finest china produced in Ireland—will create more than a hundred new jobs in a part of the country that desperately needs them."

She waved a hand to stop him. "I'm sorry, I've insulted you. I'm sure there's a rising need for thimbles and ashtrays and cups that say 'Erin Go Bragh.' It's just hard for me, you see, to picture a man who wears such wonderful suits owning a place that makes them."

"The fact that I do makes it possible for Worldwide to subsidize and offer grants to a number of artists each year. Even if they are snobs."

She rubbed the back of her hand over her nose. "That puts me in my place. And since I don't want to waste what time we have arguing, we'll say no more about it. Are you going to sit, or just stand there and glower at me? Not that you don't look fine, even with a scowl on your face."

He surrendered on a long breath. "Your work's going well?"

"Very well." She shifted, crossing her legs on the rug. "I'll show you what's new before you go, if there's time."

"We're a little behind at the gallery. I suppose I should tell you that Joseph and Patricia have eloped."

"Yes, I know. I've had a card from them."

He tilted his head. "You don't seem at all surprised."

"I'm not. They were crazy in love with each other."

"I seem to recall you claiming Patricia was crazy in love with me."

"Not at all. I said she was half in love with you, and I'll stand by that. I imagine she wanted to be in love with you—it would have been so convenient after all. But it was Joseph all along. That's not what's troubling you, is it?"

"No. I admit it took me by surprise, but it doesn't trouble me. I've come to realize I took Joseph's skills for granted. He'll be back tomorrow, and I'm grateful for it."

"Then what is it?"

"Have you had a letter from your uncle Niall?"

"Brianna has. She's the one who gets them, as she's the one who'll remember to answer back. He wrote to tell her he'd be visiting Dublin and might pass through on his way back home. Have you seen him?"

"Seen him?" On a sound of disgust, Rogan pushed out of the chair again. "I can't get near my grandmother without stepping all over him. He's settled himself in her house for two weeks past. We've got to decide what to do about it."

"Why should we do anything?"

"Are you listening to me, Maggie? They've been living together. My grandmother and your uncle—"

"Great-uncle, actually."

"Whatever the devil he is to you, they've been having a flaming affair."

"Have they?" Maggie let out a roar of approving laughter. "Well, that's wonderful."

"Wonderful? It's insane. She's been acting like some giddy girl, going dancing, staying out half the night, sharing her bed with a man whose suits are the color of fried eggs."

"So you object to his taste in clothes?"

"I object to him. I'll not have him waltzing into my grandmother's house and planting himself in the parlor as if he belongs there. I don't know what his game is, but I won't have him exploiting her generous heart, her vulnerability. If he thinks he'll get his hands on one penny of her money—"

"Hold that." She sprang up like a tiger. "'Tis my blood you're speaking of, Sweeney."

"This is no time to be overly sensitive."

"Overly sensitive." She jabbed him in the chest. "Look who's talking. You're jealous because your granny's got someone besides you in her life."

"That's ridiculous."

"It's true as the day. Do you think a man couldn't be interested in her, but for her money?"

Familial pride stiffened his spine. "My grandmother is a beautiful, intelligent woman."

"I'll not disagree with that. And my Uncle Niall is no fortune hunter. He retired from his business most comfortably set. He may not have a villa in France or wear suits tailored by the bloody British, but he's done well enough and has no need to play gigolo. And I won't have you speak of me kin in such a way in me own house."

"I didn't mean to offend you. I've come to you because, as their family, it's up to us to do something about the situation. Since they're planning a trip to Galway within the next few days, and passing by here on the way, I'd hoped you might speak with him."

"Certainly I'll speak with him. He's my kin, isn't he? I'd hardly ignore him. But I won't help you interfere. You're the snob, Rogan, and a prude as well."

"Prude?"

"You're offended by the idea of your grandmother having a rich and full sex life."

He winced, hissed through his teeth. "Oh please. I don't want to imagine it."

"Nor should you, since it's her private business." Her mouth twitched. "Still . . . it's interesting."

"Don't." Defeated, he sank into the chair again. "If there's one picture I don't want in my mind, it's that."

"Actually, I can't quite get it there myself. Now, wouldn't it be a strange thing if they married? Then we'd be in the way of cousins after all." Laughing, she slapped his back when he choked. "Could you use a whiskey, darling?"

"I could. Maggie." He took several deep breaths. "Maggie," he called again as she rummaged through in the kitchen. "I don't want her to be hurt."

"I know." She came back, holding two glasses. "It's knowing that that kept me from bloodying your nose when you spoke so of Uncle Niall. Your gran's a fine woman, Rogan, and a wise one."

"She's—" Finally, he said it aloud. "She's all I have left of my family."

Maggie's eyes gentled. "You're not losing her."

He let out a breath, stared into his glass. "I suppose you think I'm being a fool."

"No, I don't—exactly." She smiled when his eyes lifted to hers. "A man can be expected to be a bit jittery when his granny takes on a boyfriend."

Rogan winced. She laughed.

"Why not let her be happy? If it eases your mind, I'll look the situation over when they stop here."

"That's something at least." He touched his glass to hers, and they tossed the whiskey back together. "I have to go."

"You've hardly been here. Why don't you come to the pub with me and we'll have a meal together. Or"—she slipped her arms around him—"we'll stay here and go hungry."

No, he thought as he lowered his mouth to hers. They wouldn't be hungry for long.

"I can't stay." He set the empty glass aside to take her by her shoulders. "If I did we'd only end up in bed. That wouldn't solve anything."

"There doesn't have to be anything to solve. Why must you make it complicated? We're good to-gether."

"We are." He framed her face in his hands. "Very good together. That's only one of the reasons I want to spend my life with you. No, don't draw away. Nothing you told me changes what we can have. Once you realize that, you'll come to me. I can wait."

"You'll just go, then stay away again? So, it's marriage or nothing?"

"It's marriage." He kissed her again. "And everything. I'll be in Limerick for almost a week. The office knows where to reach me."

"I won't call."

He traced a thumb over her lips. "But you'll want to. That's enough for now."

🎀 Chapter Nineteen

"**Y**OU'RE being pigheaded, Maggie."

"You know, I'm tired of having that particular word applied to me." With goggles protecting her eyes, Maggie experimented with lamp work. For nearly a week everything she'd free-blown had dissatisfied her. For a change of pace she had set up a half-dozen torches, three clamped to each side of a bench, and was heating a tube of glass in the cross fire.

"Well, if it's applied to you often enough, it may be true," Brianna shot back. "It's family. You can spare one evening for family."

"It isn't a matter of time." She meant this, though for some reason, Maggie felt time was breathing down her neck like a snarling dog. "Why should I subject myself to having dinner with her?" Carefully, brows knit, she began to pull and rotate the softened glass. "I can tell you I have no appetite for it. Nor will she."

"'Tisn't just Mother who'll be coming. Uncle Niall and Mrs. Sweeney will be there. And Lottie, of course, It would be rude of you not to come."

"I've been told I'm that, as well as pigheaded." As with everything else she'd touched over the last few days, the glass refused to follow the vision in her head. The vision itself blurred, infuriating her as much as it frightened her. Pure obstinancy kept her working.

"You haven't seen Uncle Niall since Da's wake. And he's bringing Rogan's grandmother, for heaven's sake. You told me you liked her very much."

"I do." Damn it, what was wrong with her hands? What was wrong with her heart? She fused one rod to the other, burned it off, returned, burned it off. "Perhaps one of the reasons I don't want to be there is so she'll not be subjected to one of our happy family meals."

The sarcasm was as hot as one of Maggie's points of flame. Brianna faced it down with ice. "It wouldn't cost you much to put aside your feelings for one night. If Uncle Niall and Mrs. Sweeney are going out of their way to visit us before going on to Galway, we'll welcome them. All of us."

"Stop badgering me, will you? You're pecking away at me like a damn duck. Can't you see I'm working?"

"You hardly do anything else, so it's necessary to interrupt you if I want a word. They'll be here shortly, Maggie, and I'll not make excuses for you." In a gesture similar to her sister's habitual stance, Brianna folded her arms. "I'll stand right here and keep pecking until you do what's expected of you."

"All right, all right. Jesus. I'll come to the damn dinner."

Brianna smiled serenely. She'd never expected less. "At half seven. I'm serving my guests earlier so we'll have a private family meal."

"And oh, what a jolly time that will be."

"It'll go well enough if you promise to hold that

nasty tongue of yours. I'm only asking for the smallest of efforts."

"I'll smile, I'll be polite. I won't eat with me fingers." With a bitter sigh, Maggie shoved up her goggles and held the figure on the end of the tube out of the flames.

"What have you done there?" Curious, Brianna stepped closer.

"Gone mad."

"It's pretty. Is it a unicorn?"

"Aye, a unicorn—only needs a touch of gold on the horn to make it complete." She laughed, turning the mythical figure in the air. "It's a joke, Brie, a poor one. On me. It'll be swans next, I'm sure. Or those little dogs with puffs for tails." She set her work aside, briskly turned off her torches. "Well, that's that, I suppose. I'll hardly do anything worthwhile today, so I'll be along to your dinner party. God help you."

"Why don't you rest awhile, Maggie? You look awfully tired."

"Perhaps I will, after I crate up a few pieces." She tossed the goggles aside, rubbed her hands over her face. She was tired, Maggie realized. Outrageously so. "You needn't worry, Brie, you'll not have to send out the dogs for me. I've said I'll be there."

"I'm grateful." Brianna reached down to squeeze her sister's hand. "I have to go back, make certain everything's in place. Half seven, Maggie."

"I know."

She waved her sister out. To keep her mind on practical matters, she took one of the crates she'd made and packed it with padding. After spreading bubble wrap over a table, she turned to the shelves at the back of the shop. There was only one piece there, the last she'd completed before Rogan's visit.

Tall and sturdy, the trunk speared up, then curved, flooding down in slim, graceful limbs that almost seemed to sway. It would stand, she thought, like the willow that had inspired it. And it would bend, yielding, even as it remained true to itself. The color was a deep, pure blue that flooded up from the base and paled gently to the delicate tips.

She wrapped it carefully, for it was more than a sculpture. This was the last work she'd been able to draw successfully from her heart. Nothing she had attempted since then had gelled. Day after day she had labored only to remelt and remelt. Day after day she came closer to releasing the panic that jittered inside her.

His fault, she told herself as she secured the top of the crate. His fault for tempting her with fame and fortune, for exposing her vanity to such a stunning and fast success. Now she was blocked, dried up. As hollow as the tube she'd fashioned into a unicorn.

He'd made her want too much. Want him too much. Then he had walked away and let her see, brutally, what it was like to have nothing.

She wouldn't give up, nor would she give in. Maggie promised herself she would have her pride at least. While her furnace roared mockingly she sat in her chair, felt the familiarity of its shape.

It was only that she'd been working too hard, surely. She'd been pushing herself to do better and better work with each piece. The pressure of holding on to success had blocked her, that was all. She couldn't suppress the idea that as the tour moved on from Paris it would be found wanting. That *she* would be found wanting.

That she would never again pick up the pipe just for herself, just for the pleasure of it. Rogan had changed all that. He had, as she'd told him he would, changed her.

And how was it, she thought, closing her eyes, how could it be that a man could make you love him by going away?

"You've done well for yourself, haven't you, darling?" Niall, stuffed into one of his bright-hued suits like a happy sausage, beamed at Brianna. "I always said you were a clever lass. Takes after me dear sister, does Brianna, Chrissy."

"You have a lovely home." Christine accepted the glass Brianna offered. "And your gardens are simply breathtaking."

"Thank you. They give me pleasure."

"Rogan told me how he enjoyed his brief stay here." Christine sighed, content with the warmth of the fire and the glow of the lamp. "I can see why."

"She's got the touch." Niall gave Brianna a bone-crushing squeeze around the shoulders. "In the blood, you know. Blood runs true."

"So it seems. I knew your grandmother quite well."

"Chrissy was underfoot all the time." Niall winked. "Thought I didn't notice her. Shy was what I was."

"You never had a shy moment in your life," Christine said with a laugh. "You thought I was a nuisance."

"If I did, I've changed me mind." He leaned over

and under Brianna's curious eye, kissed Christine firmly on the mouth.

"It took you more than fifty years."

"Seems like yesterday."

"Well . . ." Disconcerted, Brianna cleared her throat. "I suppose I should check on . . . I believe that's Mother and Lottie," she continued when raised voices boomed down the hallway.

"You drive like a blind woman," Maeve complained. "I'll walk back to Ennis before I get into that car with you again."

"If you can do better, you should drive yourself. Then you'd have a sense of independence." Obviously unconcerned, Lottie strolled into the parlor, unwrapping a thick scarf from around her neck. "It's a chilly night," she announced, rosy-cheeked and smiling.

"And you dragging me out in it'll put me in bed for a week."

"Mother." Shoulders braced against embarrassment, Brianna helped Maeve off with her coat. "I'd like you to meet Mrs. Sweeney. Mrs. Sweeney, this is my mother, Maeve Concannon, and our friend Lottie Sullivan."

"I'm delighted to meet you both." Christine rose to offer her hand to both women. "I was a friend of your mother's, Mrs. Concannon. We were girls together in Galway. I was Christine Rogan then."

"She spoke of you," Maeve said shortly. "I'm pleased to meet you." Her gaze shifted to her uncle, narrowed. "Well, Uncle Niall, is it? You haven't graced us with your presence for many a day."

"It warms my heart to see you, Maeve." He enveloped her in an embrace, patting her stiff back with a beefy hand. "I hope the years have been kind to you."

"Why would they?" The moment she was freed, Maeve sat in a chair by the fire. "This fire's drawing poorly, Brianna."

It wasn't, but Brianna walked over to make minute adjustments to the flue.

"Stop fussing," Niall ordered with a casual wave of his hand. "It's drawing fine. We all know Maeve lives to complain."

"Doesn't she, now?" Lottie spoke pleasantly while she pulled her knitting needles from the basket she'd brought along. "I pay no mind to it myself. But that comes from raising four children, I suppose."

Unsure what step to take, Christine focused on Lottie. "What lovely wool, Mrs. Sullivan."

"Thank you. I'm partial to it myself. Had you a nice trip from Dublin, then?"

"A lovely one, yes. I'd forgotten how beautiful this part of the country was."

"Nothing but fields and cows," Maeve tossed out, annoyed that the conversation was circling out of her control. "It's fine to live in Dublin and pass through on a fine autumn day. Come winter, you wouldn't think it so lovely." She might have continued the theme, but Maggie came in.

"Why, it's Uncle Niall, big as life." With a laugh, she went into his arms.

"Little Maggie Mae, all grown up."

"As I've been for some time." She stepped back, laughed again. "Well, you've lost nearly all of it now." She rubbed an affectionate hand over his head.

"It was such a fine head, you see, the good Lord

saw no need to cover it with hair. I've heard about how well you're doing, darling. I'm proud of you."

"Mrs. Sweeney's telling you that so she can brag upon her grandson. It's lovely seeing you," Maggie said to Christine. "I hope you won't let this one run you ragged in Galway."

"I find I can keep up. I was hoping, if it's not inconvenient to you, that I could have a look at your glass house tomorrow before we go."

"Sure I'd be glad to show you. Hello, Lottie, are you well?"

"Fit as a fiddle." Her needles clacked musically. "I was hoping you'd come by the house and tell us about your trip to France."

This statement drew an audible sniff from Maeve. Schooling her features, Maggie turned. "Mother."

"Margaret Mary. You've been busy with your own doings, as usual, I see."

"I have."

"Brianna finds time to come by twice a week to see that I have all I need."

Maggie nodded. "Then it isn't necessary for me to do the same."

"I'll serve dinner now, if everyone's ready," Brianna cut in.

"I'm always ready for a meal," Niall kept Christine's hand in his, using his free one to give Maggie's shoulder a squeeze as they went into the dining room.

There was linen on the table, and fresh flowers, with the warmth of candles flickering on the sideboard. The food was beautifully prepared and plentiful. It should have been a pleasant, congenial evening. But, of course, it wasn't.

Maeve picked at her food. The lighter the mood at the table became, the darker grew her own. She envied Christine her fine, well-cut dress, the gleam of pearls around her throat, the quiet, expensive scent that drifted from her skin. And the skin itself, soft and pampered by wealth.

Her mother's friend, Maeve thought. Her childhood playmate, class to class. The life Christine Sweeney had led should have been hers, she thought. Would have been hers, but for one mistake. But for Maggie.

She could have wept from the rage of it, from the shame of it. From the helpless loss of it.

All around her the conversation bubbled like some expensive wine, frothy and foolish talk about flowers and old times, about Paris and Dublin. About children.

"How lovely for you to have such a large family," Christine was saying to Lottie. "I was always sorry that Michael and I couldn't have more children. Though we doted on our son, then on Rogan."

"A son," Maeve muttered. "A son doesn't forget his mother."

"It's true, it's a special bond." Christine smiled, hoping to soften the harshness around Maeve's mouth. "But I confess, I always wanted a daughter of my own. You're blessed with two, Mrs. Concannon."

"Cursed, more like."

"Try the mushrooms, Maeve." Deliberately Lottie spooned some onto Maeve's plate. "They're fried to a turn. You've a fine hand, Brianna."

"I learned the knack of these from my gran," Brianna began. "I was always pestering her to show me how to cook."

"And blaming me because I didn't chose to strap myself to the stove," Maeve tossed back her head. "I'd no liking for it. I'll wager you don't spend much time in the kitchen, Mrs. Sweeney."

"Not a great deal, I'm afraid." Aware her voice had chilled, Christine made the effort to lighten it again. "And I'll have to admit that none of my efforts there can come close to what you've served us tonight, Brianna. Rogan was right to praise your cooking."

"She makes a living from it. Bedding and boarding strangers."

"Leave her alone." Maggie spoke quietly, but the look in her eyes was as sharp as a shout. "God knows she bedded and boarded you as well."

"As was her duty. There's no one at this table would deny that it's a daughter's obligation to tend to her mother. Which is more than you've ever done, Margaret Mary."

"Or ever will do, so count your blessings that Brie tolerates you."

"I haven't a blessing to count, with my own children tossing me out of my own house. Then leaving me, sick and alone."

"Why, you haven't been sick a day, Maeve," Lottie said complacently. "And how can you be alone when I'm there, day and night?"

"And you draw a weekly wage to be there. It should be my own blood tending me, but no. My daughters turn their backs, and my uncle, with his fine house in Galway, pays no mind at all."

"Enough to see you haven't changed, Maeve." Niall regarded her with pity. "Not a whit. I apologize, Chrissy, for my niece's poor behavior."

"I think we'll have our dessert in the parlor." Pale

and quiet, Brianna rose. "If you'd like to go in and sit, I'll serve it."

"Much cozier," Lottie agreed. "I'll help you, Brianna."

"If you'll excuse me, Uncle Niall, Mrs. Sweeney, I'd like a word with my mother before we join you." Maggie kept her seat, waiting until the room emptied out. "Why would you do it?" Maggie asked Maeve. "Why would you spoil it for her? Would it have been so hard to give her the illusion for one evening that we were a family?"

Embarrassment only sharpened Maeve's tongue. "I've no illusions, and no need to impress Mrs. Sweeney from Dublin."

"You impressed her just the same—badly. It reflects on us all."

"Do you think you can be better than the rest of us, Margaret Mary? Better because you traipse off to Venice or Paris?" With her knuckles whitening on the edge of the table, Maeve leaned forward. "Do you think I don't know what you've been doing with that woman's grandson? Whoring yourself without an ounce of shame. Ah, he sees you've got the money and the glory you always wanted. You've only had to sell body and soul to get it."

Maggie clasped her hands beneath the table to try to stem the shaking. "My work's what I sell, so perhaps you've a point about my soul. But my body's mine. I've given it to Rogan freely."

Maeve paled as her suspicions were confirmed. "And you'll pay for it, as I did. A man of his class wants nothing more from the likes of you than what he finds in the dark."

"You know nothing about it. Nothing about him."

"But I know you. What will happen to your fine career when you discover a baby in your belly?"

"If I found myself with a child to raise, I pray God I'd do a better job than you. I wouldn't give everything up and wrap myself and the child in sackcloth for the rest of my days."

"And that you know nothing about," Maeve said sharply. "But go on this way, and you will. You'll know what it's like to see your life stop and your heart break."

"But it didn't have to. Other musicians have families."

"I was given a gift." To her own misery, Maeve felt tears burn her eyes. "And because I was arrogant, as you are, it was taken from me. There's been no music in me since the moment I made you."

"There could have been," Maggie whispered. "If you'd wanted it badly enough."

Wanted it? Even now Maeve could feel the old scar throb over her heart. "What good is wanting?" she demanded. "All your life you've wanted, and now you risk having it taken away for the thrill of having a man between your legs."

"He loves me," Maggie heard herself say.

"A man speaks easily of loving in the dark. You'll never be happy. Born in sin, live in sin, die in sin. And alone. Just as I'm alone."

"You've made hating me your life's work, and a fine job you've done of it." Slowly, unsteadily, Maggie rose. "Do you know what frightens me, frightens me down to the bone? You hate me because you see yourself when you look at me. God help me if you're right."

She fled out of the room, and into the night.

*   *   *

The hardest pill to swallow was apology. Maggie postponed downing it, distracting herself by showing Christine and Niall her studio. In the cool light of morning, the nastiness of the previous evening blurred a little. She was able to soothe herself by explaining various tools and techniques, even, when Niall insisted, trying to coach him through blowing his first bubble.

"It's not a trumpet." Maggie clasped a hand on the pipe as he started to lift it high. "Showing off like that will do no more than have hot glass spilling all over you."

"I believe I'll stick with me golf." He winked and turned the pipe back to her. "One artist in the family's enough."

"And you really make your own glass." Christine wandered around the shop, in tailored slacks and a silk blouse. "From sand."

"And a few other things. Sand, soda, lime. Feldspar, dolomite. A bit of arsenic."

"Arsenic." Christine's eyes widened.

"And this and that," Maggie said with a smile. "I guard my formulas closely, like a sorcerer with a spell. Depending on what color you want, you add other chemicals. Various colorants change in different base glasses. Cobalt, copper, manganese. Then there are the carbonates and the oxides. The arsenic's an excellent oxide."

Christine looked dubiously at the chemicals Maggie showed her. "I'd think it would be simpler to melt down used or commercial glass."

"But it's not yours then, is it?"

"I didn't realize you had to be a chemist as well as an artist."

"Our Maggie was always a bright one." Niall swung an arm over her shoulder. "Sarah was always writing me with how bright she was in school, how sweet Brianna's disposition."

"That was it," Maggie said with a laugh. "I was bright, Brie was sweet."

"She said Brie was bright as well," Niall said staunchly.

"But I'll wager she never said I was sweet." Maggie turned to nuzzle her face in his coat. "I'm so glad to see you again. I didn't realize how glad I would be."

"I've neglected you since Tom died, Maggie Mae."

"No. We all had our own lives, and Brie and I both understood that Mother didn't make it easy for you to visit. As to that . . ." She pulled back, took a deep breath. "I'd like to apologize for last evening. I shouldn't have provoked her, and I certainly shouldn't have left without saying good night."

"There's no need for apologies from you, or from Brianna as I've told her already today." Niall patted Maggie's cheek. "Maeve had settled on her mood before she arrived. You provoked nothing. You're not to blame for the way she's chosen to go through life, Maggie."

"Whether I am or not, I'm sorry the evening was uncomfortable."

"I would have called it illuminating," Christine said calmly.

"I suppose it was," Maggie agreed. "Uncle Niall, did you ever hear her sing?"

"I did. Lovely as a nightingale, to be sure. And restless, like one of those big cats you see caged in the zoo. She was never an easy girl, Maggie, happy only when the people would hush and listen to her music."

"Then there was my father."

"Then there was Tom. From what I'm told they were blind and deaf to everything but each other. Maybe to each other as well." He stroked the big hand down her hair. "It could be neither of them saw what was inside until they were bound. And when they did, what they saw was different than they'd hoped. She let that sour her."

"Do you think if they hadn't met, she'd have been different?"

He smiled a little and kept his hand gentle. "We're tossed by the winds of fate, Maggie Mae. Once we end where they blow us, we make of ourselves what we will."

"I'm sorry for her," Maggie said softly. "I never thought I could be."

"And you've done well by her." He kissed Maggie's brow. "Now it's time to make yourself what you will."

"I'm working on it." She smiled again. "Very hard on it."

Satisfied that the timing was right, Christine spoke up. "Niall, would you be a darling and give me a moment with Maggie?"

"Girl talk, is it?" His round face creased in smiles. "Take your time, I'll go for a walk."

"Now then," Christine began as soon as the door shut behind Niall. "I have a confession. I didn't go into the parlor right after last night. I came back, thinking I might be able to smooth things over."

Maggie lowered her eyes to stare at the floor. "I see."

"What I did, rudely, was listen. It took all my

control not to barge into that room and give your mother a piece of my mind."

"It would only have made things worse."

"Which was why I didn't give in to the urge—though it would have been greatly satisfying." Christine took Maggie by the arms, gave her a little shake. "She has no idea what she has in you."

"Perhaps she knows too well. I've sold part of what I am because there's a need in me, just as there is in her, for more."

"You've earned more."

"If I've earned it, or been given it as a gift, it doesn't change things. I wanted to be content with what I had, Mrs. Sweeney. I wanted so much to be, because otherwise I'd be admitting there hadn't been enough. That my father had failed us, and he didn't. Before Rogan walked through that door, I was content, or I'd talked myself into believing I could be. But the door's open now and I've had a taste of it. I haven't done a decent hour's work in a week."

"Why do you think that is?"

"He's pushed me into a corner, that's why. It can't be for myself anymore, *I* can't be for myself anymore. He's changed that. I don't know what to do. I always know what to do."

"Your work comes through your heart. That's plain for anyone who's seen in. Maybe you're blocking off your heart, Maggie."

"If I am, it's because I have to. I won't do what she did. Nor what my father did. I won't be the cause of misery, or the victim of it."

"I think you *are* the victim of it, my dear Maggie. You're letting yourself feel guilty for succeeding, guiltier yet for harboring the ambition to succeed. And I think you're refusing to let out what's in your heart, because once you do, you won't be able to take it back again, even though holding it in is making you unhappy. You're in love with Rogan, aren't you?"

"If I am, he brought it on himself."

"I'm sure he'll deal with it admirably."

Maggie turned away to shuffle tools on a bench. "He's never met her. I think I made sure he wouldn't so he couldn't see I was like her. Moody and mean, dissatisfied."

"Lonely," Christine said softly, and drew Maggie's eyes back to hers. "She's a lonely woman, Maggie, through no one's fault but her own. It'll be no one's but yours if you're lonely, too." Coming forward, she took Maggie's hands. "I didn't know your father, but there must be some of him in you as well."

"He dreamed. So do I."

"And your grandmother, with her quick mind and ready temper. She's in you as well. Niall, with his wonderful lust for life. All of that's in you. None of it makes up the whole. Niall's right about that, Maggie. So right. You'll make yourself what you will."

"I thought I had. I thought I knew exactly who I was and wanted to be. Now it's all mixed up in my head."

"When your head won't give you the answer, it's best to listen to your heart."

"I don't like the answer it's giving me."

Christine laughed. "Then, my dear child, you can be absolutely sure it's the right one."

𝒮. Chapter Twenty

BY midmorning, her solitude tucked around her, Maggie took up her pipe again. Two hours later the vessel she had blown was tossed back into the melt for cullet.

She pored over her sketches, rejected them, tried others. After scowling at the unicorn she'd set on a shelf, she turned to her torches for lamp work. But she'd hardly taken up a rod of glass before the vision faded. She watched the tip of the rod dip, melt, begin to droop. Hardly thinking of what she was doing, she began dropping the bits of molten glass into a container of water.

Some broke, others survived. She took one out by the tip to study. Though it had been formed by fire, it was cool now, shaped like a tear. A Prince Rupert's drop, no more than a glass artist's novelty, one a child could create.

Rubbing the one drop between her fingers, she took it to her polariscope. Through the lens the internal stresses in the drop exploded into a dazzling rainbow of colors. So much, she thought, inside so little.

She slipped the drop into her pocket, fished several more out of the bucket. Moving with studied care, she shut down her furnaces. Ten minutes later she was striding into her sister's kitchen.

"Brianna. What do you see when you look at me?"

Blowing a stray hair out of her eyes, Brianna looked up and continued to knead her bread dough. "My sister, of course."

"No, no. Try for once not to be so literal-minded. What is it you see in me?"

"A woman who seems to be on the edge of something, always. One who has enough energy to tire me to the bone. And anger." Brianna stared down at her hands again. "Anger that makes me sad and sorry."

"Selfishness?"

Startled, Brianna glanced up again. "No, not that. Not ever. That's one flaw I've never seen in you."

"But others?"

"You've enough of them. What, do you want to be perfect?"

The dismissive tone had Maggie wincing. "You're still upset with me about last evening."

"I'm not, no." With renewed vigor Brianna began to pound the dough. "With myself, with circumstances, with fate, if you like. But not with you. It wasn't your doing, and God knows you warned me it wouldn't work. But I wish you wouldn't always leap to defend me."

"I can't help it."

"I know." Brianna smoothed the dough into a mound and slipped it into a bowl for a second rising. "She was better behaved after you'd gone. And a little embarrassed, I think. Before she left she told me I'd cooked a nice meal. Not that she ate any of it, but at least she said it."

"We've had worse evenings."

"That's God's truth. Maggie, she said something else."

"She says lots of things. I didn't come to go over all of that."

"It was about the candlesticks," Brianna continued, and had Maggie lifting both brows.

"What of them?"

"The ones I had on the sideboard, the ones you'd made me last year. She said what pretty work they were."

With a laugh, Maggie shook her head. "You've been dreaming."

"I was awake and standing in my own hallway. She looked at me, and she told me. And she kept standing there, looking at me until I understood that she couldn't say it to you herself, but she wanted you to know."

"Why should she?" Maggie said unsteadily.

"I think it was a kind of apology, for whatever passed between you in the dining room. The best she could make. When she saw I understood her, she started in on Lottie again, so the two of them left the way they'd come in. Arguing."

"Well." Maggie had no idea how to react, how to feel. Restlessly, her fingers reached into her pocket to toy with the smooth glass drops.

"It's a small step, but a step it is." Brisk, Brianna began to dust flour on her hands in preparation for kneading the next loaf. "She's happy in the house you gave her, even if she doesn't know it yet."

"You could be right." Her breath hitched a bit as she released it. "I hope you are. But don't be planning any more family meals in the near future."

"That I won't."

"Brianna . . ." Maggie hesitated, ended by looking helplessly at her sister. "I'm driving to Dublin today."

"Oh, you'll have a long day, then. You're needed at the gallery?"

"No. I'm going to see Rogan. I'm either going to tell him I'm not going to see him again, or that I'll marry him."

"Marry him?" Brianna bobbled the next ball of dough. "He's asked you to marry him?"

"The last night we were in France. I told him no, absolutely no. I meant it. I might still. That's why I'm driving, to give myself time to think it through. I've realized that it has to be one or the other." She fingered the glass drops in her pocket. "So I'm going, and I wanted to tell you."

"Maggie—" Brianna was left with her hands full of dough, staring at the swinging back door.

The worst part was not finding him home—and knowing she should have checked before making the drive. At the gallery, his butler had said, but when she arrived there, cursing Dublin traffic all the way, he was already gone and on the way to his office.

Again, she missed him, by no more than five minutes, she was informed. He was heading to the airport and a flight to Rome. Would she care to put through a call to his car phone?

She would not, Maggie decided, stumble through one of the biggest decisions of her life over the telephone. In the end, she got back in her lorry and made the long, lonely drive back to Clare.

It was easy to call herself a fool. And to tell herself

she was better off not having found him at all. Exhausted by the hours of driving, she slept like the dead until noon the next day.

Then she tried to work.

"I want the *Seeker* in the forefront, and the *Triad* centered, precisely."

Rogan stood in the sun-washed showroom of Worldwide Gallery, Rome, watching his staff arrange Maggie's work. The sculptures stood up well in the gilded rococo decor. The heavy red velvet he'd chosen to drape the pedestals and tables added a royal touch. Something he was sure Maggie would have complained about, but which suited the clientele of this particular gallery.

He checked his watch, muttered to himself under his breath. He had a meeting in twenty minutes. There was no help for it, he thought as he called out another order for a minute adjustment. He was going to be late. Maggie's influence, he supposed. She'd corrupted his sense of time.

"The gallery opens in fifteen minutes," he reminded the staff. "Expect some press, and see that they each receive a catalog." He scanned the room one last time, noting the placement of each piece, the fold of every drape. "Well done."

He stepped outside into the bright Italian sun, where his driver waited.

"I'm running late, Carlo." Rogan shifted into his seat and opened his briefcase.

Carlo grinned, tucked the chauffeur's cap lower on his brow and flexed his fingers like a concert pianist preparing to launch into an arpeggio. "Not for long, signore."

To Rogan's credit, he barely lifted a brow as the car leaped like a tiger from the curb, snarling and growling at the cars it cut off. Bracing himself in the corner of the seat, Rogan turned his attention to a printout of figures from his Roman branch.

It had been an excellent year, he decided. Far from the staggering boom of the mideighties, but quite good enough. He thought perhaps it was best that the days when a painting could demand hundreds of millions of pounds at auction were over. Art, with so high a price tag, was too often hidden away in a vault until it was as soulless as gold bullion.

Still, it had been a profitable year. Profitable enough, he thought, that he could implement his idea of opening another smaller branch of Worldwide, one that displayed and sold only the works of Irish artists. It had been a germ in his mind for the last few years, but lately, just lately, it had grown.

A small, even cozy gallery—very accessible, from the decor to the art itself. A place that invited browsing, with good-quality art priced in a range that invited owning.

Yes, he thought the time was perfect. Absolutely perfect.

The car screeched to a halt, all but rearing up like a stallion. Carlo hurried out to open Rogan's door. "You are on time, signore."

"You are a magician, Carlo."

Rogan spent thirty minutes with the head of the Roman branch, twice that in a board meeting, then granted back-to-back interviews to promote the Concannon tour. Several hours were devoted to studying Rome's proposed acquisitions and to meeting artists.

He planned to fly to Venice that evening and lay the groundwork for the next stop of the tour. Gauging his time, he slipped away to place a few calls to Dublin.

"Joseph."

"Rogan, how's Rome?"

"Sunny. I've finished up here. I should be in Venice by seven at the latest. If there's time, I'll go by the gallery there tonight. Otherwise, I'll do the preliminaries tomorrow."

"I have your schedule here. You'll be back in a week?"

"Sooner, if I can manage it. Anything I should know?"

"Aiman was in. I bought two of his street sketches. They're reasonably good."

"That's fine. I've an idea we might be able to sell more of his work after the first of the year."

"Oh?"

"A project I'll discuss with you when I get back. Anything else?"

"I saw your grandmother and her friend off to Galway."

Rogan grunted. "Brought him by the gallery, did she?"

"He wanted to see some of Maggie's work—in the proper setting. He's quite the character."

"He certainly is."

"Oh, and speaking of Maggie, she was by earlier this week."

"By there? In Dublin? What for?"

"Didn't say. She sort of dashed in and out. I didn't even speak with her myself. She did send a shipment, with what seems to be a message for you."

"What message?"

"'It's blue.'"

Rogan's fingers paused on his notebook. "The message is blue?"

"No, no, the message reads, 'It's blue.' It's a gorgeous piece, rather delicate and willowy. Apparently she thought you'd know what she meant."

"I do." He smiled to himself, rubbing the bridge of his nose. "It's for the Comte de Lorraine, Paris. A wedding present for his granddaughter. You'll want to contact him."

"I will, then. Oh, and it seems Maggie was by your office, and the house as well. I suppose she was looking for you for some reason."

"It would seem so." He debated a moment, then acted on instinct. "Joseph, do me a favor? Contact the gallery in Venice. Tell them I'll be delayed a few days."

"I'll be glad to. Any reason?"

"I'll let you know. Give Patricia my best. I'll be in touch."

Maggie drummed her fingers on a table in O'Malley's, tapped her foot, blew out a long breath. "Tim, will you give me a bookmaker's sandwich to go with this pint? I can't wait for Murphy all bloody afternoon on an empty stomach."

"Happy to do it. Got a date, do you?" He grinned at her from over the bar, wriggled his eyebrows.

"Hah. The day when I date Murphy Muldoon's the day I lose what's left of my mind. He said he had some business in the village and would I meet him here." She tapped the box on the floor with her. "I've got his birthday present for his mother."

"Something you made, then?"

"Aye. And if he's not here by the time I've finished eating, he'll have to come fetch it himself."

"Alice Muldoon," said David Ryan, who sat at the bar puffing a cigarette. "She be living down to Killarney now, wouldn't she?"

"She would," Maggie agreed. "And has been these past ten years or more."

"Didn't think I'd seen her about. Married again, did she, after Rory Muldoon passed over?"

"She did." Tim took up the story while he built a pint of Guinness. "Married a rich doctor name of Colin Brennan."

"Kin to Daniel Brennan." Another patron picked up the tale, musing over his bowl of stew. "You know, he that runs a food store in Clarecastle."

"No, no." Tim shook his head as he walked over to serve Maggie her sandwich. "'Tisn't kin to Daniel Brennan but to Bobby Brennan from Newmarket on Fergus."

"I think you're wrong about that." David pointed with the stub of his cigarette.

"I'll wager two pounds on it."

"Done. We'll ask Murphy himself."

"If he ever gets here," Maggie muttered, and bit into her sandwich. "You'd think I have nothing better to do than to sit here twiddling my thumbs."

"I knew a Brennan once." The old man at the end of the bar spoke up, paused, blew a lazy smoke ring. "Frankie Brennan, he was, from Ballybunion, where I lived as a boy. One night he was walking home from the pub. Had a fill of porter, he did, and never had the head for it."

He blew another smoke ring. Time passed, but no one spoke. A story was in the making.

"So he went walking home, reeling a bit, and cut across a field to shorten the way. There was a fairy hill, and in his drunken state, he trod right over it. Well, a man should know better, drunk or sober, but Frankie Brennan got less than his share when the Lord passed out sense. Now, of course, the fairies had to teach him manners and respect, and so they tugged off all his clothes as he went staggering across the field. And he arrived home, stark naked, but for his hat and one shoe." He paused again, smiled. "Never did find the other shoe."

Maggie gave an appreciative hoot of laughter and propped her feet on the empty chair across from her. They could keep Paris and Rome and the rest, she thought. She was just where she wanted to be.

Then Rogan walked in.

His entrance gained him some glances, appraisals. It wasn't often a man in so fine a suit strolled into O'Malley's on a cloudy afternoon. Maggie, the pint glass nearly to her lips, froze like stone.

"Good day to you. Is there something I can get you?" Tim asked.

"A pint of Guinness, thank you." Rogan leaned back against the bar, smiled at Maggie while Tim turned the tap. "Good day to you, Margaret Mary."

"What are you doing here?"

"Why, I'm about to have a pint." Still smiling, he slid coins across the bar. "You're looking well."

"I thought you were in Rome."

"I was. Your work shows well there."

"Would you be Rogan Sweeney, then?" Tim slid the glass to Rogan.

"I would, yes."

"I'm O'Malley, Tim O'Malley." After wiping his hand over his apron, Tim took Rogan's and pumped. "I was a great friend of Maggie's father. He'd have been pleased with what you're doing for her. Pleased and proud. We've a scrapbook started, my Deirdre and I."

"I can promise you you'll be adding to it. Mr. O'Malley, for some time to come."

"If you've come to see if I've work to show you," Maggie called out, "I haven't. And I won't if you breathe down my neck."

"I haven't come to see your work." With a nod to Tim, Rogan walked to Maggie. He sat beside her, took her chin in his hand and kissed her softly. And kissed her long. "I've come to see you."

She let out the breath she'd forgotten she was holding. A frowning glance at the bar had the curious onlookers turning their attention elsewhere. Or pretending to.

"You took your sweet time."

"Time enough for you to miss me."

"I've hardly worked at all since you left." Because it was difficult to admit, she kept her eyes trained on her glass. "I've started and stopped, started and stopped. Nothing's coming out the way I want it to. I don't care for this feeling, Rogan. I don't care for it at all."

"What feeling is that?"

She shot him a look from under her lashes. "I've been missing you. I came to Dublin."

"I know." He toyed with the ends of her hair. It had grown a bit, he noted, and wondered how long it would be before she whacked away again with her scissors as she said she sometimes did. "Was it so hard to come to me, Maggie?"

"Yes, it was. As hard as anything I've done. Then you weren't there."

"I'm here now."

He was. And she wasn't sure she could speak for the pounding of her heart. "There are things I want to tell you. I don't—" She broke off as the door opened, and Murphy came in. "Oh, his timing's perfect."

Murphy signaled to Tim before heading toward Maggie. "You've had lunch, then." In a casual gesture, he scraped up a chair and snatched one of her chips. "Did you bring it?"

"I did. And you've kept me waiting half the day."

"It's barely one o'clock." Eyeing Rogan, Murphy ate another of Maggie's chips. "You'd be Sweeney, would you?"

"I would."

" 'Twas the suit," Murphy explained. "Maggie said how it was you dressed like every day was Sunday. I'm Murphy Muldoon, Maggie's neighbor."

The first kiss, Rogan remembered, and shook hands as cautiously as Murphy. "It's good to meet you."

"And you." Murphy leaned his chair on its back legs as he did his measuring. "You could almost say I'm a brother to Maggie. As she's no man to look out for her."

"And she's not needing one," Maggie tossed out. She would have kicked Murphy's chair out from under him if he hadn't been quick enough to drop it in place again. "I'll look out for myself very well, thank you."

"So she's often told me." Rogan addressed Murphy. "But need or not, she has one."

The message passed, male to male. After a moment's consideration, Murphy nodded. "That's fine, then. Did you bring it or not, Maggie?"

"I said I did." In an impatient move, she bent to grab the box from the floor and set it on the table between them. "If it wasn't for my fondness of your mother, I'd bash it over your head."

"She'll be grateful you restrained yourself." As Tim plunked down another beer Murphy opened the box. "This is grand, Maggie. She'll be pleased."

Rogan imagined so. The pale pink bowl was as fluid as water, its sides waving up to end in delicate crests. The glass was so thin, so fragile, he could see the shadow of Murphy's hands through it.

"You'll wish her a happy birthday for me as well."

"I will." Murphy skimmed a callused finger over the glass before setting it back in the box. "Fifty pounds, was it?"

"It was." Maggie held out a hand, palm up. "Cash."

Feigning reluctance, Murphy scratched his cheek. "It seems mighty dear for one little bowl, Maggie Mae—that you can't even eat from. But my mother likes foolish, useless things."

"Keep talking, Murphy, and the price'll go up."

"Fifty pounds." Shaking his head, Murphy reached for his wallet. He counted out the bills in her outstretched hand. "You know I could've gotten her a whole set of dishes for that. And maybe a fine new skillet."

"And she'd have knocked you in the head with it." Satisfied, Maggie tucked the bills away. "No woman wants a skillet for her birthday, and any man who thinks she does deserves the consequences."

"Murphy." David Ryan shifted on his stool. "If

you've finished your transaction there, we've a question for you."

"Then I'll have to answer it." Taking up his beer, Murphy rose. "'Tis a fine suit, Mr. Sweeney." He walked away to settle the wager of the Brennans.

"Fifty pounds?" Rogan murmured, nodding toward the box Murphy had left on the table. "You and I are both aware that you could get more than twenty times that."

"What of it?" Instantly defensive, she shoved her glass aside. "It's my work, and I'll ask for it what I please. You've got your damned exclusive clause, Sweeney, so you can sue me if you like for breaking it, but you'll not have the bowl."

"I didn't—"

"I gave my word to Murphy," she barreled on. "And a deal's done. You can have your cursed twenty-five percent of the fifty pounds. But if I choose to make something for a friend—"

"It wasn't a complaint." He wrapped his hand around her fisted one. "It was a compliment. You have a generous heart, Maggie."

With the wind so successfully stripped from her sails, she sighed. "The papers say I'm not to make anything that doesn't go to you."

"The papers say that," he agreed. "I imagine you'll go on snarling about it, and you'll go on slipping your friends gifts when it suits you." She shot him a look from under her lashes, so blatantly guilty, he laughed. "I see I could have sued you a time or two over the last few months. We can make what we'd call a side deal. I won't take my percentage of your fifty pounds, and you'll make something for my grandmother for Christmas."

She nodded, lowered her lashes again. "It isn't just about money, is it, Rogan? I'm afraid sometimes that it is, that I've let it be. Because I like the money, you see. I like it very much, and all that goes with it."

"It's not just about money, Maggie. It's not just about champagne showings or newspaper clippings or parties in Paris. Those are just trimmings. What it's about really is what's inside you, and all that you are that goes into creating the beautiful, the unique and the startling."

"I can't go back, you see. I can't go back to the way things were, before you." She looked at him then, studying his face feature by feature while his hand lay warm over hers. "Will you take a drive with me? There's something I want to show you."

"I have a car outside. I've already put your bike in it."

She had to smile. "I should have known you would."

With a fall wind in the air, and the leaves a riot of color, they drove toward Loop Hea. Away from the narrow road, spilling back like the sea itself, were harvested fields and the deep, sweet green so special to Ireland. Maggie saw the tumbled stone sheds that looked no different than they had when she had traveled this road nearly five years before. The land was there, and the people tended it, as they always had. Always would.

When she heard the sea, smelled the first sharp sting of it on the air, her heart lurched. She squeezed her eyes tight, opened them again. And read the sign.

LAST PUB UNTIL NEW YORK.

Shall we sail over to New York, Maggie, and have a pint?

When the car stopped, she said nothing, only got out to let the wind slap cool over her skin. Reaching for Rogan's hand, she held it as they walked down the beaten path to the sea.

The war continued, wave against rock in the echoing crash and hiss that was eternal. The mist had rolled in, so that there was no border between sea and sky, just a wide, wide cup of soft gray.

"I haven't been here in almost five years. I didn't know I'd ever come again to stand like this." She pressed her lips together, wishing the fist around her heart would loosen, just a little. "My father died here. We'd come out together, just us two. It was winter and bitter cold, but he loved this spot more than any other I can think of. I'd sold some pieces that day to a merchant in Ennis, and we'd celebrated in O'Malley's."

"You were alone with him?" The horror of it slashed Rogan like a rapier. He could do nothing for her but pull her into his arms and hold on. "I'm sorry, Maggie. So sorry."

She brushed her cheek over the soft wool of Rogan's coat, caught the scent of him in it. She let her eyes close. "We talked, about my mother, their marriage. I'd never understood why he stayed. Maybe I never will. But there was something in him that yearned, and that wanted for me and Brianna whatever that yearning was. I think I have the same longing, but that I might have the chance to grab hold of it."

She drew back so that she could look at his face as she spoke. "I've something for you." Watching him, she took one of the glass drops from her pocket, held it out in her palm.

"It looks like a tear."

"Aye." She waited while he held it to the light and studied it.

He rubbed a thumb over the smooth glass. "Are you giving me your tears, Maggie?"

"Perhaps I am." She took another one out of her pocket. "It comes from dropping hot glass in water. When you do, some shatter right away, but others hold and form. Strong." She crouched and chose a rock. While Rogan watched she struck the glass with rock. "Strong enough that it won't break under a hammer." She rose again, holding the undamaged drop. "It holds, you see. Does nothing more than bounce away from the blow and shine. But there's this thin end here and it only takes a careless twist." She took the slim, trailing end between her fingers. The glass turned to harmless dust. "It's gone, you see. Like it never was."

"A tear comes from the heart," Rogan said. "And neither should be handled carelessly. I won't break yours, Maggie, nor you mine."

"No." She took a long breath. "But we'll hammer away often enough. We're as different as that water and hot glass, Rogan."

"And as able to make something strong between us."

"I think we might. Yet I wonder how long you'd last in a cottage in Clare, or I in a house full of servants in Dublin."

"We could move to the midlands," he said, and watched her smile. "Actually, I've given that particular matter some thought. The idea, Maggie, is negotiation and compromise."

"Ah, the businessman, even at such a time."

He ignored the sarcasm. "I've plans to open a gallery in Clare to spotlight Irish artists."

"In Clare?" Pushing back her windblown hair, she stared at him. "A branch of Worldwide here in Clare? You'd do that for me?"

"I would. I'm afraid I'll spoil the heroics by telling you I'd thought of the idea long before I met you. The conception had nothing to do with you, but the location does. Or I should say it has to do with us." As the wind picked up he pulled her jacket together and buttoned it. "I believe I can live in a west-county cottage for part of the year, just as you could live with servants for the other."

"You've thought this all through."

"I have, yes. Certain aspects are, of course, negotiable." He studied the glass drop again before slipping it into his pocket. "There is one, however, that is not."

"And that would be?"

"Exclusivity again, Maggie, in the form of a marriage contract. A lifetime term with no escape clauses."

The fist around her heart squeezed all the tighter. "You're a hard bargainer, Sweeney."

"I am."

She looked out to sea again, the ceaseless rush of water, the indominable rock, and the magic they made between them. "I've been happy alone," she said quietly. "And I've been unhappy without you. I never wanted to depend on anyone, or to let myself care so much I could be made unhappy. But I depend on you, Rogan." Gently she lifted a hand to his cheek. "And I love you."

The sweetness of hearing it swarmed through him. He guided her palm over his lips. "I know."

And the fist, so tight around her heart, loosened. "You know." She laughed, shook her head. "Oh, it must be a fine thing to always be right."

"It's never been a finer thing." He lifted her off her feet, spun her around once before their lips met and clung. The wind swooped down, ribboned around them, smelling of the sea. "If I can make you unhappy, Maggie, then I can make you happy as well."

She squeezed her arms tight around him. "If you don't I'll make your life hell. I swear it. God, I never wanted to be a wife."

"You'll be mine, and glad of it."

"I'll be yours." She lifted her face to the wind. "And glad of it."

Can't get enough of Nora Roberts?
Try the #1 *New York Times* bestselling
In Death series, by Nora Roberts
writing as J. D. Robb.

Turn the page to see where it all began . . .

NAKED IN DEATH

SHE woke in the dark. Through the slats on the window shades, the first murky hint of dawn slipped, slanting shadowy bars over the bed. It was like waking in a cell.

For a moment she simply lay there, shuddering, imprisoned, while the dream faded. After ten years on the force, Eve still had dreams.

Six hours before, she'd killed a man, had watched death creep into his eyes. It wasn't the first time she'd exercised maximum force, or dreamed. She'd learned to accept the action and the consequences.

But it was the child that haunted her. The child she hadn't been in time to save. The child whose screams had echoed in the dreams with her own.

All the blood, Eve thought, scrubbing sweat from her face with her hands. Such a small little girl to have had so much blood in her. And she knew it was vital that she push it aside.

Standard departmental procedure meant that she would spend the morning in Testing. Any officer whose discharge of weapon resulted in termination of life was required to undergo emotional and psychiatric clearance before resuming duty. Eve considered the tests a mild pain in the ass.

She would beat them, as she'd beaten them before.

When she rose, the overheads went automatically to low setting, lighting her way into the bath. She winced once at her reflection. Her eyes were swollen from lack of sleep, her skin nearly as pale as the corpses she'd delegated to the ME.

Rather than dwell on it, she stepped into the shower, yawning.

"Give me one oh one degrees, full force," she said and shifted so that the shower spray hit her straight in the face.

She let it steam, lathered listlessly while she played through the events of the night before. She wasn't due in Testing until nine, and would use the next three hours to settle and let the dream fade away completely.

Small doubts and little regrets were often detected and could mean a second and more intense round with the machines and the owl-eyed technicians who ran them.

Eve didn't intend to be off the streets longer than twenty-four hours.

After pulling on a robe, she walked into the kitchen and programmed her AutoChef for coffee, black; toast, light. Through her window she could hear the heavy hum of air traffic carrying early commuters to offices, late ones home. She'd chosen the apartment years before because it was in a heavy ground and air pattern, and she liked the noise and crowds. On another yawn, she glanced out the window, followed the rattling journey of an aging airbus hauling laborers not fortunate enough to work in the city or by home 'links.

She brought the *New York Times* up on her monitor and scanned the headlines while the faux caffeine bolstered her system. The AutoChef had burned her toast again, but she ate it anyway, with a vague thought of springing for a replacement unit.

She was frowning over an article on a mass recall of droid cocker spaniels when her telelink blipped. Eve shifted to communications and watched her commanding officer flash onto the screen.

"Commander."

"Lieutenant." He gave her a brisk nod, noted the still-wet hair and sleepy eyes. "Incident at Twenty-seven West Broadway, eighteenth floor. You're primary."

Eve lifted a brow. "I'm on Testing. Subject terminated at twenty-two thirty-five."

"We have override," he said, without inflection. "Pick up your shield and weapon on the way to the incident. Code Five, Lieutenant."

"Yes, sir." His face flashed off even as she pushed back from the screen. Code Five meant she would report directly to her commander, and there would be no unsealed interdepartmental reports and no cooperation with the press.

In essence, it meant she was on her own.

Broadway was noisy and crowded, a party that rowdy guests never left. Street, pedestrian, and sky traffic were miserable, choking the air with bodies and vehicles. In her old days in uniform she remembered it as a hot spot for wrecks and crushed tourists who were too busy gaping at the show to get out of the way.

Even at this hour steam was rising from the stationary and portable food stands that offered everything from rice noodles to soy dogs for the teeming crowds. She had to swerve to avoid an eager merchant on his smoking Glida-Grill, and took his flipped middle finger as a matter of course.

Eve double-parked and, skirting a man who smelled worse than his bottle of brew, stepped onto the sidewalk. She scanned the building first, fifty floors of gleaming metal that knifed into the sky from a hilt of concrete. She was propositioned twice before she reached the door.

Since this five-block area of West Broadway was affectionately termed Prostitute's Walk, she wasn't surprised. She flashed her badge for the uniform guarding the entrance.

"Lieutenant Dallas."

"Yes, sir." He skimmed his official CompuSeal over the door to keep out the curious, then led the way to the bank of elevators. "Eighteenth floor," he said when the doors swished shut behind them.

"Fill me in, Officer." Eve switched on her recorder and waited.

"I wasn't first on the scene, Lieutenant. Whatever happened upstairs is being kept upstairs. There's a badge inside waiting for you. We have a homicide, and a Code Five in number eighteen-oh-three."

"Who called it in?"

"I don't have that information."

He stayed where he was when the elevator opened. Eve stepped out and was alone in a narrow hallway. Security cameras tilted down at her, and her feet were almost soundless on the worn nap of the carpet as she approached 1803. Ignoring the hand plate, she announced herself, holding her badge up to eye level for the peep cam until the door opened.

"Dallas."

"Feeney." She smiled, pleased to see a familiar face. Ryan Feeney was an old friend and former partner who'd traded the street for a desk and a top-level position in the Electronics Detection Division. "So, they're sending computer pluckers these days."

"They wanted brass, and the best." His lips curved in his wide, rumpled face, but his eyes remained sober. He was a small, stubby man with small, stubby hands and rust-colored hair. "You look beat."

"Rough night."

"So I heard." He offered her one of the sugared nuts from the bag he habitually carried, studying her, and measuring if she was up to what was waiting in the bedroom beyond.

She was young for her rank, barely thirty, with wide brown eyes that had never had a chance to be naive. Her doe-brown hair was cropped short, for convenience rather than style, but suited her triangular face with its razor-edge cheekbones and slight dent in the chin.

She was tall, rangy, with a tendency to look thin, but Feeney knew there were solid muscles beneath the leather jacket. But Eve had more—there was also a brain, and a heart.

"This one's going to be touchy, Dallas."

"I picked that up already. Who's the victim?"

"Sharon DeBlass, granddaughter of Senator De-Blass."

Neither meant anything to her. "Politics isn't my forte, Feeney."

"The gentleman from Virginia, extreme right, old money. The granddaughter took a sharp left a few years back, moved to New York and became a licensed companion."

"She was a hooker." Dallas glanced around the apartment. It was furnished in obsessive modern— glass and thin chrome, signed holograms on the walls, recessed bar in bold red. The wide mood screen behind the bar bled with mixing and merging shapes and colors in cool pastels.

Neat as a virgin, Eve mused, and cold as a whore. "No surprise, given her choice of real estate."

"Politics makes it delicate. Victim was twenty-four, Caucasian female. She bought it in bed."

Eve only lifted a brow. "Seems poetic, since she'd been bought there. How'd she die?"

"That's the next problem. I want you to see for yourself."

As they crossed the room, each took out a slim container, sprayed their hands front and back to seal in oils and fingerprints. At the doorway, Eve sprayed the bottom of her boots to slicken them so that she would pick up no fibers, stray hairs, or skin.

Eve was already wary. Under normal circumstances there would have been two other investigators on a homicide scene, with recorders for sound and pictures. Forensics would have been waiting with their usual snarly impatience to sweep the scene.

The fact that only Feeney had been assigned

with her meant that there were a lot of eggshells to be walked over.

"Security cameras in the lobby, elevator, and hallways," Eve commented.

"I've already tagged the discs." Feeney opened the bedroom door and let her enter first.

It wasn't pretty. Death rarely was a peaceful, religious experience to Eve's mind. It was the nasty end, indifferent to saint and sinner. But this was shocking, like a stage deliberately set to offend.

The bed was huge, slicked with what appeared to be genuine satin sheets the color of ripe peaches. Small, soft-focused spotlights were trained on its center where the naked woman was cupped in the gentle dip of the floating mattress.

The mattress moved with obscenely graceful undulations to the rhythm of programmed music slipping through the headboard.

She was beautiful still, a cameo face with a tumbling waterfall of flaming red hair, emerald eyes that stared glassily at the mirrored ceiling, long, milk-white limbs that called to mind visions of *Swan Lake* as the motion of the bed gently rocked them.

They weren't artistically arranged now, but spread lewdly so that the dead woman formed a final X dead-center of the bed.

There was a hole in her forehead, one in her chest, another horribly gaping between the open thighs. Blood had splattered on the glossy sheets, pooled, dripped, and stained.

There were splashes of it on the lacquered walls, like lethal paintings scrawled by an evil child.

So much blood was a rare thing, and she had

seen much too much of it the night before to take
the scene as calmly as she would have preferred.

She had to swallow once, hard, and force herself
to block out the image of a small child.

"You got the scene on record?"

"Yep."

"Then turn that damn thing off." She let out a
breath after Feeney located the controls that si-
lenced the music. The bed flowed to stillness.
"The wounds," Eve murmured, stepping closer to
examine them. "Too neat for a knife. Too messy
for a laser." A flash came to her—old training
films, old videos, old viciousness.

"Christ, Feeney, these look like bullet wounds."

Feeney reached into his pocket and drew out a
sealed bag. "Whoever did it left a souvenir." He
passed the bag to Eve. "An antique like this has to
go for eight, ten thousand for a legal collection,
twice that on the black market."

Fascinated, Eve turned the sealed revolver over
in her hand. "It's heavy," she said half to herself.
"Bulky."

"Thirty-eight caliber," he told her. "First one I've
seen outside of a museum. This one's a Smith and
Wesson, Model Ten, blue steel." He looked at it
with some affection. "Real classic piece, used to be
standard police issue up until the latter part of the
twentieth. They stopped making them in about
twenty-two, twenty-three, when the gun ban was
passed."

"You're the history buff." Which explained why
he was with her. "Looks new." She sniffed through
the bag, caught the scent of oil and burning.
"Somebody took good care of this. Steel fired into

flesh," she mused as she passed the bag back to
Feeney. "Ugly way to die, and the first I've seen it
in my ten years with the department."

"Second for me. About fifteen years ago, Lower
East Side, party got out of hand. Guy shot five people with a twenty-two before he realized it wasn't a
toy. Hell of a mess."

"Fun and games," Eve murmured. "We'll scan
the collectors, see how many we can locate who
own one like this. Somebody might have reported
a robbery."

"Might have."

"It's more likely it came through the black market." Eve glanced back at the body. "If she's been in
the business for a few years, she'd have discs, records of her clients, her trick books." She frowned.
"With Code Five, I'll have to do the door-to-door
myself. Not a simple sex crime," she said with a
sigh. "Whoever did it set it up. The antique
weapon, the wounds themselves, almost ruler-
straight down the body, the lights, the pose. Who
called it in, Feeney?"

"The killer." He waited until her eyes came back
to him. "From right here. Called the station. See
how the bedside unit's aimed at her face? That's
what came in. Video, no audio."

"He's into showmanship." Eve let out a breath.
"Clever bastard, arrogant, cocky. He had sex with
her first. I'd bet my badge on it. Then he gets up
and does it." She lifted her arm, aiming, lowering
it as she counted off, "One, two, three."

"That's cold," murmured Feeney.

"He's cold. He smooths down the sheets after.
See how neat they are? He arranges her, spreads

her open so nobody can have any doubts as to how she made her living. He does it carefully, practically measuring, so that she's perfectly aligned. Center of the bed, arms and legs equally apart. Doesn't turn off the bed 'cause it's part of the show. He leaves the gun because he wants us to know right away he's no ordinary man. He's got an ego. He doesn't want to waste time letting the body be discovered eventually. He wants it now. That instant gratification."

"She was licensed for men and women," Feeney pointed out, but Eve shook her head.

"It's not a woman. A woman wouldn't have left her looking both beautiful and obscene. No, I don't think it's a woman. Let's see what we can find. Have you gone into her computer yet?"

"No. It's your case, Dallas. I'm only authorized to assist."

"See if you can access her client files." Eve went to the dresser and began to carefully search drawers.

Expensive taste, Eve reflected. There were several items of real silk, the kind no simulation could match. The bottle of scent on the dresser was exclusive, and smelled, after a quick sniff, like expensive sex.

The contents of the drawers were meticulously ordered, lingerie folded precisely, sweaters arranged according to color and material. The closet was the same.

Obviously the victim had a love affair with clothes and a taste for the best and took scrupulous care of what she owned.

And she'd died naked.

"Kept good records," Feeney called out. "It's all here. Her client list, appointments—including her required monthly health exam and her weekly trip to the beauty salon. She used the Trident Clinic for the first and Paradise for the second."

"Both top-of-the-line. I've got a friend who saved for a year so she could have one day for the works at Paradise. Takes all kinds."

"My wife's sister went for it for her twenty-fifth anniversary. Cost damn near as much as my kid's wedding. Hello, we've got her personal address book."

"Good. Copy all of it, will you, Feeney?" At his low whistle, she looked over her shoulder, glimpsed the small gold-edged palm computer in his hand. "What?"

"We've got a lot of high-powered names in here. Politics, entertainment, money, money, money. Interesting, our girl has Roarke's private number."

"Roarke who?"

"Just Roarke, as far as I know. Big money there. Kind of guy that touches shit and turns it into gold bricks. You've got to start reading more than the sports page, Dallas."

"Hey, I read the headlines. Did you hear about the cocker spaniel recall?"

"Roarke's always big news," Feeney said patiently. "He's got one of the finest art collections in the world. Arts and antiques," he continued, noting when Eve clicked in and turned to him. "He's a licensed gun collector. Rumor is he knows how to use them."

"I'll pay him a visit."

"You'll be lucky to get within a mile of him."

"I'm feeling lucky." Eve crossed over to the body to slip her hands under the sheets.

"The man's got powerful friends, Dallas. You can't afford to so much as whisper he's linked to this until you've got something solid."

"Feeney, you know it's a mistake to tell me that." But even as she started to smile, her fingers brushed against something between cold flesh and bloody sheets. "There's something under her." Carefully, Eve lifted the shoulder, eased her fingers over.

"Paper," she murmured. "Sealed." With her protected thumb, she wiped at a smear of blood until she could read the protected sheet.

ONE OF SIX

"It looks hand-printed," she said to Feeney and held it out. "Our boy's more than clever, more than arrogant. And he isn't finished."

FROM THE #1 *NEW YORK TIMES* BESTSELLING AUTHOR

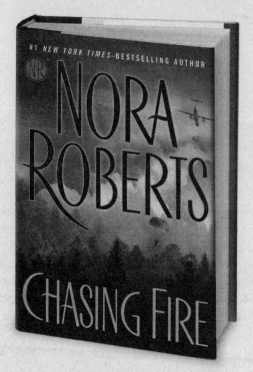

For smoke jumper Rowan Tripp, chasing fire
is not just a job—it's the ultimate thrill…

NoraRoberts.com

A MEMBER OF PENGUIN GROUP (USA) INC. · PENGUIN.COM

M806JV1110

Now available in paperback from
#1 *New York Times* bestselling author

Nora Roberts

BLACK HILLS

A summer at his grandparents' South Dakota ranch
is not eleven-year-old Cooper Sullivan's idea of a good
time. But things are a bit more bearable now that he's
discovered the neighbor girl, Lil Chance. Each year,
with Coop's annual summer visit, their friendship
deepens from innocent games to stolen kisses, but
there is one shared experience that will forever haunt
them: the terrifying discovery of a hiker's body.

Twelve years after they last walked together hand in
hand, fate has brought them back to the Black Hills
at a time when the people and things they hold most
dear need them most . . .

penguin.com

M563T1010

Share the emotional magic of
#1 *New York Times* bestselling author

NORA ROBERTS'S

BRIDE QUARTET

AVAILABLE NOW

VISION IN WHITE

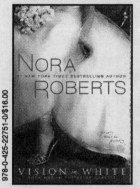

978-0-425-22751-0/$16.00

BED OF ROSES

978-0-425-23007-7/$16.00

SAVOR THE MOMENT

978-0-425-23368-9/$16.00

HAPPY EVER AFTER

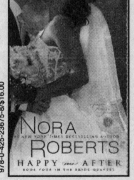

978-0-425-23675-8/$16.00

From Berkley

noraroberts.com
penguin.com

M566AS1110

Everyone's reading

NORA ROBERTS

For the thrills,

the relationships,

the adventure,

the passion,

the suspense,

the excitement.

Photo © 2005 by John Earle

The official Nora Roberts seal guarantees
that this is a new work by Nora Roberts.

penguin.com   noraroberts.com

M162AS1007